Praise for Margaret Daley
and her novels

MARGARET DALEY

Tidings of Joy

&

Heart of the Family

HARLEQUIN® LOVE INSPIRED® CLASSICS

Recycling programs for this product may not exist in your area.

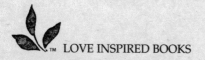 ™ LOVE INSPIRED BOOKS

ISBN-13: 978-0-373-65165-8

TIDINGS OF JOY AND HEART OF THE FAMILY
Copyright © 2013 by Harlequin Books S.A.

The publisher acknowledges the copyright holder of the individual works as follows:

TIDINGS OF JOY
Copyright © 2006 by Margaret Daley

HEART OF THE FAMILY
Copyright © 2007 by Margaret Daley

www.Harlequin.com

Printed in U.S.A.

CONTENTS

Books by Margaret Daley

MARGARET DALEY

feels she has been blessed. She has been married more than thirty years to her husband, Mike, whom she met in college. He is a terrific support and her best friend. They have one son, Shaun. Margaret has been writing for many years and loves to tell a story. When she was a little girl, she would play with her dolls and make up stories about their lives. Now she writes these stories down. She especially enjoys weaving stories about families and how faith in God can sustain a person when things get tough. When she isn't writing, she is fortunate to be a teacher for students with special needs. Margaret has taught for more than twenty years and loves working with her students. She has also been a Special Olympics coach and has participated in many sports with her students.

TIDINGS OF JOY

And ye now therefore have sorrow: but I will
see you again, and your heart shall rejoice,
and your joy no man taketh from you.
—*John* 16:22

To my family—I love you

Chapter One

Chance Taylor stepped off the bus and surveyed the town, which was nothing like where he'd spent the past two years. Yet, for a few seconds he fought the overwhelming urge to get back on the bus. Because no matter how much he wanted to, he couldn't. Not until he'd paid his debt.

The bus pulled away from the curb, leaving him behind. No escape now. The beating of his heart kicked up a notch. Chance glanced up and down the street. Sweetwater. It was exactly as Tom Bolton had described it. Quaint stores lined its Main Street. A row of Bradford pear trees down both sides of the road offered shade in the heat of summer. Even though it was the end of September, the hot air caused sweat to pop out on his forehead.

He closed his eyes to the vivid colors spread out before him—a red sign above a door, yellow pansies about the base of the trees along the street. He'd lived in a world he'd thought of as black-and-white. Now every hue of the rainbow bombarded him from all sides. Opening his eyes to the new world around him, he wiped the sweat from his brow with the back of his hand, then grabbed the one duffel bag with all his earthly possessions and strode toward Alice's Café.

Inside he scanned the diners, all engrossed in their food and conversation. People doing normal, everyday things with no idea how their life could change in a split second. But he knew.

Drawing in a deep breath, Chance took a moment to compose himself. Again the question flashed across his mind: why had he come to Sweetwater? Surely there was a better place, one he could get lost in. New York City. Chicago. Even Louisville would have been better than this small town, where according to Tom, everyone watched out for each other. He didn't want that. Nosy neighbors had led to his destruction in the past. But Sweetwater was the only place where he could fulfill his promise to himself. He was stuck here for the time being, but once he had paid his debt, he would leave as fast as a bus could take him out of town.

Chance saw Samuel Morgan in the back booth and headed toward him. Aware of a few glances thrown his way, Chance hurried over, placed his duffel bag on the floor, then slid in across from Samuel, his back to the other diners.

Samuel grinned. "I didn't think you'd come."

"I said I would. About the only thing I have left is my word."

"Tom's death wasn't your fault. He made his choice."

"I have a chance to return a favor. I intend to. That's the least I can do."

A waitress with a pencil behind her left ear paused near Samuel and dug into her apron pocket for a pad.

"Want something to eat?" Samuel asked.

Chance shook his head, aware of the open curiosity in the older woman's gaze. His stomach tightened. He should be used to people watching him, having spent the past few years with no right to any privacy. But he wasn't. All he wanted when he was through with Sweetwater was to find a quiet corner of the world where he could put his life back together.

"Alice, I'll take another cup of coffee." Samuel pushed his mug toward the edge of the table.

"Sure, Reverend. Be right back."

After Alice refilled Samuel's coffee and left, he said, "Your timing couldn't be better. Tanya Bolton has just converted the space over her garage into an apartment. She's looking for a tenant and you need a place to stay. It's perfect."

Something in the reverend's expression alerted Chance that there was more to it. "You wouldn't have anything to do with Tom's wife having an apartment, now would you?"

Samuel's grin reached deep into his eyes. "I did mention it would be a great way for her to make some extra money. She took the suggestion and ran with it."

"I can't see the lady renting to an ex-con."

"You aren't an ex-con. Your conviction was overturned because you were innocent. The police have the right guy in jail now."

The horror of the past few years threatened to deluge Chance with all the memories he desperately needed to forget. He refused to let them intrude, shoving them back into the dark corner of his mind. He didn't have the emotional strength to return to the past. His wounds ran deep, to his very soul. "It doesn't change the fact that I spent two years in prison. When she finds that out..." He couldn't finish his sentence, the words clogging his throat. The knot in his stomach grew.

Suddenly he pictured a man he'd thought was a good friend, and his expression when Chance had seen him last week in Louisville. Fear had flitted across his so-called friend's features before he could mask his reaction to seeing Chance. Although in the eyes of the law he had been exonerated, he had seen the doubt in the man's gaze. *Did they have the right guy this time?*

Samuel leaned toward Chance and said in a low tone, "I'm not telling Tanya anything about your recent past. I'll leave that for you to tell when you feel ready. But I am going to vouch for you. I know you're a good, honest man, and what you've come to Sweetwater to do is important to you."

Chance thought about being so near Tom's wife on a daily basis. He wasn't sure he could handle it, the constant reminder that he owed his life to Tom. "Is there anywhere else I can rent a room?"

"Probably. But not as convenient, that is if you really want to help Tanya. Or are you here to hide?"

Samuel's question pierced through the layers of protection Chance used to shield himself from others. If he was smart, he would leave and do exactly that.

"Look you don't have any way of getting around except walking, and Tanya's house is close to downtown so you can get just about any place you'll need to go from that apartment."

Chance held up his hand. "Okay, Reverend. You've convinced me. I'll see the lady about it."

Samuel took a long sip of his coffee. "Good. I also have lined up the interview with Nick Blackburn for that job I told you about when we spoke last week on the phone. He's looking for an assistant to help him with the part of his company he's moved to Sweetwater. Still interested?"

"I need a job while I live here, so yes, I'm still interested. What does Mr. Blackburn know about me?"

"That you are a friend of mine, that's all."

"I'll have to tell him where I've been."

"Yeah, I know, but it needs to come from you. Nick will respect that." Samuel sipped his coffee.

"When's the interview?"

"Nine o'clock tomorrow morning. His office is two blocks down on Main. The brand-new, seven-story tall redbrick building. You probably saw it coming into town on the bus."

"Yeah. He works Saturdays?" Everything was moving so fast. Was he ready to plunge back into the world of big business? Once that had been his life. Once he'd worked long hours to get ahead at his job. Now he wished he had that time back, that he'd spent it with the family he no longer had.

"Sometimes. Usually he spends his weekends with his family, but he knew you were arriving today and decided to do it tomorrow. He said something about having to be in Chicago early next week."

"I've heard of Blackburn Industries. I didn't realize he'd moved his corporate offices from Chicago to Sweetwater."

Samuel shrugged. "Love is a strong motivator. His wife is from here." Samuel finished his cup of coffee. "I'll drive you over to Tanya's."

"No, I need to do this on my own. You can call her and give her a reference so she'll open the door, but the rest will have to be up to me."

"Fine, but, Chance, you aren't alone in this world. I told you that in prison and I'm telling you that now."

"I know. I know, Reverend. God is with me. He stood by me while I watched my family taken from me and while I was on trial. He was there with me in prison when I was fighting for my life." Chance saw the disappointment in Samuel's eyes that his sarcastic words had caused.

"I know how you feel, but you didn't give Him a chance to be with you."

Chance slipped from the booth. He didn't want to hear it. Samuel knew how he felt about the Lord who had abandoned him in his time of need. They'd even had a discussion about it when Samuel had come to the prison to minister to the inmates. "How do I get to Tanya Bolton's house?"

Samuel wrote an address on a napkin and handed it to him. "Go three blocks north on Main to Second, then go five blocks east on Second and that's Berryhill Road. Sure you don't want me to at least drop you off?"

"No, the exercise will be good for me." Chance turned from the booth and headed for the door. The very act of going anywhere he wanted was precious to him. He would never take freedom of movement for granted again.

Outside he relished the warmth of the sun on his

face, the fresh air, laced with newly mowed grass and grilled meat from a barbecue restaurant on the next block. A slender man dressed in a suit passed him on the sidewalk and nodded a greeting. Automatically Chance returned it with his own nod. The sudden realization that for the next few months he would be thrust into the middle of life in a small town sent panic bolting through him. He'd grown up in a small town and knew that little was a secret for long. He didn't want to see the doubt and possibly even fear in the eyes of the residents of Sweetwater when they learned he'd been in prison.

"I've got the sign out in front and I've advertised in the paper. Now all I need is someone to rent the apartment over the garage," Tanya Bolton said as she switched the cordless phone to her other ear.

"You did such a nice job fixing the place up. I don't think you'll have any trouble finding a tenant."

"I hope you're right, Zoey, because I need the money. Having a teenage daughter who's growing out of all her clothes is expensive."

"Will I see you at Alice's Café tomorrow?"

"Of course. I wouldn't miss our Saturday get-together." Tanya lowered her voice, cupping the mouthpiece closer to her. "I don't know if I would have made it without you, Darcy, Beth and Jesse. You know I'll be there."

"See you tomorrow," Zoey Witherspoon said as a beep sounded, indicating another call on the line.

Tanya pushed a button. "Hello?"

"This is Samuel. I'm glad you're home, Tanya. I've got a friend coming over right now to see your apartment. He's going to be here for a while and needs a place to stay."

"A tenant! I was just talking to Zoey about not having shown the apartment to anyone yet."

"Then this is your lucky day. He'll be a great tenant. His name is Chance Taylor."

The sound of the doorbell ringing drew Tanya's attention. She walked toward the front door with the cordless phone still in her hand and noticed through the frosted glass a large man on her porch. "Looks like he's here. Thanks, Samuel. I really appreciate the referral." She laid the phone on the table in the small foyer, then hurriedly opened the door.

Before her stood a man several inches over six feet tall with broad shoulders, a narrow waist and muscular arms. His large presence dwarfed her small porch and blocked her doorway. Her gaze flew to his face, taking in his hard, square jaw, his nose that had been broken once, his vivid blue eyes and his short black hair. All his features came together in a pleasing countenance with just a hint of sadness in it. Surprised by that thought, Tanya wasn't sure where the impression came from.

His neutral expression evolved into a half grin. "Tanya Bolton?"

His presence filled her vision. "Yes," she managed to say, stunned by how overpowering Samuel's friend was.

"I'm Chance Taylor. Samuel was supposed to call you about me. I'd like to rent your apartment."

The deep, baritone of his voice flowed over her, smooth like a river of honey. Slowly his dark blue eyes lit with a gleam like periwinkles basking in the sunlight.

Then his mouth lifted in a full grin, causing dimples to appear in both cheeks.

"Is it still for rent?"

She nodded, for some reason her voice still unable to work properly.

"How much?"

She mentally shook herself out of her daze. This was business. "Three hundred a month plus utilities."

He dug into the front pocket of his black jeans and withdrew a wad of cash. After peeling off three one hundred dollar bills, crisp and new, he handed them to her.

She peered at the money, thinking of all the bills she needed to pay. Then common sense prevailed. "I don't want to take your money until you've seen the apartment."

"I'm not choosy about where I stay."

"The apartment is open. It's above the detached garage at the side of the house. Why don't you go and take a look at it? I wouldn't feel right if you didn't do that. I'll be along in a moment."

After repocketing his money, he tipped his head toward her. "I'll do that, Mrs. Bolton."

She watched him descend the steps with duffel bag in hand, then head for the garage. When he disappeared from view, she went into the kitchen and grabbed the lease that Beth had insisted she needed a tenant to sign and left the house by the back door.

Her daughter would be home from school in half an hour, and she hoped to have this all settled by then. After she crossed the driveway, she climbed the stairs to the apartment over the garage at the side of the house. The door stood ajar.

Inside Chance slowly turned in a full circle, surveying the place, no expression on his face. When he saw her, he stopped, one corner of his mouth hitched in a half grin, dimpling one cheek. She was beginning to wonder if that was his trademark.

"This is nice."

His compliment caused a catch in her throat. She'd worked hard on the apartment with some help from her friends and was proud of what she'd accomplished on a limited budget. "Thanks."

He faced her, his large presence filling the small two-room apartment—much like her porch—his shoulders set in a taut line, his arms straight at his sides. His gaze lit upon the paper she held in her hand. "Do you want me to sign a lease?"

"Yes. This is for six months."

"I don't know how long I'll be here. I've got an interview with Nick Blackburn about a job, but nothing's definite."

Tanya glanced at the standard lease and folded it several times. "Then we won't use the lease. Where did you come from?"

"Louisville."

"Why did you come to Sweetwater? Because of the possibility of a job with Nick?"

"No, actually Samuel has always talked so highly of Sweetwater that I decided to come pay him and the town a visit. He knew I was looking for a job and mentioned the one with Blackburn Industries." Again Chance withdrew the wad of money from his pocket and unrolled it. Covering the short distance between them, he thrust the rent toward her. "Three hundred. Do you require a deposit?"

Deposit? Tanya bit her lower lip. She hadn't thought about that. Having never been a landlord before, she realized how new this all was to her. "I guess a hundred. That should cover minor damages if there are any."

"There won't be."

"Not from what Samuel says. He basically told me I couldn't go wrong with you being my tenant."

Chance glanced away for a few seconds as if embarrassed by what Samuel had said. Clearing his throat, he returned his attention to her. "Samuel does have a way about him." He gave her the money for the deposit, then immediately stepped back as though he was uncomfortable getting too near her. He looked toward the kitchen area in one corner with a two-burner stove, a sink and a small refrigerator. "Can you give me directions to the nearest grocery store?"

Tanya thought of the bare kitchen and blurted out, "Why don't you have dinner with me and my daughter tonight? That's the least I can do for someone new to Sweetwater and a friend of Samuel's."

Chance plunged his fingers through his black hair, then massaged the back of his neck. "I don't want you to go to any trouble, Mrs. Bolton."

"My name is Tanya and it isn't any trouble. I have to warn you, though, it won't be anything fancy."

"I'm not used to fancy."

The tight edge to his words made her blink in surprise. "Well, then you'll fit right in. Sweetwater's pretty laid-back. We only have one expensive restaurant that I've never seen the inside of."

"What time is dinner?"

Tanya checked her watch and realized that Crystal would be home from school soon. "Give me a couple of hours. Say six." She backed toward the door, a sudden, awkward silence electrifying the air. "See you then."

Out on the landing she breathed deeply. Chance Taylor wasn't a chatty person. She would have to quiz Samuel about him. For some reason she didn't think her new tenant would tell her much about himself. The click of the door closing behind her penetrated her thoughts. She couldn't shake the feeling his life hadn't been easy. The sight of the school bus coming down the street sent Tanya hurrying down the stairs.

Even though Crystal was fifteen now and a freshman in high school, when her job allowed her, Tanya liked to be there when her daughter came home from school, especially lately. Something was bothering Crystal and her daughter wouldn't talk to her about it. Maybe today Crystal would say something that would reveal what was going on. She rounded the side of the garage when the bus stopped and the driver descended the steps to man the lift.

While Crystal powered her wheelchair up the driveway, the small school bus drove away. If the frown on her daughter's face was any indication, today had not been a good one. Tanya sighed and met Crystal halfway.

"We have a tenant for the apartment," Tanya said, forcing a light tone into her voice to cover the apprehension her child's expression raised.

Her daughter didn't say a word. She maneuvered

the wheelchair around Tanya and kept going toward the ramp at the back of the house. Tanya followed, trying to decide how to approach Crystal about what was happening at school. This year when she had begun at Sweetwater High, she'd quickly started trying to get out of going, even to the point of making up things that were wrong with her. Tanya had talked with her teachers, but no one knew what was going on. She had seen her usually happy, even-tempered child become someone else, someone who was angry and resentful. Was it the typical teenager angst of going through puberty? Or was it something else? Had Crystal's father's death finally manifested itself in her troubled behavior? Tom had died almost five months ago, and their daughter had gone through the usual grief associated with death but had seemed all right as her summer vacation had come to an end. Now Tanya didn't know. Maybe Crystal had suppressed her true feelings.

In the kitchen Tanya called out to Crystal before she wheeled herself through the doorway into the hall, "Our new tenant is joining us for dinner."

Crystal continued to remain quiet as she disappeared from view. Perplexed, Tanya stared at the empty doorway, wondering if Zoey, a high school counselor, or Beth Morgan, Crystal's English teacher, knew what was going on with her daughter at school. She made a mental note to call her friends later to see if anything had happened today to warrant this sullen demeanor.

Chance descended the stairs to his apartment over the garage and headed across the yard toward the back door. He noticed the ramp off the deck and remembered

Tom talking about his teenage daughter who was in a wheelchair. Until he had seen the ramp, however, he hadn't really thought about the implication of having a child who was physically disabled or the fact that he would be eating with a young girl who would only be a year or two older than the age his own daughter would have been if she had lived.

He stopped his progress toward the deck, indecision stiffening his body. He'd seen plenty of teenagers since his daughter's…death. Surely he could handle an hour in the same room with Tanya's child. How difficult could it be?

Chance discovered a few minutes later just how hard it would be when Crystal opened the door to his knock, a smile on her thin face, a black Lab standing beside her. He sucked in a sharp breath and held it. Staring up at him with open interest was a young girl who had dark brown hair and hazel eyes, so very reminiscent of his daughter's. She even had a sprinkle of freckles on her small upturned nose as Haley had.

He cleared away the huge knot in his throat and struggled against the urge to run as far away as he could. His legs refused to move forward into the house even though Tanya's daughter opened the door wider for him.

"Come in before all the insects do," Tanya said, approaching them.

He shook off the panic beginning to swell in his chest and shuffled into the kitchen. Turning to shut the back door, he took a few precious seconds to compose his reeling emotions at the sharp reminder of what he'd lost. When he pivoted back toward the pair, his feelings were tamped down beneath all the defensive layers he'd created over the past few years. Under closer inspection of Tom's daughter, he saw no real similarities between Haley and her, other than their coloring.

If he was going to repay the debt, he had no choice but to learn to deal with the teenager—and the mother. *I can do this,* he told himself and forced a smile to his lips. "I'm Chance, the new tenant," he said to Crystal, realizing he was probably stating the obvious.

The teenager's smile grew. "I'm Crystal. Welcome to Sweetwater."

"Thanks." He inhaled the aroma of ground beef that peppered the air. "It smells wonderful. What are we having?"

"As I told you earlier, nothing fancy. Just tacos. I hope you like Mexican food. Crystal and I love it." Tanya gestured toward the counter. "Everyone's going to put their own together."

"I like anything I don't have to cook." He took another few steps farther into the kitchen, committing himself to spending some time with his landlady and her daughter.

Tanya handed him a plate with big yellow and blue flowers painted on it. "You don't cook then?"

"Not unless you call heating up a can of spaghetti cooking."

Crystal giggled, patting her dog. "Even I can do that."

"My daughter's taking a Foods and Nutrition class this year. Hopefully she'll learn more than heating up what's in a can."

Chance noticed the instant school was mentioned that

Crystal's cheerful expression vanished and the young girl dropped her head, her attention glued to her lap. Did she struggle with schoolwork? He made a note to find out. Maybe he could help her with her homework, then he would be one step closer to being able to leave Sweetwater, to appeasing his guilt.

"You go first." Tanya swept her arm across her body, indicating he prepare his tacos.

Chance took two large empty shells and filled them with the meat sauce, cheese, lettuce and diced tomatoes. His mouth watered in anticipation of his first home-cooked meal in years. After he doused his tacos with chunky salsa, he made his way to the round oak table in the alcove with three large windows overlooking the deck and backyard.

He sat at one of the places already set with utensils, a blue linen napkin and a glass with ice in it. When he noticed a pitcher on the table, he poured himself some tea, then doctored it with several scoops of sugar.

Crystal positioned herself next to him and put her plate on her yellow place mat. "Mom said you're from Louisville. I went there once, when I was nine, and took a riverboat up the Ohio River."

As Tanya settled into the chair across from him, Chance said to Crystal, "I've never ridden on a riverboat. Did you like it?"

"Yeah! I'd like to take one all the way to New Orleans. I've never been to New Orleans. I haven't seen very many places." She glanced down at her wheelchair, then fixed her large hazel eyes on him as though that explained why she didn't go places.

A tightness constricted his chest. He couldn't imagine being confined to a wheelchair, every little bump in the terrain an obstacle, not free to move about as you wanted. He knew about that and had hated every second of his confinement. "You'll have time," he finally said, feeling a connection between him and Crystal that went beyond her father.

"That's what Mom says."

"I promised her a trip when she graduates from high school." Tanya poured tea for herself and her daughter. "She'll get to pick where, depending on my budget."

"Mom's got a saving account for the trip at the bank where she works."

"That's a good plan." After he picked up his taco carefully so as not to make a mess, he took a big bite, relishing the spicy meat sauce. "Mmm. This is good."

Tanya smiled. "Thanks."

She and Crystal bowed their heads while Tanya said a prayer.

When she glanced up at Chance, he'd put his taco back on his plate, a look of unease in his expression. "I don't have the time to cook like I want to, but I do enjoy getting into the kitchen when I can," she said, hoping to make him feel comfortable.

"I'm glad you invited me." Chance caught her gaze and held it for a long moment. He realized he meant what he had just said. The warmth emanating from both the mother and daughter spoke to a part of him that he thought had died in prison.

Finally Tanya dropped her regard and ran her finger around the rim of her glass. "What kind of job are you applying for with Nick?"

"As an assistant for his office in Sweetwater."

"Nick said something to me about expanding his company's presence in Sweetwater. I guess this must be the beginning. Since he and Jesse got married, I know he doesn't like to travel to Chicago as much as he used to. What have you done before?"

Tension knifed through Chance. He should have expected questions about his past. That was the last thing he wanted to discuss. "I was a financial advisor."

"Was? Not anymore?"

"I'm looking for something different. That's why this assistant's job interests me." That and the fact Samuel paved the way for him with Nick Blackburn. But even with Samuel's reference, the job wasn't a sure thing. He would have to convince Mr. Blackburn he could do the work, definitely a step down from what he'd done in the past where he'd had his own assistant.

"What happens if you don't get the job?"

"I'm still staying for a while. I'll just look for another one," he quickly said to ease the worry he heard in her voice.

He needed the conversation focused on someone else. Angling around toward Crystal, he asked, "Besides Foods and Nutrition, what else are you taking?"

The teenager downed a swallow of tea. "I'm taking the usual—U.S. history, English, algebra and biology. I'm also in the girls' choir."

"In high school I was in the show choir. I enjoyed it." Chance felt Tanya's puzzled gaze on him and shifted in his chair, feeling uncomfortable under her scrutiny as though she could see into his heart and soul. Their emptiness wasn't something he wanted exposed to the world. He busied himself by taking another bite.

"I sing in the choir at church. We can always use another man to sing."

He heard Tanya's words of encouragement and gritted his teeth so hard that pain streaked down his neck. Church. Religion. God wasn't for him. He'd believed once, and his whole life, his family, had been taken away from him. He stuffed the rest of the taco into his mouth and occupied himself with chewing—slowly. Averting his gaze, he stared out the window at the backyard and hoped the woman didn't pursue the topic of conversation.

"I thought about auditioning for the show choir, but I didn't. I can't dance very well in this thing," Crystal slapped the arm of her wheelchair, "and you have to be able to sing *and* dance to be in it. If I can't do it right, I don't want to do it at all."

The teenager's words cut through the tension gripping Chance. He looked back at her and managed to smile, hearing the need in the child's voice that twisted his heart. "Besides singing, what else do you like to do?"

"I like to draw."

"Why aren't you taking art in school?"

"I can't take everything. I'll probably take it next year." Crystal shrugged. "Besides, Mom's teaching me. She's very good."

Chance swung his attention to Tanya who looked away when his gaze fell on her. "What do you like to draw?"

A hint of red tinged her cheeks. "People mostly."

"Portraits?"

"Nothing formal like that."

"I'd love to see your work sometime."

Tanya started to say something when Crystal chimed in, "I'll go get her sketchbook. It's in the dining room." She backed up her wheelchair, made a one-hundred-eighty-degree turn, and headed for the door with her service dog following.

"I get the impression you don't show many people your drawings."

She shook her head, swallowing hard. "I'm not very good. I draw for myself."

When Crystal came back into the kitchen with the sketchbook in her lap, Chance wanted to make Tanya feel at ease so he said, "I don't want to intrude on—"

"Mom doesn't think she's good. I do. Here, see for yourself." Crystal opened the book and showed Chance.

He wasn't sure what to expect after Tanya's reluctant reaction, but what he saw was an exquisite portrait of Crystal sketching something. The drawing captured the teenager's love for art in the detailed expression on her face. The pen-and-ink picture was as good as any professional artist would have done. "I'm impressed, Tanya. This is beautiful."

"You think so?"

All the woman's doubts were evident in her wrinkled forehead, the hesitant expression in her eyes and the hidden hope that he might really be telling her the truth. As before, it was important to Chance to make Tanya feel comfortable. "Yes. I'm honored to have seen this. You should show your drawings more often."

Tanya straightened in her chair, her head cocked. "Samuel tried to get me to have one in the Fourth of

July auction this year at church. I told him I would donate my time or something else."

Chance captured Tanya's regard. "Next year take him up on the offer."

She slid her gaze away and started gathering up her plate and utensils. "I'll think about it."

"Which means she won't do it," Crystal interjected and put her dishes in her lap then wheeled herself toward the sink.

Chance followed them with his place setting. "I hope you'll let me help you clean up after being gracious enough to invite me to dinner. I might not cook very well, but I can rinse and put them in the dishwasher."

"Yeah, Mom. Let him."

Tanya laughed. "You're agreeing because you'll get out of your part of cleaning up."

"I've got homework to do."

"On Friday night?"

Crystal lifted her shoulders. "What else is there to do?"

"Fine." Tanya watched her frowning daughter and the black Lab disappear into the hallway. "Something's bothering her. I wish she would tell me."

"She's what, fifteen, sixteen?"

"Fifteen."

"Did you tell your mother what was going on with you at that age?"

"Good point. But still we've been through a lot. I…" Her voice quavering, Tanya twisted away so her face was hidden as she stacked the dishes into the sink and turned on the water.

Chance heard the thickness lacing each word and

wished he could help her. But he discovered that helping her was going to be harder than he'd thought. Actually he'd had no plan in mind other than to assist Tom's family. But how? Maybe he could reach Crystal. He had to try something or he would never be able to get on with his life—what was left of it.

Tanya handed him the first plate to put in the dishwasher. "You should come hear us sing in the choir at church this Sunday. As I'm sure you're aware, Samuel gives great sermons."

Chance gripped the glass she passed to him. "I'll think about it."

Chapter Two

Chance's clipped words caused Tanya to step back, strained uneasiness pulsating between them. She got the distinct impression thinking was all he would do about going to church.

Without really contemplating what she was saying, she asked, "You aren't going to come, are you?" The second the question was out of her mouth, she bit down on the inside of her cheek. She'd never confronted someone about not attending church. She didn't confront anyone about anything, if possible.

His gaze narrowed on her face, every line in his body rigid. "I need to get settled in."

By his tight tone, evasive answer and clenched jaw, Tanya knew that any further discussion was unwelcome. "I'm sorry I brought up the subject. I just assumed you believed."

"Because I'm friends with Samuel?"

She nodded.

"I guess Samuel would say I'm the lost sheep he's trying to bring back to the fold."

"So you've heard him speak before?"

"Yeah. But it's not going to change how I feel. Simply put, God wasn't there for me when I needed Him the most."

His statement piqued her curiosity and made her wonder even more about Chance Taylor's past. She handed him another dish and let the silence lengthen while she decided how to proceed with the conversation when tension crowded the space between them. "What happened?" She realized she was pushing when she never pushed.

"Nothing I want to revisit."

His answer hadn't surprised her. She didn't think he shared willingly much of himself with anyone. She'd seen that same defensive mechanism in Tom, especially after the riding accident that had left Crystal paralyzed. "You said you were a financial advisor. I wish I had a knack for figures. My budget's in a terrible mess. I work at a bank, but finances aren't my strong suit." There, that should be a safe enough subject for conversation.

"What do you do?"

"I started out as a receptionist, but I'm a teller now. I can count money, just not manage my own very well. There never seems to be enough to go around. I'm still paying off Crystal's medical expenses." And her deceased ex-husband's lawyer's bill, she added silently, not wanting to go into what happened with Tom. How do you explain to a person you just met that your husband was sent to prison for burning barns in retaliation for their daughter's accident?

"When was the last time you redid your budget?"

"I don't exactly have one that's written down. I pay

the most important bills first, then as much as I can on the ones left. That's the extent of my budget. Some months I do better than others." She could remember her spending spree several years back where she had bought unnecessary items—expensive clothing, inessential furniture. Thankfully she had been able to take a lot of them back—but not all. She'd finally paid off those bills a few months ago. So long as she stayed on the medication she took for manic depression, she shouldn't get herself into a bind like that again. She couldn't afford to.

After he put the last glass on the top rack, Chance closed the dishwasher. "Maybe I can help you with that."

"Would you? That would be great! If the job with Nick doesn't work out, I may be able to help you find one. I can ask around." There was something about Chance that drew her to him. She wanted to help him, especially in light of him offering to assist her with her budget.

He frowned, rubbing his hand along the back of his neck. "You don't—"

"Mom, I'm going out on the deck to do my homework. Now that the sun's going down behind the trees, it's cooler outside." With a book and pad in her lap, Crystal wheeled herself toward the back door.

Chance hurried to open it before her daughter could. "What subject are you working on?"

"English. I have an essay to write. I do my best thinking outside."

"So do I."

When Crystal was out on the deck, Chance turned toward Tanya. "I'd better go. It's been a long day, and tomorrow I have that job interview, then I need to buy some supplies."

"Pretty much whatever you need can be found on Main Street or right off it. There's a grocery store four blocks from here on Third Avenue."

"Is that right after Second?"

"Yep."

"Then I think I can find it on my walk," he said with a smile.

"You don't have a car?"

"No, I came on the bus."

"I'm going to Alice's Café tomorrow at ten. What time is your interview?"

"Nine."

"I can give you a lift, if you'd like. I have a few errands I need to run before I meet my friends."

"Thanks, but I can walk. I like the exercise."

His half grin appeared, and for a few seconds Tanya's heart responded by quickening its beat. Her physical reaction took her by surprise. After her ordeal with Tom, men hadn't interested her—until now.

Chance left and stopped next to Crystal to say a few words to her, then proceeded toward the detached garage at the side of the house. Tanya came out onto the deck and watched him. While he'd talked with her daughter, Tanya had glimpsed a vulnerability leaking into his expression. He had managed to cover it quickly, but she had seen it.

"What do you think of our new tenant?" Tanya asked when she noticed her daughter watching her staring at Chance.

"What do *you* think?"

"He seems nice. Kinda lonely."

"Yeah."

"What did he say to you?"

Crystal tilted her head, screwing up her face into a quizzical expression. "He offered to tutor me in math if I needed it."

Tanya laughed. "Did you tell him you had a ninety-eight in Algebra I and that you're taking Algebra II?"

She nodded. "I wonder why he offered."

"Did you ask him?"

"He left before I could. Maybe I will tomorrow."

"Speaking of tomorrow, I'd better get a load of laundry done tonight or neither of us will have anything to wear."

When Tanya entered the kitchen, her gaze fell on the table where Chance had sat for dinner. He was a puzzle. And one of her favorite things to do was put together jigsaw puzzles, the more pieces the better. She had a feeling there were a lot of pieces to Chance Taylor.

"Have a seat." Nick Blackburn indicated a brown leather chair in front of his large desk.

Chance quickly scanned the spacious office as he sat. The rich walnut tones of the furniture with a navy-and-brown color scheme lent a refined elegance to the room. He'd been in many offices that conveyed power and wealth. This one ranked near the top.

Mr. Blackburn perused the application Chance had filled out, and he knew the second the man read about his time spent in the state penitentiary. To give Mr. Blackburn credit, he finished the application before he glanced up at Chance and asked, "What did you do time for?"

"Murder."

The man's eyes widened slightly before he put the paper down, a bland expression veiling his curiosity. "You only served two years?"

"My conviction was overturned when the real murderer was apprehended last month."

"So you served two years for a crime you didn't commit."

Even though it really wasn't a question, Chance said, "Yes."

"That's where you met Samuel?"

"Yes, sir. He took an interest in me and we became friends."

"You know you're overqualified for this job. You have an MBA from Harvard. You've worked for several top money-managing companies in the country and were on the fast track."

"*Were* is the operative word here. That was in my past. Besides—" Chance grinned "—Blackburn Industries is well respected and a multimillion dollar business. I consider this job an opportunity to do something different."

"Because you don't see people letting you manage their money after spending time in prison?"

Chance leaned forward. "To be frank, I don't want to be reminded of the life I once had. I need to start over in something totally different. What are the duties of the job?"

After Mr. Blackburn listed them for Chance, the man said, "Do you think you can handle those?"

In his sleep, Chance thought and nodded.

"There will be some traveling to my Chicago office. The dress is casual here but not in Chicago."

"I understand."

Nick Blackburn pushed back his chair and stood. Offering Chance his hand, he said, "Then you've got yourself a job. I've never known Samuel to be wrong about a person, and he thinks you can do this job."

"When do I start, Mr. Blackburn?"

"It's Nick, and you can start Wednesday morning when I get back from Chicago. Be here at nine and I'll show you around and introduce you to the staff here in Sweetwater."

A few minutes later as Chance left the building, he couldn't resist turning his face to the sun, relishing its warmth as it bathed him. He would never tire of doing that.

He had a job. That was one worry taken care of. Now all he had to figure out was how to be there for Tanya and Crystal without them knowing why. After spending time with them the night before, he wasn't sure he wanted them ever to know his involvement in Tom's death.

"Okay, you have to tell us about the guy renting your apartment." Jesse scooted over in the booth at Alice's Café to allow Tanya to slide in beside her. "We've all been waiting with bated breath."

"Jesse Blackburn, don't you get any ideas. No matchmaking! He's only my tenant. Just passing through." Taking a sip of her coffee, Tanya looked around the group and added, "How did you know I have a man renting my garage apartment?"

Beth Morgan grinned. "Samuel told me. Do you think there are any secrets among us after all these years?"

"What else did your husband say?" Tanya thought about all she wanted to know concerning her tenant, especially what or who was responsible for the pain behind his half smile that never quite reached his eyes. She hadn't slept much the night before, her mind insisting on playing through all kinds of scenarios.

"Not much. Samuel just told me you rented your apartment to Chance Taylor, a friend from his past. You know my husband. He doesn't say much about a person he knows. He always likes people to make up their own mind. So spill the beans. What's he look like?"

An image of the first time she had seen Chance on her porch flashed into Tanya's mind. Even from the beginning she'd been drawn to his eyes where she'd seen a shadow of sadness in their depths. "He's very tall, dark hair, blue eyes, nice build, probably in his late thirties. He had an interview this morning with Nick about the assistant's job."

Surprise widened Jesse's eyes. "He did and Nick didn't tell me."

"This isn't a secretarial-type position, is it?" Zoey Witherspoon asked.

Jesse shook her head. "More like Nick's right hand. Someone he can train to take over part of his duties that demand he travel to Chicago."

"Chance's background is in finance so he should be

qualified," Tanya said, glad she knew at least that much about her new tenant.

With her elbow on the table, Darcy Markham rested her chin in her palm. "Mmm. He sounds promising."

"Hey, you're married to a very nice, good-looking man. And you're expecting your third child," Zoey said, gently punching Darcy in the arm. "Between you and Beth we'll be spending a lot of time at the maternity floor of the hospital in a few months."

"That doesn't mean I can't look at a handsome man because that's as far as it goes. No one will take the place of Joshua in my heart."

Tanya listened to her friends talk about their husbands, their children, the babies Darcy and Beth were expecting. She was the only one not married in the group, and she felt the loneliness of her situation more now than ever. A few years ago—first with Crystal's riding accident, then Tom's arson conviction that led to him divorcing her and ultimately his death in prison—her whole life had fallen apart. She was still trying to put the pieces back together and keep her manic depression under control. And she would because she had no other choice. Crystal depended on her.

"Samuel said Chance wasn't sure how long he would stay in Sweetwater," Beth said, drawing Tanya back into the conversation.

She blinked, focusing on the group of women who had been there for her through all the tragedies. "Yeah, he said he wasn't sure how long he'll be here, especially if he doesn't get the job with Nick."

"So Nick's job brought him to Sweetwater?" Zoey took a sip of her iced tea.

"I think it was more than that. I think Samuel and his description of Sweetwater had a lot to do with it." Samuel was a great counselor, and Tanya wondered if that had something to do with Chance coming to town. She just couldn't shake the feeling he was hurting inside and needed help healing. She recognized the signs because she was in the same situation.

"Where's he from?" Darcy asked.

"Louisville."

"Well, it's perfect timing. You've got a tenant and some extra money when you needed it the most. Nick might have his assistant. God works in wondrous ways." Beth wiped her mouth and put the napkin beside her empty plate. "Samuel's certainly glad Chance decided to come, even if it's only for a while."

Jesse leaned close, covering Tanya's hand. "Just remember you're not alone. Nick and I can help you financially if you need it."

Overwhelmed by all their love, Tanya smiled, fighting the lump rising in her throat. "I know. You've mentioned it half a dozen times. But as I said before, Jesse, I have to stand on my own two feet. No more handouts."

"Even with Samuel's stamp of approval, I think we should take this meeting over to Tanya's house and check this guy out." Zoey gathered up her purse as though she was preparing to leave.

"And scare him off? No way! If you all descend on him, he won't know what hit him. Remember, I need the extra money."

"Okay, we won't go over all at once. But I'll be there later this afternoon." Zoey rose.

Jesse slid from the large booth next. "I'll come over after church tomorrow."

"And I'll see you tomorrow evening," Beth added. "Samuel told me to tell you to bring Chance along to the barbecue."

Darcy, the last to exit the booth, lumbered to her feet, putting her hand at the small of her back. "That leaves Monday after you get off work. I'll come over after I visit my doctor." She patted her round stomach. "Twelve weeks to go, but then who's counting?"

"Certainly not you," Tanya said with a laugh. Standing in the midst of her circle of friends, she shook her head. "You all are gonna scare the man away, so I don't want any unexpected visits." She started for the café door. "You'll see him soon enough. Give him a chance to settle in."

Her friends' chuckles followed Tanya outside. She wouldn't put it past each one of them to ignore what she'd said and show up right on time. She was lucky to have friends like them.

Tanya slid into her six-year-old white van, equipped with a lift for Crystal's wheelchair, and backed out of her parking space. Turning down Third Avenue a few minutes later, she spied Chance, dressed in tan slacks and a black short-sleeved shirt, walking toward Berryhill Road with three large bags in his arms.

She pulled over to the curb and rolled down the window. "Want a ride?"

For a brief, few seconds he hesitated before he made his way toward the vehicle and placed one sack on the ground, then reached for the handle. After he climbed in, he settled two bags at his feet and one in his lap. "Thanks."

Did he get the job? Tanya wondered but didn't say anything. Instead, she drove in silence, aware of every minute movement Chance made. Even his clean, fresh scent saturated the air in the van.

Searching her mind for something to say, she dug her teeth into her bottom lip, painfully aware of one of her shortcomings. She wasn't good at small talk, especially with strangers. Finally she lit upon a subject as she turned onto Berryhill Road. "It's been unusually warm for even the end of September. I love winter and cold weather, but I'm afraid if this keeps up we won't have much of one." Boy, you would think she could come up with a better topic than the weather!

Silence.

Okay, maybe she should try a question. "Which do you prefer?" She threw a glance toward Chance.

His brow creased. "Prefer?"

"Cold or hot weather?" Why couldn't she think of something better to talk about? Next, she would hear him snoring because she'd put him to sleep with her scintillating conversation.

"Cold."

"Oh, then we have something in common." The second she'd said the last sentence she'd wanted to take every word back. What she really wanted to talk about was the interview with Nick. But what if Chance hadn't gotten the job?

She slid another look toward him as she pulled into her driveway. The neutral expression on his face told her nothing of what he was thinking. She decided she couldn't wait for him to say anything about the interview. "Did Nick hire you?"

"Yes. I start Wednesday."

"That's great!" Why wasn't he more excited?

When she switched off the engine, Chance opened his door and hopped out. Before he had an opportunity to escape upstairs to his apartment, Tanya hurried around the front of the van and took the bag he'd set on the ground.

"I can come back for it," he said, striding toward the stairs.

She thought about her conversation with her friends at the café and the fact she wanted to get to know him better, not because she was interested in him as a man but because she needed to know more since he was her tenant. *Yeah, right, Tanya,* she silently scolded herself, knowing in her heart that wasn't the real reason.

"Nonsense. That's what neighbors are for—to help," she hurriedly said as he put half the length of the driveway between them.

She saw him flinch when she'd said neighbors and wondered about his reaction. Somebody had hurt him. A neighbor? When he shifted at the top of the stairs so he could unlock his door, she glimpsed that haunted look again that aroused her compassion and her curiosity.

Chance disappeared inside as Tanya put her foot on the first step. Quickening her pace, she half expected him to return to the landing and take the bag she carried, then bar her from entering his apartment. But when she reached the threshold, she found him across the room. He stood stiffly at the kitchen table, staring at the floor as though a memory had grabbed hold of him and wouldn't let go. The look that flashed across his face tore at her heart.

A board creaked as she moved inside. His head snapped up, his gaze snaring hers. A shutter descended over his expression, and he turned away and busied himself by emptying his bags.

"Are you all right?" she asked and crossed the large room. His expression earlier had for one brief moment reminded her of Tom's that first time she had gone to the prison to see him.

Chance stiffened, stopping for a few seconds before resuming his task. "I'm fine."

Although the words were spoken casually, she knew something she'd said had upset him. "I'm sorry if I—"

He pivoted toward her and took the sack from her. "Thanks for helping. I can take it from here."

In other words, get lost, Tanya thought but wasn't ready to take the not-so-subtle hint. She didn't totally understand why, but she needed to help him, as though God was urging her to be there for him. Something in his past had caused him to stop believing. Her faith was the only thing that had held her life together over the past few years. Without Christ she would never have been able to piece the fragments together into a whole— albeit a fragile whole.

"That's okay. I don't mind helping. Crystal's at church at a youth group activity, and I don't have to pick her up for another twenty minutes." She began removing the groceries from the paper bag she'd brought in, ignoring the scowl on his face.

While she put the food on the table, Chance took the

items and shelved them, each movement economical. The short sleeves of his black cotton shirt didn't hide the fact the man had well-defined muscles. This prodded the thought she should do something for exercise other than walking to and from the van.

He froze in midmotion. Her gaze lifted to his, and she saw a question in his eyes as he noted her interest. Heat scorched her cheeks. She didn't usually stare at anyone, least of all a man. And then to be caught doing it mortified her.

She averted her head and asked the first thing that popped into her mind, "Did you mean it when you said you'd help me with a budget?"

"I never say anything unless I mean it." He continued putting away his food, though thankfully his back was to her now.

If she'd had to look into his face, she would have fled the apartment. She couldn't believe she had openly stared at him again and then worse been caught doing it. She really had no experience when it came to men. The only one she had seriously dated had been Tom her senior year in high school. Not long after she'd graduated, they had married. Crystal had been born two years later.

"I could use your help," she murmured, surprised at her boldness in asking him for help.

"I can come over later tonight." He paused for several heartbeats. "Unless you have other plans."

Like a date, she thought, then nearly laughed out loud. There were some people in town who still thought she might have known about what Tom had been doing after Crystal's accident. If it weren't for her church and circle of friends, she would have left Sweetwater rather

than endure their silent accusations that she had known
Tom had been setting fire to all those barns. She'd never
dreamed that her husband's rage at Crystal's accident
and her paralysis would manifest itself that way. She'd
been so wrapped up in dealing with Crystal's recovery
and her own manic depression she hadn't seen the signs.
Guilt still gnawed at her insides over not being there
for Tom when he'd needed her the most. That guilt had
plunged her into some dark times once, but she wouldn't
allow it to again.

"I don't have any plans except picking Crystal up
and then doing the chores that I leave for the weekend."

His gaze fixed on her. "I'll come over around eight
then."

"That's fine." His loneliness, a palpable force, reached
out to her and drew her to him.

She took a step toward Chance, grabbing a can of
green beans and thrusting it at him. Her hand trembled
as he took it, his fingers brushing against hers. Her
breath caught in her throat as his look delved beneath
her surface as if he searched for her innermost thoughts.

He opened his mouth to say something but instead
snapped it close, spun around and placed the can on a
shelf. "Great, then I'll see you later."

She was being dismissed again, but for some reason
she didn't want to leave just yet. Even though tension
vibrated in the air, a strong need to comfort—again she
had no idea what or why—swamped her. She curled her
hands into tight fists to keep from touching his arm.

"Listen, if there's anything—"

"Thanks for helping me put my groceries up. If
you're gonna pick up Crystal, you'd better get going."

He turned his back to her and opened another cabinet door.

Tanya backed up several paces, saying, "You're right. I'd better leave." She whirled around and hurried from the apartment.

Out on the landing she paused and stared down at her driveway and the back of her house. She couldn't shake the feeling that God was pushing her toward Chance Taylor, that he needed a friend, someone to show him the power of the Lord. With quivering hands, she gripped the wooden railing.

Lord, how can I be Your instrument when my own life is so messed up?

No answer came to mind, leaving her feeling as though God was saying everyone can help another in need. *Is that true?* There was only one way to find out. She would be Chance's friend because she knew what it was like not to have one. She also knew the difference her friends had made in her life. No one should go through life without people to care about him, and for some reason, she sensed Chance was totally alone.

With a glance at her watch, she noted the time. She had to pick up Crystal in less than five minutes. Rushing down the stairs, she withdrew her keys from her jeans pocket then climbed into the van.

Ten minutes later she pulled into the parking lot next to the church and jogged toward the back door that led into the classrooms. Usually Crystal was waiting for her by the entrance, but today she wasn't around. As Tanya headed down the long hallway, she heard voices coming from the last room on the left where the youth group met.

She started to enter when her daughter's words halted her.

"I don't know what to do about them, Sean."

"Ignore them. They aren't worth your time."

"I wish I could."

The sob in Crystal's voice contracted Tanya's heart. She hurried inside. "Honey, are you all right?"

With her daughter's back to her, she couldn't see Crystal's face as she answered, "Yeah, sure."

"I'm sorry I'm late." Tanya took a step forward.

"You aren't that late. Sean's been keeping me company."

A strange expression flitted across Darcy's son's features before he pulled himself together. "Yeah, Mrs. Bolton. Crystal's been receiving a lot of spam lately on the Internet."

If Tanya hadn't sensed the seriousness of the situation, she would have choked on her laughter. "Spam?"

Crystal finally swung her wheelchair around. "Yeah, I went to the wrong website by mistake and now I'm getting all kinds of spam."

Tanya knew that probably wasn't what Sean and Crystal had been talking about, but she also knew by the tilt to her daughter's chin she wouldn't get it out of her until Crystal was ready to tell her. Her daughter had been keeping a lot of secrets lately. But that didn't mean Tanya wouldn't do some more checking around. When she had talked with Zoey and Beth earlier about this, they hadn't known what was going on but said they would look into it for her. "I guess I can take a look at it, but I don't know much about computers."

Sean shot to his feet. "That's okay. I'll come over tomorrow after church and see what I can do."

"That's great. See, Crystal, how easy the problem can be fixed? From what Darcy says, Sean can do anything with a computer."

"Yeah, Mom," her daughter mumbled with her head down, her hands twisting together in her lap. "This may not be that easy to take care of."

The sound of his feet pounding against the pavement lured him into a rhythmic trance as Chance ran down Berryhill Road, heading toward his temporary home. Sweat drenched his white T-shirt and face. He almost went past the one-story older house with a detached garage and apartment above it. He jogged a few yards beyond, slowed and circled back around.

Freedom, as he hadn't experienced in years, called to him. He wanted to keep going, but his body screamed with exhaustion, not used to this form of exercise—not for the two years he'd spent incarcerated.

He came to a stop at the end of the driveway and bent over, drawing in lungfuls of rich oxygen, the air scented with the smells of the clean outdoors, nothing stale and musty about it. The rich colors that surrounded him no longer threw him.

He had dreamed for so long about running with the wind cooling his skin and the sun beating down to warm his chilled body that he could hardly believe he was finally doing it. He'd taken so much for granted before—not anymore, not ever again. He cherished each fresh breath of freedom, each precious day he could walk out of a place unhindered, each time he could close his eyes and not worry about whether he would wake up the next morning or not. His life began the day he'd walked out of prison.

Was his new job thrusting him back into a world he didn't want to be in? He needed a job and had been glad for a reference from Samuel, but the more he thought about the duties Nick wanted his assistant to do the more he felt as though he was being thrust back into the corporate life he'd wanted to avoid, that very life that had required hours and hours of overtime. If he had been with his wife and daughter when they had come home to find a stranger in their house, then maybe they would be alive today.

Still he needed the job. He would just have to take it one day at a time and not let his job consume his whole life. Not ever again.

With his heartbeat slowing, he strode toward the stairs that led to his apartment. A quick look toward the left halted his progress. Crystal sat on the deck, drawing something on a pad. Suddenly she threw down her pencil, tore off the sheet and crunched it into a ball. She tossed it into the yard where several other similar papers lay crumpled.

The frustration and anger that marked the teenager's face drew him toward her. If his daughter were alive, he would want to be there for her. That was impossible, of course, but he could help Tom's daughter.

"Nothing working out?" Chance gestured toward the wadded-up papers in the grass.

Crystal took the pencil her service dog had retrieved for her and looked up at him. "What's the use? I'm not any good anyway."

He descended the two steps to the yard and smoothed

out one of the sheets. He whistled. "If this isn't good, then I hate to think what you consider bad. Who is this?" He came back to sit in the lounge chair next to her.

"Just a guy. No one important."

"Are all those attempts of him?"

Crystal nodded, peering away.

"Do you always waste your time drawing someone who isn't important to you?"

She sighed, then shook her head. "He doesn't know I'm alive."

The anguish that wrenched her voice did the same to him. He cleared his throat and asked, "How do you know?"

"I just do. I might as well be dead for all he cares."

The pain her words produced stole his breath. "I'm sorry. I..." Words failed him.

Chapter Three

For a brief moment Chance thought of his daughter. He remembered Haley making a comment a few days before she'd been killed about how she would just die if she didn't get to go to a friend's party. Haley never made it to the birthday party. He turned away, aware that Crystal had clasped his arm while her service dog licked his hand.

"Are you okay, Chance?"

The alarm in her voice swung his gaze to Crystal. He forced a grin that was an effort to maintain. "I'm fine. I had a daughter. She would have been near your age if she'd lived." He couldn't believe he'd said that out loud. He didn't talk about Haley—he couldn't without—

"Oh, I'm so sorry. What happened?"

Gone were Crystal's problems as she leaned toward him, wanting to offer comfort. Most of the time he could handle it. Coming to Sweetwater had for some reason revived all those memories. Probably because Crystal was so close in age to Haley. There was only a year between them.

"She was killed." He scooted forward in the chair. "But I don't want to talk about me. Tell me about this guy you have a crush on."

Crystal started to say something but decided not to. Instead, she shrugged. "There's nothing to say. He's popular. I'm not." She put her hand on her service dog, stroking her Lab's black fur. "He's on the basketball team. Even though he's a freshman, he plays varsity because he's so good. The season will start in six weeks. I try to go to every game."

"You like basketball," he said, sensing Crystal steering the conversation away from the guy she cared about.

Her face lit. "Yes. I've even tried to play some with Sean. He's my best friend."

"Are you any good?"

Laughter invaded her features. "Are you kidding? I can't even hit the backboard now. I use to be able to before the accident. But I can still dribble."

"Maybe all you need is practice. I could fix you up a basketball hoop and backboard if you want."

"Really?"

He nodded, her enthusiasm contagious. "If it's okay with your mom."

"What's okay with me?"

The screen door banged closed, and Tanya strolled toward him. Her smile of greeting, reaching deep into her eyes, soothed some of the tension knotting his stomach. He came to his feet, facing Tanya, who was only a few inches shorter than his own six-foot-plus height.

"I offered to put up a basketball hoop for Crystal."

Her mahogany eyes grew dull. She ran her hand through her short brown hair, brushing back her wispy bangs. "I don't want—I appreciate the offer, but I'm sure you have better things to do."

He grinned, wanting to tease the smile back into her eyes, needing to lighten the mood. "Nope. I don't have anything to do except shop for some new clothes between now and Wednesday. So I'm pretty much a man of leisure in need of a project."

"Mom?"

Tanya glanced at her daughter. Eagerness replaced her earlier sadness. For the past three years Tanya had constantly depended on others to make it through. Each day she felt herself growing stronger. And with that, she had determined she would learn to stand on her own two feet. She didn't want to become any more beholden to Chance Taylor than she was. She'd already regretted asking him to help her with her budget. But how could she turn her daughter down? Basketball and drawing were the two things Crystal loved the most.

"Fine. But only if you let me help you. And I'm paying for the materials." Somehow she would come up with the money for the hoop, backboard and wood to secure it to the garage.

"Good. See you two later."

Tanya watched Chance stroll away, his hair damp from exercise, a fine sheen of sweat covering his face. He must have gone for a long run. He'd been gone over an hour. She should do more exercise. *I wonder if he would like a running partner,* she thought, realizing she'd probably never go jogging unless she did it with someone.

"Thanks, Mom."

Crystal's voice dragged her from her musings.

"You're welcome. Next time, honey, say something to me first. I could have figured out how to put one up."

Her daughter giggled. "This from the woman who until recently didn't know what a Phillips head screwdriver was?"

"But I do now. I'm getting quite handy around the house, if I do say so myself."

"I didn't ask him, Mom. He volunteered when we were talking about basketball. Did you know he had a daughter? She died."

"Really! That's horrible." Tanya peered toward the apartment over her garage, beginning to see why there was such a look of vulnerability about Chance Taylor. Losing a child was the worst thing she could imagine. She remembered when Crystal had first been taken to the hospital almost four years ago. The feeling of devastation had thrown her life into a tailspin that slowly she had managed to right, but not without a lot of heartache along the way.

"Do you think that's why he wants to help me out?"

"Possibly, honey." Then Tanya grinned. "But more likely because you're such a sweet child."

Crystal screwed up her face into a pout. "I'm not a child anymore, Mom, in case you haven't noticed."

Her daughter's fervent words wiped the smile from Tanya's face. "Oh, ba—Crystal, I've noticed what a beautiful young lady you're growing up to be."

"Then you're the only one," Crystal mumbled and wheeled herself into the house.

Stunned at the despondency in her daughter's voice, Tanya quickly followed Crystal inside only to find the door to her room closed with her Do Not Disturb sign hanging from the knob. She knocked.

"Go away."

"Crystal, we need to talk."

"I don't have anything else to say," her daughter said right before the sound of loud music blasted through the air.

Tanya stared at the door, trying to decide whether to ignore her child's request or wait for another time when she would be more willing to talk. *Lord, help me here. What do I do?*

The music grew even louder, silently giving Tanya her answer. Nothing would be accomplished this evening finding out what was at the root of her daughter's unhappiness.

"I noticed you've owned this house for ten years. Why don't you take out a second mortgage on it?" Chance asked Tanya later that evening.

"Well..." She didn't have an answer for him. Sitting at her kitchen table with all her finances spread out before her, she stared at the total figure of her debt, in large black numbers on the paper before her. "I didn't want another bill to pay."

"You could use it to pay off some of these bills and consolidate them into one payment. That'll be easier for you to keep track of rather than these seven different places." He waved his hand over the pile.

"That might work."

Chance wrote down some numbers. "I think you could comfortably handle this much a month in a payment."

"Only as long as I have a tenant for the apartment."

He looked up from the paper he was figuring on.

"Since I've taken a job with Blackburn Industries, I'll be here for a while."

Why had that simple declaration sent her heart racing as though she had just finished running alongside him earlier this afternoon? "It's gonna be more than a while until I can pay this off."

"You can always declare bankruptcy."

"No! Never! I'll pay my debts even if it takes me years." The memory of her father skipping out on her mother and her when she was a little girl materialized in her mind. The gambling debts he'd left behind had been overwhelming until her mother had nearly collapsed under their weight. But it had been a matter of pride to her mother that she didn't declare bankruptcy, sometimes the only thing that had kept her going.

"Then a second mortgage is the best way to go. I've written down a budget that should help you stay on track." He slid the paper across the table to her.

She picked it up and studied it. One large, long-term debt versus many smaller ones. She liked the idea. "I can check into it at the bank on Monday. This way I can finish paying the law—" She pressed her lips shut, wanting to snatch her last sentence back. She slanted a look at Chance to see his reaction.

He calmly stacked the sheets into a nice pile as though she hadn't spoken. "Legal fees can be staggering."

When she didn't get the question about what kind of legal fees, she relaxed back in the chair, inhaling several, calming breaths. "I can also pay a lot of the hospital bill, too. Of course, it'll depend on how much I can get as a second mortgage. I wish I was better with money." She leaned toward him and got a whiff of the soap he must have used when taking a shower. She thought of a green hillside in the spring and for a second forgot what she was going to say.

His gaze connected with hers. The beating of her heart echoed in her ears as she became lost in the sky blue of his eyes.

One corner of his mouth quirked up. "How long have you been a teller?"

"Almost two years. Don't tell the bank manager what I said about handling money. It can be our little secret."

"My lips are sealed."

A twinkle danced in his eyes, and she lowered her regard to those lips he mentioned. All she could focus on was the way they curved slightly at the end in that smile she had decided was lethal.

She slid her gaze away and took the stack of papers, then stuffed them into the manila envelopes she kept them in. Her hands shook, and she nearly dropped all of them. She scooted her chair back. The scraping sound across the tile echoed through the kitchen. After she rose, she walked to the desk by the phone and crammed them in the top drawer.

"There. Out of sight, out of mind, at least for the rest of the evening."

"Money worries can be very hard on a person."

"You speak as though you've had firsthand knowledge." She lounged back on the desk with her hands digging into the wooden edge and braced herself for him to either ignore her or shut the topic down.

He stared out the window that afforded him a view of Crystal on the deck with her service dog. "I've helped many clients in the past come up with a plan to get out of debt. Some make it. Others don't."

There was more to it than that, but his evasive look alerted her to the fact she wouldn't get an answer from him until he was ready. Had he been like one of those clients, in debt, struggling to make ends meet? For some reason she didn't think that was it, even though he had few possessions that she knew of and he had arrived in town on a bus.

Tanya pushed herself away from the desk. "I intend to be one of your success stories."

"Good." He stood. "I'd better go. It's getting late." His glance strayed again to the window that overlooked the deck. "Is something wrong with Crystal? She hardly said two words tonight."

"You know how moody teenage girls can be. She's upset with me and even ate her dinner in her room before going outside on the deck."

"Yes, I know what..." His voice trailed off into the silence.

"Oh, I'm sorry. I shouldn't have said anything. Crystal told me you had a daughter who died."

He closed his eyes for a few seconds, then when he opened them again, there was a raw look in their blue depths that turned them the color of the lake right before a storm. "I lost both my wife and daughter a few years back."

"I'm so sorry. My husband died last spring, so I understand what you must have gone through."

An expression full of doubt flickered across his face for a few seconds before he managed to mask it. He walked to the back door and thrust it open, then disappeared quickly. Tanya heard him say something to her daughter. She observed the exchange, saw Crystal's features coming alive while she spoke to Chance.

She even laughed, which thrilled Tanya. Her daughter hadn't laughed much lately—ever since the start of high school six weeks before.

Chance sensed Tanya's gaze on him and shifted his weight from one foot to the other. In prison he'd gotten used to being watched all the time, but that didn't mean he liked the feeling. It made him think of a bug under a microscope, every movement noted and analyzed.

"May I pet your dog?" he asked Crystal, the hairs on his nape prickling.

"Sure. Charlie loves people."

"He's a beauty." Chance stroked the length of the black Lab's back. "So what are you writing about?"

"About the prejudice in the book *To Kill a Mockingbird*."

"How far have you gotten?"

"I'm almost finished with the rough draft. We're supposed to compare and contrast it to the prejudice in our society today."

"How's that coming?" Chance asked, having experienced his own kind of prejudice when he had been released from prison three weeks ago. Although his conviction had been overturned, people still looked at him strangely, and he could see the question of his innocence lurking in their gazes.

"The comparing and contrasting has been the easiest part. You know, not all prejudice is racial."

"True. People can be prejudiced against anyone, an overweight person or someone who stutters. There's all kinds."

"I know."

Chance studied Crystal's solemn expression, illuminated in the light by the door. "Is something going on at school?"

Her gaze slid away from his, her head dropping until her chin nearly touched her chest.

"Crystal? What's happening?"

"Nothing," she mumbled.

He knelt and leaned close because he'd barely heard her reply. "Is someone bothering you?"

She didn't say anything.

"Crystal?" Something was wrong. Tension oscillated in waves from the teenager.

"It's really nothing. I can handle it."

He bent down farther until he caught her gaze and held it. "You'll tell someone if you can't?"

She lifted her head, visibly swallowed and nodded. She shivered. "It's getting cold. I'd better go in. Night." She guided her wheelchair toward the back door and waited for Charlie to open it for her.

Chance didn't leave the deck until the teenager had disappeared inside. Through the open blinds he saw Tanya say something to her daughter, following Crystal out of the room. He'd speak to Tanya tomorrow about what her daughter had implied. If someone was harassing Crystal, it needed to stop, especially with her earlier comment about the guy she was attempting to draw. Was he the one bothering her?

Chance hurried up the stairs two at a time and entered his apartment. Tom had been there for him in prison. He would be there for Tom's daughter. He owed the man his life.

Having no books, radio or television, he decided to go to bed early. He intended to start the basketball hoop

for Crystal early the next morning if he could find a
store open on Sunday that sold lumber and the other
supplies he would need. He wanted to give the teenager
something to smile about.

In the dark he stretched out on the double bed with
his arms folded behind his head. Staring up at the ceiling, he reviewed the day's activities. He had a job. Only
time would tell whether it was the best one for him. He'd
assisted Tanya with her budget and he knew now how
to help Crystal. Not too bad.

"I'll protect them, Tom," he whispered into the blackness, his eyelids growing heavy with sleep....

*Three men with exaggerated grins and taunting
voices surrounded him. Chance glanced from one to the
other. When his gaze finally settled on the ringleader,
tall and thin but with arms like steel clubs, Chance's
heart thudded against his chest. The instigator of this
little impromptu meeting clenched his fist around a
homemade knife, the blade long—three, exaggerated
feet—and sharp. His cackles chilled the air in the cell
as though a blizzard had swept through the prison,
freezing everything but them.*

*Trapped, with his back against the bars, Chance
didn't have to look around to know he wouldn't be able
to walk away from them without a fight. He prepared
himself, bracing his feet apart, balling his hands.*

*The ringleader charged, letting out a blood-curdling
scream that plunged the temperature in the cell even
colder. Suddenly from out of nowhere, Tom flew between him and the tall, thin man, planting himself in
front of the long, long knife. The inmate brought the*

weapon back and shoved it toward Tom and him. The blade went through Tom's chest to skewer Chance.

Chance bolted up in bed, rivers of sweat running off him as he tried to draw in a decent breath. His lungs hurt as though he really had been pierced by a knife. He couldn't seem to inhale enough air. The pounding of his heart thundered in his ears, the nightmare relived yet again. When would it ever go away? Would Tom's death haunt him forever? He dug his fingers into the bedding, trying to focus on the pain emanating from them rather than his heart.

He knew one thing. He had to tell Tanya where he'd been for the past few years. He didn't want her to find out from someone else. He owed her that much.

Tanya pulled into her driveway after church, stopped at the side of her house and stared at the scene before her. Shock trembled through her. Chance was painting a basketball backboard bright yellow. The color glittered in the bright sunlight.

"I didn't think he would do it today," Tanya murmured, amazed at how fast Chance had managed to put the hoop up. She and Crystal had only been gone three hours.

"Do what, Mom?" Crystal asked from the back of the van where her wheelchair was locked into place.

"Chance has already put up that basketball hoop for you."

"He has?" Her daughter's own astonishment sounded in her voice. "I want to see."

Tanya slipped from the front and went to the back of the van to let down Crystal in her wheelchair. Charlie bounded out before her daughter. The second she was on the ground Crystal spun about and drove toward Chance who climbed down the ladder as she approached.

A grin, wide and contagious, graced his mouth. "Well, what do you think?" He pointed toward the finished product.

Tanya noticed a streak of yellow paint slashing across his cheek. She clasped her hands together to still the urge to wipe it off. Much too intimate a gesture for someone she'd only met a few days before. Yet it seemed so natural for her to do it.

"I made it so you could adjust the height of the hoop some. Right now it's a little lower than normal. Once you master this height, I can raise it."

His comment to Crystal made it seem as though he intended to stay in Sweetwater, at least for the time being. Even though she knew he had the job with Nick, the realization Chance would be around sent a current of warmth through Tanya that she hadn't experienced in years.

Her daughter beamed as though the sun shone in her smile. "I'm gonna get my basketball." With Charlie beside her, Crystal steered her wheelchair toward the ramp that led to the deck.

"Thank you, Chance. She hasn't smiled much lately."

"Do you know anything about a boy she has a crush on at school?"

The question stunned Tanya. She knew her daughter was growing up, but Crystal hadn't said anything to her, and they had always had a close relationship, especially because of all they had been through together the past four years. "No, who?"

"I don't know. But the other day she used up a lot of paper trying to draw him. She was never satisfied.

When I said something to her about him, she said he didn't know she was alive."

Her breath jammed in her throat. Was this what had been bothering Crystal? She had a crush on someone who didn't return the feelings? Tanya's heart squeezed, an intense pressure building in her chest. How could she protect Crystal from being hurt?

"She hasn't said anything to me. I'll do some checking and see what I can find out. Something has been wrong with her lately so it's possible this might be it." Although she doubted that was what had made her daughter so unhappy lately, she would investigate. Remembering the day before and the conversation she'd interrupted between Crystal and Sean, Tanya couldn't shake the feeling her daughter was being harassed.

Chance studied her for a few seconds. "But you don't think it is?"

"No." She started to tell him what she thought it might really be, when she heard the back door closing and glanced toward her daughter making her way toward them. "Don't say anything to Crystal about us talking about the boy. It would only upset her."

"Sure, but if I can help, let me know."

Tanya tilted her head to the side and studied Chance. "Why do you want to help? Up until a few days ago we were strangers."

"Samuel told me about how rough it has been the past few years for you."

She pulled up straight, her arms rigid at her sides. "I won't take anyone's charity. Crystal and I can get along just fine by ourselves." She whirled around and started for the back door when a hand clamped around her arm.

Chapter Four

"I just want to help, Tanya." Chance released his grasp almost immediately after touching her.

But Tanya felt the imprint of his fingers on her upper arm as though he branded her. She glanced at where they had lain for a few electrified seconds, then up into his eyes, full of regret. "I can't take pity, Chance. I've had my fill of that in my life."

"No pity. Your daughter—" he peered at Crystal making her way toward them and pitched his voice low as he continued "—she reminds me of my daughter. It helps to help her—and you."

All anger dissolved as Tanya turned completely toward him, wanting to comfort, wishing she had the right to embrace him, to let him know he wasn't alone. But she didn't want him to think she pitied him because she knew, like her, he wouldn't appreciate that. "I want to pay for the supplies. That's the least I can do since you did all the work."

The sound of a basketball striking against the concrete of the driveway drew closer. Tanya looked toward her daughter and managed to give her a smile. "Sean said something about coming over this afternoon. Maybe you two could practice some."

"I gave him a call. His mom is bringing him now." Crystal continued to dribble.

"Give it a try," Chance said to her daughter who kept looking at the backboard.

"I think I'll wait till Sean gets here. Thanks, Chance." Crystal flashed him a smile, the basketball connecting with the driveway a rhythmic sound in the sudden quiet. "Mom made some lemonade. Want some?"

Chance chuckled, swiping the back of his hand across his forehead. "That sounds great." He swung his full attention to Tanya and whispered, "I think your daughter wants us to get lost so she can practice."

"But who will get the ball for her?"

"She'll manage. Besides, she has Charlie. I wouldn't be surprised if she teaches him to retrieve it for her."

Tanya began walking toward the back door. "I do have some lemonade that you are welcome to have."

Chance dropped his gaze to his cutoff jeans and dirty, sweaty T-shirt. "Although it does sound great, I think I'd better pass on it. I need a shower."

"Oh, I almost forgot. Beth and Samuel want us to bring you to a barbecue they're having this evening at their house."

"What time?"

"Six. Casual attire."

His grin dimpled his cheeks. "Good, because that's all I have at the moment."

Chance headed for his apartment and that shower. At the entrance, he stopped and glanced back at Crystal. A young man jogged up the driveway. Chance waited before entering. When Tanya's daughter smiled a greeting, he decided the teenager must be Sean and went inside.

He should have taken Tanya up on that glass of lemonade and used the time away from Crystal to explain about being in prison with Tom. The words had been on the tip of his tongue for a few seconds, then Crystal had returned with her ball and the moment passed. There was a part of him that realized he was making excuses which wasn't like him. But so many changes had occurred over the past few years. He hated to think being a coward was one of them.

No! He would tell her tonight after the barbecue. No matter what.

"You know the others are going be jealous that I'm the first to see your mysterious tenant." Beth took a huge salad bowl out of the refrigerator in her kitchen.

"So that's what was behind Chance's invitation tonight," Tanya said with a laugh.

"Well, not exactly, just a plus. Samuel wants Chance to feel at home here in Sweetwater." Beth stepped closer and looked around as though to make sure no one else was in the room and added, "I think he hopes Chance will settle down here permanently. If that happens, that will certainly solve a problem for you."

The heat of a blush singed Tanya's cheeks. "What problem?" That she was dateless and gun-shy? she wondered but kept that to herself.

"Why, your apartment needing a tenant. What did you think I meant?" Beth pinned her with an amused look.

Tanya refused to squirm under her friend's scrutiny.

"Sometimes I think all of you have taken after Jesse and her matchmaking ways. Remember trying to fix me up with Darrell?"

"Oh, that." Beth waved her hand. "I just wanted to help a fellow teacher feel at home since he moved to Sweetwater two months ago."

Tanya harrumphed, knowing good and well that wasn't all there was to it. Since she had become the only unmarried member of her circle of friends, she had noticed an increased interest in making sure she met every unmarried male Jesse, Darcy, Beth and Zoey knew, which made for quite a few.

"How's the morning sickness been?" Tanya asked, deciding to take the focus off her and dating—or rather, lack of dating.

"Much better. I haven't had any trouble in a week. And now that I've started wearing maternity clothes, my outfits are more comfortable."

"The next four or five months will go by so fast. Before you know it, your baby will be here. And then the work will really start."

Beth pulled a set of salad tongs out of the drawer. "I understand Sean helped Crystal today shoot baskets."

"Is there a secret left in this town? That just happened this afternoon."

"I didn't know Crystal shooting baskets was supposed to be a secret. The basketball hoop is out in the open where anyone can see it. It's a bright yellow. A little hard *not* to see it, if you ask me."

Peering out the window, Tanya found her daughter sitting with Craig, Beth's stepson, talking. "I don't think she wants it known all over town. I think someone is harassing Crystal at school. I wouldn't want the fact she's practicing basketball to be something she'll get teased about. She loves the game and that could kill it."

"Harassing Crystal? Who?"

"She won't say. She has a crush on a boy who doesn't return the feelings. It could be him, but I don't think so."

"Let me do some checking around, discreetly, of course. If someone is, I'll find out and let you know. That's unacceptable behavior at Sweetwater High."

"It's unacceptable behavior anywhere, but you and I know it goes on all the time."

"Sadly, it's true. C'mon. Let's join the men." Beth grabbed not only the large salad bowl but two bottles of dressing.

"What can I take outside?"

"I have tea already on the table, but get the pitcher of ice water just in case someone wants that instead."

Tanya withdrew the green plastic pitcher from the refrigerator and started for the door.

Beth paused before opening it and peered over her shoulder at Tanya. "I also heard that Chance built the basketball hoop for Crystal. That was nice of him. He's very helpful to have around."

Tanya narrowed her eyes on her good friend. "And?"

"Nothing. Just an observation I was making."

"And half the townspeople, I bet."

"What can I say?" Beth shrugged, then pulled the door open.

Chance, being the closest person to Beth and Tanya, relieved Beth of the bottles of dressing and placed them on the long picnic table, already set for dinner. Her friend murmured her thanks, her gaze shifting to Tanya as though she shared a secret with Tanya. She glanced away, feeling the warmth creep up her face. Honestly, some people in town were downright nosy. She'd forgotten that about Sweetwater. She shouldn't have since not that long ago she had been the major object of gossip with her husband's arson conviction, his demand for a divorce and then his death last spring. And from that, she knew she didn't like being the center of attention one bit. Thankfully the past few months everything had settled down.

"Come and get it," Samuel called out to the kids as he placed the grilled meat on the red tablecloth.

Allie, Craig and Jane, Samuel's three children from his previous marriage, hurried toward the picnic table. Crystal followed in her wheelchair and positioned it at one end while Tanya sat on her daughter's left and Chance on the right. For just a brief moment it seemed as though they were two families sitting down to enjoy a meal together. Then Tanya had to remind herself that wasn't exactly right—even when Chance's gaze captured hers and held it for a few extra seconds while the Morgans sat down.

"Let's pray," Samuel said and bowed his head over his empty plate.

After saying his thanks to the Lord, Samuel began passing the food—a platter of barbecue chicken, the tossed green salad and a bowl of corn on the cob, cooked over the grill. The various aromas of the meal wafted to Tanya, teasing her appetite and making her stomach rumble.

"Well, at least I know that Tanya is hungry," Beth said, laughter dancing in her eyes.

"I forgot to eat lunch. I'm not hungry. I'm *starved*." Tanya took the platter and forked a piece of chicken, then passed the food to her daughter.

When everyone's plate was full, Samuel asked Chance, "What do you think of Sweetwater so far?"

"That's a loaded question."

"First impressions."

"Welcoming, friendly and beautiful with the lake nearby. When I went jogging yesterday and today, I had several people stop me to introduce themselves. When they heard we were friends, I got the rundown on you and the fine job you're doing as the Reverend of Sweetwater Community Church." Chance stopped for a few seconds, moving his food around on his plate before he added, "Several today wanted to know why I wasn't in church this morning."

Knowing the subject was a touchy one for Chance, Tanya said, "I keep promising myself that I'll start jogging, but I never seem to get around to doing it."

"What's stopping you?" Chance asked, his gaze linking with hers.

For a few seconds a connection zapped between them, making Tanya wish that they were alone so she could pursue his reluctance to attend church. Somehow she felt it was at the heart of what had wounded him. "I'm not very motivated to exercise since it isn't one of my favorite things to do. I know it would be a good thing to do, but it's so much easier to come up with a reason not to jog. It's not hard to talk myself out of it when I think about it. There's always laundry to do or the house to clean."

"You need a jogging partner," Beth said and pointedly looked from Tanya to Chance.

Tanya took a sip of her tea to hide her smile at the obvious hint her friend had thrown out to Chance.

Being the gentleman she was discovering Chance was, he asked, "Want to jog with me tomorrow?"

"Tomorrow I work late. I won't be home until after six. I usually grab something for Crystal and me to eat on the way home."

"That's okay. I can wait until then."

"I doubt I could keep up with you."

Chance chuckled. "You *are* good at coming up with excuses. I haven't been running for long. Don't worry about me. I'll stop by at seven, and we can go jogging by the lake until it gets dark or one of us tires."

"Well, then it's settled, Tanya. You've got yourself a jogging partner." Beth shifted her attention to Crystal. "How's the paper coming?"

"Done."

"Good. I've enjoyed reading your work. You're a talented writer, Crystal."

"This paper was easy."

"You wouldn't know it from the moans from some of your classmates. There are so many ways you can deal with the subject of prejudice in our society. You would think I asked them to write a book instead of five hundred words."

"That's a good subject for a sermon." Samuel lifted a chicken leg and took a bite.

As each Morgan gave his or her opinion about prejudice, Tanya slid a glance toward her daughter who was suddenly quiet, her head down as she played with her food, eating little. She also noticed Chance didn't say much, either.

As Jane declared, "You can't let people get away with putting you down. You've got to stand up to them." Tanya saw Crystal stiffen. Her reaction to the conversation only confirmed Tanya's earlier suspicion.

"Goodness, Tanya and Crystal probably aren't used to the lively discussions we have at the dinner table." Samuel caught Tanya's attention. "Sorry, we got carried away. Let's solve the world's problems another night. We've got guests." His gaze swept each person sitting at the table to make sure his point was understood.

Silence ruled for a few minutes while everyone finished eating.

When Beth went inside to get the dessert, Samuel said, "Chance, if you've got any free time with your new job, I sure could use someone to help with the finances at the new youth center. Think you have some time?"

"Sure." He would help Samuel any way he could since the reverend had been there for him on more than one occasion.

"You might even want to help out at the center," Samuel added with a grin as his wife came out with a chocolate cake.

While Beth sliced the dessert and passed the pieces around, Chance pictured himself entrenched in the life of Sweetwater. He rubbed his sweaty palm over the napkin in his lap before reaching for his fork to eat his cake. A job. Working at the youth center. Next, he would start going to Samuel's church. He knew that would make Samuel and Tanya happy, but he couldn't go under false pretenses. That wasn't right.

"I have some cake left. Anyone want seconds?" Beth asked with Samuel and Craig sliding their plates toward her.

Twenty minutes later after Tanya had helped clear the table and he and Samuel had made sure the backyard was cleaned up, Tanya announced, "We probably better go. Tomorrow's a school day."

"Don't remind me. I still have some papers to grade." Beth hugged Tanya and Crystal. "See you in class."

On the too-short drive back to Tanya's house, Chance tried to decide how best to bring up the subject of him being in prison. *Tanya, I knew your ex-husband because I was in the same cell block.* No, that wasn't good. *Tanya, I was innocent, but I went to prison for murder.*

No! I can't say that. But what can I say?

No answer came to mind as Tanya pulled into her driveway and climbed out to man the lift for Crystal. Charlie and the teenager headed for the ramp while Tanya grabbed her purse from the front seat. Crystal let herself into the house.

A light beaming down from the garage near the basketball hoop pooled around Chance. He stuffed his hands into his pockets and tried to form the words to explain his past. Tanya turned toward him, her mouth opening to say something. It snapped closed, her forehead knitting.

"What's wrong?" she asked, moving toward him.

Tell her. He sucked in a deep breath to alleviate the tightness in his chest. It didn't work. He felt as though he were suffocating. Again he drew in some oxygen-rich air and slowly the band about his torso loosened.

"Chance?"

"I need to talk to you. Do you have a minute?"

She peered toward the kitchen door then back at him. "Yes." She came even closer until she shared the pool of light with him.

Another deep breath flooded his senses with her scent of lilacs. He thought of a garden in the springtime with Tanya standing in the middle, sun warming her, birds singing, butterflies flittering from flower to flower. The picture brought him peace, and the constriction about him fell away.

"Up until three weeks ago I was in the state penitentiary...." He paused for a heartbeat. "For murder. My conviction was overturned because the real killer was found and is awaiting trial in Louisville."

As he made his rushed announcement, the color drained from Tanya's features, her body going stiff, her eyes growing round. Silence hung between them for a long moment. Chance saw a myriad of emotions flash across her face—shock, followed by anger, then finally a wary acceptance with a touch of pain in her eyes.

She brought her hand up to smooth back her wispy bangs. Her fingers trembled. "Did you know Tom?" she asked in a voice that quavered.

He nodded, his throat closed. He hadn't wanted to hurt her, to bring up bad memories, but he saw them in her eyes. Raw pain dominated her features now.

"Is that where you met Samuel?"

He pushed down his own reeling emotions, determined to finish this conversation with Tanya. "Yes. I became friends with Samuel—and Tom."

"Why did you come to Sweetwater?"

Tell her all of it. The words wouldn't come. He

couldn't hurt her anymore. And worse, he didn't want to be sent away—at least, not until he had fulfilled his promise to himself, so he settled on part of the truth. "Samuel and Tom both told me about the town and it seemed like a good place to start over, to put my life back together."

"Who were you accused of murdering?" Again she lifted her hand and combed her quivering fingers through her short hair.

He'd known that question would be eventually asked, but hearing it created a deep ache in his heart that spread to encompass his whole body. "My wife and daughter," he whispered in a voice roughened with the memories. He had found them, and he would never forget the picture of them, lifeless, staring up at him but not seeing him.

"Oh, Chance." Tanya's face crumpled, tears glistening in her eyes. "That's how you lost your family, to a killer?" she asked in a raspy voice.

The worst part was seeing the effect his words had on Tanya. When a tear escaped, he couldn't resist brushing his finger across her cheek, the feel of her warm skin riveting him to the present. "Yes, they surprised an intruder when they returned unexpectedly."

"Then why did *you* go to prison?"

Her innocent question produced a humorless laugh that died almost immediately. "That wasn't what the police originally thought, because my neighbor had overheard a very loud argument between Ruth and me a few hours before. I had to go in to work again and she wasn't happy with all the hours I was spending at the office. We had been fighting a lot about that subject. Some of our arguments were loud."

"Married couples fight. That's normal."

Chance looked off into the darkness that surrounded them. "My fingerprints were on the gun found at the scene because it was mine. The intruder had used my own gun to kill my family. There wasn't any sign of a break-in. So I became the prime suspect, and they stopped looking for an intruder even though there were a few pieces of expensive jewelry missing. The police felt that I had done that to cover up that I had killed them." Even to this day, it was almost inconceivable that the authorities had ever thought he would murder his own child.

Tanya moved to the stairs that led to his apartment and collapsed on the second step. She turned her face up toward him, but he couldn't see her expression in the dark. "How did they find the real killer?"

"This past year there were a series of robberies where the man snuck into garages when the homeowners were leaving. While they were gone, he would rob them and leave without anyone knowing until they couldn't find their jewelry or whatever he stole. Usually he took small, easily fenced items. He would case the houses, so he knew when the occupants would most likely leave and hide near the garage until they did. Then he would slip inside. A lot of people don't lock the door from the garage into their house. He would count on that."

"Until he did something wrong?" He didn't have to see her to know that anger laced her voice. But was it directed at him or the intruder?

Chance leaned against the railing, his hands gripping

the wood so tight he felt a splinter dig into his palm. He didn't want to relive this, but he owed Tanya that much. "Yeah, the thief invaded a home that wasn't totally empty. The homeowner was a former Marine and knew how to take care of himself. When they searched the thief's place, the police found all the jewelry missing from my house. He had kept it because it was too hot to get rid of right after—after the murders." The words clogged his throat. He swallowed and continued in a husky voice, "I think he forgot about the jewelry. He lived with his mother. He hadn't robbed anyone for eighteen months because he had been in jail for assault. Once he got out he started again and with each success got bolder and bolder."

"So if he'd left Louisville, you'd still be in prison?"

He quaked. "Yes. For life."

"Are the memories of your family haunting you?"

"Yes."

She attempted to stand, swayed and grabbed the railing, her hand next to his. "I know how that is. If you allow memories to, they can take over your life."

He hadn't thought it possible to tighten his hold on the wood railing, but he did. "I should have been there. Then they might be alive. But I was too busy working!"

"So even though you are free now, you really aren't. You're living in a self-imposed prison, the bars as strong as if they were made of steel."

"You sound like you speak from experience."

"I've been there. Probably still am. I know what guilt can do to a person. Don't you think I've beat myself up over the fact that Tom needed help and I didn't see it? I was too busy trying to deal with Crystal's accident and getting her well. My husband needed me."

Her words came to a quavering stop. He wanted to hold her, take her pain away, but he didn't have the right. In fact, after this evening she probably wouldn't want to have anything to do with him. He would remind her of Tom every time she saw him.

"I wasn't there for him, and when he was sent to prison, he rejected any help I tried to give him. My concern was too late and he made it clear he wanted nothing to do with his family." Tanya released a long breath. "I could understand his feelings toward me, but not his daughter. It tore Crystal up that she couldn't see her father."

"Prison isn't any place to have a family reunion."

She thrust her face toward him. "You sound like Tom! I married him for better or worse, and he discarded me when things got bad." Her voice rose several levels.

Knowing he would provoke her further, Chance inched closer until their breaths tangled. "Do you blame Tom?"

"Yes!" Tanya shouted then immediately covered her mouth, stepping back until the pool of light revealed the shock on her face.

For a few more seconds she continued to stare at Chance, then she whirled and fled into the house. The slamming of the door reverberated in the stillness and shuddered down his length. His legs weak, he fell back onto the step. He sat there in the dark and watched one light after another go out in the house. Minutes ticked into thirty and still he couldn't move.

What had he done? What can of worms had he opened with his confession? With no lease to protect him, he could be asked to leave tomorrow morning, then where would he be with his promise to himself?

All energy siphoned from him, he rested his elbows on his knees and clasped his hands together. He stared into the blackness of the night and wished he could erase the past hour. He hadn't wanted her to find out from someone else about his past, but the truth was he hadn't wanted her to know at all. How was he going to put it behind him when every time he saw her he would think of this evening?

Lord, where are You?

Chapter Five

Lord, where are You?

Tanya sat in the dark in her bedroom, aware that Chance was still out on the stairs to his apartment. She had seen him through the slats in her blinds and for a fleeting moment she had wanted to go out and take him into her arms to ease his hurt.

I need You, God. I don't know what to feel.

After the initial shock had worn off, anger had taken hold of her until she had heard his story. How could she not feel his pain as he had spoken about his murdered wife and daughter?

But how can I help him, Lord? You ask too much of me.

The remnants of her life were held together with a glue that threatened to dissolve at the least little problem. She was a stronger person than she had been this time last year, but not this strong—to help someone discover God's love and mercy. *I just can't. I don't have what it takes.*

She lay down and turned onto her side, staring at

the thin slivers of light pushing their way through the slats of the blinds. He was still out there—hurting, confused. She didn't have to get up and look. She felt it in her heart.

Squeezing her eyes closed, she hoped to block the lone image of Chance that haunted her. She couldn't. He loomed before her, materializing on the black screen of her mind with that half grin on his mouth while his eyes were full of pain.

She twisted to her other side and pounded her pillow. It didn't do any good. Frustration clutched her in a viselike grip.

She wasn't going to have any peace until she answered God's call. *You don't realize what You're asking! I could do more harm than good.*

As she settled back on the pillow and peered up at the ceiling, she resolved to be there for Chance. She would do the best she could and prayed God would be with her every step of the way with Chance.

At a few minutes before seven Chance rang Tanya's doorbell. A long moment passed. He turned to leave, part of him surprised that Tanya wouldn't keep her jogging date with him. But the other part wasn't. Not after the night before. Not after he had told her about his past.

His foot was on the first step when the door swung open. He spun around and faced Tanya, flustered, flushed.

"Sorry, I was late getting home. I just flew in the door a couple of minutes ago and threw on these pants and T-shirt." She came out onto the porch and sat on the step to finish tying one of her sneakers. When she rose, she gave him a sheepish look. "You think this is okay for jogging?"

Chance allowed his gaze to roam slowly down the length of Tanya, dressed in the bottom half of a bright pink jogging suit with the price tag still on it and an old, several sizes too large, white T-shirt. "You look fine."

More than fine, he thought but kept that to himself. Patches of red colored Tanya's cheeks, giving her a fresh, appealing look. Although she had been through a lot, there was still a touch of innocence about her.

"What do we do first? Stretch? Run in place?"

Her large eyes charmed him. For a long moment until a little frown wrinkled her forehead, he was so entranced by her mahogany gaze, he didn't realize she had spoken. Turning away, he broke her spell, appalled that he had been caught staring at her, and said, "First, let's take this off."

As he pointed toward the price tag, her gasp of surprise sounded, followed by her laughter. "I told you I was in a hurry. I didn't have anything to jog in so I got this on my way home from work. Now that I've spent my hard-earned money, I'm committed to doing this." With a tug, she ripped the tag off and stuffed it into her pocket. "Ready."

"I always do better if I stretch first."

As Chance went through a series of stretches, Tanya followed suit. Then he set off at a slow jog down Berryhill Road toward the lake. His sneakers pounded the pavement in rhythm with Tanya's. Their synchronized pace made him yearn for a time when Tom didn't stand between them, and yet her late husband was the very reason he was in Sweetwater.

When the lake came into view, Chance found the path that edged the shoreline, often used by joggers. He headed west, the sun below the line of trees, streaks of rose, orange and light pink fingering upward.

"Doing okay?" he asked after ten minutes.

Between pants, Tanya answered, "I…think…so."

Another ten minutes and Chance slowed to a walk. "Let's go to the boulder up ahead then turn back."

She didn't reply for twenty seconds then said, "Fine."

Chance slid a glance at her face, noting the sheen of sweat glistening on her forehead, her flushed cheeks. "Or, we can stop and rest if you want."

Her gaze swept to his. "No." She inhaled and exhaled shallow breaths. "I can do this."

At the boulder he started back the way they had come and noticed Tanya's breathing was more even and the red patches were fading from her cheeks. Even though he hadn't been jogging for long, he had been in shape before this. He suspected Tanya wasn't. He shouldn't have pushed so hard earlier. He would remember next time—if there was a next time. They still needed to talk about the evening before.

He came to a place in the path only five feet from the shoreline of the lake and stopped. "We've done enough for the first day. Let's rest, then walk back at a more leisurely pace. This is a beautiful spot." He saw some huge flat rocks not far away, crossed to the first one and sat, facing the water.

Tanya stayed on the trail for a moment. If the hairs tingling on his neck were any indication, she was staring at him and trying to decide what to do.

Without looking back at her, he said, "I haven't gotten to enjoy something like this in a long time."

Her sigh drifted to him, then the sound of her footsteps as she made her way to the rock next to his. She lowered herself onto it and brought her legs up to clasp them. Keeping her head averted, she stared at the water.

"Beautiful, isn't it?" he asked to break the silence.

She nodded.

The gentle lapping of the water and the colors of the sunset reflected in the lake soothed him for the few minutes he allowed to pass before he broached the subject of last night. "Do you want me to stay in the apartment? I'll leave if I make you uncomfortable. That isn't what I intended."

Finally she looked at him. "What *did* you intend?"

"To tell you the truth. To tell you about the time I spent in prison."

"With Tom?"

"Yeah."

Peering away, she sighed. "I need the rent and I think you need a place to stay, so no, I don't want you to move."

"I didn't want you to hear about it from someone else."

"Like Samuel?"

"He wouldn't have told you. He told me that first day in Sweetwater it was my story to tell."

Tanya grinned. "That sounds like Samuel. But I'm guessing he made it clear you should tell me as quickly as you could."

"Yep. That's Samuel for you. He has this way of

manipulating you into doing what he thinks should be done."

"But you aren't attending church." She swung fully around so she faced Chance. "I know he's tried because Samuel wouldn't be Samuel unless he did."

Chance nodded.

"But because of what happened to you, you think God has abandoned you?"

"That about sums it up. Ruth was a devout Christian and look what happened to her."

"The Lord never promised us a bed of roses—at least not on Earth. He hasn't abandoned you. He's waiting for you to return to Him."

"I doubt it," Chance mumbled, pushing off the rock. He stood in front of Tanya, holding out his hand to her. "Ready to head back? We'll walk slowly."

In other words, the subject is off-limits, Tanya thought, and fit her hand in his. His touch warmed her fingers as the air began to chill with the approach of night. She shivered.

"Cold?"

"I think the heat wave has broken. This morning it was a nice fifty-five degrees when I went to work."

He inhaled. "Fall is finally in the air. About time. It'll be October in a few days."

Tanya fell into step next to him on the path. "I love fall. That means winter is right around the corner. The holidays. The cold weather."

"I'll like the cold weather, but the holidays…" His voice faded into the silence, some insects serenading the only sound heard.

That shadow passed over his features, the one that

meant he was remembering a time when life had been good, then was snatched away. "I didn't put up the outdoor decorations last year, but maybe this year." With Tom's imprisonment she and Crystal hadn't felt very festive the past few years, but Chance needed to laugh again, to be a part of a family, a community.

"I used to do that," Chance finally said a couple of minutes later. "And when it snowed, my daughter used—" He swallowed hard, coming to a halt in the middle of the path.

Tanya turned back toward him. "You should talk about Haley. She hasn't left you. She's in here." Boldly she laid her hand over his heart and felt its pounding beneath her palm—strong, a bit too fast.

He covered her hand, then pulled it away but didn't release it. "Those memories are the only thing in prison that kept me sane at times."

"I know. The thought of Crystal has been what has kept me going these past few years. She needs me. I can't let her down."

His other hand came up to cup hers between his. "You aren't. You're doing a good job with Crystal."

The dark shadows crept closer as night approached. Tanya relished his nearness for a moment before she realized the danger in that. Neither one of them was ready for anything serious and that was all she thought about as his hands held hers. Reluctantly she pulled away, breaking their physical contact.

"Not good enough. I still don't know what's bothering Crystal. She won't talk to me about it."

"She's fifteen. She'll come around. You two have

a good relationship. Did you find out anything about someone harassing her at school?"

"Not yet. Beth is looking into it for me since Crystal's in her class."

"If I can help, I will." He started walking toward the street that was lit a hundred yards away.

"You've done so much in the short time you've been here. All Crystal has been talking about is basketball since you put up that hoop. I wish I had a sports wheelchair for her. The electric one is great for getting around school and especially any large place, but when it comes to doing something like shooting baskets, it isn't as effective."

"She's adapting."

"That's my daughter. She has always been so upbeat until Tom died. His death really took a toll on her. For the first time she didn't confide in me and since then, she has drawn more and more inside herself." *Much like you,* Tanya thought, slanting a look at Chance, illuminated in the streetlight as they stepped onto the pavement.

"Has she talked to Samuel about her father's death?"

"Yes, but I don't think she was too open even with him. He told me to give her time. I know time helps us sees things in a different light, but I'm her mother and hate seeing her suffer."

Chance's expression tightened into a frown. "It's hard for a parent to watch his child hurting."

"Sometimes I wonder if life will ever get any easier. There's always something, but then I'm fortunate. I have a home, my faith, a loving daughter and wonderful friends."

"I guess if life was too easy we would get bored and complacent."

"It keeps us on our toes?"

"Yeah, something like that." Chance crossed the street and turned down Berryhill Road. "Think you can jog the rest of the way?"

"That's what I'm here for." She took off for her house, pushing herself as her long legs chewed up the length to her yard.

She heard Chance's chuckle echo in the night, then the pounding of his footsteps behind her. Out of the corner of her eye, she saw him pull alongside her, nod his head then pass her. The rest of the way she watched his back, proud that she was able to keep up the pace for the most part even though her lungs burned and her muscles protested the unusual exertion.

"The Last Chance Picnic at the beginning of November is only a week away," Zoey said as she slid into the booth at Alice's Café.

Tanya scooted over as she saw Beth enter the restaurant, the last to arrive for their usual Saturday morning get-together. The concern on her friend's face alerted Tanya that something was wrong. "What happened?"

"I'm hungry." Beth unwrapped her silverware and placed her paper napkin in her lap. "I wonder if Alice has her pecan pies made yet. I sure could use a slice."

"Okay, Beth Morgan, what's going on?" Jesse signaled for Alice to take their orders.

Beth didn't say anything until after they had all given the café owner their orders, then she drew in a deep breath and released it on a long sigh. "Some people make me so angry!"

Surprised by her fervent tone, Tanya asked, "Who made you angry?"

"Felicia. I dropped Allie off at the library to help Felicia with story time and she just had to fill my ears with lies."

Darcy shifted on the chair at the end of the booth, her brows crunching together. "What lies?"

"About Chance. She had the nerve to tell me he had been in prison for murder. If that were true, he would still be there. Why does she love to spread—"

"It's true, Beth," Tanya said and held her breath as the implication of her words sank in with each of her friends. She thought she had heard something at the bank with one of her coworkers yesterday, but when she had joined the others, the woman had changed the subject.

Her mouth hung open for a few seconds before Beth asked, "Murder! Is that where Samuel knew him? From prison?"

"Yes—"

"Is he out on parole? How many years did he serve?" Jesse leaned forward.

Alice brought their drinks, and Tanya waited until she left to reply, "The real killer was caught and he petitioned the court to have the conviction overturned, which it was. So technically he was in prison for murder, but he didn't do it. The man who did is awaiting trial."

"How horrible." Jesse covered her mouth.

"What's worse is someone is spreading false rumors

about Chance." Beth dumped more sugar than usual into her coffee and stirred so hard that it sloshed over onto the table.

"You know how it is. Someone hears a story, alters it a little when he retells it and before long a person can't recognize what the original story was." Zoey sipped her hot tea.

"I don't want Chance to suffer anymore. He's gone through enough with the murders of his wife and daughter—"

"That's who he was accused of killing?" Darcy asked, pushing herself to her feet and stretching. "Ooh, my back is really hurting."

"It won't be long," Jesse said, patting her hand, then looked at Tanya. "Was it his wife and daughter?"

Tanya nodded, remembering the night four weeks before when he'd told her that. She hurt for him. In the time since then, they'd jogged together several evenings a week, and he had joined her and Crystal for dinner a few nights then helped her daughter with shooting baskets or just talked with them on the deck. But in all that time they had spent together, there was a reserve between them, put there by what he'd shared with her that night.

Jesse clenched her hand on the table. "No one better say anything to me. He works for Nick. He's part of our family now. Nick has really been impressed with Chance's work. Usually Nick has to travel frequently to Chicago, and would have this week, but he sent Chance and he did a great job."

Tanya had heard a car dropping Chance off late the night before. She hadn't been able to go to sleep until she had known he'd returned from Chicago safely. She hadn't seen him in three days, fifteen hours, but then who was counting? Okay, she missed seeing him, even if it was only long enough to wave and say hi. She liked knowing he was nearby.

"Yeah, Dane says he's really helping with setting up the financial records for the youth center. Accounting isn't my husband's strong suit." Zoey took the plate that Alice handed her with a piece of spinach and bacon quiche.

Alice served the rest of them, then said, "Are you talking about Chance Taylor?"

Tanya stiffened, the hand holding her fork tightening. "Yes, we were."

"I heard something troubling yesterday morning. Almost said something to you when you came in, Tanya, with him being your tenant and all, but I didn't get an opportunity. He was in prison for murder. Did you know that?"

The dismay on Alice's face knotted Tanya's stomach. "I knew, and the conviction was overturned. He is innocent."

"He is? Are you sure? Wilbur said he read an article online about Chance. He went to prison for murdering his family!"

Tanya narrowed her eyes, ready to stand on the table and shout the truth to the whole café. "I'm sure. If you don't believe me, Alice, ask Samuel. He knows the truth."

"Or you can ask my husband," Jesse added, tension in her voice. "Nick would never hire someone he hadn't thoroughly checked out. He would never invite someone to his house for dinner with his family if he was a murderer."

"I guess you're right. If I hear someone talking about it, I'll tell them they're wrong." Alice hurried away.

"I've never seen Alice move so fast. I think we scared her," Darcy said, rubbing her lower back.

"At least she got the point Chance is innocent and won't be contributing to the wrong gossip spreading." Tanya forced herself to relax back against the leather cushioned booth. "By the way, Jesse, what dinner with your family?" Thinking back over the past four weeks, surprisingly she could account for Chance's where-abouts in the evenings—even when he wasn't with her and Crystal.

"The one I'm having tomorrow evening. I don't want to be accused of lying. I'll call him and ask him over. Why don't you and Crystal come, too, so he'll feel more comfortable eating with the boss's family?"

Darcy laughed. "Watch out, Tanya. She's at it again."

A few weeks ago she would have panicked over the idea that Jesse was doing her matchmaking thing with her. But after not seeing Chance for almost four days, Tanya would be glad to accompany him to dinner at Jesse and Nick's. "We'll be there. That is, if Chance says yes."

Jesse smiled. "I know you can persuade him. It can't hurt for the town to see we believe in him."

"No," Beth said. "I'll make sure Samuel is aware of what's happening, but he probably has already heard the rumors, knowing my husband."

"Well, I've got a piece of news he probably hasn't

heard yet." Jesse glanced at each one at the table, then said, "I'm going to have a baby in seven months!"

"Oh, good, you can experience what I've been experiencing for the past seven months." Darcy rose. "I'm so happy for you. Be back in a sec." She hastened toward the restroom.

"Congratulations. I didn't know you and Nick were trying," Zoey said.

"We weren't exactly, but it's great news. We're happy. That's one of the reasons we're so glad Chance is doing such a good job. It'll give Nick more time when the baby comes."

Tanya wondered if Chance would stick around that long. She wasn't sure he wanted to settle in Sweetwater permanently. She got the feeling coming to town was just a temporary thing for him. And now with the rumors flying around Sweetwater, he might not stay past the weekend. She would have to tell him. She didn't want him to find out when someone asked him about being in prison or snubbed him.

That evening Tanya stepped out onto the deck and looked toward the apartment above her garage. The fall air held a crispness, mingled with the scents of burning leaves and wood. The sun's rays peeked over the treetops to the west, streaks of pinks and oranges coloring the pale blue sky. A beautiful day. Not the kind of day to tell a man she cared about that the town knew about the time he had spent in prison.

She backed up until she pressed against the door into her house. Thoughts of escaping inside and not saying anything to Chance dominated her mind. With trembling hands, she pushed herself away from the door and strode toward the stairs that led to his apartment.

She couldn't do that to him. He deserved better than that. She could imagine him walking into a room where everyone stopped talking at once and stared at him. It had happened to her on a number of occasions a few years ago until Darcy, Jesse, Beth and Zoey had rallied around her and supported her through that dark time. Finally the rumors had died down and people had ceased speculating if she had known about her husband's activities. She'd guessed the townspeople had decided if her friends accepted that she hadn't known, then they could, too, especially when Tom had set fire to a barn that Darcy had been trapped in. But it had hurt that the people hadn't believed in her at first. She had lived in Sweetwater most of her life. They should have known she hadn't been aware.

At the bottom of the steps, Tanya paused and peered at the door above. He was in there. She had seen him come home with several bags of groceries while she had been cleaning the kitchen and occasionally staring out the window at the driveway where he would have to pass in order to get to his apartment. That had been twenty minutes ago, and it had taken her that amount of time to get up her courage to see him.

First one foot then the other settled on the steps. She gripped the railing, then hurried up before she changed her mind—again. Fortifying herself with a deep breath, she rapped on the door. She kept her hand clenched even when she dropped it to her side to stay the trembling.

Chance opened the door. A smile moved across his

mouth, slow and full with his dimples appearing. His eyes lit with warmth. "Hi, what brings you by?"

That was a perfect opening to tell him why she had come to see him. Instead, she returned his smile, the corners of her mouth quivering slightly. "How did your trip go?"

She walked inside as he held the door open. She hadn't been in his apartment in several weeks and noticed a few changes, a couple of personal touches added—a clock, a radio, a book on the table, a photo of a beautiful woman and a young girl who had to be his daughter. Tanya saw the resemblance in the smile, the eyes, the dark hair.

"I accomplished what Nick needed done."

"Then it was successful. Great!" Even to her own ears, her voice sounded strained, a little high-pitched.

Chance studied her with narrowed eyes. "Is something wrong? Is it Crystal?"

Waving her hand, Tanya twisted away from his too-perceptive gaze. "No. No, she's fine. Well, at least okay. On Thursday I think something happened at school. She came home in a bad mood and didn't say a word the whole evening. She didn't leave her bedroom except to eat dinner. She would have eaten that in her room, but I wouldn't let her."

"Has Beth discovered anything at school?" Chance moved into her line of vision.

She couldn't turn away this time. His gaze captured hers and held it. "Only what I told you before you left. There are a couple of girls she noticed talking to Crystal in the hallway last week. Afterward Crystal went into the restroom and was late for class. It looked like she had been crying, but Beth couldn't get anything out of Crystal. She sent her to Zoey, but she couldn't, either. My daughter isn't talking."

"I'll try again to see if I can find out anything. That is, if you don't mind."

"No, please try. For the longest time I wouldn't ask for help when I needed it. I've learned to now. We all need help from time to time, and there's nothing wrong in admitting that." She moistened her lips and decided the time had come. "With that in mind, Chance, I need to tell you there are some rumors going around about you having been in prison for murder."

For a second nothing registered on his expression, then it went blank as though he had completely shut down his emotions. "I figured it would be only a matter of time before someone would get wind of it. In a few months the trial of my family's killer will be all over the media in Louisville. What happened to me will come up."

"And you'll have to relive the horror all over again." She took a step closer, half afraid he would distance himself from her.

He held his ground, sadness leaking into his expression. "Yes."

"I want you to know I'll help you any way I can. So will Darcy, Zoey, Beth and Jesse. In fact, Jesse wants us to come over to dinner tomorrow night."

"I don't think—"

"She's the boss's wife. You can't say no, Chance. Besides, you can't stay holed up in here. You need to get out and let everyone know what they are saying doesn't bother you."

His half grin returned. "Who said I was gonna stay holed up in my apartment? I could have plans already."

"I just assumed—I mean—" she said, flustered. Had he met someone? The thought bothered her, for some reason.

His laughter filled the room. "Sorry. I couldn't resist. I don't have any plans. I'm gonna work at the youth center in the afternoon, but I can be ready to go. What time tomorrow?"

"Six."

"Speaking of the youth center, does Crystal ever go?"

"She hasn't yet."

"Do you think she would like to go tomorrow while I'm there? The art teacher from school is going to have a class tomorrow afternoon. I thought she might like to sit in on it since she hasn't had a chance to take art at school yet."

"I'll say something to her. If she wants to, I can drop you two off."

He covered the space between them, only a foot separating them. "You could give a class in drawing people for the kids. Dane's always looking for people to do classes that might interest the teens."

She backed away. "No. I can't teach." Her legs hit a chair, and she stopped. "I'll leave that to others."

"You've taught Crystal a lot. She's very talented. Like you."

"I merely showed her how to use her natural talent. That's not teaching."

"I beg your pardon. That *is* teaching. A teacher shows a person how to tap into his talent."

Chance shrank the space between them, his familiar scent of springtime soap drifting to her. "Don't sell yourself short. Share your talent with others."

Tanya sidestepped away and headed for the door. "I'll talk to Crystal and let you know tomorrow. I'm glad you're back." She hurried from his apartment.

Chance went to the window and watched Tanya's flight down the stairs and across the driveway. He lost sight of her, but he didn't need to see her to know every minute detail of her beautiful face—a face he had pictured more than once while he was in Chicago these past few days. When had his feelings changed toward Tanya? She was no longer just someone he had promised himself he would help, then move on. She was more. And there was no way he would allow himself to become involved with Tom's wife. How could he when he was the reason Tom was dead in the first place as though he had plunged the knife into Tom's heart himself?

Turning away from the window, Chance took in his new home, a home that was now invaded by his past. He'd known it would come out. He had just hoped he would have had more time in Sweetwater. He didn't know if he could stay and face the townspeople each day, knowing what they were thinking: did the authorities really have the right man this time?

Chance closed the program on the computer, having finished putting in the numbers for October. The simple accounting for the youth center was the closest he would be to his old life as a financial advisor. He wanted nothing to do with that life. He dreaded the time he would have to return to Louisville for the trial of his wife and daughter's murderer. He couldn't even bring himself to say the man's name.

"Oh, good. You haven't left yet," Dane said from the doorway into the office at the center.

Chance glanced up. "I'll be leaving as soon as the art class is over. What do you need?"

Dane moved into the office, perching on the side of the desk. "I don't need anything. Just wanted to see if there was anything I could do for you. You've been a blessing to us here."

Chance couldn't keep the skepticism from his expression. "Keeping the books isn't difficult. I'm sure you would have found someone to do it."

"But you saved me having to appeal to others. You stepped forward."

"Samuel has a way of persuading a person to do things."

"Yeah, he does. He's one of the reasons I'm running this place." Dane folded his arms over his chest and looked as if he were there for the long haul.

Chance's wariness tingled along his neck. "You've heard?"

"Yes, a couple of days ago my neighbor, Wilbur Thompson, wanted me to know about the kind of person I let volunteer at the youth center."

"If you don't want me to—"

Dane's eyebrows slashed downward. "I will never let Wilbur tell me what I can and can't do. We have a long history. We've come to a precarious truce since we live on the same short block and go to the same church." The anger in his expression dissolved. "I'm telling you this because I want you to know you are welcome here for as long as you want to volunteer."

"You don't have any questions?"

"About what?"

"Like did I really do it?"

Thunder lined Dane's face. "The system isn't always perfect. Occasionally the police are wrong, but thankfully they discovered their mistake and corrected it. The man I've become acquainted with this past month couldn't have done that to his family."

Chance closed his eyes, relieved to hear those words from a man he respected. He knew that Dane Witherspoon had once been in law enforcement and for him to say that meant a lot to him. "Thank you. I've come to enjoy my time spent at the center. I was gonna offer to tutor some of the kids in math if you need someone."

"Do I ever! Math isn't my strength. Now that school is underway, I'm getting some requests from the teens for different tutors to help them in their schoolwork. Math tops the list. In fact, Holly Proctor and Eddy O'Neal have asked me on more than one occasion. Let me talk with them and see if we can set something up several evenings a week. When could you do it?"

"I'm free any evening." Chance realized except for going to work and seeing Tanya and Crystal from time to time, his life was spent in his apartment reading, listening to the radio and thinking. He had too much free time on his hands. "Just let me know when to be here. I'm getting a cell phone this week so you will have a way of getting hold of me besides calling work or Tanya."

"What's next? A car?"

Chance shrugged. "It's been easy getting around Sweetwater, but I guess I'll have to get one in the near future." He thought about the time when he would have to return to Louisville. It would be easier if he had his own transportation by then.

"Let me know. I might be able to help you with getting a reliable used car."

Chance rose, his muscles tight from sitting for so long. He stretched then rolled his head around to ease the tension in his neck and shoulders. "Thanks. If you hear of anything, let me know. I can't afford much."

"You have a good job. You could get a loan."

He shook his head. "No. I don't want any debt to tie me down to material things." That was one of the reasons he had worked so long and hard before. He'd had debts to pay from accumulating a large house, two brand-new cars and some of the latest electronic devices. It had all come tumbling down around him, leaving him with nothing. Never again.

Dane pushed off the desk and walked toward the door. "That's not a bad philosophy. Pay as you go. With three children that's getting to be harder and harder."

Chance followed Dane from the office, intending to find Crystal and see if she was through with her art class. Dane headed toward the gym while he went in the opposite direction toward the hallway that led to the six rooms used for various activities like classes, counseling sessions and meetings.

When he popped his head into the room used for the art class, he only noticed the teacher and a young man left. "Do you know where Crystal Bolton is?"

"She left a few minutes ago with a couple of the girls. She shouldn't be too far," the art teacher said.

Chance retraced his steps and peered into the gym then the exercise room but didn't see Crystal. Would she have gone home without letting him know? Even if she had left, Tanya would have let him know she was taking her daughter home. So where was Crystal?

He went back to the six rooms and began to check each one. Two teenage girls came out of the last one on the right, the TV room, giggling and whispering to themselves. One hugged a sketchbook to her chest. When they saw him, they stopped talking and quickened their pace and passed him. The teen with the sketchbook tossed it on the floor halfway down the hall.

An uneasiness gripped him. Crystal's sketchbook lay discarded, opened to the page of the young boy she had a crush on.

The beating of his heart slowed for a few seconds then slammed against his rib cage. He hastened toward the last door on the right, his gut clenched into a huge knot. Just inside he found Crystal on the floor, sobbing.

Chapter Six

The sobs wrenched Chance's soul, squeezing his heart, prodding him into action. He crossed the room and knelt next to Crystal, sprawled on the floor by her wheelchair, her body shaking with her cries.

He touched her shoulder. "Crystal, are you hurt?"

"Go away. Leave—me alone," she said between her sobs, her face buried in her hands.

For a flash he pictured his daughter on the floor, crying as though the world had come to an end. And he hadn't thought it possible for his heart to hurt any more but it did. "I'm not leaving. You're stuck with me. Are you hurt?" He schooled his voice to an even level, calm, soothing.

She quieted but didn't say anything.

"Should I call your mother and have her come pick us up?"

She twisted her upper body until she glared up at him. "No!"

"I'm going to help you into your wheelchair and then you and I are going to talk." Again he made sure his voice betrayed none of the anger quickly coming to the foreground within him as he stared at her pale face, streaked with tears.

Her glare intensified, but Chance ignored it as he gathered her into his arms and hoisted her up. After securing her in her wheelchair, he backed up and sat on the couch a few feet away. His own body shook with anger that he was no longer able to suppress. Those two girls leaving the room had been responsible for Crystal lying on the floor crying. It took all his control not to storm after the two teens and demand an explanation then an apology to Crystal.

"What happened?" Chance leaned forward, resting his elbows on his thighs.

She dropped her head, staring at her hands clasped together in her lap.

"Crystal, I saw two girls leaving the room. Do you want me to go and ask them? Because one way or another, I will find out what happened."

Her head snapped up. "No! Don't!" Panic thundered in her voice.

"Then talk to me. I want to help."

"You can't. No one can." The panic slid into defeat. Her shoulders hunched over, and she returned to staring at her hands.

"I didn't tell you before, but now that some people know I figure you should hear it from me. Up until a couple of months ago I was in prison for a crime I didn't commit. They found the real killer and my conviction was overturned." When he had mentioned prison, Crystal's clasp tightened until her knuckles were white. "I knew your father. He was my friend."

Crystal raised her head and looked at him, her eyes glistening. "Dad? I—I—" She cleared her throat. "He wouldn't see me. Why?"

"Because he hated what he had done, what he had become. He didn't want you to remember him behind bars. He loved you so much he only wanted you to remember the good times you all had."

A tear slipped from her eye and rolled down her cheek. "He loved me?"

"He talked about you all the time. Believe me, Crystal, he loved you very much." Her tears produced a constriction in his throat. "I'm telling you about my time in prison because it was your father who helped me deal with some prisoners who liked to bully the new person. I learned quick to stand up for myself. You have to stand up for yourself and let these girls know what they are doing isn't going to get to you."

"But it does."

"Then don't let them see that. A bully feeds off others' fears and weaknesses."

"But look at me. How can I fight back?" Crystal scrubbed a hand across her cheeks.

"By believing in yourself. You are a beautiful, talented young lady who happens to be in a wheelchair. We all have issues we have to deal with, even those two girls."

"But still—"

"Start with your friends. Let them know exactly what is going on. Let them help you. That even includes your mother. You aren't alone. Believe it or not, those girls are the ones with the problem. They feel belittling you makes them important."

Crystal sniffled, blinking away the remaining tears in her eyes. "Mom will want to say something to them. I can't tell her."

"She's very concerned about you. She knows someone is bothering you. Please let her help by listening to you."

"I have to deal with them on my own. I can't let my mother stand up for me. That will only make it worse."

"Maybe. But being silent about being harassed won't solve the problem, either. Think about what I've said, and remember if you need someone to talk to, I'm here for you, as is your mother." Chance rose. "Now, do you still want to walk home? Or do you want me to call your mother to come pick us up?"

Crystal drew in a shuddering breath. "I need some time. Let's walk."

"Well, we couldn't have asked for a better afternoon. It's beautiful outside." He started for the door.

"I need you to switch my battery on. One of them turned it off so I couldn't go anywhere in my chair. They took my sketchbook and were taunting me with it. They said I had to reach for it. I tried but leaned too far and fell. They left laughing and giggling. They took it with them."

"No, they didn't. They threw it down in the hallway as they came out of the room. We'll get it when we leave." Chance went behind Crystal and flipped the switch on the battery. "You're all set. Let's go. I need some fresh air."

The walls seemed to be closing in on him. All the memories of the bullies he'd handled in prison inundated him, underscoring the uphill battle Crystal had in her own situation. He dragged in deep breaths to alleviate the pressure in his chest as he left the TV room.

In the hallway Chance picked up the sketchbook and gave it to Crystal, glad to see it wasn't damaged. A few minutes later they were on the street and heading toward Berryhill Road. A crisp breeze and the exertion of walking cooled Chance's anger and eased the suffocating sensation the incident with Crystal had produced. He had dealt with bullies in prison, but why did someone like Tanya's daughter have to?

Why aren't You helping her, God? Crystal doesn't deserve this on top of everything else that has happened to her in the past four years. Where is Your love?

As they neared home, Crystal said, "Don't say anything to Mom, please."

"I can't lie to her, but I won't say anything to her. You need to tell her, though."

"She's been through so much."

"She's strong, Crystal. She doesn't need protecting."

"You haven't been here. She's—" She snapped her mouth closed.

"I know she is bipolar. Your dad told me."

"Then you understand it's been tough for her. I don't want to add to her problems. She's had to deal with so many."

"Not saying anything makes the situation worse for your mother. She is imagining all kinds of things. The truth will be hard, but not as hard as what she can think of."

The front door opened and Tanya came out onto the porch, waving to them as they came up the driveway.

She descended the steps and walked to them. "How did it go? Did you enjoy the art lesson?"

Crystal pasted a bright smile on her face. "It was great. I want to take art next year under Mrs. Garrison."

"We have about an hour before we need to get ready for dinner at Jesse and Nick's." Tanya glanced at Chance and noticed a tightness about his mouth and wondered what had put it there. Had someone said something to him about being in prison?

"I'll be ready," Crystal said, heading to the ramp in back.

Chance started for his apartment.

"Did something happen at the center?"

With his back to her, he stiffened. "What do you mean?"

He didn't turn around, but Tanya didn't have to see his face to know something had gone wrong. She heard it in the clipped edge to his voice. "Did someone say something to you about your past?"

"No, not really." The tenseness in his shoulders eased. "Dane and I talked some about what he'd heard. He wanted me to know he stood behind me."

"Then what happened?"

Slowly he pivoted. "You need to talk to your daughter. I promised Crystal I wouldn't say anything."

She gritted her teeth and strode to him. "What happened? Tell me."

"I can't break a promise to Crystal. Don't ask me to."

Anger surged through her. Her fingernails dug into her palms. "You shouldn't have promised her."

"She thinks she's protecting you. Go talk to her."

"I *have* talked to her." His words cut deep into her.

Crystal had always tried to protect her and at one time she had needed that. But not now.

"After today, maybe she's ready." Chance resumed his steps toward his apartment.

Tanya watched him climb the stairs, trying desperately to tamp down her irritation at Chance's silence. She thought about following him and demanding he break his promise to her daughter but knew his integrity wouldn't allow it. Instead, she spun about and hurried into her house to find her daughter. What had happened to put such a hard edge into Chance's voice? She knew how cruel some kids could be, and she didn't want what she was thinking to be true. She didn't want her daughter to go through that kind of pain.

When is it enough, Lord? She's suffered enough. Help me!

At her daughter's bedroom door, she knocked.

"Yes?"

"We should talk, Crystal."

The sound of the wheelchair moving toward the door came through the wood. Tanya released the breath she had been holding when she realized her daughter wasn't going to shut her out—at least, not physically.

When Crystal maneuvered her chair so Tanya could enter the bedroom, her daughter asked, "What did Chance tell you?" Tension lined her face, and she appeared ten years older.

"Absolutely nothing and that's the problem. He wouldn't tell me anything, but I know something happened this afternoon at the center."

Her expression relaxed into a bland one. "Not much. I took an art lesson."

"Crystal, please don't shut me out anymore. I'm going crazy trying to figure out what's going on with you. I know you're hurting. Let me help you."

"You've got your own problems, Mom. I can take care of this by myself."

"But you don't have to. I can help. That's what family is for. To help each other." Tanya sank onto her daughter's bed, the ice-green sheets crumpled at the foot of it. She plucked at the cotton material. "Did someone bother you today?"

Crystal swiveled her chair around so she faced her desk with her outdated computer.

"Darling, you're scaring me."

The fear in Tanya's voice must have conveyed her concern more than her words because her daughter peered over her shoulder, sadness in her eyes, as she asked, "If I tell you, will you promise to let me deal with it?"

Tanya scooted to the edge of the bed, her hands gripping the bedding. "I will for as long as I can, but if you can't take care of it by yourself, I will step in. I have to. I'm your mother. That's all I can promise you."

Her daughter swung her wheelchair back around. With a deep sigh, she said, "Two girls took my sketchbook and taunted me with it. When I reached for it, I fell out of my chair. They left, laughing. That's when Chance came in."

Tanya tried to control her reaction to her child's words, but it seeped through her restraint. In Crystal's mirror over her dresser Tanya saw in her expression the shock, hurt and anger all tangled together, flashing in and out so fast they collided with each other. Finally she schooled her features into a look that didn't convey pity or rage. Her daughter wouldn't accept either of those, she instinctively realized.

"What did Chance do?" Only the last word quavered with the emotions she quelled.

"Picked me up and helped me back into the wheelchair."

"You aren't hurt?"

"Only my ego. I knew when I went into the room with them they were up to no good, but they snatched my sketchbook when I came into the hall after class. I reacted without really thinking. I won't do that again."

Her daughter shouldn't have to worry about something like that! "Who are the girls?"

"Just two sophomores. I don't want to talk about them anymore. I've let them ruin enough of my day." Crystal tilted her head to the side. "Aren't we going to Jesse and Nick's tonight? You aren't wearing that, are you?"

Tanya glanced down at her worn jeans with several holes in them. "I thought this was what all the teens like to wear." Her cleaning attire with her oversize T-shirt was only worn at home.

"Yeah. Some even buy brand-new ones with holes already in them. But, Mom, you're too—"

Tanya held up her hand to stop her child's words. "Don't you say I'm too old to. I'm changing, but only because I was anyway." She infused a lightness into her voice. "We'll leave in about half an hour." She pushed herself off the bed and strode toward the door. Before leaving, she added, "You aren't alone, honey. Remember that, if things get too hard to handle on your own."

When she left her daughter's bedroom, Tanya didn't go into hers. Instead, she headed toward the kitchen and paced its small confines, peeking out the window with each pass at the stairs that led to Chance's. Chewing on her fingernail, she debated whether to pay him a visit or not. There were details she wanted to know.

Finally ten minutes later, she made her way to his apartment. But before she could knock, the door swung open. He stepped to the side to allow her inside.

"Is Crystal okay?" Chance asked as he faced her.

"Yes—no. She said she was physically fine, but this incident really hurt her." Tanya paced from the kitchen table to the couch, then back. "How can I make this go away?"

He blocked her path back to the couch. "I'm not sure you can."

"Who are the girls?"

"She didn't tell you?"

Tanya shook her head, needing to know who would dare hurt her daughter.

"I don't know them. I thought this week when I go to the center to tutor I would ask around and find out."

"All she would tell me is that they are sophomores."

"Okay, that helps."

Suddenly the very act of standing erect tired her as though someone from above were pressing her down. She covered the short distance to the couch and collapsed onto it. The physical and emotional energy she had expended was catching up with her. "I promised her for the time being I wouldn't do anything. I don't know how I'm gonna keep that promise. All I want to do is find out who those girls are and have a few choice words with them and then their parents."

"You can't, at least not yet." Chance eased down next to her and took her hand. "You promised her."

"I told her I would give her a chance to work it out with them, but if she can't, I'll have to do something."

"What?"

She lifted her shoulders. "Beats me. Any suggestions?"

He sagged back. "No. This is out of my realm of expertise. When Haley had trouble with another girl, she went to her mother."

"I can't believe how mean some girls can be. What in the world has my daughter done to them? Do you think it's because she is in a wheelchair?"

His hand linked with hers, he answered, "Maybe."

"They might as well have pushed Crystal from her wheelchair this afternoon. They knew what their actions would do." Tears smarted her eyes, roughened her voice.

Chance slipped an arm around her and brought her up against his side. "I think you're right. Let me see what I can find out at the center."

Comforted by his presence, Tanya laid her head on his shoulder. "I'd wanted Crystal to get more involved at the center, but if girls like that are gonna be there, I probably shouldn't encourage her to go."

"Why don't I take her with me when I go to tutor? She's a whiz at math. Maybe she could tutor someone, too."

"I don't know."

"I won't let anything happen to her. I'll keep an eye

on her. Helping others always makes a person feel better."

Lately she had turned to Chance more and more. What was going to happen when he left? Already she felt the emptiness in her heart as she thought of that day. She had to protect herself from being hurt.

"Fine." She slid her eyes closed, a tear leaking out. She knew that Chance would do all that was humanly possible to protect Crystal, but this might be beyond him.

Lord, open those girls' eyes. Help them to see what harm they are doing to my daughter. And please guide me in how to deal with these growing feelings I have for Chance. I'm going to need You when he leaves Sweetwater.

"I've never seen two kids so excited to see someone," Jesse said as she brought the decaf coffee out onto the deck.

Above the squawking of the two geese by the lake, Tanya said, "Crystal's been thinking of doing some babysitting to earn some money."

"Great! I know Cindy and Nate would be thrilled." Jesse poured some coffee into two mugs.

"I don't know if it's a good idea. The logistics would be hard with her wheelchair. Most houses aren't easily accessible for her. Yours isn't too bad, but others are. That's why I haven't encouraged her."

"She wants to earn some money? Maybe she could do something else."

Tanya sipped her drink. "Like what?"

"Let me think on it."

The din caused by Fred and Ethel, two geese that lived at Jesse's house, increased. Tanya stretched her neck to look over the railing, the light on the pole enabling her to see Nick and Chance near the pier. "What are they doing down by the lake?"

"Nick's probably taunting Fred. He's never been a big fan of Fred's since that day he nipped him on the leg."

"Ah, but wasn't that the first time you met Nick?"

"Yep."

"He should be indebted to Fred."

Jesse arched a brow. "You would think. But he keeps telling me he would have discovered me eventually on his own."

The honking subsided as Chance and Nick hiked back toward the house. Momentarily the two men disappeared as the dark swallowed them. When they came into the circle of light from the deck, Tanya's heart rate accelerated. For a few seconds she recalled the sensation of Chance's arm casually about her as they'd sat on his couch. She'd felt protected and cherished while he had comforted her about Crystal. She hadn't felt so alone with him next to her.

"It's about time you two came back. I was about to go and get you. Poor Fred and Ethel."

Jesse's words dragged Tanya from her daydreaming as Nick said, "There's nothing poor about either of those geese." He climbed the steps to the deck with Chance slightly behind him. "I wanted to show Chance our new pier, offer him the use of the boat if he wants to fish."

Tanya sensed Chance's eyes on her. She swung her gaze to his and became lost in the glittering blue, much like the very lake only a hundred yards away on a sun-lit day. "You like to fish?"

"No. Well, I don't know. I've never gone fishing." Chance found the place on the love seat next to Tanya and folded his long length onto it. "Want to teach me?"

"Can't. I don't know how, either." Along the side pressed against Chance's, her body tingled from the connection.

"I guess I'll have one less opponent at the fishing rodeo." Nick took a chair across from them.

"What fishing rodeo?" Chance asked, taking a mug that Jesse had filled with coffee.

"The one associated with the Last Chance Picnic next weekend. The prize for the biggest fish is a dinner for two at Andre's." A competitive gleam shone in Nick's eyes.

"Nick Blackburn, we were just there two weeks ago," Jesse said, shaking her head.

"I know. But I'm gonna beat your granddad this year. Besides, my entry fee goes toward a good cause, the youth center."

"I'm curious why it's called the Last Chance Picnic." Chance cupped his mug between his two hands.

"It's the last chance before winter." Tanya angled herself so she faced Chance on the love seat. "It's always the first weekend in November. There have been a few years we've had to go indoors because it was raining. Once it snowed. We've always used the picnic as a fund-raiser for a worthy cause. Each year the town council comes up with a new one. It's all day. Most of the residents come for at least a short time."

Snapping her fingers, Jesse said, "I've got it. I know how Crystal can make some money."

"She's looking for a job?" Chance asked then took several swallows of his coffee before placing it on the glass table in front of him.

"Yeah, like every other teen, she wants her own money." Jesse turned toward Tanya. "What if she drew a portrait of Nate and Cindy with Bingo and Oreo? Do you think she'll do it?"

"I—I—" After what happened today at the center, would her daughter associate drawing with being harassed? Had something Crystal done in art class set the girls off? Would that stop her from drawing? "I don't know."

"I hope she will. I've seen her work and she's very talented." Jesse surged to her feet. "I'd better check on the kids. Be back in a sec."

"Jesse, don't say anything to Crystal. I'll talk to her."

Jesse gave her a funny look and shrugged. "Sure."

While her friend disappeared inside the house, Tanya wondered how her daughter would react to Jesse's proposal. Like herself, Crystal had kept her ability a private affair, only sharing with a select few. Knowing Jesse, she would frame the drawing and display it for everyone to see in her living room.

The ringing of Nick's cell phone cut into the silence that followed his wife's departure. "Excuse me. I've got to take this."

"What's wrong?" Chance asked when they were left alone on the deck.

"The girls were taunting Crystal with her sketchbook. Was there something in it that set them off?"

"Maybe. And you're worried that this incident will affect Crystal's desire to draw?"

"She doesn't have a lot she can do. Drawing and singing are two things she enjoys. I don't want to see their viciousness destroying that."

He took her hand, threading his fingers through hers. "Those girls can't destroy her talent, and as far as her desire to draw, only Crystal really controls that."

"But if I know Jesse, she'll talk my daughter into doing the portrait and then publicize Crystal's 'new' business."

"What's wrong with that? She wants to make some money."

"That will give those girls more fuel to use against Crystal."

His brows slashed downward, his forehead creased. "So she should hide her talent?"

"What if they make fun of her drawings?"

"She'll deal with it and consider the source." Chance rose and pulled her toward him. "It isn't Crystal we're talking about, is it?"

His sharp gaze snared hers. Her throat went dry. She opened her mouth but no words came out. She didn't want to think about her teenage years when a group of popular girls had taunted her, chipping away at the self-confidence that she had felt when she drew people. Only lately had she begun slowly to redevelop that desire to draw others when she'd taught her daughter what she knew.

"Tanya?"

She nodded, still not able to form an answer.

He brought his hands up and clasped her head, his

gaze seeming to bore into her. "I know one thing. Both mother and daughter are very talented, and nobody can take that away from you two unless you let them. You were given an ability most don't have. Share it with the world."

His words bolstered her spirits. Rationally she knew he was right. Emotionally she had scars that had barely healed. Exposing her inner self to others' eyes scared her. She'd spent her teenage years trying to belong and never quite feeling as though she did. It had taken Tom's love to bring her out of her shell, then his support had been pulled out from under her. Only God's love and her circle of friends had held her together since Tom's arrest and conviction.

Chance plowed one hand through her hair, gently prodding her forward—toward his mouth. When it settled over hers, her world tilted and spun as though she rode a dizzying ride. She clung to him, her fingers digging into his shoulders to steady her as her legs trembled.

When they finally parted, his shallow breath mingled with hers. Just a hint of coffee laced it.

He rested his forehead against hers. "You were given a talent. Celebrate that talent. Proclaim it to the world. Most people can't do what you can. Believe in yourself, Tanya."

"I'm trying."

"Look at what you've done so far," he said and leaned back to get a better glimpse of her. "You've raised a beautiful, caring daughter. You've shared your talent and knowledge with her. You're dealing with being bipolar."

The word *bipolar* from Chance's lips stunned her. He knew! Who had told him? Crystal? Tom? One of her friends?

"Tanya?" Chance's smile evolved into a frown.

She jerked away. "How did you find out?" She barely got the question past her suddenly parched lips.

"Tom."

She inhaled then exhaled—slow, deep breaths that weren't enough to fill her lungs. "I should have known. He was never comfortable with my—" she searched for the right word to use "—illness."

"He wasn't. He admitted it to me." Chance gathered her into his arms. "You amaze me. You've gone through so much and dealt with it well. You've befriended me when I needed it the most."

She was afraid it was more than befriending. How could she stop herself from falling off a mountain when she stood on the very tip, ready to plunge with the least push? The very thought wrung her heart.

"I don't know, Chance, if this is such a good idea. Most upperclassmen wouldn't want to be tutored by a freshman." Crystal powered her wheelchair up the ramp that led to the front doors of the youth center.

"Dane said there was a whole list of kids signed up who needed help in algebra and geometry. You're a math whiz so why not share the wealth?"

Crystal shot him a skeptical glance before she went through the door he held open. Charlie trotted in after her then Chance followed. Sounds of a basketball striking the floor echoed through the hall that led from the gym. A cheer reverberated, then another.

"We've got the first classroom on the left," Chance said, stopping next to Crystal in the doorway into the gym.

A wistful look on her face underscored her longing to be a part of the group of teens playing an impromptu game while a few bystanders watched. Stroking her service dog absently, she sighed, then turned her wheelchair toward the classroom area of the building.

Dane exited the room and smiled at them. "I've got four kids waiting. Another is coming later."

"Great. I've brought help. In fact, Crystal probably would do better than me. It's been a while since I looked at this level of math."

"It's like riding a bike, Chance. I'm sure it'll come back once you see it," Crystal said and directed her chair through the entrance into the classroom.

She came to an abrupt halt only a foot inside, causing Chance to bump into the back of her wheelchair. He peered down. The color bled from her face, Crystal's gaze riveted to a girl sitting next to Eddy O'Neal.

Chapter Seven

Chance's gut clenched. One of the girls who had harassed Crystal in the TV room sat next to Eddy. The teen with long blond hair pulled back in a ponytail laughed at something Eddy said, then glanced up and caught sight of Crystal. The smile that had accompanied the girl's laughter froze, then melted into a pout.

The teenager slammed her geometry book closed and shot to her feet. Snatching up her purse, she gathered up her work and stormed toward the door. "See ya, Eddy. I think I can figure this out."

Crystal quickly maneuvered her wheelchair out of the girl's way while Chance said, "If you change your mind and decide you need help, you know where to find us."

The blonde stabbed Chance with a withering look. "From an ex-con and—" her hard gaze slid to Crystal "—I don't think so."

Chance sidled toward Crystal, gripping the back of her wheelchair. "Your loss."

When he faced the other three teens, one girl and two

boys, in the room, he hoped that his anger didn't register on his face even though inside he shook with its force. "Why don't you all tell me what you need help with?"

"Algebra II," Eddy said with a smile.

Chance was glad to see the young man who Dane had introduced him to that first day he had come to the center. "Okay. What else?" He scanned the faces of the others.

The other boy, who Chance was almost sure was the same one that Crystal had drawn over and over, said, "Algebra I."

Chance slid a glance toward Crystal, who purposefully avoided eye contact with the boy.

"Geometry." The lone girl sat off to the side away from the others.

"Okay. I'll work with you, Eddy, and…"

"Grant Foster," the other boy said.

"And Crystal will help you." Chance regarded the girl and wondered if she were a friend of the other one.

"I'm Amanda and that's great. I can use all the help I can get. My friend will be here in a few minutes."

Still not looking at Grant, Crystal peered toward the door as though she expected the other girl to come back and dump her from her wheelchair. Chance turned his back on the group and spoke in a low tone, "If you don't want to help, I'll understand."

Crystal's eyes grew round. "No, I'll stay in here. I might as well help Amanda while I wait for you."

"I can call your mom, and she can come get you if you want."

"No, I came to help. I'm not gonna let Holly run me off." Her voice quavered with her declaration.

"Are you okay with Grant being in here?"

"Why wouldn't I be?" Crystal kept her head down.

"You're very talented, Crystal. I know he was the boy you were drawing."

She finally glanced up at him. "He needs help."

"Then let's get started."

While Chance sat across from Grant and Eddy, Crystal situated her wheelchair at the end of the table near Amanda. She gave the girl a smile that was immediately returned. The tension in Crystal's face relaxed, and Chance hoped that he hadn't been wrong in persuading her to help others with their math.

"Mr. Taylor, I'm sorry about Holly." Eddy shook his head. "I don't know what's got into her. Right before you came she was talking about the trouble she was having in geometry. I was trying to help her, but she didn't understand my explanation."

Frankly Chance didn't know what had gotten into Holly, either, but he replied, "She's the one who'll have to find the help she needs. I don't want anyone here unless he wants to be. Now show me what you're working on and what's the problem. I'll start with you, Eddy, then work with you, Grant."

As Eddy opened his book and flipped to the page, Chance heard Crystal's giggle and peered at the two girls, their heads bent over the paper Crystal wrote on. *Thank You, God.* The second he thought the words, surprise flitted through him. He'd stopped praying to the Lord over two years ago.

Tanya tossed her head back and relished the warm rays of the sun as it beat down upon her. The scent of dirt, grass and trees saturated the air. The sounds of nature—water lapping against the shore, a chirping bird sitting on a nearby limb, the buzz and hum of the insects—vied with the voices of the townspeople as they arrived at the city park along the lake for the Last Chance Picnic celebration.

The event's very name made her think of the man who had distracted her more and more each day he was in her life. When she caught a glimpse of a certain sadness in his eyes, she sensed this was Chance's last chance at happiness. Knowing his background only confirmed that impression.

When Tanya plopped into a lawn chair under a large oak, she surveyed the scene before her. Food covered the park's picnic tables while huge garbage cans filled with ice held soft drinks and bottled water. She noticed Jesse still manned the booth at the entrance, taking up the fee to attend this fund-raiser for the youth center. Off to the side in the open field Chance helped Dane and Nick set up the volleyball net while Joshua and Samuel organized the young children into groups for the fun races.

"If Zoey sees you just sitting, she'll have your head," Beth said, taking the chair next to Tanya.

"How about you?"

"Mine, too. But after setting up the food the past two hours, I'm exhausted." Beth smoothed her maternity blouse down.

"Ditto. I never knew fun could be so much work."

Beth gestured toward the crowds arriving. "But what a success. I think this is the best year yet."

"It's for a good cause."

"You can say that again. Jane told me that Dane's got the tutoring program up and running. The kids are flocking to get help. She's even volunteered to help in math."

"So has Crystal."

"Yeah, I know. Jane told me she's helping several girls with their geometry."

"Two evenings last week and she's actually been upbeat about going to school for the first time in months. Amanda, one of the girls she's tutoring, called her last night to just talk. When Crystal got off the phone, she was beaming."

"I'm glad you encouraged her to get involved."

"I didn't. Chance did." When Tanya thought about it, Chance had touched many facets of her and Crystal's lives at a time when they'd needed it. *Thank You, Lord, for sending him.* But she wanted—needed—to help him. *How, Lord? Show me.*

"Speaking of Chance, he's been quite a hit with several of the teens. I saw Eddy earlier and he was so pumped. He passed his math test yesterday. He's been spreading the word about Chance. It seems your tenant has quite a gift with teaching."

The slight emphasis on the word *your* caused heat to creep up Tanya's neck. "Yes, he is gifted." In many ways, she added silently, thinking of his quiet presence in her life that made her cherish each moment spent with him.

"I will warn you, though, that a few parents aren't happy that Chance is tutoring at the center. It was one thing when he donated his time doing the books. But some of them are upset that he is actually working with the teenagers. They've complained to Dane and Samuel."

"What is it about being innocent that they don't understand?" Tanya asked in a loud enough voice that several people nearby glanced at her with a question on their faces. She ignored them and lowered her tone, adding, "We need to do something, Beth."

"Yeah, I was thinking the same thing. Our support should help."

"There's gotta be more we can do." Tanya searched the crowd forming near the volleyball area and found Chance in the middle with Dane on one side and Eddy on the other.

"We'll need to pray about it. Something will come to mind. I'll tell Darcy, Zoey and Jesse to pray, too."

"That's an awful lot of praying power."

"Hey, we're a force to reckon with and the townspeople spreading the rumors will soon find that out."

"I almost feel sorry for them," Tanya said with a laugh.

"Feel sorry for who?" Darcy lowered herself into the vacant chair on the other side of Beth.

"The people who won't let Chance live in peace." Tanya's eyes found Chance again. Peace. Had he experienced any of that lately? She doubted it.

"I don't feel sorry for them. They are mean-spirited and need to mind their own business." Darcy folded her hands over her protruding stomach. "Bring them on. No one should mess with a woman who's suddenly carrying an extra twenty-five pounds."

Beth raised both brows. "When's your baby due?"

"Beth Morgan, you know exactly when my baby is

due. About eight weeks before yours. And yes, I've gained more weight than I wanted to."

Again Tanya couldn't resist scanning the people in the two-acre field where the activities would take place, seeking the man under discussion. She enjoyed watching him interact with others. When her gaze lit upon him, he was in the middle of his own discussion with a group of teenage boys preparing to play the first game of volleyball. Chance looked up, his eyes connecting with hers. Even from this distance she could feel the intensity in his regard. One corner of his mouth hitched up in that grin that could melt ice.

Chance's team gave a cheer, then broke their huddle and loped out onto the makeshift court. His gaze remained on her.

She'd rested enough. Rising, she said to Beth and Darcy, "Excuse me. I think I'll watch the volleyball game that's about to start."

"Hmm, I wonder why she has a sudden interest in volleyball," Darcy said as Tanya hurried toward the reason she had a sudden interest in a game she had no idea how to play.

"Hi." She came to a stop beside Chance.

"Hi, yourself. You looked mighty comfortable in that chair."

"I'm afraid if I sit too long, I'll never get up. So, can I help you with the game?"

One brow arched. "You play volleyball?"

"Well, no, but I figure it isn't too hard. Besides, I'm not offering to play, just help."

His full-fledged grin moved across his mouth. "I'm here to cheer these guys on. That's all."

"You aren't gonna play?"

He tossed his head in the direction of the grass court. "Do you see anyone out there over the age of twenty?"

She looked, then shook her head. "Then you're just coaching them?"

"No. Eddy is the team captain and very capable of coaching them. I'm their moral support."

The game started with Dane standing on the other side of the court, cheering whoever hit the ball no matter which team, while Chance supported the players with quiet words of encouragement, as though he didn't want to call attention to himself. She followed the action for a few minutes, but she couldn't shake the feeling that something was going on with Chance. The activities for the kids were off to the side away from most of the people who attended the picnic.

Finally when one side rotated, causing a lull in the game, Tanya asked, "You've been over here most of the morning. Is something wrong?"

Again one of his brows quirked as he assessed her. "I gather you've heard about the complaints against me tutoring at the youth center."

"Yep. Do you know who is complaining?"

"Dane and Samuel didn't feel they could say, but I've got a pretty good idea, starting with Holly Proctor's parents."

"Holly? The family used to go to our church. They stopped attending a few years back. Why do you think they complained?" A finely honed tension straightened her spine.

"She wasn't too happy the other evening when Crystal and I showed up to tutor. She left in a huff."

"Well, she can be dramatic at times."

"There's more. She was one of the girls who harassed Crystal in the TV room at the center."

A surge of anger zipped through Tanya. "And you're just now telling me this?"

"Yes, we've both been busy this week."

She glared at him. "Chance Taylor, you didn't think that bit of information warranted a visit even in the midst of your busy schedule?"

"Okay, I was hoping that Crystal would tell you. Obviously she didn't."

"Probably because she knows I will have a hard time not saying something to at least Holly's parents."

"See, I was trying to help you keep your promise to your daughter."

"You know there wasn't a timeline established on how long I would let her try to solve this problem."

Her gaze swept the crowd of people milling around and located the Proctor family with Holly standing off to the side slightly, a pout on her face, her arms crossed. One of the teenager's friends approached Holly and her sullen expression transformed into less grim lines. They further separated themselves from Holly's parents, whispering and glancing around them. Crystal's tormentor laughed when a younger girl walked by.

The urge to shake some sense into the teenager flooded Tanya. She started toward the pair. Chance's hand on her arm stopped her. She stared down at the long fingers clasped around her, then up into his eyes, so full of concern. "Someone needs to straighten Holly out. She shouldn't treat people like that."

"True. But I have a feeling that Crystal wouldn't

like you interfering. Remember what you said to her last weekend."

"I'm supposed to do *noth*ing?" *Her nails dug into her palms.*

"You can support Crystal. Be there to listen."

"Then how about you? You aren't gonna let those few parents stop you from tutoring, are you?"

His face tensed. "No. As long as there are kids to tutor and Dane allows me to, I will."

A cheer erupted behind Tanya. She glanced over her shoulder at the volleyball court and saw several teenagers leap into the air. Eddy came down, slamming the ball over the net. A boy on the other team dived for it and missed. The high-fives and shouts of victory drew a good part of the townspeople's attention toward them.

As Chance congratulated the winners, Tanya glimpsed Jim Proctor catch sight of Chance and frown, then say something to his wife. He strode toward Dane, still on the other side of the court with Samuel, who had joined him a few minutes ago. The man's path took him by Wilbur Thompson and Felicia Winters. Jim solicited their assistance and en masse they cornered Dane and Samuel with several other adults strolling toward the gathering.

Chance grew quiet, his gaze on the group quickly forming across the volleyball court. He flinched at the sound of a raised voice and turned away.

"I'll be right back," Tanya muttered and stalked toward the group, half expecting Chance to stop her. But the fact he didn't alarmed her more than if he had tried. The hurt expression on his face before he'd masked it behind a bland one stiffened her resolve. He was a

good man and it was about time the people of Sweetwater knew that!

"But he's been in prison," Wilbur said, glaring at
Dane. "I don't want my grandchildren around someone like him."

"Then don't let them come to the center." Dane returned Wilbur's glare.

Spying Zoey and Beth making a beeline toward the
group, Tanya pushed her way through the crowd until
she stood next to Dane and Samuel.

"The people volunteering at the center should be
checked out. My son should do a thorough background
check on them." Wilbur pounded his fist into his palm.

Behind the older man, Zach Thompson, the town's
police chief said, "Dad, I have and Chance checks out."

Wilbur huffed while Jim shouldered his way to the
center of the circle of townspeople. "My daughter can't
even get the help she needs because she's afraid."

Words of anger gushed upward, and Tanya had
to bite them back. She'd promised her daughter she
wouldn't say anything about Holly's actions—at least
not yet. But as far as Tanya was concerned, there was
probably little that frightened that young woman. Instead, Holly was the cause of scaring others.

Zoey came forward. "We have a list of tutors she can
access through the counseling office. If you want some
names, Jim, you can call me on Monday morning."

"Those tutors cost money."

"I'll help her."

The sound of her daughter's voice sent a shock wave
through Tanya. She spun around and faced Crystal, who

had maneuvered her wheelchair between the adults. Amanda walked beside her.

"For free. But she'll have to come to my house or the center if she wants help." Crystal stopped next to Tanya.

Jim opened and closed his mouth, then finally said, "*He* lives next to you."

Tanya placed her hand on her daughter's shoulder for a few seconds, then stepped forward until she invaded the man's personal space. Anger vibrated through her, but she instilled an even level into her voice as she said, "And he's a good neighbor. He doesn't judge. He helps others when he sees a need. I couldn't ask for a better neighbor. So if you want *free* tutoring, you have a choice. Take up my daughter's offer and come to the house or go to the center."

For half a minute Jim glared at her, then looked toward Zoey. "Send the list home with Holly on Monday. I refuse to expose my daughter to a man like that." Then he plunged into the crowd, disappearing from Tanya's view.

"I don't know about you, but I'm starved. I suggest we remember why we have this Last Chance Picnic and proceed to the tables set up with the food." Samuel's sharp gaze slid from one irate adult to the next, staring down each one until he hurried away.

After the instigators left, Beth said, "I've never been so embarrassed by our neighbors' behavior as today. Where in the world is this coming from?"

"It only takes a few to stir up the others." Dane clasped Zoey's hand and pulled her against his side.

"You mean Wilbur." Tanya positioned herself next to her daughter, her hand on her shoulder again. She was so proud of Crystal for offering to help the one person who was the cause of her agony.

"Yeah. Remember the problems I had with him when *I* first came to town? He just doesn't know how to keep his nose out of other people's business." Dane scanned the area. "Where's Chance?"

Tanya shifted until she made her own survey of the park. Chance wasn't anywhere to be seen, not even with Nick and Jesse or Eddy and his friends. Alarm bubbled up. *He's left. And I can't blame him. Will this push him to leave Sweetwater?* The question intensified the alarm, her stomach constricting.

Then she caught sight of him on the other side of the park near the water. When the police chief approached him, Chance stiffened. Even from this distance Tanya saw the wariness in every line of Chance's body.

"I see him. I'll be back." Tanya avoided the groups of townspeople and rushed across the expanse of the park toward him.

As she neared him, Chance shook Zach's hand, saying something to the police chief that was too low for her to hear. But when Zach left and passed her, he nodded, his features relaxed in a grin.

Although Chance saw her approach, he faced the lake, his hands stuffed into the front pockets of his jeans. The breeze from the water played with his hair, which he'd let grow out since his arrival in Sweetwater. Tanya slowed her pace, taking in his hunched shoulders, his rigid stance, as though a cold wind battered his body.

"I'm sorry you had to witness that little scene, Chance."

He didn't say anything for a long moment, then he

turned slightly. Even though his tension slipped from his expression, it still gripped his posture. "You have nothing to apologize for. This isn't the first time and I doubt it will be the last, either." He stared again at the water lapping against the shore near his feet, just missing soaking his tennis shoes.

She sidled up next to him, her gaze trained on a couple of skiffs on the lake a few hundred yards out, their occupants participating in the fishing rodeo. "What did Zach have to say?" Although she had intended for her voice to be casual, she winced at the intensity in the question.

"About the same as you, except he was more specific. He was apologizing for his father's rude behavior."

"He shouldn't apologize. Wilbur should."

"That's not gonna happen. Wilbur thinks he's protecting the people of this good town."

Tanya snorted. "From you? Wilbur is a busybody who needs to mind his own business." Even though his body language screamed stay away, Tanya slipped her arm through his. "And Jim Proctor needs to take care of his own problems. His daughter is a menace."

He chuckled, relaxing some more. "Remind me not to get on your bad side. You're fierce when riled." He twisted toward her, so near his clean scent laced the air between them and mingled with the more earthy odors surrounding them. "But I don't need you to fight my battles."

"First Crystal and now you. Will no one let me help them?"

"The best way to deal with the Wilburs and Jims of

this world is to ignore them and prove them wrong by doing the best job you can."

She caressed his face, feeling the slightly rough texture of his jawline. "But you aren't ignoring them really. I saw the look of hurt in your eyes."

Those eyes crinkled with humor now. "I didn't say I had mastered the best way yet. I'm still working on it." He searched her features, as though seeking some answers to questions she didn't know. "Let's go for a walk."

She fit her hand within his, and they started along the path that followed the shoreline. The aroma of grilled hamburgers floated to her, and she realized some of the men were cooking lunch. Even though hunger pangs tightened her stomach, she wouldn't be any other place but beside Chance. Maybe this would be the time he would let her inside, and she would be able to help him.

The large oaks, maples and pines that lined the trail shielded them from the sun, but an occasional ray fought its way through the multicolored canopy of fall leaves and struck the dirt path with its brightness. The coolness of the forest cloaked Tanya as she waited for Chance to break the silence.

"What did Crystal say about doing a portrait of Nate and Cindy?"

"I haven't said anything to her about Jesse's offer."

He slanted a look at her. "Why not?"

"Because…because…" Tanya couldn't get the words past her lips. Wasn't it obvious she was protecting her daughter?

"Tanya, what's going on? Crystal would do an excellent job."

"I'm sure she would."

"Then why haven't you told her?"

She swallowed several times. "Because it could open her up to more ridicule. She's got enough to deal with at the moment."

He stopped, angling toward her and clasping her arms. "What happened to you to make you hide your talent?"

"I made the mistake of entering an art contest at school and winning against a girl who was very popular and had many friends. She wasn't a gracious loser. She made my life a living nightmare for the rest of the year until we moved here to Sweetwater."

"And so you stopped drawing."

"I drew. Just no one saw my drawings after that. Look what happened when Holly saw Crystal at the art lesson at the center. Can you imagine what that girl would do if Crystal starting earning money with her art?"

He rested his forehead against hers. "Yes, I can imagine. But shouldn't Crystal make up her own mind what she needs to do? She wants to earn some money and that would be a good way for her to do something with her talent."

Tanya thought back to Crystal in the middle of the crowd earlier, telling Jim Proctor she would tutor his daughter for free. In her mind's eye she pictured the lift of her daughter's chin, the determination in her eyes and knew that Crystal meant every word she had uttered. She was turning the other cheek so to speak, doing what Christ would want her to do.

"I'll tell her this evening. It'll be her choice."

Chance brushed her hair behind her ears, his gaze riveted to hers. Her mouth went dry, her heartbeat pounding in her ears and drowning out all sounds. All her senses focused on him only inches from her, a tingling awareness blanketing her.

He leaned in and feathered his lips over hers. They reacted by parting. His mouth came down on hers possessing it as though there were no tomorrows. His arms entwined about her and pressed her against him while she surrendered to his kiss.

A good minute later he raised his head, the tight band of his embrace loosening slightly. A corner of his mouth lifted, his cheeks dimpling.

She brushed her finger over each indentation. "You know this was supposed to be a conversation about you and somehow we ended up discussing me. Chance Taylor, you're quite good at changing the subject."

"I'm glad I'm good at something."

"Oh, there are a number of things you are good at," she said, reliving the kiss he had just given her.

Chapter Eight

Tanya opened the drawer in the bathroom and found her medications for manic depression. She'd been feeling so well lately. In spite of all that had happened the past year, she'd done well mentally. Maybe she didn't have to take her two medicines anymore.

Fingering one of the bottles, she remembered the past few weeks since the Last Chance Picnic. Crystal seemed happier, especially with her and Amanda becoming closer as friends. She didn't think there had been another incident with those girls harassing her.

Thank You, Lord, for that.

Contentment shimmied down Tanya's length. She picked up the bottle, rolling it between her hands, the plastic container cool in her palms. Then there was Chance. Even though the weather had turned nasty, becoming colder than usual for this time of year, they jogged almost every evening after work along the lighted streets in the neighborhood. They often shared a dinner or two each week after he and Crystal tutored at the center. That was the least she could do since he was watching out for her daughter while there.

She stared at the white bottle. She hated depending on the pills to keep her even keel. The past three weeks had been near perfect. Maybe she could try not taking them today and see what would happen. If she could stop taking her medications for manic depression, then everything would really be perfect.

She tossed up the plastic container and snatched it from the air, the temptation growing within her. To be free, not sick, would be wonderful. To be whole for Chance.

"Mom, Chance is here."

Her daughter's shout penetrated the small bathroom. Sighing, she twisted the cap and shook a pill into her palm. Then she picked up the other bottle and removed her correct dose. She closed her fist around the medication. Better not take a chance with it being Thanksgiving. But perhaps she could speak with her doctor about it.

"Mom!"

"Coming." Tanya popped both pills into her mouth and swallowed some water, then opened the door. "With all your shouting you'd think it was a holiday or something."

"Funny, Mom. I'm starved. How long till dinner?"

With the house infused with the smells of the holiday, Tanya checked her watch. "About an hour. Why don't you set the dining room table and I'll finish up in the kitchen?"

Crystal made a one-eighty turn and headed down the hall. Her child's grin, which was appearing more and more, made Tanya cherish the moments. The aroma of the baking turkey finally prodded her into action. She still had to do a few things in order for dinner to be completed in an hour. Hurrying after her daughter, she started across the living room only to come to a halt with the sight of Chance kneeling in front of the fireplace as he lit the logs.

He looked at home in her house. She squeezed her eyes closed for a moment, needing to erase that image from her mind but unable to. When she peered at him again, his gaze pinned her with an intensity that stole her breath. He slowly rose and walked toward her. Her heart increased its beat, leaving her defenseless to his charm.

He clasped her upper arm and drew her to him. "You look beautiful."

She felt beautiful in his eyes. "You're not too bad yourself."

He cupped the back of her head, angling her so his lips caressed hers ever so lightly. "Happy Thanksgiving."

Hearing the sound of Crystal's wheelchair parted them. Tanya's heart still beat so rapidly her breaths came out in pants until she forced deep gulps of air into her oxygen-deprived lungs.

"We never build a fire, Chance. Thanks." Crystal sat in the entrance from the dining room with the dinner plates on her lap and her service dog next to her. "It's been so cold lately. This is perfect."

"Yeah, whatever happened to fall? We went from summer to winter in two weeks." Tanya continued her trek toward the kitchen, having enjoyed her little diversion in the living room.

At the oven she opened the door, heat blasting her in the face, and moved the large baking pan over to put in the dressing. As she made the tossed green salad, dicing the tomatoes, carrots and avocados, the added aroma of the dressing with its corn bread, onions, celery and mushrooms, filled every corner of the room.

"Can I help? Crystal says she doesn't need any and sent me in here."

Chance's deep voice flowed over Tanya, reminding her of that brief moment in the living room. He hadn't really kissed her, but her reaction had been as strong as if he had. Actually a mere look or touch could do that to her.

I'm falling in love with him.

That realization caused her to drop her knife before she cut herself. Her hands trembled with the knowledge of how important Chance had become to her in two months. She awoke each day looking forward to seeing him, perhaps sharing some time with him.

"Tanya?"

He stood behind her, her body reacting to his nearness—her mouth going dry, her palms damp, her pulse racing. *Get a grip. He can't ever know. It would send him fleeing from Sweetwater as fast as the next bus could take him. He's made it clear a relationship is the last thing he wants in his life right now.*

Plastering a smile on her face, she swung around to face him and wished she could step back, but the counter trapped her close to him. "You're our guest. I've got everything under control." *Everything except myself,* she added silently.

"It smells wonderful." He moved to the side and leaned against the counter next to where she was working.

Not far enough away. But she resumed slicing the cherry tomatoes in half and putting them in the large wooden bowl. His slightest movement registered on her brain. In light of what she'd discovered about her feelings toward him, she wasn't surprised.

"Do you have to work tomorrow?"

She nodded. "Why?"

"I thought if you didn't go to work we could run in the morning since it's so cold, especially in the evening after dark."

"Sorry. It *would* be nice to run in daylight for a change. If you want to jog in the morning, go ahead. I'll understand."

"No, I can wait until you get home. I could always get started on my holiday shopping."

"Like every other person in Sweetwater."

"On second thought, I'll hold off. I don't like crowds."

She slanted a look toward him, seeing more than she suspected he wanted to show. Crowds meant people like Wilbur Thompson and Jim Proctor. She couldn't blame him for wanting to avoid them. Although they had been quiet lately because of her circle of friends and their husbands' fierce advocacy of Chance, she was sure that wouldn't remain the case. Those two liked to cause trouble. "You might be out of luck. From here until Christmas there will be crowds."

"But nothing like the day after Thanksgiving."

"Will you be okay with the Christmas lights ceremony this evening? There will be lots of people attending."

His smile didn't reach his eyes. "But it'll be dark."

"We could go late and stand in the back."

"No, Crystal will miss some of the ceremony since she'll be sitting. We'll go early and be in the front."

"Are you sure?"

"Yeah." He pushed away from the counter. "I could always go into work tomorrow. There's plenty for me to do even though Nick has closed the office."

"Ah, working during a holiday. Better watch out. You may find yourself doing more of that." Tanya chopped up a cucumber. The sound of the knife hitting the wooden board echoed in the sudden silence. She peered toward Chance.

His face was pinched into a frown, his eyes fierce. "No, never again."

The strength behind his words took her by surprise. She scooped up the pieces of cucumber and dropped them into the salad bowl, forcing a lightness into her voice. "Why do you say that?"

"Because there was a time once when my job consumed my life to the exclusion of my family. I missed out on so much. I promised myself I would never fall into that kind of trap again. I will quit a job before I will allow that to happen."

"Is that why you aren't working as a financial advisor anymore?"

"Partly."

"What's the other reason?"

He moved away from her, his back to her. The stiffness of his shoulders meant she was treading in unwelcome territory. She waited to see if he would answer. One minute ticked into two.

"I don't think people would trust someone to advise them in financial situations when they discover I've been in prison."

"Nonsense! I mean, you're innocent." She spoke to his back as he crossed the room. "How long are you gonna let others dictate how you look at yourself? You aren't an ex-con, not really."

He spun around. "Yes, I am. I've come to accept that."

"Have you?"

"It left its mark on me whether I was innocent or not. I can't wipe those years away, no matter how much I would like to."

Tanya walked to the refrigerator and placed the salad inside, then shut the door and faced him, her hands planted on her waist. "Did Tom ever talk about Crystal and me?"

Chance blinked, surprise registering before he schooled his features into a neutral expression. "Where did that question come from?"

"I've been wondering for weeks, but since we don't talk about you being in prison, I didn't want to ask. Now we are talking about the time you spent in prison...with Tom. Did he?"

Glancing away, he heaved a sigh. "All the time."

"He did? But he wouldn't see us. He divorced me." Although she tried to keep the hurt from her voice, she heard it.

"That was the hardest thing he ever did. After your

last visit when he told me about it, he had tears in his eyes."

"Then why did he do it? I know he didn't want his daughter to see him like that, but he would have gotten out eventually. Didn't he want us in his life?"

"I don't think he thought he would get out. I'll never forget the hopelessness on his face that night when we talked. Prison has a way of killing hope. It was dead in Tom."

Tanya pressed herself back against the refrigerator, her legs weak. She clutched its edge to hold herself upright. "I could have helped him. I could have reminded him that God was with—"

"Don't give me that. God isn't in prison, no matter how much Samuel wants to believe He is. He may be other places, but not there."

Tanya gasped at his harsh tone. "He *is* everywhere, even prison." Her limbs trembling, she covered the space between them. "God doesn't give up on people. People give up on Him. Give Him a second chance. Open your heart and let Him in again." She laid her hand over his chest and felt the thumping of his heart. "We have so much to be thankful for. Come to church this Sunday with Crystal and me. We have a special service where we offer our thanks to the Lord for the past year. You're free. That's something to celebrate."

He gripped her hand touching him. "I can't—"

"Please."

He slid his fingers over the back of her hand to link with hers, searching her features for some kind of answer. "I'll think about it."

"If you want a ride, I leave on Sunday at nine o'clock."

When he didn't say anything, Tanya tightened her hold on his hand and in order to fill the silence asked, "I expect you to pull into the driveway any day with a car. Wasn't that on your list of items to buy?"

"I have something else I'm saving my money for first, then I'll get a used car."

"With winter coming, walking everywhere will be harder. If I can give you a lift, just ask."

"Thankfully Sweetwater isn't so big that I can't usually get where I need to go in a short amount of time. Besides, I like to walk."

Finally she slipped her hand from his and immediately missed the physical contact. "Well, at least you're doing your bit for the environment. We probably all should walk more." Tanya checked to see how the peas were simmering, then removed the turkey from the oven and stuck in the biscuits. "Did I tell you I finally got up the nerve to apply for a better-paying job at the bank?"

"No. What?"

"A loan officer."

"When will you find out?"

"Tomorrow."

"Then you might have something to celebrate tomorrow night."

She shrugged as she withdrew a pan to make the gravy in. "I know of several other women who applied that are very qualified."

"But so are you and you're dedicated to your job."

The heat scored her cheeks, and it had nothing to do with the steam rising from the turkey pan that was several feet away on the counter. Using the pan juices, Tanya mixed the ingredients for the gravy in the pot and stirred it while it simmered, the whole time aware of Chance's presence in the kitchen.

He made himself busy by giving Crystal some assistance in getting the table set, even though she had insisted she could manage by herself. He took the salt and pepper shakers, container of real butter, the salad dressing bottles and the salad into the dining room.

We work well together—Crystal, Chance and myself. That thought fueled her overactive imagination, and she immediately pictured them as a family, sharing more than a Thanksgiving dinner.

"When am I going to get to see that portrait of Nate and Cindy you drew?" Chance followed Crystal back into the kitchen, Charlie walking beside him.

"Jesse is stopping by this evening before the lighting ceremony to pick it up. I guess it's done," her daughter said.

"It's hard sometimes to let something you've created go." Chance took his place again at the counter not far from Tanya, leaning against it casually while facing Crystal and her Lab in the center of the room.

"Yeah, what if she doesn't like it?"

"I don't think you have to worry about that," Tanya said, switching off the burners and the oven.

Crystal sighed. "I know Jesse would never say anything about not liking it. She'll like it because I'm your daughter. But I want her to *really* like it because it is good."

"You want someone to tell you the truth." All casualness drained from Chance as he straightened, picking up the platter that the turkey was on. "Go get it and I'll tell you the truth—or at least my real opinion. I will always tell you the truth."

Tanya bit down on her lower lip, the quiet heavy after her daughter's exit.

Chance stepped into the dining room and placed the platter on the table then came back into the kitchen. "I know it's good, Tanya, but I meant it when I said I would tell her the truth. Nothing good comes from lies, not even little white lies."

The sound of Crystal's approach silenced Tanya's response. The serious expression on her daughter's face tautened her nerves. Her breath lodged in her throat as she waited for Crystal to show them the picture. When she lifted it from her lap to unveil the portrait, tears misted Tanya's eyes.

The pen-and-ink drawing revealed a young boy kneeling in the grass holding his dog while a younger girl stood beside him cradling her cat to her chest. The expressions of joy on the children's faces made a person seeing the portrait smile. Her daughter's talent was amazing.

Chance studied it for a good minute.

"Well?" Crystal fidgeted in her wheelchair.

"You know, I am at a loss for words." He plowed his hand through his hair.

"Good or bad ones?"

The grin that encompassed his whole face said it all. "It's beautiful. Great. Wonderful. Stupendous." He swung his attention to Tanya. "Help me here. I'm running out of synonyms for an absolutely stunning piece of art."

"Oh, I think she's got the picture." Tanya gestured toward the beaming expression on her daughter's face.

"You really like it."

"No."

Crystal blinked, her smile fading.

"I *love* it! And if Jesse Blackburn doesn't, then something is definitely wrong with her."

Crystal blew out a rush of air. "I think I'll be able to eat now. I'm starving, but my stomach has been tied up in knots, thinking about her coming to pick it up."

"Speaking of eating, let's get the rest of the food on the table. I didn't have breakfast, and I'm starved, too," Chance said.

As if they were a true family, all three worked to put the meal on the table, then sat down and held hands while Crystal said a prayer of thanksgiving.

On the ride to Main Street where the Holiday Lights Ceremony would take place, Chance thought back over the afternoon with Tanya and Crystal. A warmth suffused him that scared him. Even the prayer that Crystal had said before the meal hadn't bothered him—it had actually soothed him. Memories of the times he, Ruth and Haley had done that very thing before eating had inundated him and hadn't sent panic through him.

What was happening to him? He didn't want to forget his wife and daughter, and yet he had found himself not thinking about them every day. Instead, he'd wondered what Tanya or Crystal was doing. He'd look forward to seeing Tanya and her bright smile of greeting when he came home. She usually managed to be around either outside or at the window if it wasn't one of their days to run or the occasional times she had to work late at the bank. And if she wasn't at the window or outside, he'd come up with a reason to knock on her back door and see how her day had gone.

He needed to leave soon—before he became so involved in their lives he couldn't. And Tanya didn't need someone like him in her life permanently. He was emotionally damaged and with her manic depression she had enough to deal with herself.

He'd been reading about manic depression and admired her even more for being able to pull her life together as she had. It hadn't been easy and would always be something she would have to deal with. He was still amazed to discover people like Abraham Lincoln and Winston Churchill had been bipolar. Look what they had accomplished!

Tanya parked behind Alice's Café, and he hopped out to man the lift for Crystal. A cold breeze shivered down his length. He needed to buy a heavier coat for the winter. He hated to spend the money when he almost had saved enough for Crystal's sports wheelchair. Although there was only one other youth in a wheelchair who expressed an interest in playing basketball, Chance knew there were several adults in Sweetwater who wanted to try forming a team. If not here in town, Lexington wasn't too far away. He wanted Crystal to have the option of playing on a team if she wanted to. It would be the perfect Christmas gift, especially since he would be leaving town right after the new year. He wanted to give Crystal and Tanya something meaningful and lasting.

He just hadn't thought of the perfect gift for Tanya yet.

"Hey, Chance, are you going to stand around staring into space all evening? We'll get lousy seats," Crystal said as she drove her wheelchair around the corner of the building that housed Alice's Café.

"It's good to hear her eager to do something again." Tanya slipped her arm through his and snuggled closer.

"Jesse had a lot to do with her good mood. As I predicted, she loved the drawing."

"Don't sell yourself short. She laughed all the way through dinner today and that's because of you."

Her compliment warmed him in the cold. "It's really not any of that. It's Amanda. They are inseparable at the center."

Walking beside him, Tanya took the same path as her daughter around the building. "And on the phone in the evening. Sean and Craig complain they never talk to Crystal like they used to. Hopefully this thing with Holly is over."

Chance chilled suddenly, all the warmth gone. "Don't count on it, Tanya. Bullies don't just go away like that." He snapped his fingers.

"I can hope, can't I?"

"Sure, but don't let that keep you from seeing what's going on." *How can I leave until the problem with Holly is taken care of? And yet, the trial is the first full week in January. I've got to be there to see justice done.*

He and Tanya emerged onto Main Street, and immediately he saw Crystal near the stage with Amanda next to her. Another girl he'd seen around the center occasionally with them joined the pair. Then two boys, one being Grant Foster, came up and stood with them. Laughter sounded as Tanya and he approached.

"Maybe we should leave them to their own devices." Seeing Crystal happy caused that same emotion in him. For so long he'd forgotten what happiness meant—until he'd come to Sweetwater, until he'd met Tanya.

"Are you suggesting we would put a damper on my daughter's fun?"

He nodded. "We're over thirty. That's a given."

"You don't believe that, do you?"

He chuckled. "No. I just want to have you to myself." Where in the world did those words come from, he thought, shocked by them as much as Tanya obviously was if her wide eyes and open mouth were any indication.

She cuddled next to him, his arm slung over her shoulder. Shortly, Jesse and Nick joined them, then Darcy and Joshua. Before long Samuel, Beth, Zoey and Dane completed the group. Surrounded by Tanya's friends—no, his, too, he had to acknowledge—he realized he had a lot to be thankful for this Thanksgiving.

He leaned down close to Tanya's ear and whispered, "I'll go to church with you and Crystal this Sunday, that is, if the invitation is still open." He added the last part in a teasing tone just so he could see her expression light up before she playfully jabbed him in the side.

"Funny. You know the invitation is a standing one."

The mayor of Sweetwater came to the mike and began the ceremony with a speech. Chance tuned out the man and scanned the crowd gathered. He spied Wilbur glaring at him with Jim and his family not far from the older man. Jim Proctor refused to look toward him as though to do so would acknowledge that he was alive and part of the town.

Chance noticed one of Holly's friends pull her away and Crystal's tormentor joined a group of teenage girls, some he had seen at the center. What he had seen he hadn't cared for. They had often been cruel and callous toward others. They had always made sure they were together in a group because it gave them a sense of power. He'd seen that in prison and he'd seen what could happen. Tom's death was a result of one of those bullying gangs.

He shuddered.

"Cold?"

Tanya's question thankfully drew him away from his past. "Are you kidding? It must be twenty."

She wound her arm around his waist. "I wouldn't be surprised if it snowed before the weekend is over. I can smell it in the air."

"All I smell is wood burning. I could use a hot cup of coffee."

"Will hot apple cider do?" Tanya whispered, close enough that the familiar scent of lilacs rivaled the aroma of burning wood.

"Sure. Hot is the operative word."

"Good. Alice invited some of us to the café after the ceremony."

"How long does it take to throw a light switch?" Chance asked as the mayor concluded his speech about the upcoming holiday season.

"Let's see, we'll sing a few songs, then the mayor's wife will turn the lights on."

"How many songs?"

"Six, maybe seven."

"That's not a few!"

As the crowd launched into "Joy to the World," Tanya murmured close to Chance's ear, "It used to be twelve—one song for each of the twelve days of Christmas. And we ended with that one."

"Then I should count my blessings?"

"Always."

In the soft glow of the streetlight, Chance became transfixed by the intensity in Tanya's gaze. He didn't hear one word of the second or third song. His attention fixed upon the woman at his side. He savored her beauty that was on the inside as well as the outside.

Finally he joined in with the others and sang the last song, "Silent Night." As the last chord rang out in the square, the mayor's wife flipped on the lights and a brilliance filled the whole length of Main Street and the park in the middle where a massive twenty-foot Christmas tree shone with hundreds of tiny twinkling clear lights.

"The power company must be ecstatic right about now." Chance took in the whole park, lights in almost every tree, lights running along the fence that separated the children's playground from the rest of the area.

"We do tend to go all out. I figure an astronaut can see Sweetwater from outer space. What do you think?"

"Yep. I figure you're right." He hugged her against his length, enjoying her warmth, her own radiance that vied with the brilliance of the lights.

Tanya's becoming too important to me. He needed to back off. And he would tomorrow, he told himself as the crowd began to disperse, people strolling toward their parked vehicles. Some of them made their way toward Alice's Café, lit with its own bright lights, the

owner standing in the doorway greeting her guests as
they entered.

Tanya started for the restaurant, stopped after a few
feet and said, "I forgot I have a present for Darcy. I left
it in the van. I'll be right back."

Before she could move away, Chance captured her
hand and halted her progress. "I'll get it. You go on
inside."

She tossed him the keys, and he snatched them up.
Then in a lope he headed toward the back of the building and the few parking spaces behind it. Coming
around the corner, he stopped when he heard yelling.

"Can't you do anything right?" Jim stood only inches
from Holly, his face thrust in hers, his hands balled into
fists. "You don't need a tutor to learn math. You just
need to study harder. When were you going to tell me
you failed that test? If your teacher hadn't said anything
tonight, I wouldn't have found out, would I?"

"Dad—"

Jim glimpsed Chance and stepped back. "Get in.
We'll talk more at home."

Chance watched Holly jerk open the back door and
slide inside while her mother and younger brother got
into the car. Silhouetted in the dim light from the cars
passing on the side street, Jim Proctor stared at Chance.
The man's anger was evident by the stiff lines of his
body.

So much for the perfect family, Chance thought as
the Proctors pulled away, Jim gunning the car. Bullies
were made and Holly had been expertly molded by her
father. But still that didn't excuse the teenager's actions
toward Crystal.

Quickly Chance retrieved the wrapped present for Darcy and jogged back to the front of Alice's Café. He wanted to feel sorry for Holly, but Crystal's pain made it hard for him.

When he entered the restaurant, he searched for Tanya and found her with Darcy and Joshua in the corner. Chance wove his way through the crowded café and joined them, giving the present to Tanya who immediately handed it to Darcy.

"I saw this yesterday and couldn't resist, especially since we know you're having a little girl."

Darcy took the gift. "You shouldn't have. You've already given me something."

"Yes, I should have. Darcy, you were the first person to reach out and help me when I was in trouble. I'll never forget that."

"We've helped each other." Darcy's eyes filled with tears. "See, you're gonna make me cry. I cry at the drop of a hat lately."

"Tell me about it," Joshua said with a laugh.

Darcy jabbed her husband in the side. "Are you complaining?"

He held up his hands. "No way am I answering that question."

"Unwrap the present." Tanya shifted from one foot to the other.

Darcy ripped into the gift. When she opened it to reveal a music box with painted pink roses on it, a tear slid down her face. "Oh, Tanya. It's beautiful. What song does it play?"

"That's the best part—'Amazing Grace.'"

"The one Sean and Crystal sang together."

Tanya nodded. She turned to Chance. "That was the first time they sang together and they got a standing ovation."

"It's one of my favorites," Darcy murmured, running her finger along the edge of the music box. "Thank you, Tanya. I will treasure this."

A few seconds of silence reigned before Joshua cleared his throat and said, "Hey, I don't know about you all, but I'm gonna fight my way to the counter and get some hot apple cider and a few of Alice's cookies."

"I'll help you." Chance followed Joshua, leaving the women by themselves.

"Call me tomorrow whether you get the job or not. I want to know either way." Darcy tossed the crumpled wrapping paper and box into the trash can near the kitchen door.

"I'll have more responsibility. If I get it, I'll need to go to a seminar in Lexington for three days in a couple of weeks. I'll have to drive back and forth since I can't stay overnight because of Crystal."

"She can come out to the farm and stay with us."

"No, I'd rather drive. It's only a little over an hour. I can do it for three days. With all that's happened this year at school, I don't want to be gone."

"I don't blame you, but you know we're here to help if you need it." Darcy cradled the music box to her chest. "Sean says things are a little better at school."

"The situation has improved some, especially since Crystal's begun to tutor some of the kids at the center. I think they appreciate the help."

"A bully feeds on the reactions of bystanders and if there are no bystanders..." Darcy's voice trailed off into silence as she shrugged. She looked toward Chance and Joshua who were making their way back and asked, "How's it going with Chance?"

"Fine."

"Fine? That's all you're gonna say. I saw you two at the ceremony looking all cozy. I want details."

"There are no details. We're good friends. That's all." Tanya noticed the men stopped to say something to Dane.

"That's all? That's not the way it looked to me."

"Darcy, I don't know that Chance will ever get over his family's deaths. Not only does he have a picture of his daughter up in his apartment but one of his wife, too. I know they are together but still..."

"You need to give him a drawing of you and Crystal so he has something besides them. Life is for the living. He needs to move on and you need to help him do that."

"It's not that simple."

"Sure it is. Wouldn't that be a great Christmas gift for him? A portrait of you and Crystal. I bet he would treasure it like I will this." Darcy held up the music box. "You're not asking him to get rid of the photo of his wife and daughter. You're just giving him an alternative."

"I don't do drawings for other—"

"Shh. Here they come. Think about it." Darcy plastered a smile on her face and directed it at Joshua and Chance who broke through the crowd with their drinks in their hands.

Tanya took the mug Chance handed her and sipped the apple cider, relishing its spicy flavor. Its heat slid down her throat warming her insides.

When Chance bent forward and whispered, "I discovered something about the Proctor family that I want to share with you," the warmth from his nearness replaced the warmth from her drink.

She nearly melted into him. "What?"

"I'll tell you later, but it explains some things."

Her curiosity aroused, Tanya hardly listened to the conversation flowing around her, even when Samuel and Beth joined them. But the mention of the Proctor family caused her to scan the café to make sure her daughter was all right. Crystal sat in her wheelchair at a table with Jane, Eddy, Craig, Grant and Amanda. The grin on her daughter's face eased any tension the Proctor name produced. And it didn't return until her friend got up on a chair and gave a loud whistle to get everyone's attention.

Jesse held up the drawing Crystal did of Nate and Cindy so the crowd could see. Murmurs flew around the café. The noise level rose.

"I wanted you all to see what a beautiful job Crystal Bolton did on a drawing of my children that I commissioned. From what I understand she wants to earn some money and what better way than sharing her talent with us." Jesse gestured toward Crystal, who blushed from head to toe.

But a huge grin still graced her daughter's face as several people openly commented on the portrait. Two women approached her immediately and Tanya could see her pleasure at their compliments.

"Her work was shown and nothing bad happened. Crystal is doing a great job of handling the praise. I predict she will have to turn people down before the evening is over. She's gonna be quite busy this holiday season. Maybe you could help her out with some of the portraits?"

Chance's suggestion stirred Tanya's interest for all of two seconds until she pictured people staring at her work, analyzing it, criticizing it. No, her art was a private affair between her and her daughter—and maybe Chance. Because Darcy's idea of a portrait for Chance for Christmas wasn't half-bad. With him she felt safe enough to share an important part of herself—her art.

Chapter Nine

"What do you think about putting some more lights up there?" Tanya pointed toward the roof of her house.

Chance stepped back several feet and surveyed it. "You already have twenty-five strands up. Are you trying to outshine the park downtown?"

"I got these lights on sale. I know I probably shouldn't have bought them, but with my new job, I got a raise. I wanted to use a little money to celebrate it. What better way than lots of holidays lights?"

Chance studied Tanya for a moment. Something was wrong. He wasn't sure what, but he felt it in his gut. He took the red string and started for the ladder. "How's the job going?"

"Okay. There's a lot to learn. I'm glad the seminar is over. Driving back and forth took more time than I thought." While she laid clear lights over the bushes in front, she described her new duties.

Chance half listened to her words. What he really tuned in to was her tone of voice. It sounded as if Tanya had been up for the past several nights and was going through the motions of living on little sleep and a lot of caffeine.

When there was a lull in Tanya's discourse on her new job, he asked, "Is everything okay with Crystal?"

"Sure." Then she launched into an account of her daughter's week at school which Chance already knew from Crystal herself. Tanya described in detail Crystal eating lunch with Grant the day before in the school cafeteria.

He descended the ladder after stringing the lights on the roof then walked to where Tanya continued her task of putting up lights along the porch railing. "Is everything okay with you?"

Her brow crunched into a frown. "Yes, why would you ask? Crystal seems happy. I've got a new job I like."

Kneading the back of his neck, he tried to decide how to put his concerns. "You're acting different. I thought maybe something was wrong." He paused, drew in a deep, fortifying breath and added, "Have you been taking your medication?"

"Why would you ask that?" Anger laced her voice.

He shrugged. It had been over a month since he'd read about manic depression, but Tanya wasn't acting right. He needed to check online, maybe call one of her friends.

He cut the distance between them and brushed his finger under each eye. "Are you sleeping? You've got dark circles under your eyes."

Shrugging away, she moved toward the porch steps. "I just told you that the driving back and forth between Sweetwater and Lexington was more than I anticipated. So naturally I haven't got as much sleep as I usually do." She finished putting up the strand of lights, twisting it around the poles.

Chance watched her hurried movements. He started to say something when she gathered up the few strings left and said, "I think that's all for today. I still have to clean my house." She hoisted the almost-empty box of lights and climbed the stairs to the porch. "Thanks for your help. We'll have to pick Crystal up at the center in two hours."

"Fine. But—"

Tanya opened the front door and disappeared inside. Chance swallowed his words, his mouth hanging open for a few seconds before he quickly closed it.

He strode toward his apartment, removing his cell and punching in Darcy's number.

"Chance, what do you need?"

"I'm worried about Tanya. She's not acting like she usually does. What are some of the signs of manic depression?"

"Not sleeping. Recklessness. Impulsiveness. Too much energy. Talking fast. Poor judgment. Easily distracted. Heightened moods. Irritable and sometimes aggressive. That's some of the symptoms for mania. Do you want them for depression?"

"No. If there's a problem, it's mania. Tanya told me she hasn't been sleeping. The whole morning all she did was talk and talk while she was working. Half the time she would start one string of lights, get distracted and do a new one across the yard. I had to go back and finish up for her. She had so much nervous energy she made me edgy."

"I'll come over. She once told me she wished she

could stop taking her medication. She was raised to believe that a pill wasn't the answer to everything."

"Don't, Darcy. Let me take care of it." He hung up before she could protest.

He stood on the small landing into his apartment and stared at the front lawn with every bush, tree and pole covered with lights, not to mention the house. When she switched them on tonight, he'd need a pair of sunglasses. A laugh threatened to erupt until he thought of the seriousness of the situation. He didn't want Crystal to know what was going on and have her worry. He headed back down the stairs to the driveway, then jogged to the back door and pounded on it.

Tanya rushed across the kitchen and flung open the door. "Forget something?" She flashed him a smile and whirled around to hurry to the refrigerator. "Want something to drink? How about some brownies?" She left the refrigerator and rummaged through the pantry.

He took hold of her arms and pulled her away from the cabinet. "What I want is for you to sit and talk with me."

She glanced at her watch then the clock on the wall. "I don't know. Remember we need to get Crystal. I need to make her something to eat before we go to Darcy's farm. Maybe I should make her something to drink, too. She hates apple juice." She checked her watch again. "There's just not enough time in the day to do everything."

Tugging her away from the pantry, Chance scooted out a chair and sat her in it, then took a seat in front of her so he faced her. He held both of her hands between them and stared at her. She wouldn't meet his gaze.

"I realize you didn't really answer me earlier. Have you been taking your medication lately?"

She averted her head. "Partly."

"What do you mean partly?"

"This week I cut back on my mood stabilizer. With the holidays and my new job, I've had so much to do that I thought if I didn't have to sleep as much I could get—" The color drained from her face. She brought her hand up to her mouth. "What have I done?"

"Nothing that can't be fixed. Why don't you get your medication and take it now? Then call your doctor and check in with him."

She rose and left the kitchen. A moment later she came back in with a bottle in her hand. After speaking with her doctor she took what he prescribed, then eased down onto the chair.

With a shudder, she hugged her arms to her chest. "I wish I didn't have to take the medication."

"I know." He moved his chair closer until their legs pressed together. "You have to think of yourself like a diabetic who can't live without insulin."

"Everything was fine. I thought I could cut back and be fine. I wasn't going to stop taking the medication, just not take as much."

"But you were all over the place. You weren't fine."

Tanya buried her face in her hands. "I'm so ashamed."

The steel case around his emotions cracked open. "Why? You have no reason to be ashamed. You have an illness and you're under a doctor's care. You need medication and counseling to help you live a healthy, happy life. You have done nothing wrong. People deal with all kinds of illnesses every day. Yours happens to be manic depression." He covered her hands and massaged his fingers into her skin, willing his touch to heal her hurt.

She lifted her head, her eyes swimming with tears. "I didn't make a fool of myself out there in the front yard this morning?"

"Nope. But it was obvious to anyone who knows you well that you weren't acting like you usually do."

"My doctor wants to see me on Monday then have me make an appointment with my counselor."

"Do you want me to go with you?"

She shook her head. "I can do it by myself. As much as I wish things were different, they aren't. I have to accept that. I have no choice because I won't go back to the way I was right after Crystal's accident."

"And if you slip, you've got friends who are here to help."

"Who helps you?"

"I don't—"

She silenced his words with the touch of her fingers against his lips, the warmth of his skin against the tips electrifying. "Everyone needs help from time to time, even you." She pushed the last of her tears back and asked, "If I slip in the future, will you be one of those friends who is here to help me find my way back?"

The question hung in the air between them.

His large hands clasped her smaller ones. "I can't answer that. Probably not. But you have Darcy, Jesse, Beth and Zoey to help you. You have Crystal."

But not you. That hurt worse than the realization she would be on medication for her manic depression for the rest of her life. Her little experiment hadn't worked.

She'd known better, but she had wanted so badly to be totally free of her illness.

She pushed a smile through the hurt and said, "Well, at least my yard is decorated for the holidays. Now all we need is the Christmas tree."

"And we're picking that out later this afternoon."

"Yeah, Darcy's latest idea is a good one. I can't wait."

"Good? You aren't the one who will be chopping the tree down."

"True." She squeezed his upper arm. "But you've got the muscles to do the job. I don't." She flexed hers. "Not promising."

"You've got a point there. When do we meet everyone at the farm?"

"In a little over an hour. I volunteered to bring some cookies." She slapped a hand over her mouth. "Oh, no. I forgot. I volunteered to bring some homemade cookies."

"You don't have any?"

"Nope."

Chance rose and held out his hand. "C'mon. We've got an hour until we pick Crystal up at the youth center. I can help you with the cookies. That is, if you have the ingredients."

"You bake?"

He tugged her to her feet. "Nope, but I can follow directions. Lead the way."

The scent of freshly baked chocolate chip cookies saturated the van with its scintillating aroma. After parking in front of the youth center, Tanya hopped down and hurried toward the building with Chance right behind her. The cold, crisp air wrapped its icy fingers around her, prodding her to move even faster. She side-stepped a mound of dirty snow plowed off the sidewalk and mounted the steps.

Inside the warmth of the center chased away the chill gripping her. "Crystal should have finished tutoring Amanda and Brady." Tanya looked up and down the long hall. "I thought she would be out here waiting since we're a little late."

"You called her to let her know we were running behind. Maybe she's in the gym. The Saturday Basketball League is playing a game right now and Grant is one of the players. Maybe she's watching."

"I guess," she murmured, listening to the stomping and shouting coming from the gym. But the hairs on her nape tingled.

For the past month everything had been calm with Crystal as if Holly had decided to stop harassing her daughter. Crystal had even insisted on going to the center without Chance there to watch over her. Now, however, Tanya had second thoughts. She'd asked Crystal to be in the front hall waiting since they were behind schedule.

Chance stared at her for a few seconds. "I'll look in the gym. You take the classrooms on the right. Then I'll check the ones on the left."

Amanda was with her daughter. She would be okay. She was overreacting. She noticed some doors were open, some closed. Those rooms were the ones she would check first.

Tanya opened the door to the nearest room. Empty. She moved to the second one. A group of twelve-and thirteen-year-olds were talking. Her hand shook as she gripped the handle on the third one. For some reason she inched it open quietly. Low voices, furious and sharp, accosted her as she peeked inside.

"We've had enough of you spreading rumors and gossip about Crystal and now Amanda." Eddy stood in a warrior's stance in front of Holly and her friend. On one side of the young man was Jane and on the other Brady. "It's wrong. It's against what Christ taught us is right. Crystal and Amanda have tried to be nice to you this past month and all you've done is make their lives unbearable. Not anymore. We won't let it happen." Eddy gestured toward his friends around him.

Holly pushed against him. "Get out of my way. I'll tell my father."

Eddy crossed his arms over his chest. "Go ahead. And then we'll tell about the graffiti about Crystal and Amanda that you wrote on the girls' bathroom walls here and at school."

"I didn't do it! *She* lies!" Holly pointed toward Crystal sitting in her wheelchair off to the side with Amanda next to her.

"I saw you," Jane said, stepping in front of Eddy. "I expect you to have the walls here at the center cleaned off today and the ones at school on Monday."

"I won't—"

"It isn't negotiable, Holly." Jane held her ground.

"I have friends that—"

"I think you'll discover your 'friends' won't fight this battle with you. You need to take lessons from Crystal on what a good friend is. You aren't one."

Tanya sensed Chance come up behind her. He put his hands on her shoulders and squeezed them. Tears crowded her eyes as she watched the group of teens deal with Crystal's tormentors.

"We will not stand by and watch you hurt our friend." Eddy walked to Crystal and positioned himself next to her.

When Brady followed, standing beside Amanda, Jane said, "So what's your choice? Leave or take care of your mess."

Holly glared at Crystal, her hands curling and uncurling. A tense silence vibrated the air. Finally Holly huffed and said, "I'll clean it up," then flounced out of the room, throwing a glare at Tanya as she passed her.

Tears ran down Tanya's cheeks, matching the ones that coursed down her daughter's.

The older teens circled Crystal's wheelchair with Eddy saying, "There isn't a place at this center or in this town for a bully. If she bothers you again, Crystal, let me know. There are a group of us dedicated to taking care of people who try to bully. We won't tolerate it."

"But she does have a lot of friends who don't care—"

Eddy knelt in front of Crystal, taking her hand. "No, she doesn't. They just don't know what to do when she bullies someone. Dane is gonna start some classes on bullying and what to do in a situation where you're harassed by a classmate or you witness someone bullying another. If we allow bullying," Eddy pointed to himself, "then it will happen. But if we don't, we can stop it."

Jane grinned. "Hey, kid, I haven't been watching you grow up for nothing. I'm your friend. Come to me if there's a problem. What are friends for but to help?"

Tanya turned away from the scene, a lump lodged in her throat. She knew Crystal had seen her, but she wanted to give her daughter some privacy with her friends. Besides, she needed time to gather her own composure after what she had witnessed. Friends coming to the aid of a friend in trouble. Crystal would be all right as long as she had good friends around her. And so would she as Chance had pointed out earlier that day. Even if he left—and she knew he would—she would be all right. Her heart would break, but she would make it because she had the support she needed in place with her friends and the love of the Lord.

Tanya waited by the front door with Chance. She saw Holly and her friend go into the girls' bathroom with some cleaning supplies. The anger in the teen's expression saddened her.

Chance stared at the restroom door through which the two girls had disappeared. "Bullies aren't born. Holly was made. Remember when I witnessed her dad yelling at her and telling her how stupid she was? They are not the perfect family everyone's been led to believe. As I told you after the Holiday Light Ceremony, I have a feeling Holly learned the tactics of a bully from her father."

"That doesn't surprise me after what he's tried to do with you."

"But the tactics aren't working with me. I don't care what he thinks, and I have friends to help me. Jim and Wilbur are nothing compared to the predators in prison."

"Most people in Sweetwater are seeing what you're doing. Some of their children are getting the help they need in math because of you."

"It's not just me tutoring." He straightened as he saw Crystal driving her wheelchair toward them. "Your daughter has a natural talent for teaching."

"I'm discovering my daughter has a lot of talents. She may not be able to walk, but God has gifted her with so much." Tanya pushed open the front door. "You all ready? The best trees are probably gone by now."

Crystal with a huge grin on her face headed out into the cold. "Nah. I bet Darcy is waiting for us to arrive before they start."

When everyone was settled in the van and the heater blasted warm air, Tanya backed out of her parking space and drove toward Darcy's family farm. Anticipation of the fun to come hummed through her veins. For the first time in months she experienced hope that her daughter would be all right. Crystal might have to deal with being in a wheelchair the rest of her life, but then people often had something they had to deal with their whole life—like her manic depression.

Fifteen minutes later Tanya parked next to a horse barn, noticing that they were the last to arrive at Darcy's. Several other vehicles were already there, which meant everyone was inside the brown structure, waiting for them just as Crystal had said. In the barn some of the horses were saddled while others were being readied to ride.

Tanya noticed that everyone had horses. "I don't know why I agreed to this. I don't ride."

Darcy lumbered over to them. "I've been having some contractions so I'm giving you the sled. Dad and Sean are gonna get our tree while Joshua and I stay back, just in case."

Tanya pointed at her friend's large round stomach. "Just in case you have the baby today? You should have called and canceled this outing."

"No way. We need a tree and we have a whole forest of Christmas trees waiting for everyone to choose one for their living rooms." Darcy smiled at Crystal. "Sorry, but you have to ride with your mom and Chance. Though it's probably a good thing. You can keep those two in line."

Tanya sidled next to Chance and whispered, "Okay, do I look as red as Crystal's scarf?"

He studied her—a mistake to ask him, Tanya decided because the heat intensified on her face.

His dimpled grin appeared. "Your friends have a refreshing candor."

"I wasn't gonna call their meddling refreshing."

"Let's go, Mom, Chance. Everyone's ready to go. The sled's out back."

Sean wheeled Crystal toward the back doors. A blast of cold swept into the barn when he opened them. Samuel mounted after Craig got on his horse and Allie rode behind him. Beth stayed behind because of her pregnancy. Jane climbed into her saddle, her animal tied next to Jesse and Nick's. Nate and Cindy were already on two small mares which their parents were going to lead. Darcy's dad was at the front of the group with Sean next to him. Zoey and Dane were the last to get on their geldings. Joshua handed up Mandy to Zoey and Dane took Tara. Blake hopped onto his own horse.

"When you get the perfect tree and cut it down, head back here. There will be hot chocolate and sweets waiting," Darcy announced to the group while Tanya ascended the sled.

Chance lifted Crystal out of her wheelchair and placed her next to Tanya. Then he climbed up onto the sled and took the reins. "Ready? Joshua told me a great place to look for the perfect tree."

All the horses and riders headed out into the snow-covered pasture near the barn. Chance directed the two horses pulling the sled along the road that led to the back part of the farm. Tanya wrapped the wool blanket around their legs, then snuggled down into the warmth created by being sandwiched between her daughter and Chance.

The tinkles of bells, hanging off the sled, echoed through the cold air as they glided farther away from the barn. Gray clouds roiled across the sky, churning and eating up the blue. The wind, scented with the hint of snow, picked up.

Away from people and animals the cover of snow was unbroken, a white carpet lying over the ground with trees and bushes poking up out of it. In the distance she saw the pines that Chance was heading toward. Some shot up toward the sky, tall, majestic. No way one of them would get inside her house. Maybe a seven-foot tree, she thought, excited at the prospects of sharing the holidays with Chance.

He pulled back on the reins and stopped the horses at the edge of a copse that fed into a larger forest bordering the lake. "Anything call to you?"

Crystal giggled. "Nothing's calling 'cut me,' but I like that one."

Tanya looked toward the four-foot tree that stood slightly apart from the others as if it had been shunned because its scraggy branches would hold only a third, possibly a half, of her ornaments. "Don't you want something bigger? Our living room could take a tree up to maybe seven feet tall."

Her daughter cocked her head to the side and studied the scrawny pine. "Nope. It needs us. No one else would pick it." She turned toward Tanya, excitement gleaming in her eyes. "It's small enough that we could dig it up instead of cutting it down and maybe after Christmas plant it in our yard. Do you think we could?" Her hopeful gaze traveled from Tanya to Chance.

He peered at Crystal for a few seconds, then slid his regard back toward the pine, its limbs gently waving in the light breeze. "I'll have to come back. All I have is an ax."

"Will you, Chance? Please?"

Her daughter's enthusiasm infused each of her words, making Tanya excited, too. "I can help. We can come back tomorrow after church."

"I can try, but it might not make it. I might not be able to get all of its root system."

"Maybe Joshua knows what to do. He loves to work in his yard." Tanya surveyed the undersized Christmas tree and warmed to the idea of loading its branches down with the ornaments that meant the most to her and Crystal.

Chance prodded the horses forward and swung the sled in a wide circle. "I'll ask him when we get to the barn. We can all come back tomorrow afternoon if Darcy will loan us the sled again. I don't think this snow will melt anytime soon."

"It's supposed to snow tonight. What if we can't come back?" Crystal threw a glance over her shoulder at her tree.

"The van has snow tires. If we can't come tomorrow, we will as soon as possible since Christmas is only two weeks away." Tanya scanned the darkening clouds, a few flakes falling. She held out a gloved hand and caught a flake which melted immediately.

Tanya tugged the blanket up and made sure that Crystal was completely covered. She snuggled closer to Chance, placed her arm around her daughter's shoulder and pulled her against her side to warm her as much as she could. The temperature in the past hour they had been out had dropped at least five degrees. The wind gusted.

"That hot chocolate sounds so good right now," Crystal said, shivering.

"It's only a few more minutes." Chance directed the horses onto the road that led to the barn. "I wonder what the others got."

Five minutes later Chance brought the horses to a halt right outside the barn's back doors. He hopped down and went inside to retrieve Crystal's wheelchair.

Dane helped him get Crystal out of the sled. "Darcy and Joshua were gone when we got back a little while ago. She went to the hospital. Lizzie and Beth were waiting for us and insisted we have the hot chocolate and sweets. Darcy doesn't want us all to go to the hospital. She wants us to wait until she calls. It could be a false alarm."

"This could be it. She's only a couple of weeks early. If she has the baby now, she won't spend Christmas in the hospital. She told me once she was afraid she would have her baby on Christmas Day and miss the celebration." Tanya climbed down from the sled and followed Crystal, Dane and Chance into the barn.

Inside everyone was back except Nick and Jesse's family. Beth helped Lizzie, Darcy's stepmother, pour three mugs of hot chocolate, then carried them over to Tanya, Chance and Crystal.

After tying his pine to the roof of his car, Samuel and his son came in from the front. "Where's your tree?" the reverend asked Chance, taking his own mug from his wife's hand.

"Still in the ground. I'm coming back to dig it up."

"That's ambitious. The ground may be too frozen to do it."

"I've got to try. Crystal fell in love with this one and wants to plant it in the yard after Christmas. It hasn't been that cold until lately."

"And winter has now hit with a vengeance." Tanya joined Chance and Samuel, cradling the heated mug between her hands. She relished the warm steam, laced with the scent of chocolate, wafting to her face.

Shamus Flanaghan's cell phone rang. After he answered it, he said to the group, "It's official. She's gonna have the baby tonight, God willing."

"Let's say a prayer for Darcy and Joshua." Samuel moved into the middle of the circle and bowed his head.

Tanya clasped Crystal's and Chance's hands, remembering back to when her daughter was born.

"Lord, You are about to give a loving couple another child. Please protect them and be with Darcy and the new baby through her birth and the days to follow. Also, help Joshua to give Darcy the support and encouragement she will need tonight. We will be here to teach their new daughter Your importance and the love You and Your son, Jesus, have for us."

Amid the others' *amens,* Tanya heard Chance's clear strong voice utter the word. Her heart swelled with the sound. He had attended church with her and Crystal the past two weeks. His presence added a joy and hope that she hadn't felt until he had started going to church. Maybe he was ready to forgive and put his trust in God again.

Jesse and her family came into the barn. "Darcy's in labor?" she asked, looking around at the smiles on everyone's faces.

"Yes, they just wheeled her into delivery." Shamus hugged his grandson to his side.

"Well, what are we standing around here for? Let's get to the hospital." Jesse nudged her husband who dragged the tree they selected behind him.

"The staff isn't gonna know what hit them when we come," Tanya said with a laugh.

"Nah. Remember the last time? Granted, we have added a few more people, but I think they expect us to all turn out." Beth looped her arm through Samuel's.

"We've practically doubled in size." Jesse held up her hand, counting off the people as she named them. "There's Samuel, his children, Chance, Dane."

"Just wait until you have yours." Tanya started for the front doors. "Less than six months to go."

Jesse moaned. "Don't remind me. Six months of gaining weight and looking like a beached whale."

Chance opened the massive double doors. "You can drop me by the apartment on the way to the hospital."

Tanya halted halfway to the van. "You don't want to come and celebrate the birth of Darcy and Joshua's daughter?"

"I don't belong. It's a family—well, not a family affair but...you know what I mean?"

She placed her hand on her waist, aware that it was beginning to snow a little harder. A couple of flakes caught on her eyelashes and she blinked. "No, I don't understand. You're a part of this group. Darcy would be disappointed if you weren't there."

"I don't—"

"Going by the house is out of my way. I want to get to the hospital before it really starts snowing." Tanya walked to the back to operate the lift for Crystal.

When she secured her daughter in the van, she moved around to the driver's side and slipped in. "Besides, you are at my mercy. You go where I go."

Chance opened his mouth to say something, but no words came out. He pressed it closed and stared straight ahead.

Chapter Ten

At the end of the church pew Chance sat between Tanya and Crystal in her wheelchair. He stifled a yawn as Samuel rose to give his sermon. Being up half the night took its toll on him, especially when he didn't sleep the other half because of the woman sitting next to him and her insistence that he accompany her and Crystal to the hospital. To be a part of Darcy and Joshua's celebration of their new daughter. To be a part of the close friendship the five families had for each other. No matter how much Tanya wanted it, he was still an outsider. He would always be the outsider.

But for a few minutes last night, it had been nice to wonder what it would feel like being a part of this close-knit group of friends.

As Samuel began to talk about hope, using the illustration of the birth of Joshua and Darcy's daughter, Tanya slipped her hand over his, sending him a smile. Deep in her eyes he saw a connection forged between them with the shared experiences of the past few months. A strong urge to tug his hand away deluged him with panic.

Then Samuel's words came to Chance, calming him. "Jesus died for us. God gave us hope with His Son's resurrection. Peter best said it, 'Blessed be the God and Father of our Lord Jesus Christ, which according to His abundant mercy hath begotten us again unto a lively hope by the resurrection of Jesus Christ from the dead.' Remember those words when you think there is no hope in your life. Remember what Christ went through for us in the end, all because He loved us. Believe in Him and you will always have that hope."

Was it that simple? Chance wanted it to be. Mentally recapping his life, he needed to do something. He needed a purpose. Soon his job would be done here. Then what?

As everyone around him rose for the final song, Chance stood and joined in with Crystal and Tanya. The calm that had started with Samuel's sermon spread outward to encompass his whole body. By the time Chance left the pew and followed Crystal and Tanya toward the exit where Samuel greeted his congregation, Chance latched onto the feelings developing inside him. He liked those feelings—the peace. He hadn't had that in a long time.

"Nice service, Samuel," Chance said and shook his friend's hand.

"After being up most of the night, I wasn't sure I would be able to string more than a few sentences together."

"Well, you managed just fine."

Samuel studied him. "Did they give you something to think on?"

He nodded.

"Then this has been a good day." Samuel turned to Tanya and Crystal. "Are you all staying for refreshments?"

"For a few minutes. We still have to go get our Christmas tree this afternoon." Although Tanya answered Samuel's question, her gaze never left Chance's face.

The second they were out in the church foyer, she stopped him while Crystal continued toward the rec hall. Off from the others milling about, Tanya leaned close and whispered, "You felt God's presence, didn't you?"

"Yes."

She beamed. "He hasn't abandoned you. Let's go get something to drink and eat. We've got hard physical work ahead of us this afternoon. I want the Christmas tree up and decorated this evening. Think that's possible?"

He chuckled. "Yeah. I definitely think it is."

Later that evening, a fire burned in the fireplace. The scent of wood permeated Tanya's living room. Cozy. Romantic. With only the lights from the Christmas tree and the blaze, for a while, the rest of the world didn't exist. There were only the three of them—Crystal, Chance and her. Charlie slept in front of the fire, oblivious to what was going on around him.

Tanya stood back and surveyed the small pine with so many ornaments on its limbs that they drooped, the bottom ones almost to the carpet. "I won't be surprised if one morning we wake up and find all the balls have slid off the tree." Her head tilted to the side, she tapped her finger against her chin.

"We can always remove some." Crystal positioned her wheelchair next to the pine and reached for a cardboard circle colored with red and green markers and a silver glittered glob in the middle.

"No! Not that one. Remember you made that for me in first grade."

Crystal went for another homemade one, and Tanya shook her head. After going through several more, her daughter blew out a breath, her bangs lifting.

"Mom, half of these are ugly."

"Not to me. They're precious. There's a story behind every ornament on that tree."

Chance moved forward, his arm brushing against Tanya's. "We had ornaments like that."

The roughened edge to his voice riveted Tanya's attention to his face. Pain etched his features. "Where are they? Maybe we can get another small tree and you can have one in your apartment."

"No!" he said as forcefully as Tanya a moment ago.

"You need something." She itched to smooth away the creases in his expression.

"Why? I'm perfectly content to come look at yours when I need a Christmas fix. Besides, I don't want anyone to go to any trouble. I don't spend enough time there."

Crystal yawned loudly. "I'm tired. We did a lot today. Since I have some homework I need to finish, I'd better do it before I fall asleep. Good night, Chance, Mom."

"Night, Crystal." Chance's gaze drilled into Tanya's.

"If you need some help, let me know, honey." Tanya refused to look away from him.

When the sound of the wheelchair faded down the hall, Tanya asked, "What happened to your Christmas decorations?" He would never get on with his life if he didn't deal with his loss, every aspect of it. She knew; she'd been there with Tom.

Pain still reflected in his expression, Chance pivoted away and walked to the fireplace, staring down at the flames as they licked the huge logs in the grate. He stuffed his hands into the front pockets of his black jeans. Focusing on the plaid pattern of his flannel shirt for a moment, Tanya gave him some time to bring his emotions under control.

As his rigid stance dissolved into a relaxed one, Tanya strode to him and laid her hand on his arm. "What happened?"

After taking in a calming breath, he visibly swallowed and said, "Ruth's parents took them, along with most of her and my daughter's things."

"Why haven't you gotten them back?"

"I don't want them. The picture I have in my apartment is all I need. I can't bring either one back. They are in my past and as much as I wish they hadn't been murdered, I can't change what happened." His gaze sought hers. "Today, for the first time in a long while, I felt hope when I listened to Samuel's sermon. I don't want to let that feeling go."

"Then don't. I have fond and loving memories of Tom, but I have had to learn to move on with my life. I can't afford for Crystal's sake to live in the past."

His smile deepened the dimples in his cheeks and

the pain disappeared completely from his gaze. "I'm working on it. I enjoyed decorating your—" he looked at the small pine "—uh, tree this evening."

She basked in the teasing that shone in his eyes. "It's not too bad. I'm beginning to think like Crystal. That tree was calling out for someone to take it, and after Christmas, we can plant it in our backyard so we can remember this holiday for years to come." *I know I will.* Chance's presence made the first Christmas since Tom's death bearable to her and Crystal. "I've got some more hot chocolate. Want a refill?"

"Sure. But you sit and I'll go get it. I know my way around your kitchen."

Tanya settled on the couch before the fireplace with the tree off to the side, listening to Chance rummaging around in her kitchen. When he reappeared with the two mugs, steam floating upward, her stomach flip-flopped with his look that said he only had eyes for her. She wanted to savor this moment so she could revisit it in the future when Chance left Sweetwater. If only he would stay, then— She shook that wish from her mind. She had to be practical for once and steel her heart as much as possible against the hurt that would follow his departure.

Pausing in front of her, Chance held her mug out. She slipped her fingers around the warm ceramic, brushing against his. He eased down next to her, close but not touching. All Tanya wanted to do was feather her lips across his, be surrounded by his embrace. But she stayed where she was and concentrated on taking one sip, then another of her hot chocolate.

"I love chocolate, and this is great on a cold night," she said to break the silence after a few minutes.

He placed his mug on the coffee table, half his drink gone. "You get no complaints from me."

Tired from a long, productive day, she set her mug next to his, relaxed back against the cushion and watched the flames dancing in the fireplace, the red-orange blaze mesmerizing. Her eyelids slid closed. From afar she heard the crackling of the fire, felt the warmth it generated....

"Tanya, we'd better call it a night."

Chance's voice penetrated the fog that shrouded her mind. Tanya blinked her eyes open and found herself pressed against his side on the couch, his arm along the back of the cushion, her head resting on his shoulder. What a great way to spend an evening. Content, she didn't move for a good minute. Then slowly she straightened.

"Yes, you're right. Six o'clock tomorrow morning will come soon enough." Tanya glanced at her watch and realized she must have dozed about fifteen minutes, cuddled in his arms. That thought sent her heart beating a shade faster.

Chance unfolded his long length and rose, then tugged her up. He wound his arms around her waist and brought her near. "As much as I'm enjoying myself, I agree. Tomorrow starts a long work week."

He bent his head a few inches closer, and Tanya could smell the chocolate on his breath. "Thank you for digging up the tree for us. It really is a nice one. Just don't tell Crystal I said so. I love how protective she is over it."

"My lips are sealed."

Her gaze fixed upon those lips, and she couldn't take her eyes off them. She wanted him to kiss her. Every part of her screamed for it.

Slowly his mouth settled over hers, ending her frustration. His kiss stamped her his, even if he would never know how much she really cared about him. She would never forget this time with him.

As he deepened the kiss, she melted against him, clinging to him. With each second that passed, she became more and more connected to him on a level that left her shaken. He was a man who had suffered greatly and was trying to put his life back together. And today he had taken the first step in his journey back to the Lord.

Chance pulled away and firmly put some space between them. His breathing was short and raspy. His look nearly undid her all over again. It proclaimed the connection in his glittering blue depths. Her mind wiped blank, she stared at him as he collected himself, the rapid rise and fall of his chest slowing.

"I need to leave. See you tomorrow," he finally said in a voice rough, intense with emotion.

She didn't follow him to the door but just watched him stalk toward the front hallway. A few seconds later she heard the door shut. She pressed her hands to her cheeks. The warmth beneath her palms seared the past few minutes into her mind.

Their relationship had moved to another level tonight. She could no longer kid herself that she and Chance were just good friends. The kiss they had shared made a mockery of that. She had wanted more, and in his expression she'd seen he had, too.

Chance stormed into his apartment and headed for the closet. He dragged out his duffel bag, emptied the top drawer of the chest and stuffed his T-shirts, jeans and socks into his only piece of luggage. Halfway back to the closet to get his pants and shirts, he halted.

Staring at the overflowing duffel bag, he realized how many material items he had acquired in the past three months. But most of all, he realized he couldn't run away. He wasn't a man who went back on a promise, even though he had made it to himself. He would stay through the holidays and make sure that Tanya and Crystal were cared for.

He just couldn't kiss her again.

Too dangerous.

Chance shoved the bag over and sank down onto the couch that converted into a bed. Why had he ruined a wonderful day by kissing her like that? Why had he poured his heart into it?

I find a few moments of peace earlier in church, and all of a sudden I'm wanting to build a life with Tanya and Crystal. Leaning forward, he buried his hands in his hair and stared at the floor. He hadn't come to Sweetwater to get involved romantically with anyone, especially Tom's wife.

He'd had a family once. He couldn't go through losing another. *Lord, I'm asking for Your help. Stop these feelings for Tanya from growing. I don't want to care about her like that. I want to help her, then I want to leave. Please, God, that is the only way.*

* * *

After finishing the last sip of coffee, Tanya cupped her chin in her hand and rested her elbow on her kitchen table. "Jesse, Christmas is ten days away and I can't think of a thing to get Chance. He's gonna have dinner with Crystal and me on Christmas Day. He's gotta have something under the tree. Buying him something like clothes doesn't convey what I want to convey."

Jesse relaxed back in the chair opposite her. "And what *do* you want to convey?"

"I…" Tanya toyed with the rim of her mug, running her finger around and around it. What did she want to convey? Everything she had looked at in the store hadn't seemed right. She didn't know why but each time she had gone shopping she had come away empty-handed. "I'm not sure. I guess I want to thank him for helping out with Crystal."

Jesse quirked a brow. "Is that all?"

She sat up straight. "What's that supposed to mean?"

"You're only thinking of Crystal?"

"Okay, I want to thank him for being my friend, too."

"Just a friend?"

Tanya huffed. "Don't you start matchmaking, Jesse Blackburn. We are friends. Nothing more." She had to keep reminding herself of that in spite of the kiss they had shared recently, or when he left, she would fall apart. She'd done enough of that in the past four years to last a lifetime.

"For being just friends, you two have been spending a lot of time together lately."

"Look, we haven't even seen each other since last Sunday when we decorated the tree. He's been busy.

I've been busy. We haven't had a chance even to jog because of the weather."

"That's only five days."

"Six. Today's Saturday." Tanya stood and took her mug over to the sink, needing to move, to do something to keep herself from dwelling on the six *long* days she hadn't seen Chance except in passing. Crystal had seen him at the center a lot more than she had.

"Today isn't over yet." Jesse brought her mug to the counter and lounged back against it.

"Where did he and Nick go?"

"Can't say."

Tanya spun around and faced her with a hand plunked on her waist. "Jesse, you can't keep a secret from me."

"Sorry. He needed Nick's SUV. That's all I know. They wouldn't even tell me."

"He could have borrowed my van."

"He thought you might need it." Her friend crossed her arms and tilted her head to the side. "Now, back to your problem. What to get Chance for Christmas. Does he have any hobbies?"

"Besides jogging, which I don't consider a hobby, I can't think of anything. He's either working or helping out at the center or—" Tanya glanced out the window over the sink "—helping Crystal and me."

"Well, I guess you two are his hobby." Jesse laughed.

"You aren't helping."

"Sorry. Back to your dilemma. Why not do something for him?"

"What? His apartment is sparse and always clean. He—" Two ideas began to form in her mind. Tanya turned away, taking Jesse's mug and rinsing it out before putting both of them in the dishwasher. "Come to think of it, there is something I could do."

"What?"

"He needs his own tree. His apartment might as well be a motel room. I have a key and both him and Nick are gonna be gone all afternoon. Want to help me get a small tree and decorate it? I have leftover ornaments that I didn't have room for on mine."

Jesse pushed away from the counter. "Sure. I'm game. Do you think he'll be okay with you using your key?"

"He knows I have it and doesn't mind. Personally I don't even think he sees that apartment as his place. I just want to spread a little joy. He's made the past few months so much easier for Crystal and me." Although he'd declared last Sunday he didn't spend much time in his apartment, she wanted him to enjoy the holidays even when he was there.

"Well, then we've got some work to do."

Later that afternoon, Tanya paced her kitchen, glancing at the clock every few minutes. Restless energy surged through her. She couldn't sit. She couldn't do anything until she knew what Chance thought of his Christmas tree.

Reflecting back over the day, she recalled the letter she had seen lying on his kitchen table from the district attorney in Louisville about the trial of the man who had killed his wife and daughter. While setting the box of ornaments down, she had glimpsed the date of the trial before she realized what she was looking at.

She'd quickly averted her gaze, but guilt had taken hold of her. Although she had known about the impending trial, seeing the date written in black and white made it very real and looming.

At first she had wanted to leave and hoped that Chance didn't figure out that she'd been in his apartment. But the damage had been done. She'd seen the letter and couldn't ignore what Chance would be going through in less than a month. All the old hurts would be exposed again. The least she could do was give him something festive to look at when he awakened each morning—and her apology for intruding.

Nick's SUV pulled into the driveway as it started to get dark. In the headlights Tanya saw snowflakes falling. The roads had been finally cleared today, and now it looked as if it would start all over again. She wasn't distressed one bit. She loved the cold, the snow. Its soft white blanket made everything quiet and pristine as though God had laid a cover of pureness upon the earth.

She closed the blinds, turned away from the window and stared at her kitchen. She chewed her thumbnail. *Should I go see him now? Or wait to see if he comes over here?*

She didn't know what to do. Fifteen minutes later when Chance hadn't come to see her, she knew she had to go to him. Throwing on a sweater, she hurried across the yard and quickly climbed the stairs. Snow coated her hair and clothes as it began to fall harder. In another half an hour she would have to go pick up Crystal at the youth center. But for the time being, she needed to see Chance.

The door stood ajar a few inches. She knocked on

it, causing it to swing inward a couple of more inches. Although Chance hadn't responded to her knock, she glimpsed him sitting on the couch, staring at the tree as though in a trance, an expression of disbelief on his face.

"Chance?"

He blinked but didn't glance toward her.

"I'm sorry. I shouldn't have done this. I shouldn't have come here without you knowing. I know what you said last time—"

He finally twisted completely toward her, a sheen in his eyes. His look, full of awe and something she couldn't quite identify, snatched her words and breath.

She stepped into his apartment and closed the cold and snow out. "I wanted to surprise you."

One corner of his mouth tilted upward. "That you did," he murmured, his voice thick.

"Then you aren't upset?"

He started to say something but had to clear his throat before he proceeded. "Upset? Until I came to Sweetwater, I hadn't had many nice things done for me in a long time. That all changed the minute I stepped off that bus. You and your friends have welcomed me as though I was one of you." He rose and waved his hand toward the lit tree. "And now this."

"Then you like it?" She took another step farther into the room.

"Like it? I love the gesture, Tanya. If you had asked me, I would have told you no. In fact, I did. I didn't think I needed anything for the holidays. But when I walked in here and saw the tree, I realized I was wrong."

Swallowing visibly, he made his way to her but stopped short of touching her.

She yearned for his arms to be around her, but he had kept his distance the past six days because of the kiss they had shared Sunday night. He didn't have to come right out and tell her but she knew. He didn't want to take their relationship beyond friendship, and she had to respect his wishes. She was determined to enjoy what he could offer her and mourn his loss when he left—not one minute before.

She smiled. "Good. It was a spur-of-the-moment plan. Jesse was over here, and I decided that you needed your very own tree after helping Crystal and me with ours. So Jesse helped me with it."

"A few of those ornaments look familiar."

"They should. They're the ones I couldn't use. I hope you don't mind my castoffs."

He peered at the three-foot pine sitting in the middle of his kitchen table with small twinkling lights and a few homemade balls interspersed among gold and red glittery ones hanging from the tree's small branches. "Not at all."

"I did buy that star at the top when I got the tree. I knew it would look perfect where it's sitting."

The gold sequined star blinked on and off, its soft light sending out a radiance that shone down on the whole small pine. Chance walked the few feet to the table and fingered the star.

"My own Star of Bethlehem, right here in my apartment."

"It can be left on separately from the strand of lights."

"Do you think it will help me find my way home?"

Chance's gaze fell to the letter not far from the tree. "Did you see they set the date for the trial?"

Suddenly, all emotion fled his voice, and Tanya shivered. "Yes," she whispered as she realized she could say nothing else but the truth.

"I knew it would be soon after the first of the year. But until you see it on paper, it's still an abstract event that will happen sometime in the future."

The heaviness in her heart threatened to cut off her next breath. She'd thought the same thing. She drew in deeply and said, "Chance, I'll help you any way I can. That's the least I can do for all you've done for me and Crystal."

He flinched as though she had hit him. Averting his face, he folded the letter, strode to a drawer and laid it inside.

Something coiled in her stomach. The tightness in her chest expanded. "Don't shut me out. Please." She remembered the times Tom had and what it had led to: her husband turning his anger outward and burning down horse barns. If only she could have reached Tom in time, maybe then things would have been different.

Chance pivoted. "What do you want me to say? The trial has been set. I knew it was coming. It really was no big surprise." Scanning the apartment as though searching for a way to escape, he said, "Where's Crystal?"

He was so good at letting her see small glimpses inside him, then slamming the door. Tanya wanted to demand he let her help him. But then that never worked. If he wasn't ready, nothing she did would make a difference. "She's at the center. I've got to pick her up—" she checked her watch "—now. I told Dane I would help with cleanup after the holiday party. It should be over soon."

"I'll ride with you."

She walked toward his door. "You don't have to."

He leaned around her and turned the knob. "In case you didn't notice when you came up here, it's snowing. I would feel better if you would humor me and let me tag along."

She shrugged and said, "Sure," then darted out into the gently falling snow. "I just need to get my heavy coat."

Fifteen minutes later, Tanya pulled into the handicapped parking space right in front of the youth center. She and Chance hurried up the steps and into the warm building. A few teens and their parents headed out of the gym, bundled up against the cold. Wilbur Thompson, with his grandson next to him, nodded at Tanya while he glared at Chance.

In spite of the icy greeting, Chance said, "Good evening, Wilbur, Tyler."

Wilbur snorted. "There's nothing good about it. It's snowing *again*. This has got to set some kind of record for us."

As the older man passed them in the foyer, Chance asked, "Do you need any help?"

For a step, Wilbur looked surprised by the offer, then he covered it by wrapping his scarf around his neck and murmuring, "No, Tyler can help me."

"Just let me know if you do." Chance started forward, nearing the large double doors.

"You may win Wilbur over before long," Tanya whispered as she heard the Christmas music coming from the gym.

"I don't know if that's possible, but it won't be because I didn't try. There are still a few holdouts, but thanks to you and your friends, most people have accepted my presence here at the center."

"I'm glad it doesn't bother you working around teens."

He paused, his hand on the swinging door. "Because of Haley? I can't go through life avoiding kids who are the same age as she. If my daughter were alive, she would have loved a place like this." He pushed the door open and moved into the gym.

Tanya followed him. Three months ago she wasn't so sure Chance had felt that way. He'd been a little leery of Crystal at the beginning. Now she realized why. Crystal and Haley, if she had lived, were only a year apart in age.

Tanya searched the crowd of teens still at the holiday party and found her daughter with Amanda, Jane and Grant at one of the tables. The sound of Crystal's laughter sweetened the air as Tanya walked toward her. Chance went in the other direction to see Dane.

"Mom, you're early."

"No, I'm a little late."

Crystal looked down at her watch. "I guess you are. I didn't realize it was so late."

"Hello, Mrs. Bolton. We were talking about the presents Crystal gave us." Grant held up a caricature of himself, showing him playing basketball with his head twice its normal size and his jersey number huge on the front. "Isn't it neat?"

"Yes." Tanya looked at her daughter. So that was what she had been working so hard on for the past few weeks.

"And here's mine." Jane showed her picture, which showcased Samuel's daughter's talent as an artist. "I'm gonna have to do this."

Tanya saw others as some teenagers came over to thank Crystal. In each caricature her daughter had taken one of the teens' talents and played it up. Sean's was working with computers. Nate's and Craig's were their band. Amanda's was talking on the phone.

"I need to check about cleaning up. I just wanted to let you know I was here," Tanya said.

"We'll be right here." Jane took a sip of her hot chocolate. "Dad and Beth are in the kitchen, cleaning up."

Tanya made her way to the kitchen where Samuel, Beth and Zoey were working. "Need any help in here?"

All three glanced at her and shook their heads while Zoey said, "Got everything under control. You might check with Dane."

Back in the gym Tanya saw Dane and Chance directing some of the youths in cleaning up the trash left on the tables. More of the teenagers were leaving. Relieved they would be home before the snow caused too much trouble on the roads, Tanya walked toward Chance. She peered at Crystal and Amanda, who had begun to pick up the discarded paper cups, and glimpsed Holly stop by her daughter. Tanya tensed and made a detour toward Crystal. She wouldn't allow that teen to ruin her daughter's mood and this successful holiday party.

As Tanya neared Holly from behind, she heard the

teenager say, "You're really good at drawing. Thanks for the picture."

Before Tanya could reach Crystal, Holly left, the caricature in the girl's hand. All Tanya could make out of Holly's picture was that the teen was portrayed in her cheerleading outfit with pompoms.

What her daughter had done touched Tanya. Her throat tightened. "You drew a caricature for everyone, even Holly?"

"Well, the ones who come regularly, and those I knew would be here tonight at the party," Crystal said, peering after Holly as she slipped out of the gym. "She thanked me."

"I heard."

"For the past few weeks Holly has avoided me. I almost didn't draw her, but that's not what Jesus taught us. If I believe in Him then I can't ignore His Word." Her daughter's mouth lifted in a sassy grin. "Even though I was sorely tempted. After I finished last night, I knew it was the right thing to do. Now I'm glad I did it."

"Is everything okay here?" Chance asked, approaching them. "I saw Holly talking to you."

Throwing a glance over her shoulder toward Grant helping Eddy clean up, Crystal smiled. "Yeah, everything is great!" Then she drove toward the large trash can to deposit the paper goods she had collected.

Obviously Grant Foster wasn't unaware of her daughter any longer. More and more when she came to pick Crystal up at the youth center, she would find her talking with Grant. Perhaps he was discovering Crystal's inner beauty as others were. "She continues to amaze me. My daughter gave Holly a gift."

"And how did Holly feel about it?" Chance moved to the nearest table and held the plastic bag open while Tanya dumped the remains of the party into it.

"She was okay about it."

"I guess Eddy and Jane's intervention helped. If more people would stand up and say no to someone bullying another, then we wouldn't have as much of a problem as we do."

Tanya walked to the next table and began cleaning up. "You were right. Bullies aren't born, they are made."

"And after what I saw between Holly and her father, I can imagine where the girl learned her ways."

"Jim Proctor has always thrown his weight around, steamrolling over others." She dropped some more trash into the plastic bag.

"Maybe it isn't too late to teach his daughter there are better ways to interact with peers than to harass them and make fun of them."

"When's Dane starting the antibullying classes?"

"After the new year."

"Do you think anyone will come?"

Chance shrugged. "We have to start somewhere. Even if it means there are only a handful who take the class, it's a beginning."

"We?" Tanya completed removing the used paper goods from the last table. "You sound pretty vested in this."

"I did some research and found the program Dane's going to use. That's all of my participation."

"Because you won't be here?" Tanya held her breath waiting for the reply she knew was going to come.

"Yes."

Chapter Eleven

From across Jesse's large living room Christmas Eve, Tanya watched Chance interact with Dane, Nick and Samuel. The ease with which he fit in with the other men didn't surprise her. He was the same kind of man as her friends' husbands—caring, loving and ethical. Her friends were blessed to have found such men. She didn't envy them their happy marriage; she just wished she was as blessed.

Ever since she and Chance had cleaned up at the youth center after the party, she couldn't get out of her mind that he had told her yet again he was leaving soon. The very thought brought such intense, sad emotions to the foreground. Chance deserved some happiness; she deserved some. Why couldn't he see she would be good for him?

"You're drooling," Jesse whispered close to her ear.

"Am I that transparent?" Tanya turned her attention to her friends standing near her.

"Written all over your face, so if you don't want him to know you need to get better at hiding your feelings."

Zoey took a bite of a small sandwich square with cream cheese and cucumber. "This is good, Jesse."

That's it! If she didn't risk her heart and tell him how she felt, how was she ever going to know if she and Chance might work out? She needed to find a time soon to let him know she loved him. There, she'd admitted it. *I love Chance! I want to make a life with him.*

Now to convince him she was the right woman for him. Even if he needed more time to heal, she understood that and would give it to him. She just didn't want him to move away. Her gaze drifted back to Chance, his face lit with laughter, the hard lines of life almost gone.

He may not know it yet, but this is his home now. Every time she looked at him, she saw it in his relaxed stance, the humor in his eyes, the peace that he conveyed.

"I'm thinking if we want Tanya to participate in our conversation, we need to drag Chance over here to join us," Beth said.

Tanya exaggerated a pout and faced her friends. "I had to suffer through you all going all dreamy eyed over your husbands so you will just have to put up with me doing it."

"Ah, there, she has admitted it finally. Congratulations." Jesse patted her on the back.

As Beth and Zoey offered their congratulations, Tanya said, "Shh. You'll have everyone in the room, including Chance, looking over here." She lowered her voice. "Yes, I admit I'm in love with him, but if you all say anything…" She let the threat trail off into the sudden silence as her three friends stared at her wide-eyed.

Beth was the first one to recover, saying, "I can't believe you said the words."

"No regrets?" Zoey asked.

Tanya shook her head.

Jesse glanced toward Chance then back. "No more we're just friends?"

"Nope. I'm not gonna fight these feelings anymore. It's exhausting."

Laughter erupted from her friends, drawing everyone's attention.

"Shh. You can't say anything until I've said something to Chance." Tanya stared each of her friends directly in the eye.

After they agreed, Jesse sighed. "Of all the times Darcy can't be here. She'll be so upset she wasn't. I can say something to her, can't I?"

"Fine." Tanya's neck tingled. Peering over her shoulder, she caught Chance studying her.

"Thankfully Alexa is all right. I know how it can be when one of your children, especially a baby, spikes a fever," Zoey said.

"I'm glad she called to let us know or I would have worried all night."

Tanya heard Jesse's comment that led to a discussion of children's illnesses, but her friends' voices slowly faded from her consciousness. From across the room all she could focus on was Chance looking at her as though no one else existed. They were the only two people in the room filled with over twenty guests.

Chance smiled, his dimples showing.

She returned his smile, then said to the group, "Excuse me."

Chance left the men and walked toward her. They met in the middle of the living room with people all around them. But the others didn't really register on her brain. Every sense fixated on the man before her, looking so incredibly handsome. The faint scent of the outdoors, from when he had helped Nick bring in the wood for the fire, clung to him.

"Hi, are you enjoying yourself?" Tanya asked, wanting every second of the holiday season to be perfect for Chance, especially in light of her discovery that she loved him.

"Yes, how about you?" His eyes twinkled with merriment.

"Yes," she murmured as though she were a teenage girl again and dating for the first time. She was beginning to understand what Crystal was going through with her feelings for Grant Foster. "Good friends and good food. What more can you ask for?"

He took her hand and tugged her out of the path to the food table to a more secluded spot off to the side. "I want to thank you."

Every nerve ending in her hand responded to his fingers closed about hers. For a few seconds she couldn't put two coherent words together to reply to his statement. "Why?"

"I know you have gone out of your way to make sure I am included in your holiday activities as well as others."

"Am I that transparent?" She worried that she wore her feelings on her face. Did he see her love for him?

"Yep. I haven't had much downtime in the past month."

"Have I worn you out?"

"No way. Bring it on. I can keep up with you."

"Well, we need to leave for church in a while. I'm in charge of the birthday party."

A question entered Chance's eyes. "Birthday party?"

"Jesus's. After the service this evening, we have cake and punch to celebrate Christ's birth. I want to lay everything out before the service so I don't have to leave during it."

"I like that."

"What? My superb organizational skills or the celebration?"

The humor in his eyes brightened. "Both actually. Are we picking up Crystal at Amanda's beforehand?"

"Yeah, Amanda's coming to church with us. Her parents will come later." Their discussion underscored how meshed their lives had become—almost as though they were a couple talking about their daughter, their plans as a family. *I want that. I want what my friends have, a husband to complete my family.*

"We'd better say our goodbyes. With the roads still snow covered it might take us longer to get to church." He placed his hand at the small of her back and guided her toward Jesse.

After they thanked Jesse for inviting them, Tanya started for the front door. In the large foyer she paused while Chance retrieved their coats from the bedroom. He assisted her into her wool wrap, then swung her around to face him. He pointed upward, his look full of mischief.

She tilted her head and saw the mistletoe with a red bow. Leave it to the town matchmaker to have mistletoe in her foyer, Tanya thought with a laugh. "Do you have something in mind, sir?"

"One or two things come to mind." He leaned forward, framing her face with his large hands. "We can't go against tradition," he whispered right before kissing her.

His mouth claimed hers in a union that rocked her to her core. His hands fell away from her cheeks, and he fit her against him, his arms trapping her in the very place she wanted to be—his embrace.

When they parted, his forehead touching hers, he murmured, "I couldn't resist. I haven't seen mistletoe in years since…" Suddenly his arms about her tensed and he straightened, pulling slightly away.

She wasn't going to let him retreat. "Since when?"

A wistful look entered his eyes. "Since the last Christmas I spent with my family. Haley had wanted to buy some when we bought the tree. She was eleven and into boys. I think she had visions of kissing a boy under the mistletoe."

Having seen her photo in Chance's apartment, Tanya knew how pretty his daughter had been. "And you got some?" she asked in mock horror, desperate to lighten the mood.

He grinned, relaxing. "I was a sucker for her smile, but I also knew I wouldn't let a boy within ten yards of her and the mistletoe."

"Now that's the picture I see of you and your daughter."

He quirked a brow. "Tyrant and princess?"

"Yep."

His chuckle filled the air. "C'mon. Let's get Crystal and Amanda and get to church."

Hearing him say those words put a spring in her step as she and Chance made their way to her van. Bundled up against the cold night, she slipped into the passenger seat and he got behind the wheel. He'd been driving more and more. She expected him to buy a used car soon. She knew he had been saving his money. It wouldn't be long before he would have a good down payment for one.

"Mom! Mom! Time to get up."

Tanya buried herself under the blankets. She didn't want to get up even though it was Christmas morning. They hadn't gotten home from church until after one, then she hadn't been able to go to sleep for hours, thinking of her tenant. She'd wrapped Chance's presents, excitement building, making sleep impossible.

The door opened. "Mom! It's past nine. We usually have our gifts opened by now."

Tanya peeped out of the mound of covers and saw the dim light in her bedroom. "It seems like dawn."

"That's because it's snowing again."

Tanya struggled to sit up, the pull to lie back down strong. "It is? I thought it was clouding up last night when we got home."

"Yep. Big flakes. I went out on the deck for a few minutes until I got too cold."

She smiled at her daughter. "You just can't resist snow."

"Nope. C'mon, sleepyhead. I told Chance to be over in half an hour. That I'd have you up and going by then."

"You've seen him this morning?" Half an hour? Running her hands through her messy hair, Tanya scooted to the edge of her bed. Her heart already began to pound in anticipation of seeing him again in such a short time.

"He was drinking coffee on his step and enjoying the snow so he came over to keep me company while I was on the deck. He likes snow like you and I do." She turned her wheelchair around and headed out into the hall. "I promised him I would wait until he could join us to open my presents."

The second her daughter disappeared down the hall Tanya flew into action, amazed her body could move so fast when only a few minutes ago sleep weighed her limbs down. Motivation was a powerful mover. She didn't have much time, and she wanted to look her best today for Chance. She'd decided she would tell him how important he was to her. Now all she had to do was find the perfect time today.

Half an hour later she stood before her full-length mirror analyzing how she looked. With her body trimmer since she started jogging with Chance, she fit easily into last year's holiday outfit of red slacks, white lace blouse and Christmas sweater with decorated trees. Her short brown hair, still a little damp from her shower, framed her face in wisps. She moved to the mirror and put red lipstick on as the final touch.

The sound of the doorbell echoed through the house. Strange. Chance usually came to the back door, and Crystal knew that and would be waiting for him. Tanya left her room and hurried toward the front, anxious to see Chance.

When she opened the door and found Nick standing

on her porch with a huge box behind him, she had to snap her mouth closed at her surprise. "What are you doing here?"

He grinned. "Making a delivery for Chance. Is he here yet?"

"I'm right here."

Tanya gasped and whirled around, her hand going to her mouth. "How did you get in here?"

"The usual way, through the back door. Crystal let me in."

"I know I'm used to the cold and everything being from Chicago, but just in case you didn't notice, it is snowing and it's Christmas morning. I promised my family I would only be gone a few minutes." Nick shifted to get hold of one side of the box with a big red bow on it.

Chance walked past Tanya and got the other side. "How did you get it to the porch?"

"Nate. He's waiting in the car. I think he thinks if he waits in the car I won't stay long."

"Clever boy," Chance said, looking toward Nick's SUV. "Tell him thanks for me."

Chance backed through the door while Tanya stepped to the side, shivering in the cold. Peering outside, she noticed the snow falling more heavily.

"Take it in the living room, then Nick, you'd better get on home. It's getting worse." Tanya closed the door to shut out the frigid air and followed the men.

After they set the gift in front of the fireplace next to Charlie, Nick said his goodbyes and left. Tanya along with Crystal stared at the box wrapped in gold paper.

"You must have used several rolls of wrapping paper." Tanya circled the present. "Who's it for?"

"Crystal."

"Me?" Her daughter wheeled close and stopped next to it, fingering the gold paper. "This isn't one of those presents you open and there's another smaller box inside, then another one and another one?"

Chance chuckled. "No. This is a huge present."

"But I can't think of anything—"

"Open it, honey, before your mother dies of curiosity." Tanya moved to Chance's side, seeing the excitement in his expression.

The excitement was contagious as her daughter peeled off one strip of wrapping paper. It built as each piece of the box was revealed. But when the gift was finally unwrapped, a brown box with no writing on it still kept the present hidden.

Chance shifted from one foot to the other. "Do you want me to help with the box? I've got my pocketknife." He retrieved it and flipped it open.

"Yes, please." Crystal patted Charlie while she waited.

Chance slit the top open. Her daughter maneuvered close and stretched to see inside at the same time she did. The sight of the sports wheelchair took Tanya's breath away. She glanced back at Chance who had stepped away to let them look. His expression radiated with a bright smile.

Words congealed in her throat. She knew how expensive the wheelchair was. This was what he had been saving for—not a used car. "Chance?" was all she managed to say as she looked at Crystal, stunned, her fingers pressed to her flushed cheeks while her mouth hung open.

Silence ruled.

"What do you think? Can you use it?" Chance finally asked.

Tears welled in her daughter's eyes as she swung around to stare at Chance. One after another slipped down her face, setting off Tanya's own tears.

Crystal gestured toward the gift. "I—I—" She swallowed several times. "I love it! It's perfect. But you shouldn't—"

Chance held up his hand. "Don't say it. The joy I see on your face is the best present I could receive. I want you to be able to play basketball and whatever else you want to that requires that kind of wheelchair."

The pressure in Tanya's chest made breathing difficult. She swiped at her tears and thought of the sacrifice this man had made for her daughter. The love she felt doubled in that instant.

"Let me get it out for you. Do you want to try it out?" He stepped to the box.

Crystal nodded while she wiped her own tears away, a huge smile on her face as she watched Chance lift it up and then place it beside Crystal's electric wheelchair. He leaned over her daughter who put her arms around his neck. He picked her up and transferred her to the shiny chrome and black sports chair, much lighter than her other one, with big wheels that were set at a slant.

Before he straightened, Crystal kissed his cheek. "Thank you doesn't seem enough."

Red patches colored his face. "That's plenty."

His roughened voice underscored how affected he

was by her daughter's appreciation. Tanya kissed him on the other cheek. "Thank you. We will remember this Christmas for a long time."

He glanced at her, his dark blue gaze capturing hers. "So will I."

For a long moment no one said anything. Tanya continued to stare into his eyes, drowning in his regard that from the beginning had always made her feel so special, so womanly.

"Hey, we have other presents to open, you two."

Crystal's statement broke the connection between her and Chance. He looked away. She peered at her daughter wheeling the new chair around the living room.

"Yes, we have a gift, or rather *gifts,* for you." Tanya forced herself to step away from him and knelt by the tree to retrieve a bright package with red and green ornaments on it. "Here, open this first."

Chance sat on the couch and shook it. "It doesn't rattle." He squeezed it next. "It gives a little. A big book?"

Tanya laughed. "Open it and find out."

He tore into the wrapping and had it removed in seconds. When he saw the gift and opened to the first page of the sketchbook, he sucked in a deep breath. As he slowly flipped through the sketches, his hand trembled. "You *both* drew these," he said in awe.

Tanya eased down next to him. "We wanted you to remember this holiday and we didn't think a camera would do it justice so we drew different pictures to convey the things you did with us."

He paused and ran his finger over the pen-and-ink drawing of them decorating the four-foot tree only a few feet away. "I will cherish this always." His voice thickened with each word he said.

"Good. It wasn't easy because these sketches are big, but we made a copy of them for ourselves. We don't want to forget this Christmas, either." Crystal did a tight circle in her new chair.

Chance closed his hand over Tanya's, and her pulse rate soared. "Your presence has been such a nice treat for us."

She didn't tell him that both her and her daughter felt as if this holiday was a new beginning for them—the past finally behind them. They had loved Tom and mourned his loss, but they needed to move forward. Crystal's accident, Tom's conviction and ultimately his death in prison had shaped so much of the past four years. Her daughter deserved more—a life as normal as possible. She prayed one day that he could move forward, the past behind him, too.

Chance shifted so he could face her on the couch. "I could say the same for you two. I'm the grateful one getting to share in your Christmas celebration."

When Crystal wheeled herself into the kitchen, Tanya sandwiched his hand between hers. "You shouldn't have spent so much. I know those chairs are expensive. You were supposed to be getting yourself a car."

His grin reached deep into his eyes. "I will, just later. I like to walk."

"But it's snowing, has been a lot these past few weeks."

"The cold is invigorating to me. I like to walk in the snow. After dinner let's go for a walk."

"I've got another gift for you." She released his hand

and hurried to the tree, getting the second present—the most important one. Back at his side, she laid it in his lap.

He hefted it up. "This I know has got to be a book." Again he ripped the silver wrapping paper off quickly to reveal a black Bible with his name engraved in gold on the front at the bottom right hand corner. He touched the lettering then slanted a look at her. "Thank you, Tanya. This means a lot to me. One of the things I wish I hadn't lost was my family Bible. Now I have a new one."

When she had first met him and realized how he had felt about God, she hadn't thought she would hear him say something like that. But he had found his way back to the Lord. That was the best gift she could have received the whole season. "I have marked a few places you might want to read."

Tanya heard Crystal opening and closing a cabinet door, probably searching for something to eat. "I'd better get the prime rib in the oven if we're gonna have dinner at a reasonable hour." She started to rise.

He stopped her. "First, I want to give you your present."

"Me? But you've already spent too much on Crystal."

"Did you think I would neglect to give you something to remember me by?"

Her heart slammed into her ribs. The way he'd phrased the question made it seem as if he was leaving Sweetwater soon. She supposed after the New Year was soon. Before she could say anything, he held out a long, thin box in his palm. She stared at the gold-wrapped present.

Can't he see Sweetwater is perfect for him? That I

am? Lord, that's all the gift I need. For him to return to Sweetwater after the trial.

"Aren't you gonna open it?"

She blinked, willing the hammering of her heart to slow. He might not have really meant he was leaving for good. *Perhaps he sees how good this town is for him.* "Of course." Slowly she took it from him but not before he clasped her fingers and tugged her to him, kissing her, quick and hard.

She carefully unwrapped the present and lifted the lid. Beneath some tissue lay a beautiful gold chain with an outline of a heart dangling from it with a diamond sparkling in its right corner. She held up the necklace, the gem gleaming. "It's beautiful."

"When I saw it in the store, I immediately knew it was perfect for you. You have such a good heart. You're so caring of others."

The swelling in her throat captured her words. All she could do was hand him the chain and turn so he could hook the necklace around her neck. The feel of his fingers on her nape sent tingles down her spine. She squeezed her eyes closed and imagined they were a real family, celebrating Christmas.

"There," he whispered close to her ear, his lips brushing her lobe.

She melted back against him, weak with wanting him. His hands clasped her upper arms, his breath feathering her neck. She turned her head to the side, and he planted tiny kisses along her jaw.

"Don't let anyone ever tell you otherwise, Tanya. You're a beautiful, loving woman who deserves the very best."

Even though he said all the right words, she felt as if there was a "but" at the end of the last sentence. She twisted around to face him, trying to read his expression which suddenly blanked. "What are you trying to tell me?"

"The truth as I see it. Those sketches you did for me were great. Share your talent with others. Look what it has done for Crystal. Let people see what you're capable of."

Again she sensed something left unsaid but realized Chance wouldn't expound on it unless he wanted to. "I'll think about it."

He stared long and hard into her eyes, then rose and offered her his hand. "Let's put that roast in the oven. I'll help you."

He pulled her to her feet, then headed to the kitchen. Crystal sat at the table, drinking some milk and eating a bowl of cereal.

When her daughter saw them, she said, "I'm gonna have to lift weights to build up the muscles more in my arms."

"You can use the weight room at the center to get started." Chance planted himself at the counter, lounging back against it.

"Yeah. I'd been thinking about it anyway, and now with this chair, I have to if I want to play sports and be any good."

"Besides basketball, what are you thinking about?" Tanya removed the prime rib from the refrigerator.

"There's track-and-field events. I could do some racing."

As Crystal and Chance discussed the possibilities

open for her daughter, Tanya prepared the roast and
stuck it into the oven. With all that had happened this
morning she was even more determined to tell him
how she felt about him. Then if he still left, at least he
would have all the facts. She wanted no regrets when
it came to him.

Tanya matched her strides with Chance's as she
strode beside him later Christmas Day. Crystal had
urged them to go for a walk while she talked with her
friends on the phone, no doubt comparing presents.

The snow continued to fall but lightly now. The
clouds cast the sky in different hues of gray. The scent
of burning wood laced the crisp winter air. The snow
blanketed the terrain in pristine white, undisturbed in
most places as the majority of the townspeople stayed
indoors.

"I think a lot of people miss the beauty of winter
holed up in their houses." Tanya swept her arm across
her body to indicate the area before them.

"I agree, but then it wouldn't be as beautiful if they
were all trampling through the snow."

"Like us? So you think we should keep this a secret
from them?"

"Yep. It's here if they want to partake of its beauty."

Tanya laughed. "That's kinda hard when some have
pulled their drapes already." She pointed toward the
house they were passing.

"Yeah, it's only four. We have another hour of daylight." He cut down another street and headed for
the lake.

"And the ones who see us walking are probably thinking we're crazy for being out here."

At the lake the water appeared dark gray-blue and icy. With no wind blowing its surface was mirror smooth. Tall pines, the only green in the landscape, skirted the shoreline, poking themselves up out of the white cover of snow. Tanya paused at the edge and stared across the lake. She needed to tell Chance her feelings, but for the life of her she didn't know where to begin.

Lord, help me to say the right words. I feel as if my tongue has swollen in my dry mouth all of a sudden.

The large boulder she had often used to sit on by the water beckoned. Tanya dusted the snow off its surface and sat. Chance stood in front of her wearing his heavy black coat with no gloves or cap.

"You aren't cold?" Tanya touched her red hat that kept her ears warm.

"Nah. The cold makes me feel alive. In winter we didn't get outside as much so I enjoy any time I can be outdoors."

Tell him. "Your ears are red."

"They'll survive. A few minutes in front of your fire and they'll be toasty warm."

"Do you have a busy week at work?"

"No, Nick let a lot of people off because of the holidays. I've got a project I need to finish up, but that's all."

She glanced at the water lapping gently against the shore, the only sound in the quiet. "You know what I miss the most during the winter is the animals, especially the birds. We have a few, but most of them go south for the winter." *Tell him!*

At that moment a red cardinal left his perch on a

branch of an oak tree that still retained its brown leaves. She followed his flight for a minute before looking back at Chance. The regret in his eyes stole her breath. He lowered his lashes and veiled it.

"When are you leaving?" she blurted out the question without really thinking.

His sharp intake of air filled the silence. "The trial starts in less than two weeks."

Will you be back afterward? she wanted to ask but was afraid of the answer. Instead she pushed herself off the large rock, positioning herself only a few feet from him. "You aren't alone, Chance. God is with you."

"I know. There's a part of me that doesn't want to go to the trial."

"Then don't. If you're testifying only go for that part."

His intense gaze riveted to hers. "I have to go. I want to say goodbye and this is my chance to do that."

"God's not the only one with you. I am, too."

"I know. You're a good friend." His intensity faded. *Tell him.* "I want to be more than a friend, Chance. I've fallen in love with you."

His eyes widened. He dropped his gaze, twisting around to stare at the lake. "You shouldn't have, Tanya. I'm not free to love."

His past continued to haunt him, holding him prisoner as if he were still in prison. His rigid stance conveyed the barrier that might always be between them. For the first time since she'd begun the walk, cold seeped in, straight to the marrow of her bones, leaving her frozen with despair.

Chapter Twelve

Blessed be the God and Father of our Lord Jesus Christ, which according to His abundant mercy hath begotten us again unto a lively hope by the resurrection of Jesus Christ from the dead. The words from Peter, that Samuel had quoted in his sermon, leaped off the page, entwining themselves into Chance's heart. Christ offered him hope—hope that one day he could have a life rid of this guilt that ate into his soul.

Closing the Bible that Tanya had given him, Chance rose and walked to the window. The sound of the basketball striking against the concrete then the backboard drew him. He watched Crystal take another shot at the hoop. When the ball bounced off the rim and landed in the grass alongside the driveway, Charlie went after it and nosed it toward Crystal. She dribbled then set up for another shot. Chance turned toward the door.

He had avoided Tanya all week since Christmas day and her declaration of love. She deserved to be loved by someone who could come to her with a clear heart—not him. And above all, she deserved to know the whole story about him and Tom before he left for Louisville.

His hand on the knob, Chance rested his forehead against the wood. He loved her. But he wasn't free to love Tanya as she should be. Hate and guilt crowded his heart. How could he enter into a relationship she deserved when he couldn't straighten out his own life? She had endured so much these past few years. He would never forgive himself if he added to her pain.

Once he told her he was the reason Tom was killed, her love would die and he could leave. Turning the knob, he opened the door and stepped outside onto the landing.

The basketball slamming into the driveway over and over echoed in the air. He descended the stairs.

When Crystal saw him, she smiled and cradled the ball in her lap. Although the temperature was only in the low fifties, beads of sweat pebbled her forehead. She swiped the back of her hand across her forehead.

"This is hard work, but since the snow melted yesterday, I've got to grab the chance to practice while I have it." She lined up the ball toward the hoop and sent it flying. It swished through the net. "Yes!"

Chance loped toward the ball as it hit the concrete and caught it before it bounced a second time. He tossed it toward Crystal who trapped it against her body.

"You've done a good job teaching Charlie to help retrieve your ball."

She called her service dog to her and stroked the length of his back. "He's always been a quick learner." With the ball in her lap, she rolled toward the deck ramp.

When Chance saw Crystal struggling up the ramp, easily accessible for an electric wheelchair, he started toward her but stopped. He gave her a few more seconds to see if she would make it on her own. That was important to Crystal. When she reached the top of the ramp, she swung around, her grin wide.

"I started working out at the center. Before long going up this ramp will be a piece of cake."

"Your arms have to be tired. You've been practicing for the past hour."

"Yep. I hear we might have another round of snow next week. You would think we live in Alaska the way it has been snowing this past month."

Chance took a wooden lounge chair opposite Crystal. "Have you played any basketball at the center yet?"

"Not yet. I will when I get better. I'm thinking in the spring of joining a wheelchair basketball team that's part of a league that meets in Lexington. Mom said she would drive me to the practices and the games." She leaned forward. "Thank you again for this chair. I've always loved sports, and now I can participate in them more."

Chance glanced toward the back door and wondered where Tanya was. He really needed to talk to her, but he realized sitting with Crystal was his way of avoiding what he must do. He didn't want to see the pain, disappointment and anger in Tanya's face. But it was better this way. A quick sever would be less painful than a prolonged one.

"Have you decided on what sports besides basketball that you want to do? I know you mentioned track and field once."

"I've been researching some different ones online and I think racing would be the best one for me. Also, I'm gonna talk with Darcy about getting more involved with riding."

"Your mom told me you've gotten back up on a horse since your accident, but you aren't riding like you used to."

"I want to again. I don't blame the horse for my paralysis." She stared down at her lap for a good minute then lifted her gaze toward him. "Blame is such negative energy. I've decided I don't have room for that in my life. I used to blame myself for what my father did."

"But you weren't at fault."

"I know that now. I prayed a lot about it, especially after he died. For a time I thought I had killed him."

No, I did. Chance clenched his teeth, unable to say the words.

Crystal sought Charlie, who laid his head in her lap. She scratched him behind his ear. "Guilt is like blame. It's negative energy. It doesn't do any good for a person. If God can forgive me, then why shouldn't I forgive myself?"

"It's not always that easy," Chance murmured, thinking of his own guilt that he carried around.

"'But if we walk in the light, as He is in the light, we have fellowship one with another, and the blood of Jesus Christ His Son cleanseth us from all sin.' I remember Samuel telling me that one day last summer and it all made sense."

The creak of the back door opening sounded. Chance glanced toward Tanya. A piercing pain knifed through his heart. He was going to hurt her. There was no way around it. The idea cut him deeply.

For a few seconds while he and Tanya stared at each other, he thought about fleeing as far from Sweetwater as he could get. And he would. But first he had to tell her everything concerning Tom.

"Hi, Mom. Did you see me shooting? I made a couple of baskets. Before long, Chance, I'm gonna have you raise the basket to regulation height."

He stood. "It's easy. Anyone can for you."

Crystal gave him a questioning look but didn't say anything. Instead, she rolled her chair into the house while Tanya held the door open. He followed, his throat jammed with emotions of regret and a much more intense feeling he wished he could deny.

"I need to clean up. Tonight is New Year's Eve and I've got a feeling this next year is gonna be a good one so I want to be up to greet it."

"Do you hear her?" Tanya stood in the middle of the kitchen watching her daughter disappear into the hallway. "She is happy." She swung around to face him. "And part of the reason for that is you, Chance."

"If that is so, then I've accomplished one of the things I wanted to do when I came to Sweetwater."

Confusion created deep creases in her brow. "What do you mean?"

Lord, I need Your help. How do I tell Tanya without hurting her? But nothing came to Chance's mind as he stared at the woman who had come to mean so much to him. He sucked in a deep, fortifying breath then released it slowly. "It wasn't Samuel who brought me to Sweetwater. It was you."

"Me? But you didn't even know me."

"Yes, I did. Tom often talked about you and Crystal. We had a lot of downtime while in prison and he would tell me different stories."

"What did he say?" Curiosity replaced her puzzlement.

"I heard about your vacation to the Smoky Mountains. I heard about the baby squirrel Crystal found and raised until it was big enough to live on its own. Through all the stories I heard the love he had for you and Crystal. He told me right before he died that he regretted everything he had done to you two. He didn't understand your manic depression, but he thought you were a loving, caring woman. He didn't understand how God could have allowed something like Crystal's paralysis to happen to her. Toward the end he was filled with hopelessness and bitterness, but he always loved you two."

Tanya spun around and took two steps to the table to settle onto a chair. Her hand shook as she smoothed back her hair. "I still don't understand why he thought he had to go it alone. He would have gotten out of prison, and we could have been a family again."

"I think in his mind he thought his life was over." The pounding in his chest echoed in his ears. If he didn't say something now, he might never. "I'm the reason Tom was killed."

Lifting her head, she looked at him. "You? I don't understand."

"A couple of inmates had me cornered and were intent on killing me. Tom stepped in and took the knife meant for me. I had had enough of being pushed around and had stood up to the wrong person. Tom was killed because of me."

She blinked.

A long silence fell between them.

Finally she rose, slowly. "Why didn't you tell me before?"

"I wanted to help you and Crystal, and I didn't think you would let me if you knew."

"So you kept it a secret!" Tears glinted in her eyes as she stepped toward him, her hands clenched at her sides.

"Yes."

"Why say anything now?"

"I wasn't gonna say anything to you, but you deserve to know everything."

"So Crystal and I were a charity case for you, and now that you've done what you set out to do, you're ready to leave." Anger sliced through her words.

"Yes," he said, even though she hadn't asked a question. The thunderous beat of his heart continued to vibrate through his mind. "I have unfinished business in Louisville."

"And afterward?" Steel strengthened her voice.

"I don't know. I can't think beyond the trial."

Her usual expressive face evolved into a neutral facade. She walked to the back door and opened it. "Thanks for letting me know about how Tom really died."

He strode toward her, wanting so badly to take her into his arms and hug her until her anger melted. When he came alongside her, her words stopped him.

"And you don't need to worry about Crystal and me.

We're doing just fine, and don't need any more of your help."

"Tanya," he started but couldn't find the words to express his feelings. He still had to deal with his past and put to rest the guilt and anger that choked him when he thought about the murder of his family. He wouldn't involve Tanya in that. She'd been through enough. "Happy New Year," he murmured finally and left.

Outside on the deck he flinched at the sound of the door slamming behind him. Glancing around at the shadows of dusk creeping over the yard, he knew what he needed to do next. He couldn't stay until the start of the trial. He needed to leave now. A clean break was best for Tanya, and he'd already hurt her enough today. He didn't want to cause her any more pain by lingering a few extra days. He strode across the driveway to the stairs that led to his apartment.

Tanya watched Chance head for the apartment above the garage. Numbing shock gripped her in a tight vise. Tom died trying to break up a fight between Chance and two other inmates. Her emotions lay frozen within her. She didn't know what to feel.

There had been no future for her and Tom for years. Ever since he had set fire to the first barn, their future had been sealed in her husband's mind. But even before that, there had been a rift in their relationship partly due to the fact he hadn't been understanding about her manic depression. She had struggled alone dealing with it, and it had taken a toll on her marriage that Crystal's accident had completely torn apart.

Tanya turned away from the window and made her way toward her bedroom and lay on her bed, staring at the ceiling. Darkness slithered into the room, and she welcomed it as she willed her mind empty of any thoughts. But on the black screen of her mind all she could see was Chance, the pain in his eyes when he had looked at her the last time before leaving her house. She wasn't even sure he was aware of his expression.

But she was sure of one thing: she had moved on in her life. She no longer felt guilty about Tom. And she was no longer angry at Tom for what he had done to their lives, to his life.

Finally she sat up and swung her legs over the edge of the bed. After switching on the lamp on her bedside table, she pulled her Bible onto her lap and opened it, searching for peace in its pages.

Dawn broke on the horizon. Tanya saw the streaks of red-orange entwined through the dark blue and wished she had some answers to the hundreds of questions that had plagued her through the night. The overriding one, what did she do now, still demanded an answer she didn't have.

The scent of perking coffee drifted to her, and she walked to the pot to pour herself a huge mugful. The gritty feel in her eyes reminded her of the sleepless night that had passed. Some time in the middle of the night she had closed her Bible. Peace had eluded her, but the need to see Chance had grown as she had read the Word.

Sipping the brew, she stared out the window at the stairs to Chance's apartment. She loved him and realized that hadn't changed even with the new information she had learned the day before.

Was she going to allow Tom to continue to dictate how she lived her life? He had chosen his path, even when he had stepped in front of the knife meant for Chance. Tom's death wasn't Chance's fault.

But Chance felt it was. Could she find a way to make him understand it wasn't? Even if Chance didn't love her, he deserved to forgive himself for what happened to Tom. That was the least she could give Chance. Peace of mind. Then maybe she would have her own peace.

Still dressed in her jeans and sweatshirt from the day before, she took one last swig of her coffee, placed it on the counter and strode to the back door. Outside the crisp winter air chilled her. She hurried toward the stairs that led to his place. She took them two at a time and started to knock when she noticed the door wasn't totally shut.

He was gone! She knew it in her heart. Her hands quivered as she opened the door and entered the apartment. Scanning the large room through a sheen of tears she saw that every trace of Chance was wiped away. Her gaze rested on the kitchen table where a note propped next to a wad of money sat. Slowly she crossed to it and reached for the paper with her name on it.

Her hand clutched it as she read the short letter.

Tanya, the time spent with you and Crystal has been wonderful. I have left you this month's rent as my notice. May you find a man who one day deserves your goodness. Love, Chance.

Love, Chance. Did that mean he loved her? Was that just a casual closing to his note that really meant nothing? Frustration at no answers churned in her stomach.

She crumpled the letter into a ball and threw it across the room. Anger consumed her. How dare he leave without saying goodbye in person! How dare— Then she remembered the last time she had seen him, yesterday when confusion reigned in her. She couldn't blame him. She had basically kicked him out of her house.

She collapsed onto a chair and buried her face in her palms. She'd made a mess of the situation. And now Chance was gone. She had no idea where he was, at least not until the trial started next week.

Chance stood at the window of his hotel room, glimpsing the Ohio River in the distance. The gray day reflected his mood. The first day of the trial had gone smoothly with the selection of the jurors in the morning and the opening remarks in the afternoon. He'd held up, even through the attorneys' remarks to the jury, mostly by shutting down his emotions totally and staring a hole in the back of the chair in front of him. He'd barely gotten out of there before all his feelings had inundated him.

Gripping the window ledge, he leaned his forehead against the cold pane. Icy fingers spread through him, cooling the heat of his anger. The man who had destroyed his life had sat next to his lawyer, smug, unaffected by the trial.

Lord, I can't do this!

Even though the trial wasn't expected to last long, he didn't know how he was going to make it through all the testimony day in and day out. Flashes of his past blinked in and out of his mind—finding his family murdered, being charged with those murders, the years spent in prison knowing he was innocent and the real killer was walking free, something he never thought he would do again.

God, help me! I have to do this much for Ruth and Haley, see this trial through to the end. I owe them that.

A knock sounded at the door. He spun around and stared at it as though he hadn't really heard anything.

Another rap filled the silence.

As though his legs had a will of their own, they carried him across the room. He reached for the handle in slow motion and pulled the door open. When he saw Tanya before him, he nearly fell apart. Her inner beauty shone from her eyes, her smile of greeting melting the icy shroud that blanketed him.

Time faded away as he stared at her here in the hallway outside his hotel room, not in Sweetwater where she belonged.

Finally one of her delicate brows rose. "Can I come in?"

"How did you find me?"

"Nick helped me. He figured you would be staying near the courthouse. I wish I could have been here yesterday, but I had to work in order to get the rest of the week off."

"The rest of the week?"

She peeked around him. "Let's talk in your room."

"Oh," he said, realizing he still blocked the entrance. He stepped to the side to allow her inside.

"I'm here to support you through the trial." Tanya turned in the middle of the room to face him.

"Why?"

"Because no one should have to go through what you're going through alone. You need your...friends. Nick and the rest of them are coming tomorrow."

"But..." He didn't know what to say. "Everyone?"

"Yep."

"Why would—"

Tanya covered the space between them in two quick strides. She placed her fingers against his mouth to still his words. "Whether you want to admit it or not, you have a lot of people in Sweetwater who care about you and don't want you to go through the trial alone so there's nothing you can do but put up with us."

The feel of her fingers pressing into his lips, the look of love in her eyes, released the dam on his emotions. They flooded him, rendering him humble in the power of the Lord. Tanya was here because God had sent her. She had been there all along for him, but he hadn't wanted to see it, had fought it all the way.

Chance gathered Tanya to him, burying his face in her hair, the apple-scented shampoo she used washing over him. Tears crowded his eyes. He squeezed them closed, holding them inside, but they clogged his throat, making any comments impossible.

Minutes later he finally pulled back, keeping his arms loosely about her. He swallowed several times before he was able to ask, "You took vacation days to be here?"

She nodded. Lifting her hand, she cupped his jaw. The sheen in her eyes indicated the depth of her feelings for him. They humbled him anew. How in the world did he deserve someone like Tanya?

The question put some emotional distance between him and Tanya. There was so much baggage that stood in the way of having any kind of future together.

Tanya must have sensed his thoughts because a cloud masked the joy in her gaze. "We have a lot to talk about, but first you need to get through the trial. The rest can come later."

"I wish it were that easy."

"It won't be easy. I never said that. But you need to let me help you as you helped me. Lo—friendship is a two-way street." Tanya slipped her fingers from his face. "What time do we need to be at the courthouse?"

"Nine."

"Then we'd better get moving. But first let's pray." Tanya took both his hands and bowed her head. "Dear Heavenly Father, watch over Chance in his time of need. Help to ease his pain and pave the way for him to forgive the man who took his family. In Jesus Christ's name, amen."

Chance yanked his hands free. "Forgive! How can you expect me to forgive that man after all he did to me and my family?"

"Because until you do, you won't be totally free to move on. He will pay for his crimes, but I don't want to see you continue to pay because you can't forgive him."

He spun around. "I don't think I can. We'd better get going. I don't want to be late."

Hopefully it will be over tomorrow, Chance thought by Thursday evening after spending the whole week in the courtroom. The jury was deliberating as he sat in his darkened hotel room. He didn't think they would be out long because the evidence had been compelling. But then a jury had convicted him on circumstantial evidence that had thrown his already messed-up life into a tailspin so it was hard to tell what a jury would do.

Only in the past few days with first Tanya and later her circle of friends and their husbands sitting around him as support had he experienced again the peace he had felt that time in church with Tanya. He could still feel the comfort of her hand within his throughout the closing statements by each of the lawyers. Each look, touch had soothed his pain until now all he wanted to do was let go of this anger that had consumed him for years while he had sat in a cell—imprisoned physically, and as he knew now, mentally, too.

Lord, I don't want to feel this way anymore. What do I do?

In the dark he caught sight of his Bible on the table in front of the window, a stream of light illuminating it. Every night before going to sleep he had read it until his eyes had drooped closed.

He flipped on the lamp beside him and reached for his Bible. Tanya had insisted he had to forgive his family's killer in order to be totally at peace and able to move on. *How do I do that, Father?*

He turned to Luke and read the account of Christ's ministry, his death. "Then said Jesus, 'Father, forgive them; for they know not what they do.' And they parted his raiment, and cast lots."

The words leaped off the page, striking Chance with their meaning. *If Christ can forgive the people who tormented and killed him, then the least I can do is the same: forgive the man who murdered my wife and daughter.*

After finishing Luke, Chance closed his Bible and fingered the gold letters of his name engraved in the black cover.

He imagined the killer in his mind. "I forgive you," he whispered into the silence of the room. Then in a stronger voice he repeated, "I forgive you."

With each word uttered, a part of his anger dissolved. Left in its wake was the peace he had craved.

Tightening her grasp on his hand, Tanya slid a glance toward Chance as the verdict was read. His somber expression evolved into relief as the word "guilty" was spoken in the quiet courtroom. The taut line of his shoulders sagged and he dropped his head, his eyes closing for a few seconds.

"It's over," he whispered to her, his voice raw.

Tanya released his hand and opened her arms to him. He went into her embrace. His shudder passed through his body and into hers.

"I'm finally free. Really free."

Around them people stood, talked, moved about, but Tanya sat in the front row with Chance and held him for minutes. When he pulled back, she saw a new man in his eyes, a man who had closed the door on his past and faced his future with hope. Joy spread through her.

Her arms fell away. She smiled. "Justice was finally done today."

"Yes, Gary Kingston has to face the consequences of what he did. I hope he finds some kind of peace over it."

This was the first time Chance had said the man's name out loud to her. He'd always used "murderer" or "killer" before this. "You do?"

He nodded. "I had to forgive him. I—"

Nick approached and sat in the vacant chair behind Chance. "We want to celebrate. Do you two feel up to dinner at the hotel before we all head back to Sweetwater?"

Tanya scanned her friends and their husbands waiting near the entrance into the now almost-empty courtroom. Even Darcy was here with her new baby to support Chance. Emotions crammed her throat at how lucky she was to have friends like Darcy, Jesse, Beth and Zoey.

"Sure. You all go ahead. I want to have a word with Tanya. We'll be along in a few minutes." Chance shook Nick's hand. "Thanks for being here."

"Anything for a friend. We'll save you a seat." Nick made his way toward his wife, slipping his arm around her shoulder as the group left.

"Let's go find a quiet place in the hall." Chance rose and held his hand out for her.

After fitting hers in his grasp, she walked beside him out into the foyer. Chance quickly found an empty bench and drew her to it. As she leaned against the hard back slats, her heart slowed. Was he going to tell her goodbye? Did he want to move on without her? Maybe he didn't love her enough to marry her. And she realized more than ever she wanted to get married again. She wanted the happiness her friends had.

Chance swallowed hard, clasping her other hand, too. "Thank you for being here with me. After that first day, I didn't know how I was going to get through the trial, then you showed up on my doorstep and gave me a way. I know about all you had to do to be here with me."

"I'd do it again."

He grinned. "I know. And I have several people back in Sweetwater to thank. Amanda's parents who agreed to take Crystal in and trade cars with you so they could transport Crystal in the van. Your boss, for letting you take time off suddenly. Not to mention all your friends who came."

"They're your friends, too."

"Until this week I hadn't really realized that. I never had friends like them. I was always working too hard to have time for other people except my family and even then I didn't spend enough time with them. I can't get that back, but I can move forward, live the type of life Christ spoke of. Learn from my mistakes."

Little creases lined his forehead as he spoke. Tanya wanted to smooth them away, but he held her hands and she loved the feel of his fingers entwined with hers.

"And the most important thing I've learned in the past few months is that I love you, Tanya. I want to spend the rest of my life with you."

One small seed of doubt nibbled at her. "You aren't saying that because of your guilt over how Tom died, are you? This isn't some kind of payback?"

He shook his head. "Tom wanted to die. He made the choice to step in between me and my attacker to take that knife. I know that now. Last night when I forgave Gary Kingston, I also forgave myself."

"I never really blamed you for Tom's death. I didn't get a chance to tell you because you left before I could. And we've been busy with the trial. I came over to see you New Year's Day early in the morning to let you know that. But you were gone. I was angry because you didn't trust me earlier with knowing the details of how Tom had died."

"I was wrong. I should have. But I had become so used to seeing people shun me that I didn't want to see that in your eyes. I realize now that I was falling in love with you and was scared to do anything to change that so I kept quiet."

"Why did you tell me then?"

A full-fledged grin returned. "Because I was in love with you and was scared to be in love again. I used it to put distance between us, an excuse to leave you. I won't make that mistake again."

"I'll hold you to that." The joy she had held at bay burst out of its restraints and flooded her. She slipped her hands from his and drew him to her. "I love you, Chance. I want to spend the rest of my life with you."

His mouth claimed hers in a deep kiss. She relished the sensations he generated in her.

His breathing ragged, he asked, "Will you marry me?"

"Yes! Yes!"

Again he possessed her mouth with his, leaving no doubt in her mind that he loved her with all his being.

When Chance finally rose, he laced his fingers through hers and tugged her gently to her feet. "I guess we'd better not keep our friends waiting. After all, we have a lot to celebrate tonight, and if I can't have you alone, then I can't think of any better way to celebrate than with friends."

Fifteen minutes later, Tanya strode into the hotel

restaurant with Chance by her side. She knew her love for the man next to her was written all over her face. That was shortly confirmed when the waiter showed them into the small room that Nick had secured for their dinner.

When her friends looked at them, one by one they rose, clapping, with smiles that matched the grins plastered on her face and Chance's.

"I don't think we need to ask what has kept you two. Care to share any news with us?" Jesse reseated herself next to her husband.

"Tanya has agreed to become my wife."

More applause and cheers followed Chance's announcement. Tanya squeezed his hand and slanted a look his way. His gaze, trained on her, flared with the promise of friendship *and* love.

"When?" Beth asked when everyone quieted.

Tanya eased into the chair that Chance held for her. "We haven't set a date, but I've always wanted a June wedding."

"A June bride! How wonderful!" Darcy patted her baby on the back. "That gives us time to really plan a beautiful wedding."

As Jesse, Beth, Zoey and Darcy began to discuss their ideas for the wedding, Chance leaned down, kissed Tanya's neck by her ear and whispered, "We can always elope. It's your call."

Epilogue

"The last item up for bidding is an opportunity to have a portrait painted by our very own Tanya Taylor. Just in case a person hasn't seen the wonderful work she does, I have a portrait here to show you." Samuel held up a picture of Beth and his children that Tanya had done for him.

The heat of a blush tinged Tanya's cheeks as she heard the admiration of her neighbors. She snuggled closer to Chance, never comfortable being in the limelight.

"You'd better get used to hearing people comment on your work. You're garnishing quite a reputation. This is bound to bring in the largest amount for the Fourth of July Auction." Grinning, Chance kissed her cheek.

"Hey, the honeymoon ended two weeks ago, you two," Zoey said next to Chance.

Tanya felt her blush deepen and spread down her neck. She and Chance had had a wonderfully planned wedding, given to her by Jesse, Darcy, Beth and Zoey, followed by a honeymoon to the Bahamas that had been Nick and Jesse's wedding present to them. The joy that had come into her life with Chance blossomed each day she spent with him.

Ten minutes later the president of the bank where she worked had indeed set a record for what one item brought in for the church's outreach program and put an end to the auction. Chance, Nick and Dane cleared off the gym floor at the center so the next part of the afternoon's activities could begin.

When Chance settled next to Tanya in the bleachers, he took her hand. "Okay?"

"Nervous."

"She'll do great. She's been practicing for months. And I don't think Crystal's minded all the practice one bit since Grant has been giving her pointers."

At that moment Crystal and the rest of her team rolled out onto the floor to give an exhibition of wheelchair basketball for the spectators. Tanya held her breath as the ball was set in motion. One of her daughter's teammates dribbled down the court, passed it to Crystal and she took a shot. It circled the rim and swished through the net.

Tanya jumped to her feet and cheered, Chance right next to her, yelling even louder than her. Through the exhibition Crystal's smile grew as the enthusiasm of the crowd grew.

At the end, Tanya threw her arms around her husband. "She is good!"

He captured her gaze. "Just like her mom." His hand cupped the back of her neck. "I never thought I would be so happy, Mrs. Taylor."

She stood on tiptoes and brushed her lips across his. "Me neither. You have brought me such joy, Mr. Taylor."

* * * * *

Dear Reader,

This was the last book in *The Ladies of Sweetwater Lake* series. I will miss these characters, having really gotten to know them over the course of five books. Tanya's story was the hardest one to write. She was wounded and hurting and, until Chance came into her life, didn't realize she could help another to heal.

In *Tidings of Joy,* Crystal and, to a certain extent, Chance, had to deal with a bully. I teach in a high school and have seen firsthand the harm a bully can do to another. If you or a loved one are dealing with a bully, get help. Don't try to cope on your own. If you witness a bullying situation, speak up for the person who is targeted. Bystanders can make a difference in a bullying situation.

There are some excellent books about bullying and what can be done to stop it. I had the pleasure of listening to Barbara Coloroso speak on bullying in our school. Her book *The Bully, the Bullied, and the Bystander* offers good suggestions to parents and teachers about making changes in how we raise our children, to break the cycle of violence we've seen in our cultures and schools.

I love hearing from my readers. You can contact me at P.O. Box 2074, Tulsa, OK 74101, or visit my website, at www.margaretdaley.com, where you can sign up for my quarterly newsletter.

All the best,

Margaret Daley

Questions for Discussion

1. Tanya dealt with manic depression, an illness she would have to take medication to control. She didn't like having to depend on the medicine, but she didn't have a choice. What things have you had to do that you had no choice over? Did your faith help you deal with it? How?

2. Chance couldn't move on in his life because he couldn't forgive himself or the man responsible for his wife's and daughter's deaths. How hard is it to forgive another? Have you ever not been able to forgive? How does that affect you spiritually, emotionally?

3. Crystal was being harassed by a couple of girls at school. Have you ever been bullied? How did you deal with it? What are some things we can do to prevent bullying?

4. Crystal, and even Chance, learned to turn the other cheek against the people bothering them. When have you done this? How did it make you feel?

5. Tanya hid her talent as an artist because she feared rejection. Fear of rejection is a powerful emotion that controls our actions, as it did in Tanya's case. How has fear of rejection controlled you? How have you overcome its hold on you?

6. Chance went to prison, even though he was innocent. He lived in a nightmarish situation for over

two years. Even after he left prison, he still lived in a self-imposed one, built by guilt and the inability to forgive. Have you ever lived in a self-imposed prison? How did you move on? Did your faith play a part in breaking those bonds? How?

7. When Holly needed a tutor for math, Crystal came forward and volunteered to do it. In Romans 12:20 it states, "Therefore if thine enemy hunger, feed him; if he thirst, give him drink." That can be hard to do when you have been hurt by another. What has helped you to forgive your enemy?

8. John 14:27 says, "Peace I leave with you, my peace I give unto you: not as the world giveth, give I unto you. Let not your heart be troubled neither let it be afraid." In the end, through the Lord, Chance found the peace he had been seeking. Has this happened to you? How did you find your peace?

9. Tanya worried about her daughter—so much had happened to Crystal over the past four years. To Tanya, God and her circle of friends were the ones who had gotten her through the hard times. Who do you rely on during the tough times? How?

10. Crystal was in a wheelchair. Tanya had manic depression. We all have some kind of disability we have to cope with, whether physical, emotional or spiritual. What is yours? How do you cope? Does your faith help? How?

HEART OF THE FAMILY

Then said Jesus, Father, forgive them; for they know not what they do. And they parted his raiment and cast lots.
—*Luke* 23:34

To my family: my husband, mother-in-law, son,
daughter-in-law and granddaughters

To all the foster parents who have done such a
great job helping out in a difficult situation

Chapter One

The child's name on the chart held Jacob Hartman's gaze riveted. Andy Morgan. The eight-year-old from Stone's Refuge had possibly another broken bone. Flashes of the last time the boy had been in his office, only a few weeks before, paraded across his mind.

With a sigh, Jacob entered the room to find the boy perched on the edge of the exam table, his face contorted in pain as he held his left arm, in a makeshift sling, close to his body. A woman Jacob wasn't familiar with stood to the side murmuring soothing words to Andy. She turned toward Jacob, worry etched into her face—and something else he couldn't decipher. Her mouth pinched into a frown that quickly evolved into an unreadable expression.

Jacob shook off the coolness emanating from the young woman. "Hi, Andy. Remember me? I'm Dr. Jacob," he said, using the name the children at the refuge knew him by. "How did you hurt your arm?" He gently removed the sling made from an old T-shirt and took the injured, swollen limb into his hands.

When he probed the forearm, Andy winced and tried to draw it back. "I fell." The child's lower lip trembled, and he dug his teeth into it.

"He was climbing the elm tree next to the barn and fell out of it." When Jacob glanced toward her, taking in the concern in the woman's dark blue gaze, she continued in a tense voice that had a soft Southern lilt. "I'm the new manager at Stone's Refuge. Hannah Smith. I was told when there was a medical problem to bring the children to you. This is only my second day, and no one else was around. The other kids are at school. Andy was supposed to be there, too. I—" she offered him a brief smile that didn't reach her eyes "—I talk too much when I'm upset."

No doubt the tension he felt coming from the refuge's new manager was due to Andy's accident. "I take care of the children's medical needs." Jacob buzzed for his nurse. "Andy, can you do this for me?" He demonstrated flexing and extending his wrist and fingers.

With his forehead scrunched, the boy did, but pain flitted across his features. He tried to mask it, but Jacob knew what the child was going through. He'd experienced a few broken bones in his own childhood and remembered trying to put up a brave front. He learned to do that well. Jacob unlocked a cabinet and removed a bottle of ibuprofen.

He handed the boy the pain pills and a glass of water. "Why weren't you at school?" Children like Andy were the reason he had become a pediatrician, but he hadn't quite conquered the feelings generated when he was confronted with child abuse.

The boy dropped his head, cradling his arm against

his chest. "I told the other kids I was going back to the cottage because I didn't feel good. I hid instead. I don't like school. I want to go home."

"Just as soon as I get a picture of your arm and we get it fixed up, you can go home."

Andy's head snapped up, his eyes bright. "I can? Really?"

Hannah Smith stepped closer and placed a hand on the child's shoulder. Apprehension marked her stiff actions. "Back home to the refuge."

"No! I want to go *home*." Tears welled up in Andy's brown eyes, and one slid down his thin face.

"Andy, you can't. I'm sorry." Calmness underscored her words as tiny creases lined her forehead. Her concern and caring attitude accentuated her beauty.

Having realized his mistake, Jacob started to respond when the door opened and the nurse appeared. "Teresa, Andy's visiting us again. We need an X-ray of his left arm."

"Hello, Andy. What did you do to your arm?" Teresa, a petite older woman with a huge, reassuring smile, helped the child down from the table. "I bet you remember where our prize box is. Once we get the X-ray done, I'll let you check it out."

"I can?"

"Sure. If I remember correctly, you were also eyeing that red car the last time. It's still there."

"It is?" Andy hurried out of the room, still holding his arm across his chest.

The refuge's manager started to follow the pair. Jacob blocked her path and closed the door. Frowning, she immediately backed up against the exam table.

"I'd like a word with you, Ms. Smith. Teresa will take care of Andy. He knows her. She spent quite a bit of time with him several weeks ago."

Her dark blue gaze fixed on him, narrowing slightly. "I haven't had a chance to read all the children's files yet. What happened the last time he was here?"

Obviously she was upset that something like this occurred on her watch. But beneath her professional demeanor, tension vibrated that Jacob suddenly sensed went beyond what had occurred to Andy. "His mother brought him in with a nasty head wound, and I called social services. Her story didn't check out. Thankfully he was placed quickly at Stone's Refuge."

"I was in the middle of reading the children's files when the school called to find out why he wasn't there. I found Andy lying on the ground hugging his arm and trying his best not to cry, but his face had dry tear marks on it." She pushed her long blond hair behind her ears and blew a breath of air out that lifted her bangs. "When I approached him, he tried to act like nothing was wrong."

"Sadly, Andy is used to holding his pain in. I took several X-rays last time because he was limping and discovered he'd broken his ankle and it was never set properly. He probably will always limp because of the way his bone healed without medical attention."

"His mother didn't seek care for him?"

He shook his head. "I think the only reason she came in last time was because there was so much blood involved. She thought he was dying. He'd passed out briefly. She flew into a rage when he was taken from her." Jacob didn't know if he would ever forget the scene

Andy's mother created at the clinic that afternoon. If looks could kill, he would be dead, but then he should be accustomed to that from an angry mother.

"Is there a father?"

"No. I don't think there ever was one in the picture. His mother clammed up and hasn't said anything about the new or old injuries." Jacob picked up the child's chart. "I want you to know what you're dealing with since you haven't been on the job long. The only time Andy cried was when he found out he wasn't going with his mother when he left the hospital. He kept screaming he needed to go home. When he settled down, he whimpered that his mother needed him, but I could never get him to tell me why he thought that." He jotted his preliminary findings down on the chart. "Have you been a social worker for long?"

A gleam glittered in her eyes. "No, I got my degree recently."

A newbie. No wonder she'd wanted to know if Andy's mother had sought help. He would hate to see that light in her eyes dim when the reality of the system sank in. But having dealt with the Department of Human Services and the lack of funding that so often tied its hands when it came to neglected or abused children, he knew the reality of the situation, first as a boy who had gone through the system and now as a pediatrician.

"I've been impressed by the setup at Stone's Refuge, especially since it hasn't been around for long. We could use more places like that." Hannah hiked the straps of her brown leather purse up onto her shoulder. "I'm glad they've started building another house at the ranch. Mr. Stone has quite a vision."

Jacob laughed. "That's Peter. When he came up with using the students from the Cimarron Technology Center to help with the construction of the house, it was a blessing. They're learning a trade, and we're getting another place for kids to stay at a cheaper rate."

"I heard some of his ideas, as well as his wife's when I interviewed with them. It's quite an ambitious project." She started forward. "I'd better check and see—"

The door opened, and Andy came into the room with Teresa and a red car clutched in his hand. "It was there, Dr. Jacob. No one took it."

The child's words, *no one took it,* stirred a memory from Jacob's past. He'd been in his fourth foster home, all of his possessions easily contained in a small backpack. Slowly his treasures had disappeared. The first item had been stolen at the shelter after he'd been removed from his mother's care. By the age of twelve he hadn't expected any of his belongings to stay long, so when he had received a radio for Christmas from a church toy drive, he hadn't thought he would keep it more than a day or so. But when he had moved to his fifth foster home seven months later, he still had the radio in his backpack. No one had taken it. His body had begun to fill out by then, and he'd learned to defend himself with the older children.

"Here's the X-ray, Dr. Hartman."

Teresa handed it to him, drawing him back to the present.

After studying the X-ray, Jacob pointed to an area on Andy's forearm. "That's where it's fractured. Teresa will set you up with Dr. Filmore, an orthopedic surgeon here in the clinic, to take care of your arm."

Andy's eyes grew round. "What will he do?"

"He'll probably put a cast on your arm."

"Can people sign it?" Andy stared at the place where Jacob had pointed on the X-ray.

"Yep, but you won't be able to get it wet. You'll have it on for a few months."

Andy grinned. "You mean, I don't have to take a bath for months?"

Jacob chuckled, ruffling the boy's hair. "I'm afraid a few people might have something to say about that."

"But—"

"We'll rig something up to keep your arm with the cast dry while you take a bath." Hannah moved next to Andy, her nurturing side leaking through her professional facade. "And I'm thinking when we get home, we'll have a cast signing and invite everyone. I've got some neat markers we can use. We can use different colors or just one."

"My favorite color is green."

"Then green it is." Hannah glanced toward Jacob. "Where do we go to see Dr. Filmore?"

Jacob nodded toward Teresa who slipped out of the room. "He's on the third floor. He owes me a favor. If he isn't in surgery, he should be able to see Andy quickly. Teresa will arrange it."

Hannah smiled, her glance straying to Andy. "Great."

It lit her whole face, transforming her plain features into a pretty countenance. It reached deep into her eyes, inviting others to join her in grinning. Jacob responded with his own smile, but when her attention came back to him, her grin died. An invisible but palpable barrier fell into place. Was she still worried about the accident on her second day on the job? Or something else?

As Teresa showed Hannah and Andy out of the room, Jacob watched them leave. He couldn't shake the feeling he'd done something wrong in Hannah's eyes, that her emotional reaction went beyond Andy's accident. Jacob was out at the refuge all the time, since he was the resident doctor for the foster homes and on the board of the foundation that ran Stone's Refuge. But the ice beneath her professional facade didn't bode well for their working relationship. As he headed into the hall, he decided he needed to pay Peter a visit and find out what he could about Hannah Smith.

The sun began its descent toward the line of trees along the side of the road leading to Stone's Refuge. Tension gripped Hannah's neck and shoulders from the hours sitting in the doctor's office, waiting for Andy's arm to be taken care of. No, that wasn't the whole reason. The second she'd seen Dr. Jacob Hartman she'd remembered the time her family had been torn apart because of him. After the death of her older brother, Kevin, everything had changed in her life, and Jacob Hartman had been at the center of the tragedy.

But looking at him, no one could tell what he had done. His bearing gave the impression of a proficient, caring doctor. Concern had lined his face while interacting with Andy. Even now she could picture that look in his chocolate-brown eyes that had warmed when he'd smiled. The two dimples in his cheeks had mocked her when he had turned that grin on her. And for just a second his expression had taunted her to let go of her anger. But she couldn't.

The small boy next to her in the van had been a trouper the whole time, but now he squirmed, his bottled-up energy barely contained. "Mrs. Smith, ya ain't mad at me, are ya?" Andy stared down at his cast, thumping his finger against it over and over.

The rhythmic sound grated on Hannah's raw nerves, but she suppressed her irritation. Andy wasn't the source of her conflicting emotions. "Mad? No. Disappointed, yes. I want you to feel you can come talk to me if something is bothering you rather than playing hooky from school."

Andy dropped his head and mumbled, "Yes, ma'am."

"Please call me Hannah. You and I are the new kids on the block. Actually, you could probably show me the ropes. How long have you been at the house? Two, three weeks?"

He lifted his head and nodded.

"See? This is only my second day. You've got tons more experience at how things are done around here." *Why had she accepted this job? How was she going to work with Dr. Hartman?* The questions screamed for answers she couldn't give.

"Sure. But I don't know too much. The other kids…"

When he didn't continue his sentence, Hannah slanted a look toward him, his chin again resting on his chest, his shoulders curled forward as though trying to draw inward. "What about the other kids?"

"Nothin'."

She slowed the van as she turned onto the gravel road

that led to the group of houses for the foster children at Stone's Refuge. "Is anyone bothering you?"

His head came up, and he twisted toward her. "No. It's not that."

In the short time she'd been around the boy, she felt as though she was talking to a child two or three years older, especially now after the half a day spent at the clinic and his staunch, brave face. But after reading part of his file and hearing what the doctor had said, she understood where the boy was coming from. He'd seen the ugly side of life and experienced more than most kids his age. "Then what's wrong?"

"I don't fit in."

Those words, whispered in a raw voice, poked a dagger into old wounds. She had always been the new kid in school. After her family had fallen apart with Kevin's death and her parents divorced, she and her mother had moved around a lot. "Why do you say that?" she managed to get out, although her throat tightened with buried pain she'd thought she had left behind her. But coming back to her hometown where she had lived for the first nine years of her life had been a mistake. How had she thought she wouldn't have to confront what had happened to Kevin? Of course, she hadn't discovered Dr. Jacob Hartman's involvement with the refuge until yesterday.

Andy averted his gaze, hanging his head again. "I just don't. I never have."

The pain produced from his declaration intensified, threatening her next breath. She slowly drew in a lungful of rich oxygen and some of the tension eased. "Then maybe we could work on it together. The staff at the refuge has been there since it opened last year. In fact, I just moved here last week." Cimarron City had been the only place that had resembled a home to her in her wayfaring life. She'd spent much more time here than any other place. Even while attending college, she'd moved several times. She wanted stability and had chosen the familiar town to be where she would put down roots. Maybe that was a mistake.

"You did?"

"Yep." She parked between the two houses she managed—still wanted to manage. This job had been a dream come true—until she realized that Jacob Hartman was involved. "Up until recently, I'd been in school."

"Aren't you too old for that?"

Hannah grinned. "In your eyes, probably. I had to work my way through college as a waitress, which took longer than normal."

Andy tilted his head. "How old are you?"

"Don't you know you aren't supposed to ask a woman how old she is?" she said with a laugh, then immediately added when she saw the distress on his thin face, "But I'll tell you how old if you promise not to tell anyone. I'm twenty-nine."

"Oh," he murmured, as though that age really was ancient.

She almost expected him to say, "I'm sorry," but thankfully he didn't. Instead, he shoved open the door, slowly climbed from the van, and walked toward the house. Seeing him limp renewed her determination to do well in her first professional job, to help these children have a better life.

But she couldn't help thinking: her second day at work and a child in her care had broken a bone. Not good. She would make sure that Andy went to school if she had to escort him every day. She needed to let Laura and Peter Stone, the couple who ran the Henderson Foundation that funded the refuge, know that they were back and what happened with Andy. Hannah looked toward the main house off in the distance, on the other side of the freshly painted red barn.

The refuge was perfect for children who needed someone to care about them. At the moment there were two cottages but the foundation for a third had been poured last week. The best part of the place was the fact it was on a ranch, not far from town. The barn housed abandoned animals that the children helped take care of. The wounded helping the wounded. She liked that idea.

Before she went in search of the couple, she needed to check on Andy and the other seven children in the house where she lived. Meg, her assistant at the cottage and the cook, should be inside since the kids had come home from school an hour ago.

Ten minutes later, after satisfying herself that everything was fine, Hannah trekked across the pasture toward the Stones' place. When she passed in front of the large red double doors thrown open to reveal the stalls inside, she heard a woman's light laugh followed by a deeper one. She changed her direction and entered the coolness of the barn. In the dimness, she saw both Laura and Peter kneeling inside a pen with several puppies roughhousing on the ground in front of them.

"We're going to have a hard time not keeping these."

Peter gestured toward the animals that had to be a mix of at least three different breeds.

Laura angled her head toward him. "What's another puppy or two or three when we have so many? They're adorable."

"Are you going blind, woman?"

"Okay, they're so ugly they're cute." Laura caught sight of Hannah and waved her to them. "Don't you think they're cute?"

Hannah inspected the black, brown and white puppies with the elongated squat body of a dachshund, the thick, wiry coat of a poodle and the curly tail and wrinkled forehead of a pug. *Ugly* was an understatement. "I can see their attraction."

Peter's laughter reverberated through the cavernous barn. "I meant that we would have a hard time finding homes for them since they are so—unattractive."

"But that's their appeal. They're different, and you and I love different." Laura stood, dusting off her jean-clad knees.

He swept his arm in a wide arc, indicating the array of animals that had found a refuge at the ranch along with the children. "That's for sure."

Laura stepped over the low pen and approached Hannah. "I heard about Andy. Is he okay?"

"Yes. Broken left forearm. He told me he'd wanted to climb to the very top of that elm tree you have outside the barn."

Laura chuckled. "I've found my twins up there more than once." She glanced back at Peter. "Maybe we should cut it down."

"And rob the kids of a great tree to scale? No way! We'll just have to teach Andy the art of climbing."

"There's an art to climbing trees?" Hannah watched as Peter came up to Laura's side, draped his arm over her shoulder and cradled her against him. Wistfulness blanketed Hannah—a desire to have her own husband and family. She'd almost had that once when she'd married Todd. Would she ever have that kind of love again? A home she would stay in for more than a year?

"Of course. The first rule is to make sure you have good footing before you reach up. I'll talk with Andy."

"He's gonna be in a cast for a few months."

"When he's ready, I'll show him how to do it properly." Peter nuzzled closer to Laura.

"I'm sorry I didn't realize he wasn't on the school bus. If I had, he would—"

Laura shook her head. "Don't, Hannah. Boys will be boys. I have three, and believe me, I know firsthand there's little we can do when they set their minds to do something. I gather you took him to see Jacob."

The name stiffened Hannah's spine. "Yes. He got Andy in to see Dr. Filmore, who put the cast on him."

"We don't know what we would do without Jacob to take care of the children for free." Laura looked up at her husband, love in her eyes. "We've taken up more and more of his time as the refuge has grown."

"Wait until we open the third home. Before we know it, there'll be eight more children for Jacob to take care of." Peter shifted his attention to Hannah. "That should be after the first of the year. Are you going to be ready for the expansion?"

"I'm looking forward to it. The more the merrier." By

that time she would know how to deal with Jacob without her stomach tensing into a knot. And hopefully she would become good at masking her aversion because she could do nothing to harm the refuge.

"I knew there was a reason we hired you to run the place. I like that enthusiasm. I've got to check on a mare." Peter kissed his wife's cheek, then headed toward the back door.

"Don't blame yourself for Andy's accident." Laura pinned her with a sharp, assessing regard.

"I'm that obvious?"

"Yep." Laura began walking toward the front of the barn. "Kids do things. They get hurt. Believe me, I know with four children. The twins get into more trouble than five kids. I'm always bandaging a knee, cleaning out a cut."

Outside Hannah saw an old black car coming down the road toward them, dust billowing behind the vehicle. As it neared her, Hannah glimpsed Jacob Hartman driving. Even with him wearing sunglasses, she knew that face. Would never forget that face. She readied herself mentally as the car came to a grinding stop and Jacob climbed from it.

In her last year in college she had discovered the Lord, but she didn't think her budding faith had prepared her to confront the man responsible for her brother's death.

Chapter Two

Jacob's long strides chewed up the distance between him and Hannah. Her heartbeat kicked up a notch. Even inhaling more deep breaths didn't alleviate the constriction in her chest.

A huge grin appeared on his face. He nodded toward Laura, then his warm brown gaze homed in on Hannah. "It's good to see you again. How's Andy doing?"

Lord, help! When she had decided to come back to the town and settle down, she'd discovered Jacob Hartman still lived in Cimarron City and was a doctor, one of nine pediatricians, but why did he have to be involved with *her* children?

"Hannah, are you all right?"

His rich, deep-toned voice penetrated her thoughts. She blinked and focused on his face, his features arranged in a pleasing countenance that made him extra attractive—if she were interested, which she wasn't. His casual air gave the impression of not having a care in the world. Did he even comprehend the pain his actions caused?

"I'm fine." Hannah stuffed her hands into her pants pockets. "Andy's doing okay. He's going around, having everyone sign his cast. If any good has come out of the accident, I would say it has been an icebreaker for him with the others." When she realized she was beginning to ramble, she clamped her lips together, determined not to show how nervous and agitated she was.

Jacob's smile faded as he continued to stare at her. "I'm glad something good came out of it."

Tension invaded his voice, mirroring hers. She curled her hands in her pockets into fists and forced a grin to her lips as she turned toward Laura. "I'd better get back to the house. I just wanted to let you know about Andy. Good day, Dr. Hartman." If she kept things strictly formal and professional, she would be all right.

Hannah started across the pasture toward the refuge, the crisp fall air cooling her heated cheeks. Keep walking. Don't look back. She thought of her Bible in her room at the house and knew she needed to do some reading this evening when the children were settled in their beds. Somehow she had to make enough peace with the situation to allow her to do her job. She wanted what was best for the children and if that meant tolerating Dr. Hartman occasionally, then she could do it. The needs of the children came first.

"Do you get the feeling that Hannah Smith doesn't like me?" Jacob followed the woman's progress across the field.

Laura peered in the same direction. "There was a certain amount of tension. I just thought it was because of Andy's accident. I think she blames herself."

"I think it's something else." Jacob kneaded the nape of his neck, his muscles coiled in a knot. "Tell me about our new Stone's Refuge's manager."

"She just completed her bachelor's degree in social work from a college in Mississippi."

"What brought her to Oklahoma? The job?"

Laura laughed. "In our short existence we are garnering a good reputation but not that good so we can attract job candidates from out of state. She used to live here once and wanted to come back. She heard about the job from a classmate, who lives in Tulsa, and applied. Personally I think the Lord brought her to us. She's perfect for the job and beat every other candidate hands down."

"High praise coming from you."

"When the third house is finished, we're going to need someone highly organized and capable. We'll have almost thirty children, ranging in ages from five to eighteen. I'm hoping to bring in another couple like Cathy and Roman for the third home and eventually have one in the second cottage, too."

"What happens to Hannah Smith then? I understand she's living in the second cottage right now." He had heard and sensed Hannah's passion for her job earlier and agreed with Laura she would be good as the refuge's manager.

"We'll need someone to oversee all three homes. I can't do it and run the foundation, too. Raising money is a full-time job. If she wants to continue living on-site, we'll come up with something, but I'd like a man and woman in each cottage in the long run, sort of like a surrogate mother and father for the children."

He had pledged himself and his resources to the Henderson Foundation because he knew how lacking good care was for children without a home and family. "I'll do whatever you need."

"I want you to find out what's going on with Hannah. If there's something concerning you, take care of it. She's perfect for the job, and I don't want to lose her. You can charm the spots off a leopard."

"I think you've got me confused with Noah." He peered toward the group homes. "Are you sure there isn't something else I could do?" He wished he had the ease with women that Noah did. His foster brother rarely dated the same lady for more than a month while lately he had no time to date even one woman.

"Yeah, while you're over there, check and see how Andy is faring. I worry about him."

"You worry about all of them."

"Hey, I thought I heard your car." Peter emerged from the barn, a smile of greeting on his face. "What brings you out this way? Is someone sick?"

"Do I have to have a reason to pay good friends a visit?"

Peter slipped his arms around Laura's waist, and she leaned back against him. "No, but I know how busy you've been, and it isn't even flu season yet."

Watching Peter and Laura together produced an ache deep in Jacob's heart. He wanted that with a woman, but Peter was right. His work and church took up so much of his life that he hadn't dated much since setting up his practice two years ago. And you have to date to become involved with a woman, he thought with a wry grin. Maybe Noah could give him lessons after all.

Laura's gaze fastened on him. "Jacob's just leaving. He's going over to check on Andy."

A scowl descended over Peter's features. "Andy's situation is a tough one. His mother is fighting the state. She wants him back."

"To use as a punching bag." Jacob clenched his jaw. He couldn't rid himself of the feeling Andy and his situation were too similar to his own experiences growing up, as though he had to relive his past through the child. He'd been blessed finally to find someone like Paul and Alice Henderson to set him on the right path. "If at all possible, I won't let that happen." He needed to return the gift the Hendersons had given him.

"Stop by and have dinner with us when you're through. I want to discuss the plans for a fourth house."

"Peter, I love your ambition, but the third one isn't even half-finished." Jacob dug into his pocket for his keys.

"But maybe it will be by the holidays. What a wonderful way to celebrate Christ's birthday with a grand opening!"

"I can't argue with you on that one, but the weather would have to cooperate for that to happen and you know Oklahoma. When has the weather cooperated?" Jacob headed toward his car. He twice attempted to start it before he managed to succeed and pull away from the barn. He had a woman to charm, he thought with a chuckle.

Andy held up his cast. "See all the names I've gotten. All in green."

Hannah inspected it as though it were a work of art. "You even went to the other cottage."

"Yep, I didn't want to leave anyone out."

Because he knew what it was like to be left out, Hannah thought and took the green marker from Andy to pen her own name on the cast. "There's hardly any room left."

He flipped his arm over. "I had them leave a spot for you here."

Hannah wrote her name over the area above his wrist where a person felt for a pulse.

"I've saved a place for Dr. Jacob, too."

Andy's declaration jolted Hannah. She nearly messed up her last letter but managed to save it by drawing a line under her name. "You aren't going back to see Dr. Jacob. Dr. Filmore will be seeing you about your arm." She realized Jacob Hartman was at the barn talking with Peter and Laura, but hopefully he would leave without coming over here. She needed more time to shore up her defenses. The walk across the pasture hadn't been nearly long enough.

"He told me he would come see me. He'll be here. The others said he never breaks a promise."

That was just great! She was considering retreating to her office off her bedroom when the front door opened and the very man she wanted to avoid entered the cottage. His dark gaze immediately sought hers. A trapped sensation held her immobile next to Andy in the middle of the living area off the entrance.

"Dr. Jacob. You came! I knew you would." With his hand cradled next to his chest, Andy hurried across the room and came to an abrupt halt inches from the doctor. The boy grinned from ear to ear. "See all the names I have!" He held up the green marker. "Will you sign it?"

"Where?"

"Right under Hannah's."

"I'd be honored to sign your cast." Jacob again looked at her and said, "I'm in good company," then scribbled his signature on the plaster, a few of his letters touching hers.

The adoring expression on Andy's face galled her. If the boy only knew—Hannah shook that thought from her mind. She would never say anything. She couldn't dwell on the past or she would never be able to deal with Jacob in a civil way. She had to rise above her own anger if she was going to continue to work at Stone's Refuge and put the children's needs before her own.

Was she being tested by God?

She didn't have time to contemplate an answer. Kids flooded into the living room to see Dr. Jacob. In less than five minutes, every child in the house surrounded him, asking him questions, telling him about their day at school.

How had he fooled so many people? Maybe she was here to keep an eye on him. But in her heart she knew that wasn't the reason, because she couldn't see Peter and Laura having anyone but the best taking care of the foster children.

Jacob tousled Gabe's hair. "I see you've got your baseball. How's that throwing arm?"

"Great. You should see me." Gabe grasped Jacob's hand and tugged him toward the front door. "I'll show you."

Jacob allowed himself to be dragged outside, all the kids following. Hannah stepped out onto the porch and observed the impromptu practice in the yard. Laughter floated on the cooling air while the good doctor took turns throwing the ball to various children. They adored Dr. Jacob. She should be cheered by that thought, but Hannah couldn't help the conflicting emotions warring inside her.

If God had put her here to forgive Jacob, she had a long way to go.

"I thought I saw Jacob's car." Cathy, the other cottage mom, came up next to her at the wooden railing. "It's the ugliest—thing. I can't even call it a car. I sometimes wonder how he even makes it out here in that rolling death trap."

Hannah's fingernails dug into the railing. She hadn't even been able to see Kevin for one last time at his funeral because of how messed up he had been after the car wreck. Although seven of the children were running around and throwing the ball, all she could see was Jacob standing in the middle, smiling, so full of energy and life. Not a care in the world.

Before long several of the boys ganged up on him, and they began wrestling on the ground even though Jacob had on nice khaki pants and a long-sleeved blue cotton shirt. The gleeful sounds emphasized the fun the kids were having. But the scene was tainted by Hannah's perception of Jacob Hartman.

"He's so wonderful with them. If he ever decided to take time for himself, he might find a nice woman to marry and have a boatload of children. He'd make a great dad. Too bad I'm already spoken for."

Seizing the opportunity to turn her back on Jacob, Hannah swung her attention to Cathy. "To a very nice young man."

Her assistant smiled. "I know. Roman is the best husband."

"Where is he?"

"He went over to help Peter at the barn with one of the animals."

"It's nice he works at a veterinarian clinic."

"One day he hopes to go back to school to become a vet even if he's the oldest student in the class."

Hannah relaxed back against the railing, allowing some of the tension to flow from her body. The sounds of continual laughter peppered the air. "I was beginning to think that would be the case with me. It's hard working and going to college at the same time, but it's worth it when you do finally graduate."

"I almost forgot the reason I came out here. I passed through the kitchen and Meg said dinner will be ready in fifteen minutes." Cathy left, walking back to the other cottage next door.

Good. That should put an end to the doctor's visit. Hannah wheeled around and called out to the nearest two girls who were standing off to the side, watching the melee with the boys. "Let's get everyone inside to wash their hands for dinner."

Shortly the group on the ground untangled their limbs and leaped to their feet. They raced toward the door while Jacob moved slowly to rise, his shirttail pulled from his pants, his brown hair lying at odd angles. He tucked in his top and finger combed his short strands.

Andy, who had been standing off to the side watching the fun, shuffled toward Jacob, taking his hand. "Why don't you eat with us, Dr. Jacob?"

The too-handsome man glanced toward her. The child followed the direction of his gaze and asked, "Can he, Hannah?" When she didn't immediately answer, he quickly added, "He'd better check me out before bedtime to make sure I'm okay."

Having stayed behind, too, Gabe took Jacob's other hand. "Yeah. Don't forget you promised me the last time you were here that you'd read a story to me before I went to bed."

That trapped feeling gripped Hannah again. She really didn't have a reason to tell the man no, and yet to spend the whole evening with him wasn't her idea of fun.

Hannah shifted from one foot to the other, realizing everyone was staring at her, waiting for an answer she didn't want to give. She pasted a full-fledged smile on her face that she fought to maintain. "Sure, he can— if he doesn't mind hamburgers, coleslaw and baked beans."

He returned her grin. "Sounds wonderful to a man who doesn't cook. Meg can make anything taste great, even cabbage."

His warm expression, directed totally at her, tempted her cold heart to thaw. "Cabbage is good for you," was all she could think of to say.

"Yeah, I know, but that doesn't mean it tastes good."

"Yuck. I don't like it, either." Gabe puffed out his chest as though he was proud of the fact he and Dr. Jacob were alike in their food preferences.

"Me, neither." Andy followed suit, straightening his thin frame.

Jacob peered down at both boys. "But Meg makes it

taste great, and Hannah is right. It's good for you. I'll play a board game with you guys if you finish all your coleslaw. Okay?"

"Yes," the two shouted, then rushed toward the door.

Oh, great. The evening was going to be a long drawn-out affair with games and reading. Maybe she could gracefully escape to her room after dinner while he entertained the children. Hannah waited until he had mounted the porch steps before saying, "Nice recovery."

He gave her another heart-melting grin. "I keep forgetting how impressionable these children can be. They're so hungry for attention and love. I wish I had more time to spend with them."

No! Please don't! She pressed her lips together to keep from saying those words aloud. But she couldn't keep from asking, "Just how involved are you with the refuge?"

He chuckled. "Worried you'll have to be around me a lot?"

Heat scored her cheeks. Obviously she wasn't a very good actress, a fact she already knew. She forced a semi-smile to her lips. "I was curious. I just thought you were the refuge's doctor and that's all."

He planted himself in front of her. "I'm more than that. Peter, Noah and I were the ones who started this. Peter is the one in charge because he lives on the property, but I keep very involved. I'm on the foundation board. This project is important to me."

His words and expression laid down a challenge to her. "It's important to me, too." She took one step back. *He's on the foundation board. It's worse than I thought.*

"Why?"

Although the space between them was a few feet, Hannah suddenly had a hard time thinking clearly. A good half a minute passed before she replied, "I went into social work because I want to make a difference, especially with children who need someone to be their champion. Stone's Refuge gives me a wonderful opportunity to do my heart's desire." *If I can manage my feelings concerning you.*

"Then we have something in common, because that's why I'm involved with the refuge."

The idea they had anything in common stunned Hannah into silence.

The front door opened, and Gabe stuck his head out. "Dr. Jacob, are you coming?"

"Sure. I'll be there in a sec." When the door closed, he turned back to her, intensity in his brown gaze. "I sense we've gotten off on the wrong foot. Somehow we'll have to manage to work together. I won't have the children put in the middle."

She tilted up her chin. "They won't be."

"Good. Then we understand each other."

He left her alone on the porch to gather her frazzled composure. He was absolutely right about never letting the children know how she really felt about their "Dr. Jacob." She had two choices. She could quit the perfect job or she could stay and deal with her feelings about him, come to some kind of resolution concerning Jacob Hartman. Maybe even manage to forgive him.

There really is only one choice.

Trembling with the magnitude of her decision, Hannah sank back against the railing and folded her arms across her chest. She'd never run from a problem in the past, and she wasn't going to now. She didn't quit, either. But most of all, these children needed her. She had so much love to give them. A lifetime of emotions that she'd kept bottled up inside of her while she had been observing life go by her—always an outsider yearning to be included.

So there's no choice. Lord, I need Your help more now than ever before. I want this to work and I can't do it without You. How do I forgive the man who killed my brother, because I can't expose his past to the others? The children adore him, and I won't hurt them.

Jacob finished the last bite of his hamburger and wiped his mouth with his napkin. "So next week is fall break. What kind of plans do you all have for the extra two days off from school?"

Several of the children launched into a description of their plans at the same time.

He held up his hand. "One at a time. I think you were first, Gabe."

"Peter wants us to help him when he takes some of the animals to several nursing homes on Thursday."

"And there's a lot of work to be done on the barn expansion." Susie, the oldest child in this cottage, which housed the younger kids, piped up the second Gabe stopped talking.

"He's getting new animals all the time." Terry, a boy with bright red-orange hair, stuffed the last of his burger into his mouth.

Jacob laughed. "True. Word has gotten around about this place."

Nancy nodded. "Yep. I found a kitten the other day in the trash can outside."

Jacob caught Hannah's attention at the other end of the long table. "Do you have any activities planned that you need a chaperone for next week? Maybe I—"

"I think I've got it covered." She looked down at her plate, using her fork to stir the baked beans around in a circle as if it were the most important thing to do.

"I'm sorry, Hannah, I didn't get a chance to tell you I won't be able to go to the zoo with you on Friday." Meg, the cook and helper, stood and removed some of the dishes from the center of the table. "That was the only time I could get in to see the doctor about the arthritis in my knees."

Nancy's blond pigtails bounced as she clapped her hands. "Then Dr. Jacob can go with us!"

Hannah lifted her head and glanced from Meg to Nancy before her regard lit upon him. For a few seconds anxiety clouded her gaze. He started to tell her he didn't have to go when a smile slowly curved her lips, although it never quite touched her eyes.

"You're welcome to come with us to the zoo. It'll be an all-day trip. We leave at ten and probably won't get home until four." Her stare stayed fixed upon him.

The intensity in her look almost made Jacob squirm like Andy, who had a hard time keeping still. She might not have meant it, but deep in her eyes he saw a challenge. Determined to break down the barrier she'd erected between them, he nodded. "I'll be here bright and early next Friday, and I even know how to drive the minibus."

"That's great, since I don't think Hannah's had a

chance to learn yet. If you aren't used to it, it can be a bit awkward." Meg stacked several more plates, then headed for the kitchen.

"You can take that kind of time off just like that?" Hannah snapped her fingers.

"I always leave some time during a break or the holidays for the kids."

"Yep." Terry, the child who had been at the cottage the longest, stood to help Meg take the dishes into the kitchen.

"Well, then it's settled. I appreciate the help, especially with the minibus." Hannah rose. "Who has homework still to do tonight?" She scanned the faces of the eight children at the dining-room table.

Several of them confessed to having to do more homework and left to get their books.

Gabe, short for his nine years, held up his empty plate. "I ate all my coleslaw."

"Me, too." Andy gestured toward his as Susie took it.

"You two aren't part of the cleanup crew?" Jacob gave the girl his dishes.

Both boys shook their heads.

"Then get a game out, and I'll be in there in a minute."

"Can I play, too?" Nancy leaped to her feet. "I don't have to clean up."

Gabe frowned and started to say something, but Jacob cut him off with, "Sure you can."

Nancy, being in kindergarten, was the youngest in the house. Jacob suspected that and the fact she was a girl didn't set well with Gabe, and judging by Andy's pout, him, either. But Jacob knew the importance of bonding as a family and that meant every child, regardless of sex or age, should have an opportunity to play.

Gabe and Andy stomped off with Nancy right behind them, her pigtails swinging as she hurried to keep up. Jacob turned toward Hannah and noticed the dining-room table had been cleared and they were totally alone now. That fact registered on her face at the same time. Her eyes flared for a second, then an indecipherable expression descended as though a door had been shut on him.

"I'm glad we have a few minutes alone." The look of surprise that flashed into her eyes made him smile. "I forgot to tell you earlier that Andy's mother is fighting to get him back. Peter just found out today."

"She is?"

"And I'm not going to let that happen. I've seen his injuries." *I've been there. I know the horror.* "He's better off without her."

"If she cleans up her act and stops taking drugs, he might be all right going back home. In the short time I've been around him, I've seen how determined he is to get back there."

"He isn't better off if he returns to her. Believe me."

A puzzled look creased her forehead. "Then why does he want to go home?"

He shook his head slowly. "You're new at this. Take my word in this situation—he shouldn't go back to his mother. He's the caretaker in that family of two and he feels responsibility as a parent would. Certainly his mother doesn't."

Hannah's face reddened. She came around the side of

the table within a few feet of him. "How do you know this for a fact? Has Andy said anything to you?"

"No, I just know. I was in foster care for many years. I've seen and heard many things you've never dreamed of. Give yourself a year. Your attitude that the birth parent is best will change."

"I believe if it's possible a family should be together. Tearing one apart can be devastating to a child."

The ardent tone in her voice prodded his anger. His past dangled before him in all its pain and anguish. His heartbeat thundered in his ears, momentarily drowning out the sounds of the children in the other room. "Keeping a family together sometimes can be just as devastating." He balled his hands at his sides. "Why did you really go into social work?" he asked as though her earlier reason wasn't enough.

Her own temper blazed, if the narrowing of her eyes was any indication. "As I told you earlier, to help repair damaged families. But if that isn't possible, to make sure the children involved are put in the best situation possible."

His anger, fed by his memories, sizzled. Before he said anything else to make their relationship even rockier, he spun around and left her standing in the dining room.

The children's laughter, coming from the common living area, drew him. He needed that. For years he'd dealt successfully with the wounds of his childhood by suppressing them. Why were they coming to the surface now?

Lord, what are You trying to tell me? Aren't I doing

enough to make up for what I did? What do You want of me?

Jacob stepped into the room and immediately Gabe and Andy surrounded him and pulled him toward the table in front of the bay window where the game was set up. Nancy sat primly, toying with a yellow game piece. Her huge grin wiped the past few minutes from his mind as he took his chair between the boys.

He lost himself in the fun and laughter as the three kids came gunning for him. He kept being sent back to the start and loving every second of it. Until he felt someone watching him. Jacob glanced up and found Hannah in the doorway, a question in her eyes—as though she couldn't believe a grown man was having so much fun playing a kid's game. He certainly hadn't done much of this as a child.

Across the expanse of the living room that challenge he had sensed earlier reared up. If she was staying at the refuge as its manager, then he would have to find a way for this situation to work. He didn't want the kids to feel any animosity between him and Hannah. They'd had enough of that in their short lives. Before he left tonight, he would find out exactly why she was wary of him.

Chapter Three

Hannah stood in the entrance into the living room and observed the children interacting with Jacob. She hadn't intended to stay and watch them play, but for some reason she couldn't walk away. Jacob had a way with the kids, as if he knew exactly where they were coming from and could relate to them on a level she didn't know she would ever reach.

The bottom line: he was good with them. Very good.

When the trip to the zoo had come up at dinner, she hadn't wanted Jacob to come. Now though, she saw the value in him being a part of the outing.

A fact: if she stayed, Jacob would be in her life whether she wanted him to or not. She was a realist, if nothing else, and she would come to terms with her feelings concerning him for the children's sake.

Andy yawned and tried to cover it up with his palm over his mouth. When he dropped his hand away, however, his face radiated with a smile as Jacob directed a comment to him.

"Gotcha! Sorry but you've got to go back to the start,

buddy." Jacob triumphantly removed Andy's peg from its slot and put it at the beginning.

Gabe took his turn and brought one of his pieces home. He pumped the air and shouted his glee. "I've only got one more out. I'm gonna win!"

Hannah needed to check to see if the others were doing their homework. But she found she couldn't leave. There was something about Jacob that kept her watching—after years of hating the man for what he'd done to her family.

At Gabe's next turn he jumped up and pranced about in a victory dance as if he'd crossed the goal line. "I finally won!"

Andy tried to grin but couldn't manage it. Instead he blinked his eyes open wide and yawned again—and again.

Hannah entered the room. "Gabe, please put the game up. It's time for bed."

"But we haven't played enough." Gabe stopped, a pout pushing his lips out.

Jacob began removing the pegs from the board. "You'd better do as she says or I might not get to read you a story. If there's not enough—"

Gabe leaped toward the table and scrambled to put up the game. Andy's head nodded forward. Nancy stifled her own yawn.

Hannah made her way to Andy's side and knelt next to him. "Time for bed."

His head snapped up, his eyes round as saucers. "No. No, another game. I haven't won yet."

"Sorry. You'll have to wait for another day." Hannah straightened.

"Andy, I'll make you a promise, and you know I don't go back on them. The next time I'm here, we'll play any game you want." Jacob stood and moved to the boy, saying to Hannah, "Here, I'll take him to his room," then to Andy, "I think everything has finally caught up with you, buddy. You've been great! I can't believe you went this long. Most kids would have been asleep hours ago after the day you had."

As Jacob scooped up the eight-year-old into his arms and headed to the boys' side of the house, Andy beamed up at him, then rested his head on Jacob's shoulder.

After hurriedly putting the game away, Gabe raced to catch up with them. "We share a room."

Nancy looked sleepily up at Hannah. "I want a story, too."

"How about if I read one to you? You get ready for bed while I check on the others finishing their home-work."

Nancy plodded toward the girls' side while Hannah went back into the dining room where Terry and Susie were the only ones still doing their work. "How's it coming?"

Susie looked up, a seriousness in her green eyes. "We're almost done."

"Need any help?"

"Nope." After scratching his fingers through his red hair, Terry erased an answer to a math problem on his paper. "Susie had this last year in school. She's been helping me."

Leaving the two oldest children, Hannah walked to Nancy's room and found the little girl in her pajamas, stretched out asleep on her twin bed's pink coverlet.

Her clothes were in a pile on the floor beside her. Her roommate was tucked under her sheets, sleeping, too. Hannah gently pulled the comforter from under Nancy and covered her, then picked up the child's clothes and placed them on a chair nearby.

With the youngest girls in bed, Hannah made her way to the boys' side to see how Gabe and Andy were doing. The evening before, her first night in the cottage, both of them had been a handful to get to bed. Even with Andy half asleep, Jacob could be having trouble.

Sure, Hannah, she asked herself, *is that the real reason you're checking on them?*

At the doorway she came to a halt, her mouth nearly dropping open at the scene before her. Andy was in bed, lying on his side, desperately trying to keep his eyes open as he listened to the story Jacob was reading. The doctor lounged back against Gabe's headboard with the boy beside him, holding the book on his lap and flipping the pages when Jacob was ready to go on to the next one. Neither child was bouncing off the walls. Neither child was whining about going to bed. Jacob's voice was calm and soothing, capable of lulling them to sleep with just the sound of it.

Cathy is right. Jacob would make a good father.

That thought sent a shock wave through her. She took a step back at the same time Jacob peered up at her, the warmth in his gaze holding her frozen in place. For several seconds she stared at him, then whirled and fled the room. She didn't stop until she was out on the porch. The night air cooled her face, but it did nothing for the raging emotions churning her stomach.

How could she think something like that? For years

she had hated Jacob Hartman. In her mind he wasn't capable of anything good. Now in one day her feelings were shifting, changing into something she didn't want. She felt as though she had betrayed her family, the memory of her brother.

Her legs trembling, she plopped down on the front steps and rubbed her hands over her face. *Lord, I'm a fish out of water. I need the water. I need the familiar. Too much is changing. Too fast.*

She leaned back, her elbows on the wooden planks of the porch, and stared up at the half-moon. Stars studded the blackness. No clouds hid the beauty of a clear night sky. The scent of rich earth laced the breeze. Everything exuded tranquility—except for her tightly coiled muscles and nerves shredded into hundreds of pieces.

She'd lived a good part of her life dealing with one change after another—one move after another, the accidental death of her husband after only one year of marriage. She had come to Cimarron City finally to put down roots and hopefully to have some permanence in her life. *Instead I'm discovering more change, more disruption.*

"Hannah, are you all right?"

She gasped and rotated toward Jacob who stood behind her. So lost in thought, she hadn't even heard him come out onto the porch. She didn't like what the man was doing to her. She wanted stability—finally.

"I'm fine," she answered in a voice full of tension.

He folded his long length onto the step next to her. She scooted to the far side to give him room and her some space. His nearness threatened her composure. Leaning forward, he placed his elbows on his thighs and loosely clasped his hands together while he studied the same night sky as she had only a moment before. His nonchalant poise grated along her nerves, while inside she was wound so tightly she felt she'd break any second.

She didn't realize she was holding her breath until her lungs burned. She drew in deep gulps of air, suffused with the smells of fall, while grasping the post next to her, all the strain she was experiencing directed toward her fingers clutching the poor piece of wood.

He was no fool. He would want to know what was behind her cool reception of him. And she intended to keep her past private. After today she knew now more than ever the secret could harm innocent people—children. She couldn't do that for a moment of revenge. Their shared past would remain a secret.

"Have we met before this morning?" he asked, finally breaking the uncomfortable silence.

She sighed. This was a question she could answer without lying. "No." She was relieved that her last name was no longer the same as her brother's.

"I thought maybe we had, and I'd done something you didn't like."

"I've never met you before this morning." Which was true. Kevin and Jacob hadn't been friends long when the car wreck occurred. She felt as though she were running across a field strewn with land mines and any second she would step in the wrong spot.

"I get the feeling you don't care for…my involvement in the refuge."

Thank You, Lord. His choice of words made it possible for her not to reveal anything she didn't want to.

"I've seen how you interact with the kids this evening. They care very much for you. How could I not want that for them? They don't have enough people in their lives who do."

Jacob faced her. "Good. Because I intend to continue being involved with them, and I didn't want there to be bad feelings between us. The children can sense that. Gabe already said something right before he went to sleep."

"He did? What?"

Although light shone from the two front windows, shadows concealed his expression. "He wanted to know what we had fought about. He thought I might have gotten mad at you because Andy got hurt. I assured him that accidents happen, and I wasn't upset with you."

Hannah shoved to her feet. "I should go say something to him."

"What?"

"Well…" She let her voice trail off into the silence while she frantically searched for something ambiguous. "I need to assure him, too, that we haven't fought."

"By the time I left him he was sound asleep. I've never seen a kid go to sleep so fast. I wish I had that ability."

Had he ever lost sleep over what he did, as she had? "You have a lot of restless nights?" slipped out before she could censor her words.

He surged to his feet, and his face came into view. "I have my share."

The expression in his eyes—intense, assessing—bored into her. She looked away. "It's been a long second day. I need to make sure the rest of the children go to bed since they have school tomorrow. Good night."

She'd reached the front door when she heard him say in a husky voice, "I look forward to getting to know you. Good night, Hannah."

Inside she collapsed back against the wooden door, her body shaking from the promise in his words. Against everything she had felt over twenty-one years, there was a small part of her that wanted to get to know him. His natural ability to connect with these children was a gift. She could learn from him.

On the grounds at the Cimarron City Zoo Hannah spread the blanket out under the cool shade of an oak tree, its leaves still clinging to its branches. Not a cloud in the sky and the unusually hot autumn day made it necessary to seek shelter from the sun's rays. She'd already noticed some red-tinged cheeks, in spite of using sunscreen on the children. Susie, the last one in Hannah's group to get her food from the concession stand, plopped down on the girls' blanket a few feet from Hannah's.

Where were the boys and Jacob? She craned her neck to see over the ridge and glimpsed them trudging toward her. Jacob waved and smiled.

Terry hurried forward. "I got to see a baby giraffe! Giraffes are my favorite animal."

"I'm not sure I can pick just one favorite." Out of the corner of her eye she followed Jacob's progress toward her. He spoke to the guys around him, and they all headed toward the concession stand. "You'd better go get what you want for lunch." Hannah nodded toward the departing boys and Jacob.

Terry whirled around and raced after them. Ten minutes later everyone was settled on the blankets and stuffing hamburgers or hot dogs into their mouths.

Nibbling on a French fry, Hannah thought of the trip this morning to the zoo on the other side of Cimarron City with Jacob driving. Not too bad. She'd managed to get a lively discussion going about what animals they were looking forward to seeing.

Quite a few of the children had never been to a zoo and were so excited they had hardly been able to sit still in the minibus. Andy literally bounced around as though trying to break the restraints of the seat belt about him. Since his accident he had gone to school every day and the minute he returned to the cottage he would head to the barn to help with the animals. Last night he had declared to her at dinner that he wanted to be a vet and that he was going to help Peter and Roman with "his pets."

"May I join you?"

Jacob's question again took her by surprise. She swung her attention to him standing at her side. She glanced toward the other two blankets and saw they were filled with the children. "Sure." She scooted to the far edge, giving the man as much room as possible on the suddenly small piece of material.

"How are things going so far?" Jacob sat, stretching one long leg out in front of him and tearing open his bag of food, then using his sack as a large platter.

"Good. The girls especially liked the penguins and the flamingos."

"Want to guess where we stayed the longest?" Jacob unwrapped his burger and took a bite.

"The elephants?"

"Haven't gone there yet."

"We haven't, either."

"Why don't we go together after lunch? They have a show at one."

"Fine." Her acceptance came easier to her lips than she expected. He'd been great on the ride to the zoo. He'd gotten the kids singing songs and playing games when the discussion about animals had died down. Before she had realized it, they had arrived, and she had been amazed that the thirty-minute trip she had dreaded had actually been quite fun. "So where did y'all stay the longest?"

"At the polar bear and alligator exhibits. Do you think that means something? The girls like birds and the boys like ferocious beasts?"

Her stomach flip-flopped at the wink he gave her. Shock jarred her. Where had that reaction come from? "I had a girl or two who liked the polar bears. One wanted a polar bear stuffed animal."

"Let me guess. Susie?"

She shook her head. "Nancy."

He chuckled. "I'm surprised. She's always so meek and shy."

"She's starting to settle in better." Nancy had only been at the refuge two weeks longer than Andy, and being the youngest at the age of five had made her adjustment to her new situation doubly hard on her.

"That's good to hear," he said in a low voice. "Her previous life had been much like Andy's, except that her mother doesn't want her back. I heard from Peter this morning that she left town."

Hannah's heart twisted into a knot. How could a mother abandon her child? Even with all that had happened in her life, she and her mother had stuck together. "I always have hope that the parents and children can get back together."

Jacob's jaw clamped into a hard line. He remained quiet and ate some of his hamburger. Waves of tension flowed off him and aroused her curiosity. Remembering back to her second night at the cottage, she thought about his comments concerning Andy and his mother fighting to get him back. What happened to Jacob to make him feel so fervent about that issue? Was it simply him being involved with the refuge or something more personal? *And why do I care?*

For some strange reason the silence between her and Jacob caused her to want to defend her position. She lowered her voice so the children around them wouldn't overhear and said, "I was up a good part of the night with Nancy. I ended up in the living room, rocking her while she cried for her mother. It tore my heart to listen to her sorrow, and I couldn't do anything about it."

"Yes, you did. You comforted her. Her mother wouldn't have. She left her alone for days to fend for herself."

"But her mother was who she wanted."

"Because she didn't know anyone else better."

The fierce quiet of his words emphasized what wasn't being spoken. That this conversation wasn't just about Nancy. "But if we could work with parents, give them the necessary skills they need to cope, teach them to be better parents—"

"Some things can't be taught to people who don't want to learn."

"Children like Nancy and Andy, who are so young and want their mothers… I think we have to try at least."

"Andy wants to go home. He never said he wanted his mother. There's a difference."

Hannah clutched her drink, relishing the coldness of the liquid while inside she felt the fervor of her temper rising. "Maybe not in Andy's mind. Just because he doesn't say he wants his mother doesn't mean he doesn't. The biological bond is a strong one."

"Hannah, can we play over there?" Susie pointed to a playground nearby with a place to climb on as though a large spider had spun a web of rope.

All the children had finished eating while she and Jacob had been arguing and hadn't eaten a bite. A couple of the boys gathered the trash and took it to the garbage can while Terry and Nancy folded the blankets. "Sure. We'll be done in a few minutes."

"Take your time." Susie raced toward the play area with several of the girls hurrying after her.

When the kids had cleared out, Hannah turned back to Jacob to end their conversation, since she didn't think they would ever see eye to eye on the subject, and found him staring at her. All words fled her mind.

One corner of his mouth quirked. "Do you think she heard?"

Granted their words had been heated, but Hannah had made sure to keep her voice down. "No, but I'm glad they're playing over there." She gestured toward the area where all the children were now climbing on the spiderweb, leaping from post to post or running around. "While in college I helped out at a place that worked to find foster homes for children in the neighborhood where their parents lived."

"I'm sure that was a complete success." Sarcasm dripped over every word.

"Actually they had some successes and some failures, but those successes were wonderful. They went beyond just placing the children near their parents. They counseled the parents and tried to get help for them. While I was there, several made it through drug rehab and were becoming involved in their child's life again. The children still stayed in their foster home while the problems were dealt with, but the kids didn't feel abandoned by their parents. That went a long way with building up their self-esteem."

"What about the child's safety and welfare when that parent backslides and starts taking drugs or abusing alcohol again?" Jacob pushed to his feet and hovered over her.

His towering presence sent her heart hammering. She rose. "You can't dismiss the importance of family ties."

He glared at her. "I've seen too many cases where family ties meant nothing."

She swung her attention to the children playing five yards away, but she sensed his gaze on her, drilling into her. "Family is everything."

"I'm not saying family isn't important—when it is the right one. When it isn't, it destroys and harms a child."

She noticed Andy say something to a woman. "I can understand where you're coming—"

"Don't!"

Out of the corner of her eye she saw Jacob pick up the blanket they'd been on and begin folding it. When she looked back to the children, she counted each one to make sure everyone was there. Shoulders hunched, Andy, now alone, sat on a post and watched the others running around and climbing on the ropes.

Jacob came up to her side. "I was in foster care. I got over it and moved on."

"So these children will, too?"

"With our help."

Andy walked a few feet toward her and stopped. "Hannah, I'm going to the restroom."

"Sure, it's right inside the concession stand." She started toward the boy.

Andy tensed. "I can go by myself. I'm eight!"

"I'll just be out here on the porch waiting for you, then we're going to the elephant exhibit."

He grinned. "Great."

Five minutes later Jacob rounded up the children on the playground when Andy came out of the concession stand.

"I can't wait to see the elephants." The boy limped toward the large group heading toward the other side of the zoo.

Hannah took up the rear as they made their way to the elephant building. Inside, the kids dispersed to several different areas. Andy and Gabe crowded around the skeleton with another group. People packed the Elephant Enclosure with a few youngsters running around, shouting.

Jacob stared toward the entrance, a frown descending.

"What's wrong?"

He shook his head as though to clear it. "I thought I saw someone—" he scanned the area "—but I guess I didn't."

"Who?"

"Andy's mother."

Alarm slammed Hannah's heartbeat against her rib cage. "Let's get our children together." She began gathering the girls into the center of the exhibit.

One pair of boys joined the four girls. Hannah counted six. She searched for Jacob, Gabe and Andy. She found Jacob with Gabe off to the side of the skeleton. The fear and concern in the man's expression told Hannah something was wrong—very wrong. She corralled the kids near her and hurried toward the two.

"Where's Andy?"

Tears streaked down Gabe's face. "Andy told me to be quiet. Then he left with a lady."

Jacob leaned close to her and whispered, "It *was* his mother I saw. She has him."

Chapter Four

The fury in Jacob's words scorched Hannah. She stepped back and scanned the throng at the zoo, checking the exits. All the children were watching her. She schooled her expression into a calm one. When she faced Jacob again, his jaw clenched into an impenetrable line.

"I'll notify security. Keep the kids together." He didn't give Hannah a chance to say anything. He strode toward a man wearing a zoo uniform.

"Hannah, will Andy be all right?" Terry stood in front of the children as if he were their spokesman.

"He isn't with a stranger. He's with his mother. He'll be fine." She prayed she was right. "There's nothing to worry about. Let's go outside where it's less crowded." She took Nancy's and Gabe's hand and headed for the door nearest them.

As she left the building, she caught Jacob's attention and pointed toward the exit. The grim look on his face didn't bode well. *Lord, please bring Andy back to us safe and sound.*

Hannah sought a shaded area where she could keep an eye on the door into the Elephant Enclosure. The children circled her with Gabe off to the side. Tears ran down his cheeks. She drew him to her and draped her arm over his shoulder.

"I didn't…mean—" Gabe released a long sob "—to do anything wrong."

"Sometimes keeping a secret isn't a good thing."

Gabe looked up at her, fear invading his blurry gaze. "Am I in trouble?"

Hannah gave the boy a smile. "No." Then she surveyed the other six children and added, "But this is a good time to talk about what y'all should do if someone approaches you and wants you to go with them. Don't go without first checking with one of the staff at the refuge. Even if you know that person." She made eye contact with each child.

Susie broke from the circle and hurried past Hannah. "Dr. Jacob, did you find Andy?"

Hannah pivoted and saw relief in Jacob's expression as he nodded. The tautness in her stomach uncoiled. "Where is he?"

"Security has him and his mother at the front gate. I told them we'd be right there."

Hannah gathered the children into a tight group, then they headed toward the zoo entrance. A member of security waited in front of a building. The young man indicated a door for them to go through. Inside Andy sat in a chair with another security guard at a desk.

Hannah hurried to Andy and sat in the vacant seat beside him while the other children milled about the room, trying not to look at them. "Are you all right?"

Swinging his legs, Andy stared at his hands entwined together in his lap and mumbled, "Where's my mom?"

Hannah scanned the area and noticed Jacob talking with a man who appeared to be in charge. "I don't know."

He lifted his tear-streaked face. "They took her away."

"Who?"

Andy pointed toward the guard nearest him, his hand shaking. "One of them."

Hannah patted his knee. "Let me find out what's going on. Stay right here."

His head and shoulders sagged forward. "I want to see my mom." He sniffed. "She came to see me."

The quaver in the child's voice rattled Hannah's composure. All she wanted to do was draw him into her arms and hold him until the hurt went away. Instead she rose and crossed the room to Jacob and the security guard by the desk.

Susie approached. "Is Andy all right? Can we help?"

"He'll be fine. And if you can keep the others quiet and together over there—" she waved her hand toward an area off to the side " —that would be great."

"Sure. I'll get Terry to help me." The young girl hurried to her friend and whispered into his ear.

As Susie and Terry gathered the children into a group and lined them up along the wall, Hannah stopped near Jacob by the desk. "Where's Andy's mother?"

"Security has called the police for me. They're on their way. She violated a court order. She can't see Andy unless it's a supervised visit arranged ahead of time."

Hannah glanced over her shoulder to make sure Andy—for that matter, the other children, too—hadn't heard what Jacob said. Thankfully he'd kept his voice low. The boy continued to look down at his hands. "Andy wants to see her."

"No!"

Although whispered, the force behind that one word underscored Jacob's anger. From the few comments he'd made, Hannah wondered what was really behind his fury. She moved nearer in order to keep their conversation private, aware of so many eyes on them. "She's still his mother. We could be in the room with them to make sure everything is all right."

He thrust his face close. "I won't have that woman disrupt his life any more than she already has by pulling this stunt."

She met his glare with her own. "I am the manager at the refuge, and I do have a say in what is done with the children."

Jacob started to speak but instead snapped his jaw closed.

"I'll talk with Andy's mother first and see what prompted this action today."

"It won't do any good. She doesn't deserve a child like Andy."

There were so many things she wanted to retort, but she bit the inside of her mouth to keep her thoughts quiet. It was important that Andy not realize they were arguing over him. "Beyond that day in your office, have you had any contact with the woman?"

His eyes narrowed. "No."

"Then let me assess the situation." Again she sent a quick glance toward Andy then the other seven kids to make sure they weren't hearing what was said. "If

I don't think her intentions are honorable, I won't let her see Andy. Deal?" She presented her hand to seal the agreement.

Jacob looked at it then up into her face. His fingers closed around hers, warm, strong. "Deal. But I want you to know I don't think this is a good idea."

She wasn't sure it was, either, but for Andy's sake, she needed to try. Maybe there was a way to salvage their family if the mother was trying this hard to see her son.

"Where's Andy's mother?" she asked the head of security, not sure that Jacob would have told her.

The man pointed toward a door at the end of the hall where another guard stood. She made her way down the short corridor, stopping for a moment in front of Andy to give him a reassuring smile. His tear-filled eyes reinforced her resolve to try and make this work for him.

At the door she paused and peered back. Jacob's sharp gaze and the tightening about his mouth emphasized his displeasure at what she was attempting. Then she swung her attention to Andy, and the hopefulness she saw in his expression prodded her forward.

Lord, let this work. Help me to reach Andy's mother somehow.

When Hannah entered the room, she found Andy's mom sitting at a table, her head down on it as though she was taking a nap. The sound of the door closing brought the woman up, her gaze stabbing Hannah with fury.

"You don't have no right to take my son away. I wanna see Andy."

Calmness flowed through Hannah. She moved to the table and took the chair across from Andy's mother.

"I'm Hannah Smith, the manager at Stone's Refuge where your son is staying." She held her hand out.

The young woman glared at it, then angled sideways to stare at the wall.

"Mrs. Morgan, Andy wants to see you, but I want to be assured that you won't upset him and cause a scene."

Again her angry gaze sliced to Hannah. "He should be with me. This ain't none of your business. He's my son!"

Hannah assessed the woman, focusing on her eyes to try and discern if she was on any drugs. Other than anger, she didn't see anything that indicated she was high. "The court has taken Andy away from you and is reviewing your parental rights. You may see Andy when you make prior arrangements with his case manager. You can't see him alone."

Some of the anger leaked from her expression. "I just wanna see my baby. I shouldn't have to ask for permission. I haven't taken no drugs in days."

"That's good. Would you consider going into a rehab facility?"

Her teeth chewed on her lower lip. "Yes. Anything. Will I get Andy back then?"

"That isn't my decision. It will have to be the court's. But it will be a step in the right direction." Hannah folded her hands on the table, lacing her fingers together. "How did Andy get hurt the last time you were with him?"

Tears sprang into the young woman's eyes. "It was an accident. He fell and hit his head." Her gaze slid away from Hannah.

"Why did he fall?"

Silence. Andy's mother bit down hard on her lip.

"If I'm going to help you, I need to know everything. I need the truth."

The young woman opened her mouth to speak, but clamped it closed without saying anything. The indentation in her lower lip riveted Hannah's attention. When she finally peered into Andy's mother's eyes, a tear rolled down her cheek.

"If you're serious about being in Andy's life, you have to trust me."

The lip with the teeth marks quivered. "My boyfriend pushed him away." More tears welled into Andy's mother's eyes and fell onto the table.

"Why did he do that?"

Mrs. Morgan dropped her head, much as Andy often did. "Because he was hitting me and Andy wanted to stop him."

"I see."

Her head jerked up. "No, ya don't! He didn't want me to take him to the doctor. Andy was throwing up. When my boyfriend passed out, I brought my baby to see Dr. Hartman. That's when everything went bad. They took Andy from me. I went home and my boyfriend had left me. He's—he's— I'm all alone." She swiped her trembling hands across her cheeks. "I don't—" she sucked in a shuddering breath "—wanna be alone."

"So all Andy's injuries were caused by this boyfriend?"

"Yes, yes, I'd never hurt my baby. Never!" Tears continued to flow from her eyes.

"But staying with your boyfriend did hurt your child."

"I know, but I don't have no money. I'm—" Andy's

mother sagged forward and cried. "I love Andy. I…"
The rest of the words were lost in the woman's sobs.

Hannah came around the table and touched her shaking shoulder. "Let's start with you talking to Andy. If that goes well, we can discuss the next step, Mrs. Morgan."

The woman lifted her head, rubbing her hands down her face. "My name is Lisa Morgan. I ain't never been married."

"How old are you?" Hannah went back to her chair.

"Twenty-three. I can't pay for rehab. I don't have no money." She dashed her hands across her cheeks then through her hair.

"Let me worry about that. When you think you're ready, I'll go get Andy."

Lisa straightened, smoothing her shirt. "I'm ready to see my baby."

Hannah pushed to her feet and headed for the door. She hoped she was doing the right thing, that Jacob was wrong. Lisa had been a child when she'd had Andy. Maybe she'd never had a break.

Out in the hall she motioned for Andy to come to her. She caught Jacob's regard over the heads of all the kids who had surrounded him in the security office. "We won't be long. Maybe the children would like to ride the train."

"Yeah!" several of them shouted.

"Can we?" Terry asked Jacob.

"Sure."

His gaze intent on her, Jacob crossed to her while she opened the door into the small room where Lisa was. Andy slipped inside. Out of the corner of her eyes, she saw the boy throw himself into his mother's outstretched arms and plaster himself against her. His cries mingling with his mother's could be heard in the hallway.

"This is a mistake," Jacob whispered while he peered inside at Andy and his mom.

"What if it isn't?" Hannah lifted her chin a notch. "I'm going to have security call the police back and tell them they don't have to come."

"She should be held accountable for breaking the court order." A steel thread weaved through each word.

"That will only happen if, as a member of the foundation board, you overrule me." She directed a piercing look at him. "Are you?"

He met her glare for glare while a war of emotions flitted across his face. Finally resignation won. "No, I'm not going to. But don't leave them alone together." He pivoted and strode to the group of children hovering around the head of security's desk, asking him tons of questions.

Hannah paused in the entrance into the room and said to the guard nearby, "Please call the police and tell them it isn't necessary to come." Then she went in and closed the door.

"Mom, when can I come home?" Andy pulled back from his mother. "I miss ya."

Lisa shifted in the chair until she faced her son, clasping his hands. "And I missed ya, too. I have some things to work out, but once I do, you'll be able to come home with me."

"When?"

Lisa shook her head. "I ain't sure." She slid her gaze

to Hannah, then back to her son. "I'm gonna do everything I can, but it'll be up to the judge when."

Andy puffed out his chest. "I'll tell him I want to come home. He'll listen to me."

"Baby, I'm sure he will, but I hafta do a couple of things before we go in front of the judge. Then ya can tell him what ya want. Okay?"

Andy frowned. "I guess so."

"Good. I know I can count on ya, baby." Lisa drew her son to her and held him tightly.

Emotions clogged Hannah's throat. She swallowed several times before she said, "Andy, I'm sure we'll be able to arrange for your mother to come see you at the refuge. You can show her your room. She can meet your friends."

Hope flared in the boy's expression. "Yes. How about tomorrow?"

Hannah rose. "Let me see what I can arrange, Andy. It may have to be some time next week."

The light in his eyes dimmed. "Promise?"

"I can promise you I'll do everything I can to make it happen." *Please, Lord, help me to keep that promise.*

Jacob leaned into the railing on the porch of the cottage and stared up at the crystal clear night sky, littered with hundreds of stars. The cool fall air soothed his frustration some as he waited to speak with Hannah after the children were in bed. He didn't want to have this conversation where the kids might overhear.

Not only didn't Lisa Morgan get hauled down to the police station for defying a court order, but now Hannah was making arrangements for the woman to see Andy here at the refuge. Dinner, no less, in two nights! And worse, she'd persuaded Laura and Peter to go along with this crazy plan of hers.

The sound of the front door opening and closing drew Jacob up straight, but he didn't look at Hannah. He kept his gaze glued on the stars.

Lord, give me the right words to convince Hannah of the folly of getting Andy and his mother together except in a courtroom.

"You wanted to talk to me." Hannah moved to the other side of the steps and leaned against the post. "I'm tired so can we make this quick."

He clenched the wooden railing. Patience. He faced her, a couple of yards between them, her expression hidden in the shadows of evening, although Jacob didn't need to see her to imagine her glower. "We need to talk about Andy and his mother."

"No, we don't. You may be on the board, but I was hired to be the manager." She pushed away from the post, her posture stiff. "That means I run the refuge. I have Peter and Laura's support."

Which he intended to change the first opportunity he got a chance to speak with them. "And what happens when Lisa Morgan takes Andy again and harms him. Or comes to the cottage on drugs. Or lets her son down by not showing up when she's supposed to."

"She isn't the one who hurt Andy. It was her boyfriend, who isn't around anymore."

"She allowed it to happen. That's the same thing in my book."

"One of the calls I placed this afternoon was to a

drug-rehab facility. I got her in. She can start the program next week."

Jacob snorted. "So she goes through the motions of getting clean, and the second she gets Andy back she's taking drugs again and hooking up with that boyfriend or some other who is equally abusive to Andy." As much as he tried to keep visions of his past from flashing across his mind, he couldn't. The first time his mother had come out of drug rehab, he'd had such hope that she would stay clean. She'd lasted one whole day. He could still remember as if it were yesterday finding her passed out on the floor in the living room. "Then where does that leave Andy?"

"I have to try."

"Why?"

"Andy loves his mother. He wants to be with her. He told me he called her to come to the zoo." She could never share the pain she had gone through when her family had fallen apart. Even though it was under different circumstances and she had continued to live with her mom, she'd essentially lost her that day her older brother was killed. And the person responsible stood in front of her. She tamped down on the words of anger she suddenly wanted to shout at him. They would do no good. She needed to learn to work with this man—somehow.

"He'll get over it."

Hannah drew in a sharp breath. "How can you say something like that?"

"Because I did."

His whispered words hung in the air between them.

Did she hear him right? She stepped closer. "What did you say?"

He pivoted away from her, gripping the railing. "My mother was like Lisa Morgan. On drugs. Nothing else was important to her. Certainly not me. Or where the rent and food money was going to come from. And when she didn't have enough money for her drugs, she took her frustration out on me with a fist or a belt."

Her anger disintegrated at the anguish in his voice. She wasn't even sure he was aware of it lacing each word. A strong impulse to comfort inundated her. She held her ground for a few seconds before she covered the distance between them to stand next to Jacob.

"I'm sorry," she whispered, meaning it. She caught a glimpse of his expression in the moonlight. Painful memories etched deep lines into his face as though he was reliving his past.

Finally as if he realized he had an audience to witness his agony, he blinked and shook his head. "I don't need your pity. All I want from you is to put a stop to getting Andy together with his mother."

As though she had no control over her actions, she lay her hand on his arm. "I can't. Andy is so excited about his mother coming to dinner."

He jerked away. "What you mean is, you won't! You want to try some little social experiment to see if it works." He thrust his face close to hers. "You're experimenting with a young boy's life."

Hannah stepped back. "And you're not? What happened to you was a tragedy, but that doesn't mean it will happen to everyone in the same situation. What if Lisa can successfully kick the habit? Wouldn't Andy be better off with his mother rather than in the foster-care system, possibly never adopted? We owe it to him to try."

"We owe him protection and a quality life."

"I'm not going into this with my eyes closed. I know what can happen and I plan to be there every step of the way."

"And I plan on being here, too. Plan to have another person at dinner on Sunday night."

"Fine. You're welcome to come here anytime." The second she said it she wanted to take it back. That meant she would see him more than an occasional call to the doctor's office or a social visit from him to see the children every once and a while.

"Good, because I'll be here a lot."

Her earlier exhaustion assailed her. Her legs weak, she sank down onto the steps. Her emotions had taken a beating today, and it looked as if it wouldn't be over with for a long time. Again she thought about walking away from the job, but then she remembered Andy's huge smile at bedtime because his mother was coming to visit him in a few days. He'd already started cleaning his room so it would be perfect for her.

"You know, I'm not going into this lightly. I told you about my involvement in a program where the children lived in the same neighborhood as their parents and saw them frequently in supervised situations. The program also worked with the parents, helping them address whatever forced the state to take their children, whether it was anger management, drug or alcohol abuse."

He sat next to her. "And what was the success rate?"

"Thirty to forty percent."

"What happened to the sixty or seventy percent it didn't work with?"

"Other arrangements were made for them. No one was left in a bad situation."

"That you know of."

"The program had long-term follow-up built into it. When I interviewed with Laura and Peter, they knew my desire to try something like that here."

His expression displayed surprise. "They did?"

"We need to explore all opportunities for the children. One is trying to get them back with their parents. Do you feel every child in the foster-care system should never go back home?"

"No."

"Then why are you against this?"

He closed his eyes for a few seconds. "Because Andy could be me."

"But he isn't."

"That remains to be seen." Jacob shot to his feet and dug into his pocket for his keys. "I'll be here Sunday." He stalked toward his old car in front of the cottage.

She sat on the porch step watching him drive away, stunned by what she had discovered about the person she had grown up hating. He had been abused. It didn't change what he had done to her brother, but it did alter her feelings. It was hard to look at him and not see what he must have gone through as a child.

She thought about a sermon she'd heard a few months ago about being careful not to judge another. How could we know what that person had gone through unless we walked in his shoes? Until this moment she hadn't really contemplated its true meaning.

Chapter Five

"You're early for dinner." Hannah glanced up from reading the paperwork needed for Lisa's rehab facility.

Jacob fit his long length into the small chair to the side of her desk. "I promised some of the kids I'd play touch football. The day has turned out to be great so here I am." He spread his arms wide.

Indeed, he was, looking ruggedly handsome with tousled hair and warm brown eyes. "Who?"

"Some of the older boys in the other cottage, but Gabe and Terry want to play, too."

"Is that safe?" She stacked the papers to the side to give to Lisa later.

He grinned, his two dimples appearing. "I'll protect them. They've always watched before, but both boys love football so I said yes."

"Still...aren't they a little young to play?"

He pushed to his feet, giving her a wink. "I promise they will be fine, and you know I don't break a promise."

"You can't control everything."

The merriment in his eyes died. "I, more than most, realize that. Your life can change instantly and take you in a completely opposite direction than you ever imagined." He headed for the door. "I'm going to have a few words with the older guys about making sure Gabe and Terry have fun but aren't hurt." He peered back at her. "Okay?"

"Yes," she said as he disappeared out into the hall.

She had a report to read, but maybe she should go watch the game just in case something unforeseen happened. *Yeah, right. Is that the only reason?*

She had to admit to herself that since Friday night, when Jacob had told her something about his childhood, she hadn't been able to get the man out of her mind. And only a moment before he'd referred to life changing so quickly. Perhaps he hadn't walked away from the wreck unscathed.

She left her office and went in search of the touch-football game. She found a group of kids in the area between the two cottages and among them was Jacob giving instructions on the rules. Gabe and Terry, smaller than the other boys, flanked Jacob. How good he was with the children was reconfirmed as she watched.

"Will Terry and Gabe be all right?" Susie asked, coming to Hannah's side with Nancy.

"Dr. Jacob told me they would be."

"Then they will. Good. I wouldn't want anything to happen to them. Terry wants to try out for the basketball team at school and tryouts are next week."

"He didn't say anything to me. When?" She shouldn't be surprised Susie knew before her. The young girl was a mother hen to the kids in the cottage.

Susie shrugged. "He probably forgot. It isn't until Thursday after school."

Nancy tugged on Hannah's hand. "I'm gonna be a cheerleader. Susie taught me some cheers."

Hannah scanned the children assembled. "Where's Andy? I thought he would be out here in the thick of things, even if he can't play."

"He's cleaning his room—again." Susie clapped as the two teams lined up, with Nancy mimicking the older girl's action.

"I'll go check on him and get him to come out here." Hannah hurried toward the house. She didn't want to miss the game—in case there was a problem. *Yeah, sure. You're fooling yourself again. Jacob Hartman is the reason you're out here and not inside reading that report you need to go through.*

In the cottage she discovered Andy folding his clothes in his drawer and having a hard time with only one hand. "Hey, there's a big game being played outside. Dr. Jacob is here and in the middle of it."

"I know. But my room isn't clean enough." Andy attempted to refold the T-shirt.

Hannah surveyed the spotless area. She walked to Andy and took the piece of clothing. "You want to talk?"

"Nope. I've got to get this done." He averted his gaze.

"This looks great."

"It isn't good enough yet."

She thought about leaving him alone, but the quaver in his voice demanded her full attention. She drew him around to face her. "Andy, I won't lie to you. You can't do anything else to this room to make it better. I wish all the children's bedrooms were this clean."

"But—but it's got to be perfect for Mom."

"Why, hon?"

"Mom needs to know I can keep our place clean."

Hannah tugged Andy to the bed and sat with him next to her. "Then she will know. Why do you feel that way?"

"'Cause—" he sniffled "—'cause her boyfriend got mad at me for leaving the cereal out. He started to hit me when she came in between us. He hurt her instead."

She settled her arm along his shoulders. "He moved out so you won't have to worry about him."

Sniffing, Andy wiped his sleeve across his face. "But he could come back. He's left before and come back."

Hannah hugged the boy to her. "Let's not worry about that right now. I want you to have a good time showing your mother around and introducing her to your friends." She stood. "C'mon, let's see what everyone else is doing."

Andy remained seated. "Can I tell ya a secret?"

"Sure."

"He gave Mom money to live on. She's tried some jobs, but they never last long. Do you think if I get a job it'll help? 'Course, I can't quit school. Mom didn't finish, and she told me how important it is I do."

Staring down at Andy, Hannah felt she was talking to a little adult. Her heart broke at the worry and seriousness she saw in the boy's eyes. "Tell you what. If you promise me you won't worry about finding a job, I'll help your mother find one after she gets out of drug rehab. Okay?"

"You will?" Joy flooded his face as he leaped to his feet. "That would be so good!"

She held out her hand. "Let's go see what's going on outside."

As they strolled toward the yard between the cottages, Hannah mulled over what Andy had told her. She knew Lisa wasn't well educated from the way she talked. Getting her help with her drug problem was only the beginning of what Lisa and Andy would need if reuniting the family were going to work. She hadn't really thought beyond getting Lisa through a drug-rehab program. Maybe she was naive. Jacob certainly thought so.

I'm just going to have to prove him wrong.

Outside, Hannah positioned herself on the sidelines of the makeshift football field with Andy on one side and Nancy on the other. Watching Jacob playing with the children, Hannah decided he was a big kid at heart. The laughter and ribbing filled the cool fall air. Before she knew it the sun began to slip down the sky toward the western horizon.

"Shouldn't Mom be here by now?" Andy asked as the losing team shook hands with the winners.

Hannah checked her watch. "She's only a few minutes late." *Please, Lord, let Lisa show up. If she doesn't...* Hannah didn't have any words to express her regret if the woman didn't come.

Jacob jogged toward her, his shirttail hanging out of his jeans, some dirt smudges on his face, his hair tousled even more than usual where some of the children tackled him to the ground at the end. Gabe and Terry had hung back until all the bigger kids were on the pile, then they joined the others on top.

Jacob peered toward the road that led to the cottages

and mouthed the words, "Not here?" so that Andy, who was staring at the same road, wouldn't hear.

She shook her head. "Everyone needs to clean up. Dinner is in an hour." She eyed Jacob and his smudges. "Including you."

"I brought an extra shirt in case something like this happened, which it does every time." With a wink, he loped toward his car.

"What if something happened to Mom?"

Hannah put her hands on Andy's shoulders and pulled his attention away from the road by blocking his view. "We have an hour until we eat. Don't you know women are notorious for being late to important events. We have to make our grand entrance."

"Ya think that's it?"

I hope so. "Yes," she said, and sent up another prayer.

She and the children walked toward the cottage as Jacob joined them, carrying his clean shirt. He slipped into the house ahead of them and made his way to the bathroom off the kitchen. The kids dispersed to their bedrooms to clean up. Hannah stood in the foyer with Andy, Nancy and Susie.

The boy glanced back at the front door. "I'm gonna wait out on the porch."

After Andy left, Hannah said to Susie, "Will you make sure everyone really cleans up? I'll be outside with Andy."

"Sure. I hope his mother comes. He's been so excited." Susie took Nancy's hand to lead her back to the bedrooms.

Nancy stuck her thumb into her mouth and began to suck it. Hannah watched them disappear down the hall, wondering why the five-year-old was sucking her thumb. She hadn't seen that before, and it now worried Hannah.

Out on the porch Hannah eased down next to Andy on the front steps. He cradled his chin in his palm and stared at the road. Her heart contracted at the forlorn look on the boy's face. *Maybe Jacob is right. I should have left well enough alone.*

She searched her mind for something to make the situation better when she heard the door open and close. She glanced back at Jacob, who came to sit on the other side of Andy. She saw no reproach in Jacob's expression, which surprised her. Lisa was a half an hour late, and a lot of people would now be gloating about how she had been wrong.

"You know, I want a rematch tonight. I can't let Gabe's win stand. Want to join us in the game, Andy?" Jacob lounged back, propping himself up with his elbows and appearing as though he had not a care in the world.

Until you looked into his eyes, Hannah thought, *and glimpsed the worry deep in their depths.*

"Can Mom play, too?"

It took Jacob several heartbeats to answer, "Sure." But again nothing was betrayed in his expression or tone of voice.

Andy jumped to his feet. "Look! She's coming." He pointed toward a woman walking down the road toward the cottage.

Before Hannah could say anything, the boy leaped off the steps and raced toward his mother. Relief trembled through Hannah at the sight of the woman. Lisa scooped up Andy into a bear hug, then looped her arm around him.

"She came," Hannah murmured, tears smarting her eyes.

The silence from Jacob electrified the air. She resisted the urge to look at him and instead relished this step forward in Andy and his mother's relationship. *Maybe my plan will work after all. Thank you, Lord.*

"I'm glad she's here," Jacob finally said, straightening.

When Hannah peered at him, relief replaced the worry in his gaze as he observed the pair make their way toward him. She realized in that moment that he wanted what was best for Andy, even if he was wrong. They didn't agree what was best, but they had a common goal: Andy's safety and happiness. There was a part of her that was unnerved that she would have another thing in common with Jacob, but she couldn't deny it. In that moment she felt close to him, and that sensation surprised her even more than his earlier lack of reproach.

Hannah brushed her hand across her cheek and rose as mother and child approached. "It's so good to see you, Lisa, but how did you get here?"

Lisa stopped at the bottom of the steps with Andy cradled against her side. "I walked from the bus stop."

"That's two miles away." She couldn't believe she hadn't thought about the fact that Lisa might not have transportation out to the farm.

Andy's mother grinned. "I need to get in shape. It took me a bit longer than I thought." She splayed her hand across her chest. "I had to rest about halfway. But I'm here now."

Hannah stepped to the side. "Welcome to Stone's Refuge. The children are waiting inside to meet you."

Andy took his mother's hand and led her into the house. Jacob nodded his head and indicated Hannah go through the entrance before him. She did and felt his gaze burning a hole into her back. She paused in the foyer to watch the children greet Andy's mother in the living room. The only one who didn't was Nancy. She hung back with her thumb in her mouth and her gaze trained on the floor by her feet.

"What's wrong with Nancy?" Jacob whispered into her ear.

Nearly jumping, Hannah gasped and spun around. She'd been so focused on Andy and his mother that Hannah hadn't heard Jacob approach from behind her. "Give a gal some warning."

"Sorry. I haven't seen Nancy sucking her thumb before. When did it start?"

"I think this afternoon. At least that's the first time I've seen it since I've been here."

Jacob frowned and peered at the little girl, still off to the side while everyone else was crowded around Andy and Lisa, all trying to talk at the same time. A dazed look appeared in Lisa's eyes.

Hannah moved forward. "Andy, why don't you give your mother a tour of the house and show her your bedroom? Dinner will be in half an hour."

En masse the group started for the back of the house. Except for Nancy. She stayed in the living room, continuing to stare at the floor. Hannah covered the distance between her and the little girl and knelt in front of Nancy.

"What's wrong?"

With thumb still in her mouth, Nancy shook her head.

"Are you sure I can't help you with something?"

She nodded, hugging her arms to her, her eyes still downcast.

"Well, I sure could use someone to help me set the table. Will you, Nancy?"

"Yes," the child mumbled around her thumb.

"I'll help, too." Jacob came up to join them.

"Great. We'll get it done in no time." Hannah held out her hand for Nancy to take. She did.

Jacob flanked the little girl on the other side and extended his palm to her. She stared at it for a long second before removing her thumb from her mouth and grasping him. "Are you looking forward to going back to kindergarten tomorrow after your fall break?"

"My teacher's so nice. I'm gonna tell her about the zoo and the pla—mingos."

Hannah left Nancy and Jacob in the dining room while she went into the kitchen to get the place mats and dishes. Arms loaded, she backed through the swinging door and nearly collided with Jacob. Nancy giggled. He took the plates, set them on the table, then passed the mats to the girl.

"I'll do these while you put those down." Jacob gestured toward the mats held in Nancy's hands.

Hannah hurried back for the rest of the dishes. In ten minutes the dining-room table was set. She stood back with Jacob on one side and Nancy on the other. "We're a good team. Next time I need some help, I'll have to ask you, Nancy."

She peered up at Hannah, a question in her eyes. "How about Dr. Jacob? He helped."

"Yeah, a team has to stick together," Jacob said with a laugh.

"Him, too." The heat rose in Hannah's cheeks. The idea of them being a team wasn't as disturbing as she would have once thought.

Hannah examined the piece of paper Nancy held up. "I like your flamingo. Are you going to share it with your class tomorrow?"

The little girl nodded. "Just in case they don't know what one looks like."

"Well, they will now with this picture." Hannah tilted her head, tapping her chin with her finger. "You know, it seems I remember someone has a birthday coming up."

"Me!" Nancy pointed to herself. "I'll be six in four days."

"We'll have to think of something special to celebrate such an important birthday."

Shouts of victory permeated the living room. Hannah glanced toward the game table by the bay window.

Andy stood by his chair, pumping his good arm into the air and dancing around in a circle. "I won finally!"

"Why don't you take this back to your room and start getting ready for bed." Hannah handed the paper to Nancy.

"But I'm not tired."

"Tomorrow will be here soon enough."

As Nancy trudged from the room, Hannah rose and

walked to the table where Jacob sat with Andy, Gabe and Lisa playing a board game. Gabe began to set up the pieces again for another game.

"Sorry, guys. It's time for bed."

Moans greeted Hannah's announcement.

"But Dr. Jacob hasn't won yet," Gabe said, continuing to put the pieces on the board.

"Too bad. He'll have to win some other day."

Gabe pouted. "But—"

"Gabe, Hannah is right. This just means we'll have to play again at a later date." Jacob picked up the game box.

Andy jumped to his feet. "Mom, can you put me to bed?"

Lisa peered at Hannah. "If it's okay?"

"That's great. I'll help Jacob clean up while you two boys get into your pajamas." Hannah surveyed the other children in the room. "That goes for everyone." As the kids filed into the hallway, Hannah stopped Lisa. "May I have a word with you?"

"Andy, I'll be there in a sec." Lisa waved her son on.

"How are you getting home?" Hannah asked when the room emptied of children.

"Walking to the bus stop. The last one is at ten."

"I'll drive you home. I don't want you walking at night on the highway."

"I don't want ya to go—"

"I'll take you home. I have to go that way." Jacob boxed up the last piece of the game and put it in the cabinet.

Appreciation shone in Lisa's expression. "I won't be long. I'll go say good-night to Andy."

"I'll go with you." Jacob started after Andy's mother.

Hannah halted him. She waited until Lisa had disappeared from the room before asking, "Are you sure? I don't mind taking her. Meg is still here to watch the children. I won't be gone long."

"No, I need to get to know her better. This will be a good opportunity to see what her intentions are toward Andy."

"Maybe I'd better take her after all."

He chuckled. "Afraid I'll scare her away?"

"No."

"Good, because if I can then she shouldn't be involved with Andy and finding out now would be better than later."

Hannah's eyes widened. "You're going to interrogate her?"

He saw the concern in her gaze that quickly evolved into a frown. "No, I'll be on my best behavior. I offered because there really is no reason for you to drive her into town." Shrugging, he flashed her a grin. "I'm going that way."

"Just so you'll know, tomorrow I'm taking her to the rehab facility to begin the program. Don't frighten her away."

"Who, me?" He thumped his chest. "I'm wounded. I want it to work out for Andy. I just don't think it will." He held up a hand to ward off her protest. "But I'm willing to go along so long as Andy isn't hurt. The second he is—"

Hannah walked toward the entrance, cutting off his

words with a wave. "I have the child's best interest at heart, so you don't have to threaten me."

"Excuse me?"

She wheeled around at the door. "What are you going to do? Come riding in on your white steed and save the day?"

"Why, Ms. Smith, I do believe that's sarcasm I hear in your voice."

She put her hand on her waist. "I think we can agree on disagreeing about how to handle Lisa and Andy."

"Hey, I'm willing to give it a try. I behaved at dinner."

Her other hand went to her waist. "If you call behaving giving the poor woman the third degree, then, yes, you behaved like a perfect gentleman."

"Ouch! I do believe your barb found its mark." He flattened his palm over his heart. "I wanted to know how she was going to support Andy."

"I could have told you she doesn't have a job. I intend to find her one."

"You do?"

"Well, yes, when she's completed the drug-rehab program. Do you know of anyone who might hire her?"

"Not off the top of my head. But let's wait and see what happens in a few weeks before you go out pounding the pavement looking for a job for Andy's mom." He strode to her, gave her a wink and headed down the hallway. "You may not have to worry about it."

Jacob heard Hannah's gasp and chuckled. He enjoyed ruffling her feathers, so to speak. He expected Hannah to follow him to Andy's room, but when he stopped at the boy's door, she still hadn't come down the corridor. Disappointment fluttered through him.

Cradled against his mother, Andy sat on his bed in his pajamas, listening to her read a story. When she closed the book, Andy said, "Again."

Lisa glanced toward Jacob. "I have to go, but I'll be back."

"Promise."

"If it was just me, I would, but the judge makes the decisions now. I hope so." Emotions thickened her voice.

"I love you, Mommy." Andy threw his arms around her.

She kissed the top of his head, then stood. "I'm gonna get help, Andy. This time it'll work."

This time? As Jacob had thought, Lisa had gone through rehab before and it hadn't been successful. He backed away, not wanting Andy to see anything in his expression. But in his mind Lisa represented his mother and his concern skyrocketed.

Jacob waited in the front foyer for the woman to emerge from the back. She said goodbye to Hannah then approached him. He wrenched open the door and stepped to the side to allow Andy's mother to go first. When he glanced toward Hannah, her look communicated a plea for understanding, as though she could read the war going on inside of him.

After asking for Lisa's address, Jacob fell silent on the drive into town. Memories of his own mother assailed him. He'd known he would be reminded of his childhood when he chose to work with children in the foster-care system. He'd thought he was prepared and usually he was. But not this time. His grip on the steering wheel tightened.

Jacob pulled to the curb in an area of town that had seen better days. Trash littered the streets and even with the windows rolled up, a decaying smell seeped into the car. "You live around here?"

Lisa grasped the door handle. "No, but I can catch a bus on the corner."

He scanned the area and wondered who or what lurked in the darkness between the buildings. "I said I'd drive you home, and I meant all the way."

"But—"

His gaze fixed on a broken-out storefront window. A movement inside the abandoned building made him press his foot on the accelerator. "I can't leave you here. It's too dangerous. Where are you staying?"

Silence.

Jacob slid a glance toward Lisa who stared at her hands in her lap. "You were staying back there?"

She nodded.

"Where?"

"In one of the buildings."

"You're homeless."

"It was my boyfriend's place Andy and I was staying at. He came back last night and kicked me out."

"So now you don't have anywhere to live?"

"No."

When Jacob turned onto a well-lit street, he sighed with relief. "How did you get to the zoo?"

"By bus."

Jacob made another turn, heading into the heart of the city. "I'm taking you to a shelter that's run by a couple from my church. They're good people. You'll be safe there." Again he looked toward Lisa and caught the tears streaking down her cheeks. "Okay?"

"Yeah," she mumbled, and dropped her head.

Something deep in his heart cracked open when he glimpsed Lisa's hurt. "I'll let Hannah know where you're staying so she can come there to pick you up tomorrow."

Her sobs sounded in the quiet, and another fissure opened up in his heart. Conflicting emotions concerning Lisa and her situation swirled through him.

"Why are ya being so nice? Ya don't like me," Lisa finally said between sniffles.

"For Andy." Jacob pulled into a parking space at the side of the shelter in downtown Cimarron City near his church.

Lisa lifted her head. "I love my son."

"Enough to stop taking drugs?"

She blinked, loosening several more tears. "Yeah."

"I'll be praying you do." Jacob opened his door, realizing as he slid out of the car that he meant every word. He would pray for Lisa's recovery. In the past he'd always thought of the child, never the parent in the situation. He was finding out there were two sides to a story.

Inside the shelter connected to his church, Jacob greeted Herb and Vickie Braun. "Lisa needs a place to stay for the night."

"We've got a bed. I'll show you the way." Vickie gestured toward a hallway that led to the sleeping area.

As the two women left the large hall where the residents ate their meals, Herb slapped Jacob on the back.

"I wondered when we'd see you again. We've missed you down here."

"I've been so busy with Stone's Refuge and my practice."

"Eighteen children can keep you hopping. What you, Peter and Noah have done is great and definitely needed."

"We've appreciated you keeping an eye out for any children in need of a safe place to stay." Jacob walked toward the front door. "In a few months the third house will be finished."

"We'll take care of Lisa. She'll have a place to stay for as long as she needs it."

Back in his car Jacob rested his forehead on the steering wheel. He hadn't wanted to tell Herb the reason he didn't volunteer at the shelter, as many did from the church, was that it hit too close to home. There had been many times he had stayed in a shelter with his mother, but none were as safe and nice as this one. He'd comforted himself with financially supporting the place, but he knew now he should do something more. He needed to face his past and deal with it. He'd been running for a long time.

He started his car and drove toward his apartment near his practice. Emotionally exhausted, he plodded into the building and punched the elevator for his floor. Five minutes later, he plunked down on his bed and lay back, still fully dressed. He needed to get up and check his messages, then finish making some notes on a case, but a bone-weary tiredness held him pinned to the mattress. His eyes slid closed....

Darkness loomed before Jacob, rushing toward him.

"Let's go faster," Kevin said, turning the radio up louder, the music pulsating in the air.

"I can't see well." Jacob squinted his eyes as if that would improve his vision so he could see out the windshield better.

His friend shifted toward him until he spied the dashboard. "You're only going forty. What's the point taking Dad's car if we don't do something fun?"

"You're the one who wanted to come out here." Jacob's gaze swept the road in front of him, then the sides he could barely make out. Piles of snow still lined the highway.

"Yeah, so we could put the pedal to the metal. If you don't want to, I'll drive again."

To keep his friend quiet, Jacob increased the speed to forty-five but looked for a place to pull over so Kevin could drive. Suddenly he lost control of the car, the darkness spiraling around him. Screams pierced the quiet, sounds of glass breaking....

Jacob shot up in bed, sweat drenching him. His whole body shook from the nightmare that had plagued him for years—one of his punishments for surviving the wreck that killed Kevin.

Chapter Six

Hannah stared at the shelves full of medical books with titles that made her head spin. Why was she standing in the middle of Jacob's office waiting for him? She rotated around to grab her purse on the chair and leave before he came into the room. As she gripped the leather handle, the door opened, and she knew she was stuck.

"I was surprised to hear you were here." Jacob's smile wiped the weariness from his face. "I'm assuming everything is all right at the refuge or Teresa would have said something about it to me."

"Everything's fine. I just dropped Lisa off at the rehab center and wanted to stop by and thank you for finding a place for her to stay last night." Hannah released her strap and straightened. "I didn't realize she was living on the street. She didn't say anything to me about that."

"It was nothing. At this time of year Herb and Vickie always have a spare bed at the shelter. Now, if it had been winter, it might have been different."

"I should have figured something like that had happened to her when she mentioned she wasn't working. I'm learning." She attempted a smile that quivered. "At least she has a place to stay for the next few weeks."

"If she stays there." Jacob dropped a file on his desk, releasing a long sigh.

Exhaustion, etching tiny lines into his face, sparked her compassion. "Long day?"

"Nonstop since I arrived this morning. The beginning of the flu season."

"Don't mention that word to me. I have eighteen children to keep healthy. I know you gave them a flu shot, but that's not the only illness they can get."

"As I well know. You've got your work cut out for you." He leaned back against his desk and folded his arms over his chest.

"I think you're right."

His eyebrows shot up. "You're admitting I might be right. Hold it right there while I get my recorder and you can repeat it for the microphone."

"Funny. I could say the same thing about you. You think I'm naive and idealistic."

"You are, but the world needs all kinds of people."

"So they don't all have to be cynical and realistic?"

He thrust away from the desk. "I hope not or we are in big trouble. Are you hungry?"

"Why?"

"Now, that question sounds cynical." He grinned. "Because I am hungry, and I'd like to take you to Noah's restaurant for dinner."

"According to all the kids that's their favorite place to eat."

"According to Noah it's the best in the whole Southwest."

"Will your friend be there?"

"If he's not out on a date, he's usually there. He's worse than me about working all the time. The one on Columbia Street was his first restaurant so he has a soft spot for it." Jacob snatched his jacket from the peg on the back of the door and slipped it on.

"I know he's a board member of the Henderson Foundation, but I haven't met him yet." Hannah exited the office first, into the dim light of the hallway.

Jacob came up behind her. "I guess everyone skedaddled out of here the first chance they got. Did I tell you it has been a long, crazy day?"

"I believe you mentioned that fact." She was very aware they were probably the only two people left in his suite of offices.

His chuckle peppered the air, making Hannah even more conscious of the fact they were alone. She'd come by to thank him for helping Lisa, and now she was going to dinner with him. How had that happened? For a moment in his office she'd forgotten who Jacob was. She needed to remember it at all times.

Hannah hurried her step toward the outer door. When she emerged from the building, she headed for her vehicle. "I'll follow you. I'm not sure where the restaurant is."

"Fine." Jacob unlocked his car door and climbed inside.

While she dug her keys out of her pocket, Hannah listened to him try to start his engine. A cranking sound that grated down her spine cut into the silence, then nothing. Dead. She peered over her shoulder as he tried again. Frustration marked his expression as he exited his vehicle.

He strode to her. "I knew it was only a matter of time before she died. I was hoping to get a few more months out of her."

"Maybe you can get it fixed."

"That baby was my first car, and I need to say good-bye to her. Can I hitch a ride with you?"

"Sure." Why hadn't she brought the van? She stared at her very small car that practically forced people to sit on top of each other. "Do you still want to go to dinner?"

"A guy's got to eat, and if you could see my refrigerator, you'd take pity on me. I don't live too far from the restaurant or here. In fact, it'll be on your way to the refuge. If you need to get back, we can skip dinner and grab a quick bite at some fast-food joint."

A way out. She pushed the button to unlock her doors. "I don't have to be back at the refuge for a while. Laura relieves me on Monday to give me some time off."

"That's great." He walked around the back of her vehicle and slipped into the passenger seat. "After rushing around all day, it would be nice to kick back and have a relaxing dinner."

Oh, good. She blew her one chance to end the evening early. She didn't understand what was going on with her. A week ago she would have avoided any time spent in Jacob's company. But that was before she had gotten to know him better. Nothing was ever black-and-white and the gray areas were tripping her up.

Her car purred to life, and she pulled out of the parking lot onto the still-busy street. In the small confines she smelled his distinctive male scent, laced with a hint of the forest. Too cozy for her peace of mind.

"Turn right at the next corner and go three blocks. The restaurant is on the left side of the road."

His deep, baritone voice, edged with exhaustion, shivered through her. "Do you eat at your friend's a lot?"

"Probably once a week. Sometimes I bring the kids from the refuge."

"You do?" She was constantly discovering he was more involved in the children's lives than she had ever thought possible. "All of them?"

"Not usually. I rotate six different ones each time. I don't want to play favorites and cause any problems."

"Do you have a favorite?"

"I try not to. They all need love and understanding. But…"

His voice faded into the quiet.

"What? Fess up. Which one has stolen your heart?"

"It's hard for me not to be drawn to Andy."

Although she thought she knew the answer, she asked, "Why?" She pulled into a parking space next to the restaurant and looked at him, the light from the building washing over his face.

"Because he reminds me of myself when I was his age."

"And that's why you're being so hard on Lisa." Knowing how he felt about Andy's mother, she should be surprised he had taken the time to help her the evening before, but she wasn't, because the more she got acquainted with Jacob the more she realized that would be exactly what he would do.

"No, I'm skeptical of her motives because I've seen that kind of situation before and it didn't turn out well."

"I'm sorry about your mother, but Lisa isn't her."

"It's not just my mother I'm talking about. I've seen a lot over the years as a foster child and a doctor."

"Were there any situations where a parent was able to stay off drugs and take care of her child?"

He thought for a moment and answered, "One of my friends was lucky."

She placed her hand on the handle. "Then maybe Andy and Lisa will be like that one." She opened the door and left her car before they got into a heated discussion as they had in the past when they'd talked about the little boy's situation.

Inside the restaurant wonderful smells of spices, tomato and meats caused Hannah's mouth to water. "I didn't realize how hungry I was until now."

After they ordered at the counter, Jacob found them a table in the back in a less-crowded section and pulled out her chair as if they were on a date. She stared at it for a few seconds before she sat and let him scoot it forward. His hand brushed her shoulder as he came around to his side, and she nearly jumped at the casual touch.

Get a grip. This is not a date. It is simply two people who are acquainted sharing a meal. It could never be anything more than that.

"They're usually pretty fast here, so it shouldn't be long before they bring us our pizzas. And this is my treat."

"You don't have to," she immediately said, not liking how that made this sound more like a date.

"Yes, I do. You're helping me out, and I always pay my debts."

"Is that why you have a car that should have seen the inside of a salvage yard a long time ago?"

For a couple of heartbeats his jaw tightened, a veil falling over his expression. Then it was gone and he grinned. "Contrary to how a lot of men feel about their cars, I don't care what I drive. I wanted to pay off my educational loans before I took on any more debt."

"When will you be finished?"

"In a few months." He looked beyond her and his smile grew. "I wondered if you were here. Hannah, this is Noah, the guy who is responsible for adding at least five pounds to my waist."

A tall man with long brown hair pulled back with a leather strap paused at the table. "I must admit this isn't something I see often. I had to come out and meet the woman who could make my friend stop long enough to go out on a date."

Hannah shook Noah's hand. "Oh, this isn't a date. We're just…" How did she describe what they were?

"We're friends enjoying some pizza," Jacob finished for her.

"Sure. Sorry about the mistake." Noah's gaze danced with merriment as it lit upon first Jacob then Hannah.

"Hannah is the new manager at Stone's Refuge. Why she was interested in meeting you, I don't know."

Noah laughed. "She probably heard of my charming personality."

"No doubt," Jacob grumbled good-naturedly. "Are you leaving?"

Noah's laughter increased. "I can take a hint. You don't have to wound me."

"I couldn't wound you. Your hide is too thick."

The restaurant owner shifted his attention to Hannah. "Don't listen to a thing he says. He doesn't know how to have fun. He's too busy working all the time." He took her hand. "It was nice meeting you. I'm sure I'll see you around the farm."

As Noah strolled away, Hannah turned to Jacob. "Did you tell me y'all are friends?"

"Afraid so. Actually Noah and Peter are like brothers to me."

"Then that accounts for your ribbing."

"You sound like someone who has siblings. A brother or sister?"

The reminder of Kevin struck her low. She struggled to keep herself composed while she sat across from the man who caused her brother's death. Trembling, she clutched the sides of the chair.

"Excuse me." She bolted to her feet and searched for the restrooms.

Seeing the sign across the room, she quickly fled the table. Inside she locked the door and collapsed back against it. When she lifted her gaze to the mirror over the sink, she saw two large eyes, full of sorrow, staring back at her. She covered her cheeks, the heat beneath her fingertips searing them. His question had taken her by surprise and dumped her past in her lap.

She crossed to the sink and splashed cold water on her face, then examined her reflection in the mirror for any telltale signs of her grief. Blue eyes filled her vision, pain lurking just beneath the surface. She stamped it down.

She needed to get through dinner. Thinking about Kevin—the fact she had never been able to say goodbye to him because her parents wouldn't let her go to the funeral—was something she couldn't afford to do right now.

"You can do this." She blew out a breath of air, lifting her bangs from her forehead, and left the restroom.

Jacob stood when she approached. Worry knitted his forehead. "Are you all right?"

She took her chair, noticing that the pizzas had been delivered while she was gone. "I'm fine."

"Did I say something wrong?"

"I did have an older brother. He's dead. Your question took me by surprise. That's all."

He covered her hand on the table. "I'm so sorry about your brother."

Somehow she managed not to jerk back. She forced a smile to her lips and said, "I'm hungry. Let's dig in."

As Hannah took her first bite of the Canadian bacon slice, she knew what she had to do soon. She needed to go out to her brother's grave site. She needed to say goodbye.

The next afternoon at the cemetery, Hannah's steps slowed as she neared where her brother lay at rest. A vase of brightly colored flowers drew her immediate attention. Where had those come from? She had no relatives living in Cimarron City.

Hannah put her mum plant next to the vase, then moved back. The bright sunlight bathed her in warmth she desperately needed. Hugging her arms to her, she wished she had worn a heavier sweater. The north wind cut through her, and she positioned herself behind the large oak that shaded the area, its trunk blocking the worst of the chill.

"Kevin, I'm sorry I told on you that last day. If you

hadn't gotten in trouble with Dad, you might not have gone out joyriding that night. If I had only known…" The lump in her throat prevented her from saying the rest aloud. But for years she had wondered: if she hadn't tattled on her brother, would that have changed the outcome of that night? That was something she would never know the answer to.

Lord, I need Your help in forgiving Jacob. I can see he is a good man. I don't want to carry this anger anymore. Please help me.

The evening before hadn't been torture. She wouldn't have thought that possible until recently. But she had seen a side of Jacob—even if they didn't agree about Andy and Lisa—which she liked. He cared about the children at the refuge. He cared about his patients. He cared about his friends.

If Jacob could move past Kevin's death, then so could she. She would find a way because she wanted to continue working at the refuge and that meant being involved with him.

"We need to stop meeting like this," Jacob said several weeks later as he closed the door to the exam room.

Hannah held Nancy in her lap, the child's head lying on her shoulder. "Just as soon as they come up with a cure for the common cold and a few other illnesses."

He knelt next to Hannah. "What's wrong, Nancy?"

"I don't feel good."

He leaned closer to hear the weak answer. "Let's take your temperature first."

While he rose, Nancy's eyes grew round. "I don't want a shot."

Hannah cradled the child against her. "I gave her something for her fever last night, but she didn't sleep well. She ended up in my bed. She complained her throat hurts."

"Nancy, can you hop up here and let me take a look?" Jacob patted the exam table.

The little girl nodded, then slipped off Hannah's lap. Jacob helped her up, then placed a digital thermometer into her ear.

Hannah stood next to Nancy. "What is it now?"

"Hundred and four. When was the last time you gave her something for her fever?"

Hannah checked her watch. "Four hours ago."

When the nurse came into the room, Jacob examined the child, then took a swab of her throat. "Strep is going around. We should know something in a few minutes."

He handed the sample to Teresa, who left, then shook out two children's pain relievers and gave them to Nancy. After chewing them, she sipped the cup of water Jacob filled for her.

"If it's strep, you'll need to keep her away from the other children. It can be very contagious. I often see it make the rounds in a family." Jacob jotted something on the girl's chart.

"I'll have her stay in my room, but she ate dinner and breakfast with the whole crew."

"I'll give you a maintenance dose of antibiotics. I don't want you getting sick, too."

The door opened as Nancy leaned against Hannah as if the child didn't have the strength to keep herself upright. Teresa entered and handed Jacob a slip of paper.

He frowned. "It's strep." He scribbled on a prescription pad, then ripped it off and handed it to Hannah. "Get her started on that right away. I'll come by this evening to check the rest of the kids, as well, and see how Nancy is doing after she's had a dose of antibiotics and lots of rest. I'll bring maintenance doses for the children to take when they get home from school." He smoothed the child's hair from her face. "You'll rest for me, Nancy?"

She nodded and buried herself even more against Hannah.

"Great. I bet Teresa has a toy for you from the box. Do you want one?" Jacob sent his nurse a silent message.

Nancy's dull gaze slid from Jacob to the nurse. "Yes, please."

"What would you like?" Teresa took the child's hand and assisted her down from the exam table. "We've got some coloring books. Do you like to color?"

"Uh-huh."

"Then you can pick from several different ones." Teresa left the room with Nancy in tow.

The second they were gone, Hannah rounded on Jacob. "What didn't you say in front of Nancy?"

"This could be serious. Both Terry and Susie get strep throat easily. Last time Terry was very sick from it. I'll be there not long after they get home from school. Has Nancy been around them much, other than at dinner and breakfast?"

"Susie read to her last night. She's the one who came and told me Nancy wasn't feeling well and was hot." Hannah pictured the children all in bed with sore throats and fevers. "So do you think I'd better dust off my tennis shoes and get ready to run between bedrooms?"

He chuckled. "That's a possibility, but I'll help as much as I can."

The barrier around her heart crumpled a little as she looked into his eyes. Since he'd come into her life, he was doing that a lot—helping her out.

Hannah collapsed onto the couch in the living area and rested her head on the back cushion. "Thankfully Terry doesn't have strep yet, but I'm worried about Susie."

"I've got her on an antibiotic. We caught it early this time so she should be all right in a few days." Jacob settled across from her in a lounge chair.

"Are you as tired as I am?"

"I could fall asleep sitting up in this chair."

"Are you going to be all right driving home?"

One corner of his mouth lifted. "Sure, if I can persuade you to fix me a cup of coffee."

"Won't that keep you up after you get home?"

"I'm just hoping it will keep me up *until* I get home."

"If you think there'll be a problem, you are welcome to stay here and sleep on this couch." She patted the black leather cushion.

"No. My new car practically drives itself."

Summoning her last bit of energy, Hannah pushed to her feet. "One cup of java coming up then."

In the kitchen she quickly brewed some coffee, amazed that she actually invited him to stay over. It wasn't as though they would be alone, not with eight children in the house—six of them sick and probably up and down the whole night until the antibiotic really took effect.

But a picture of his tired face popped into her mind as she stared at the dark liquid dripping into the pot. It was after one, and he'd spent over nine hours here, helping her with the children—and that was after working a full day at his office. With Meg off, she'd needed the help, and she hadn't wanted to expose anyone else to strep.

Thank You, Lord, for sending him to us.

The aroma of coffee permeated the kitchen, tempting her to drink a cup herself. But she needed to get what rest she could so she only filled a mug for Jacob, then walked back into the living room to find him sound asleep. Even in relaxation he appeared exhausted, his pale features highlighting the dark circles under his eyes.

After placing his coffee on the table beside his chair, she grabbed the coverlet from the couch and threw it over him, pausing for a long moment to stare at him. Until she realized what she was doing. Quickly she dimmed the lights and tiptoed out of the living area. On her way to her bedroom, she checked on the children. The sick kids were separated from the two who were still healthy and she hoped stayed that way.

All seemed well as she headed for her room and bed. She was so tired she didn't even bother removing her clothes. She plopped down on the bedspread and fell back onto the pillow. The softness cocooned her in luxury that her weary body craved.

A thought seeped into her mind. She needed to get

up and take her maintenance dose. She'd forgotten earlier. She would…soon.…

The next thing Hannah knew someone was shaking her arm. She popped one eye open to find Nancy by her bed, her thumb in her mouth, her face flushed. "Baby, what's wrong?" She pushed herself up on her elbows.

"I can't sleep," she mumbled with her thumb still in her mouth.

Hannah touched her forehead, then cupped her cheek. Fever radiated beneath her palm. She slid her glance to the clock. Four. She'd slept almost three hours. "Let me give you some more pain reliever."

Hannah hurried into the bathroom off her room and retrieved the medicine and a paper cup full of water. When she returned, she found Nancy curled on her bed, still sucking her thumb. "Here, chew these first then drink some water."

Nancy did, then lay back down, her movements lethargic.

"I'll carry you to your room."

"Not mine. It's Susie's. Can I stay here?"

Hannah pulled a chair near the bed and sat. "Okay. This time. I'll take you…"

The child's eyes drifted closed. She'd wait until Nancy was asleep then take her back to the bedroom she shared with the two other girls. Fifteen minutes later she scooped up Nancy into her arms and strode out into the hallway and nearly collided with Jacob, who held Andy against him.

"What happened?" Hannah stepped back.

"He's sick, too. He woke me up in the living room."

"That makes seven now."

"Put him in my bed. I don't want him going back into the room with Terry."

Jacob passed her and entered her bedroom while she quickly took care of Nancy. She tucked the little girl in and brushed her fingers along her forehead. Her skin was cooler to the touch. Relief flowed through Hannah as she checked on the other two girls then slipped out into the hallway. Hopefully by this evening the children would be much better with no complications from the strep.

When Jacob came out of her room, she asked, "Are you hungry? I'll fix you an early breakfast or a late-night snack, whichever way you want to look at it."

"I never turn down a chance at a meal I don't have to fix. And after the past—" he glanced at his watch "—twelve hours I'm starved."

As she made her way to the kitchen, the hairs on her nape tingled as though Jacob was staring at her. She didn't dare look back to see if he was. Just thinking about it caused her cheeks to flame.

After flipping on the light, she crossed the room, opened the refrigerator and removed ingredients for scrambled eggs. "Frankly I love having breakfast at any time of the day. Mom used to fix pancakes for dinner once a month."

When he didn't say anything, she peered back at him. A shadow dulled his eyes until he saw her staring and a veil descended over his expression.

He moved to her. "Can I help?"

"Someone who professes not to cook? I don't think so. Have a seat. This is the least I can do for all your help with the kids."

"I'm their doctor."

"Who's gone above and beyond the call of duty."

He scooted back a chair from the kitchen table and sank down onto it. His gaze captured hers and for a moment she forgot everything but the charming smile that tilted the corners of his mouth and the gleam that sparkled in his eyes.

She blinked and he looked away. She quickly turned back to the counter, found a mixing bowl and began cracking eggs into it. "What made you become a doctor?"

A good minute passed before he answered, "I wanted to heal."

The anguish that slipped through his words froze Hannah. Heal himself? Or heal others? Suddenly she remembered anew who was sitting a few feet away from her. For a while she'd forgotten that he'd been responsible for her brother's death. Her hand trembled so badly she had to grip the edge of the counter.

"Hannah, are you all right?"

The sound of the chair scraping across the tile floor focused her on the here and now. Jacob had asked a question. She needed to answer him. She cleared her throat and said, "I'm just tired and concerned about the kids."

"They're a tough bunch. I think we caught it early." He stood right behind her.

His presence electrified the air. *Lord, help me to forgive. How did You do it on the cross?*

"Are you sure I can't help?"

Fortifying her defenses, she swung around and took a step back. "Yes, I'm sure. You're my guest. Now, sit and behave." She needed him across the room. She needed some space while she mended her composure, and it was hard to think straight with him so near.

He held up his hands. "Okay. I'm going." After he resettled in the chair, he asked, "Has being a social worker been everything you wanted it to be?"

That was an easy question thankfully. She turned back to finish preparing the scrambled eggs. "Yes, I love kids and wanted to make a difference in their lives, but I couldn't see myself as a teacher." She poured the mixture into the heated skillet. "I like a challenge, and I think social work is definitely challenging."

"That's putting it mildly."

She stirred the eggs. "I would think being a doctor is one, too."

"I guess you and I are alike. I enjoy a good challenge. It keeps life interesting."

The third thing they had in common. At this rate there would be no differences between them. After sticking four pieces of bread into the toaster, she withdrew some dishes from the cabinet and brought them to the table.

Before she went back to the stove to get the food, Jacob caught her hand and held it, drawing her full attention to his handsome face. "Thank you for covering me with a blanket." His voice dropped a level, a huskiness in it.

His hand about hers, warm and strong, robbed her of words. For the life of her, she couldn't look away, as though his eyes lured her into their brown depths. "You're welcome," she managed to say, her mouth parched.

The silence grew until she thought he must hear her heart pounding. All she could remember was his dedication to helping the children the evening before. A connection between them sprang up that staggered Hannah, a connection that went beyond what they had in common.

Finally he released her grasp. A smile dimpled his cheeks. "You'd better get the eggs."

She spun around and hurried to the stove, gripping the wooden spoon and counter to keep her hands from quivering. What just happened? How could she betray her brother's memory like that? It was one thing to forgive—but to forget? No!

While she saved the breakfast from being ruined, she tried to bring her rebellious emotions under control. It was because she was so exhausted, she told herself, that for a moment she looked beyond what Jacob had done in the past to what he was doing in the present.

Chapter Seven

Hannah sat at the kitchen table, trying to drink a cup of warm milk to help her sleep. It curdled her stomach. She pushed it away and buried her face in her hands. Fever singed her palms. Her throat burned. She didn't need a doctor to tell her that after a day and a half taking care of the sick children, she'd caught what they had. Thankfully most of them were on the mend, except Terry who had come down with it earlier today. Jacob didn't think the boy would have it too badly since he'd already taken two doses of the maintenance antibiotic. Up until an hour ago when she began to feel sick, she'd forgotten to take hers. Obviously she was too late to prevent it totally.

The sound of the door opening alerted Hannah she wasn't alone. Dropping her hands onto the table, she straightened as Meg came into the room.

"Everyone's in bed. Anything else you need before I go home?" Meg stopped near her, her eyes narrowing on Hannah. "You've got a rash, Hannah!"

"A rash?"

"All over your face and neck."

Hannah glanced down as though she could see it in the surface of the table.

The older woman touched Hannah's forehead. "You've got a fever. Come on. You're going to bed now." She took her arm to help Hannah rise.

She tried to stand and swayed. The room spun. "But the kids need—"

"I'll take care of the children. Don't you worry." Meg supported most of Hannah's weight as she headed toward the bedroom area.

"But you might get sick, too."

"If I do, then I'll deal with it. Right now you worry about taking care of yourself. I wonder why the maintenance dose didn't work for you. You've been on it for a while."

"I forgot until an hour ago. I was too busy taking care of the others."

Meg flipped back the coverlet and helped Hannah ease down onto her bed. "I'll get you some aspirin."

Hannah slid her eyes closed, listening to Meg move about the room, the sound loud to her sensitive ears. Her face felt on fire. Pain gripped her throat and drummed against her skull.

"Here." Meg slipped her arm underneath Hannah and lifted her up to take the pills and drink some water.

The second Hannah managed to swallow the aspirin she sagged back onto the mattress, shutting her eyes to the swirling room.

As the pain continued to do a tap dance in her head, she embraced the darkness.

* * *

"Why didn't she say anything to me before I left this evening?" Jacob stared at Hannah sleeping fitfully on her bed.

"I don't think she was thinking about herself. She's got a bad rash," Meg said.

The tiny red spots stood out like a neon sign against the otherwise pale skin. He brushed back a strand of hair from her face, feeling the warmth beneath his fingertips. "That can happen sometimes with strep. I'm going to give her a shot." He opened his medicine bag and took out a syringe and a vial of antibiotics. "I hate to wake her up, but she needs this now."

"I'm staying tonight to make sure the children are taken care of. You take care of her." Meg crossed to the door and left.

Gently, he shook Hannah awake. Her eyes blinked, then drifted closed.

"Hannah, I need to know if you're allergic to any medicine."

"Medicine?" she mumbled.

"I want to give you a shot of an antibiotic."

Her eyes popped open and focused on him. "A shot? I hate them."

Jacob pulled a chair close to the bed and sat. "I'm worried about you. Are you allergic to anything?"

"No—you don't need to worry…" Her voice floated into the silence as she surrendered to sleep again.

She flinched when the needle pricked her skin, but her eyes stayed closed. Again he combed the wayward lock back from her forehead, then went to the living room to settle into a chair for the long night ahead. He wouldn't leave until he was sure she would be all right.

Hannah moaned. Every muscle ached. She tried to turn over onto her side, but someone held her hand. Easing one eye open, she stared at Jacob stretched out in a chair next to her bed, asleep. She tugged herself free at the same time he snapped upright, disoriented. His hair lay at odd angles, making him appear younger.

He chuckled. "I guess you caught me napping on the job."

Her mind still shrouded in a fog, she mumbled, "What job?"

He bent forward, taking her wrist and placing his fingers over her pulse. "Caring for you."

She struggled to sit up. "I don't need you…" She collapsed back onto the pillow.

"What were you saying?"

She inhaled a shallow, raspy breath. "I'll be fine with some rest." She shifted her head until she glimpsed her clock on the bedside table. "I've only been sleeping a few hours…" The light slanting through the slits in the blinds attracted her attention. "What time of day is it?"

"It's eleven in the morning."

"I slept all night?" Again she tried to sit up and managed to prop herself on her elbows. "What about the children?"

"Meg has been here taking care of them. I've looked in on each one, and all of them are recovering nicely. And there were no cases at the other cottage."

"What about your patients?"

His chuckles evolved into laughter. "I know I work

a lot, but today is Saturday. I'd planned to spend it here making sure the kids were all right."

"You were? I mean, I don't remember...." She rubbed her temple, the pounding in her head less but still there. She swallowed several times to coat her dry throat. "Can I have some water?"

"Sure." He rose and settled next to her to hold her up while she sipped some cold liquid. Despite its coolness, it burned going down. "I need you to take these." Jacob produced some pills. "And there's no forgetting this time."

She winced each time one went down. "I guess I forgot to tell you I used to get strep throat every year while growing up."

"No, you left that out."

"It wouldn't have made any difference. I'd still have taken care of the children. They needed me." The sound of her voice grew weak in her ears.

Jacob laid her gently back on the bed and stood. "Somehow I figured that. But now I'm your doctor, and I'm telling you to sleep and not worry about anything."

"You're a pediatrician." Her eyes fluttered closed.

"But I'm free and here. You aren't going to get rid of me."

That last sentence comforted her as sleep descended.

"She's awake, Dr. Jacob! She's awake!"

Nancy's shrieking voice thundered through Hannah's head, threatening to renew the earlier hammering pain.

"Shh." Jacob filled the doorway with several children standing behind him, peeping into the room.

He looked good to her tired eyes. Very good. Slightly

worn but handsome as ever with his tousled brown hair and gleaming eyes that held hers. "How long have I been asleep?"

"It's Sunday afternoon and Laura and Peter are here."

"I lost another day."

Nancy appeared in her face. "I was worried about you."

Other than the ashen cast to the little girl's features, she looked all right. The dullness in her eyes was gone and a smile brightened her face. "I'll be as good as new in a day or so."

"Okay, everyone, Laura and Peter have dished up some ice cream for you in the kitchen. You'd better eat it before it melts."

The sound of running footsteps faded down the hall, leaving Jacob alone with her. He moved into the room.

"I have news for you, Hannah. You won't be up and about in a day or so. You had a bad case of strep on top of exhaustion. You need to get a lot of rest if you want to be as good as new by Thanksgiving."

She frowned. "You aren't going to be one of these demanding doctors who insists I follow your instructions."

He stood with his feet slightly apart and his hands on his hips, glaring at her. "Yes, I am." But the merriment in his eyes mocked his fierce stance. "I came close to taking you to the hospital."

"You did?"

The implication threw her. If her aching body was any indication, she realized she had been very sick. But the hospital?

"Oh, you are awake? The kids said you were." Laura walked to the bed and positioned herself on the other side of Jacob. "I brought you some ice cream." She held up the bowl.

"Vanilla?"

Nodding, Laura sat in the chair nearby and scooped a spoonful of it for Hannah. "Peter could use your help, Jacob. By now all eight children are clamoring for more ice cream."

"Make sure she stays in bed," was his parting remark.

Laura laughed. "He can be so demanding when a patient doesn't follow his instructions."

Hannah scooted up against the headboard and took the bowl from Laura. "This does make me realize I have to find a doctor. I haven't yet."

Laura's laughter increased. "Jacob has a way with children, but I can see his bedside manner might be lacking with an adult. He does mean well, though."

Hannah slid the spoonful of ice cream into her mouth and relished the coldness as she swallowed the treat. "I wouldn't know about his bedside manner. I was pretty out of it. I remember him making me take some pills, though."

Laura's expression sobered. "Yes, I know. Peter and I have been here helping Meg with the children. You should have let us know how bad it was. We could have come sooner."

Hannah stared at her ice cream. "You have four children. I didn't want you to be exposed to strep, so I played it down when we talked."

"And got Meg and Jacob to go along."

"I thought we were handling it. We did. I just got sick."

"Running yourself into the ground. In fact, I tried

to get Jacob to go home and take care of himself, but he wouldn't leave your side."

"He didn't?" Warmth, that had nothing to do with a fever, spread through her.

"He told me he wouldn't be able to sleep until he knew you were out of the woods. For the past day and a half he has stood guard over you." Laura glanced toward the doorway. "Now, I'm gonna insist he go home and get some rest."

Hannah took another scoop of the ice cream. "Do we have any Popsicle treats left?"

"You must be getting better. You have an appetite. I'll see if I can find any. The children have been eating them right and left. I had Peter go get some more." She rose and headed for the hallway.

Hannah finished her treat and placed the bowl on the table, tired from the brief exertion. How was she going to look after eight children? She couldn't even feed herself without getting exhausted.

She tried to concentrate on that dilemma, but she kept thinking about what Laura had told her about Jacob. He hadn't left her side. He'd watched over her. She should be upset by that news, but after the past few days working with him to take care of the sick children, she wasn't. A bond of friendship had formed between them.

Lord, if any good has come out of the illness that took hold of this house, it was that. I don't hate Jacob anymore. I can forgive him for what happened to Kevin. The man I've gotten to know would never have done something like that on purpose. The car wreck was an unfortunate accident that I suspect has left a mark on Jacob, too.

She sank farther into her pillow, propped up against the headboard, and closed her eyes. Total peace blanketed her for the first time in years. *This is why you forgive someone. This is why you let go of your anger. I understand now, Jesus, why You forgave them on the cross. Thank You, Lord.*

Footsteps announced she wasn't alone. She opened her eyes, expecting to see Laura, but instead Jacob entered with a cherry Popsicle in his grasp.

"I hear you're hungry." He sat in the chair by the bed and gave her the treat.

"I thought Laura was making you go home to sleep."

"She tried."

"And obviously failed."

"I can be a very determined man."

"I appreciate all you've done, but she's right. I don't want you to get sick, too." She nibbled on her Popsicle.

"I'm not going to. I've built up quite a resistance. Remember I deal with sick kids all the time."

"Now I see why the children love having you come. The gifts you brought them to keep them occupied and in bed were great."

"I love those handheld video games."

"You sound like you've played your share of them."

"I'm a kid at heart."

His smile encompassed his whole face and sent her heart beating a shade faster. "I'll have to try one sometime."

"I'll loan you one of mine. A great stress reliever."

"I thought exercise was."

"I'm exercising my mind."

Seeing his well-proportioned body, she knew he also

had to exercise physically, too. "I like to ride my bike but haven't had a chance yet."

"There are some great places around here to visit. If the weather stays nice, I could show you one weekend."

"You have a bike?"

He nodded. "A great stress reliever."

"Maybe I could get some bikes for the kids, and we could all go on an excursion one Saturday."

"Let's get you well first, then we can plan something."

"I'll be up in no time." She fluttered her hand in the air, but immediately dropped it into her lap, her arm feeling as though it weighed more than a twenty-pound barbell.

He rose. "I'd better let you get some rest. Besides, I promised Laura I would deliver the Popsicle and leave. I don't want to make a liar out of me."

The second he left, Hannah felt the energy level in the room diminish. He charged the air wherever he was. He had a presence about him that drew a person to him. Why hadn't she noticed that before?

Because I had been too busy trying to avoid him.

It was nice having a friend in Cimarron City.

A friend? a little voice questioned.

Yes, a friend. Anything else would be taking this forgiveness thing too far.

"Dr. Jacob has pulled up," Gabe shouted from the window in the living room.

"Mom's here!" Andy jumped up and down, then raced for the front door.

Hannah laughed. "I think he's excited."

"He's been marking off his calendar until Thanksgiving." Susie followed Andy outside.

Hannah heard the car doors slamming shut. She hurried after the children who flooded out of the house and down the steps. Excitement bubbled up in her. She wished she could attribute it totally to the fact that Lisa had just finished her drug-rehab program and was going to join them for Thanksgiving dinner today. She couldn't, though. After she was up and about at the end of last week, she hadn't seen much of Jacob other than at church on Sunday. But today he was spending Thanksgiving with them.

Whenever he was at the cottage, it seemed to come alive. His relationship with the children was great.

How about his with you?

She ignored the question and greeted Lisa with a hug. "It's good to see you."

The young woman slung her arm around Andy who was plastered against his mom. "Thanks for the invitation. I've been looking forward to today."

Andy yanked on his mother's arm. "Come inside. I want to show you what Dr. Jacob got me."

"I'll show you my gift, too," Gabe said.

"Talk to you later," Lisa said laughingly as her son dragged her up the steps and into the house.

Hannah turned to Jacob. "I appreciate you picking her up."

"No problem. I was coming this way." He produced a bouquet of fall flowers from behind his back. "These are for you."

"Me?" She took them, her eyes probably as round

as the yellow mums she held. The scent of the lilies teased her senses.

"Dr. Jacob, have you heard about the bike trip we're going on this weekend?" Nancy asked, tugging on his arm to get his attention.

He knelt down so that they were eye to eye. "I'm going, too."

"Oh, yeah. I forgot." The little girl hugged her worn pink blanket to her and stuck her thumb into her mouth.

"C'mon, Nancy. You need to help me set the table." Susie clasped the child's hand and mounted the steps.

"Where are the other kids?"

Still stunned by the gesture, Hannah was momentarily speechless. She could not recall anyone ever bringing her flowers—not even her husband.

"Hannah?"

"Oh. At the barn feeding the animals. They'll be here shortly. Roman took several of them over with some of the older kids."

"I bet Terry led the way."

"You know that boy well."

"He has been here the longest. I wish someone would adopt him, but he's nearly twelve, which makes it harder." Jacob held the front door open for Hannah.

"Yeah, everyone wants a baby or a young child when they're looking to adopt."

The aroma of the roasting turkey seeped into every corner of the house. "Ah, the best smell. Did Meg make her cornbread dressing?"

"Yes, and my contribution is dessert. Pecan pie."

"A woman after my heart. That's one of my favorite desserts."

"Meg made her pumpkin pie and a chocolate one, too."

"Stop right there. You're driving a starving man crazy."

"Tell you what. Dinner isn't for another hour. Let me put these flowers into water and check with the kids to see if anyone wants to go to the barn. That oughta take your mind off food."

"Great. If I stayed here, I'd probably be raiding the kitchen, and Meg doesn't take too kindly to snacking before a meal."

She waved her hand toward the living room. "Two are in there. See if they want to go," she said while she walked to the dining room and peered in.

Susie gave Nancy a plate to set on the table.

"Want to come to the barn with Dr. Jacob and me?"

Nancy thrust the dishes she still held at Susie. "Yes!"

The older girl scanned the near-empty table. "I promised Meg I would help her. You all go on without me."

Next Hannah found Gabe and Andy in the boys' bedroom, showing Lisa how to play one of the handheld video games. "We're going to the barn. Want to come?"

Gabe leaped to his feet at the same time Andy did. The boy pulled his mother up.

"I guess that's a yes," Hannah said, and went to the kitchen to let Meg know where they would be and put the flowers in water.

Five minutes later the group passed the unfinished third house and started hiking across the meadow. With just a hint of crispness, the air felt nice. The scent of burning wood lingered on the light breeze that blew a few strands of Hannah's hair across her face. Andy practically hauled Lisa behind him at a fast clip while the other children ran and skipped toward the red barn.

"After the busy week I've had, I don't have that kind of energy." Jacob chuckled when Andy's mother threw them a helpless look.

"Do you think Lisa will be successful this time?"

"Honestly? No, I don't but then my experience hasn't been a good one when it comes to successful stories with drug rehab."

"I'm praying you're wrong."

Jacob paused in the middle of the field and looked long and hard at Hannah. "Truthfully I hope I am, too."

The more she was around Jacob, the more she realized she'd never met a man like him. He was honest, caring, and when he was wrong, admitted it. If she weren't careful, she would forget who he was. Yes, she had forgiven him, but she hadn't forgotten what happened all those years ago. To do so would have been to betray her family.

Peter came out of the barn as the children with Lisa raced by him. "The kids are almost through feeding the animals." He swung his attention from Hannah to Jacob. "Now I know why you turned Laura and me down for Thanksgiving dinner. The kids told me you were joining them today."

"I got an offer I couldn't refuse." Jacob's grin accentuated his two dimples.

"Laura and I will eventually get over it." Peter shifted toward Hannah. "I hope you have enough food. You should have seen him last Thanksgiving."

"Hannah, look." Nancy walked toward her with a

puppy cradled against her chest. "I got to pick her up this time."

"Yeah, she's just about ready for a home." Peter started for the interior of the barn.

"I can give her a home," Nancy said, trailing after Peter with the mutt still in her arms. "I'm good with puppies."

"So far I've managed to discourage any pets at the cottage, but I've got my work cut out for me this time." Hannah hurried to follow Nancy.

"Why? I think a pet around the house would be good for the kids."

She stopped in the middle of the cavernous building. "And how do you suppose I should pick the pet? Each child wants a different one."

Jacob scratched the top of his head. "I don't know. I'll have to think on that one."

"Fine. You come up with a fair way and they can have one."

Terry entered through the back door, carrying a lamb. "I found him." He passed the animal to Peter, then waved at Hannah. "I'm finished. Is it time for dinner?"

"About half an hour." Hannah swung her attention back to Nancy and saw the little girl put the white puppy back in its pen with the other ones. The child stooped down and continued to stroke the mutt.

Jacob was right. There needed to be some pets at the cottage, not just down at the barn. She'd never gotten to have one because they had always been moving to a new place. She remembered her yearning and her promise to herself that when she had her own home she would have several to make up for the lack while growing up.

"I've got it." Jacob leaned close, his voice low. "Paul used to have a family meeting every week and everyone had an equal say in what was discussed. That's where we often hashed out problems that came up. When something like having a pet needed to be decided upon, we would talk about it at the meeting, then vote. Majority ruled."

His warm breath tingled along her neck. She stepped a few feet away and tried to slow her suddenly pounding heart. "That might work."

"He set up ground rules. One person at a time spoke. No one was allowed to cut in until that person was through speaking. Everyone had to be respectful of the others. Our voting was done by secret balloting and no one was to be questioned how they voted."

"He sounds like an amazing man."

"He was. I miss him. Thankfully Alice, his wife, lives with Laura and Peter."

"Alice was your foster mother? I didn't know that." She'd met the older woman while visiting Laura once.

"Yes. Both of them were lifesavers to a lot of kids."

"Including you?"

"Especially me. I was pretty messed up when I went to live with the Hendersons at fifteen."

"Why?"

A frown marred his face and his eyes darkened with storm clouds.

Hannah wished she could snatch the question back. Would he say anything about the wreck? Was that even what he was referring to?

Chapter Eight

For a few seconds the urge to share inundated Jacob. He'd never told anyone but Paul. Jacob stared into her gaze, void of any judgment. The words formed in his mind.

"Jacob?"

He turned away from Hannah in the middle of the barn and strode to the entrance. How could he tell her what he'd done, that he'd been responsible for another person's death? He valued her friendship and didn't want to see disappointment, or something worse, in her eyes. Their rocky start had finally smoothed out. He didn't want to go back to how it had been in the beginning.

Hannah's hand settled on his arm. The touch went straight to his heart. The guilt he'd lived with for twenty-one years whisked the words away. He couldn't tell her, but he had to say something.

He glanced at her slightly behind him and to the side.

"Before I came to the Hendersons, I was an angry teen who had even run away from several foster homes."

"Because of your childhood?" Sympathy edged her voice.

"Yes. Paul's the one who taught me about Jesus. He showed me there was another way besides giving in to my anger."

"Anger can consume a person."

"It nearly had me. I never want to go back to that place." He shuddered.

Hannah moved to stand in front of Jacob. Her fingers skimmed down his arm, and she grasped his hand. "I don't see that happening."

"Not as long as the Lord is in my life."

"Hannah, I'm finished. I forgot to eat breakfast," Terry said.

She looked beyond Jacob and grinned. "Gather the others and we'll head back."

In the past few years he'd done a pretty good job of throwing himself totally into his work and putting the past behind him. But lately he hadn't been able to do that. *Why, Lord? Why now?*

Nancy took his hand. "I don't want to leave Abby."

"Abby?" That was Nancy's mother's name.

She pointed toward the pen. "The puppy. I named her Abby. I love that name."

His heart ripped in half, and he had no words for Nancy, having been in her shoes and remembering the pain of rejection he'd suffered as a child. Racking his brain for something to say, Jacob cleared his throat. "I like the name, too."

Nancy tugged him down and whispered in his ear, "Will you talk to Hannah about Abby?"

A lump lodged in his throat. "Sure."

Hannah sat at one end of the long dining-room table with Jacob at the other end. For the past minute silence had ruled because all the children were stuffing bites of pie into their mouths.

Jacob pushed his empty plate away. "That's it. I'm full up to my earlobes. Any more and it will come out the top of my head."

A couple of the children giggled.

"Dr. Jacob, you're funny," Nancy said, shoving her plate away. "I'm full up to my earlobes, too."

"That was the best Thanksgiving dinner I've had, Meg." Jacob wiped his mouth with his napkin.

The older woman blushed. "Oh, it was nothing."

"Who agrees with me?"

Everyone's arm shot up into the air. Meg beamed from ear to ear.

"And to show my appreciation, I'll clean up the dishes. Who's going to help me?" Jacob scanned the children's faces.

Everyone's arm dropped.

Hannah fought to keep her expression serious. "I guess you're stuck doing them by yourself."

"Who's going to take pity on me and help?" Jacob's gaze again flitted from one child to the next.

"I will," Lisa said.

"I can." Andy stood and gathered up his plate.

"Thanks, you two, but you enjoy your time together. I'll help Dr. Jacob." Hannah rose.

Before she had a chance to reach for the dishes in front of her, the children fled the dining room with Lisa and Meg following at a more sedate pace.

"I've never seen them move quite so fast," Jacob said with a chuckle.

"Not cleaning up is quite a motivator."

"Wash or dry?"

"You're the guest. You choose." She stacked the plates and carried them into the kitchen.

Five minutes later with the table cleared, Jacob rolled up his long sleeves and began rinsing the dishes off for the dishwasher. "Noah said something about coming over after eating at Peter and Laura's."

"Speaking of Noah, I've been thinking. Do you think he'll give Lisa a job at one of his restaurants?"

"You'll have to ask him. He's always looking for good help. Why? Did Lisa say something to you?"

"Well, no, but she doesn't have a job. I thought I would help her find something."

"Don't you think you should talk to her first?"

Hannah took the glass that Jacob handed her. "I didn't want to get her hopes up if it wasn't possible. She doesn't have many skills and has only worked in a fast-food restaurant."

"It'll be hard finding a decent job without a high-school diploma. Will she be able to stay at the halfway house?"

"Yes, and they have a program there that assists people in getting their GED."

Jacob shifted to face her. "Hannah, you can't live Lisa's life for her. She has to want it— especially being off drugs—if it's going to work."

She averted her gaze, uncomfortable under the intensity of his. "I know. She loves Andy. I know it. They belong together."

"Then she'll stay off the drugs if that's the way to be involved in his life." Sharpness sliced through his words.

Reestablishing eye contact with him, she glimpsed the pain he experienced as a child who hadn't meant much to his mother—at least not enough to stop taking drugs. "I have to try to help. That's why I went into social work in the first place." She took another dish from him. "In fact, I found Nancy's mother. She's only thirty miles from here in Deerfield."

He arched a brow. "And what do you intend to do with that information?"

"I'm going to see her next Wednesday."

"Do you want some company?"

Surprised, she immediately answered, "Yes," then took a harder look at Jacob and noticed the tightening about his mouth and the inflexibility in his eyes. "Why do you want to come?"

"I don't want you to go alone. I've read Nancy's file. I know the rough characters her mother has hung out with." Censorship sounded in his voice.

Hannah straightened, thrusting back her shoulders. "I have to try. Have you seen how upset Nancy is when she sees Andy with his mother?"

"Yes, I've seen her carrying her blanket and sucking her thumb more and more since Lisa has come into Andy's life."

"She misses her own mother."

"Maybe. But maybe she's just plain scared her mother might come get her."

"I don't think so. She's asked me tons of questions about my mother."

Mouth tightening, Jacob squirted some detergent into the sink and filled it up with hot water. "What time did you want to go? I can rearrange my afternoon appointments if that's okay with you."

"Fine. How about after lunch?"

"How about lunch then we can go?"

"Lunch?"

His chuckle tingled down her spine. "Yes, you've got to eat. I've got to eat. Let's do it together then leave from there."

"Sure."

"Then it's a date."

A date? No, it wasn't a date, she wanted to shout, but realized her panic would be conveyed. Instead she clamped her teeth together and didn't say another thing until they had finished up with the pots and pans.

While she put away the meat platter, Jacob wiped down the counters. "Does Nancy's mother know you're coming?"

Jacob's question in the quiet startled her. She whirled around. "No, I thought I would surprise her."

"I hope you're not the one who is surprised."

She frowned. "I'm not totally naive. I don't expect the woman to welcome me with open arms."

"That's good because she won't."

Tension pulsated between them as he stared at her.

Terry burst into the kitchen. "Noah is here! You've got to come see what he brought us." The boy spun around and disappeared back through the entrance.

"Was that Terry who blew in and out of here?" Hannah asked with a laugh, needing to change the subject.

"Yep."

The huge grin on Jacob's face prompted her to ask, "Do you know what Noah brought?"

He nodded and quickly followed the boy out of the kitchen.

Exasperated at the lack of information, Hannah left, too, and found all the children out front, surrounding a pickup filled with bicycles, many different sizes. She stopped at Jacob's side. "I guess that answers my problem about bikes for a ride. I'd only been able to come up with a few. Peter said he would work on it for me."

"He did. Noah and I were his solution."

"Y'all donated them?"

Jacob's smile grew. "Yep. It should have been done before now. Sometimes I'm so focused on their well-being physically that I forget about their mental health."

He waded his way through the crowd of children to help Noah lift the bikes out of the truck bed. As the two men did, they presented each one to a different kid.

Nancy hung back next to Hannah. The little girl glanced up at her. "I don't know how to ride. I've never had a bike."

Hannah pointed toward one still in the bed of the pickup. "That's why there are training wheels on that one. Before you know it, you'll be riding everywhere."

The child stared at it, doubt in her eyes, a tiny frown on her face. "I guess." She lowered her gaze to the ground at her feet.

"I'll work with you this afternoon since Dr. Jacob and I want to take all of you on a bike ride this Saturday. He said something about there being a small lake near here that we could go to and have a picnic. What do you think?"

"Can I bring Abby?"

Hannah knelt in front of Nancy. "A bike ride probably isn't the best place for a puppy."

Jacob approached the little girl. "Here's yours." He set Nancy's small bike with training wheels on it next to her.

She put her thumb in her mouth and looked up shyly at him, mumbling, "Thanks."

Hannah settled her hand on the child's shoulder. She saw the concern in Jacob's expression and said, "I'm going to teach her how to ride over the next two days. She never has."

Before he could say anything, the children encircled Noah and him, vying for the men's attention with their enthusiasm.

"Andy's always wanted a bike. He used to ride the boy's in the apartment across the hall." Lisa said, while watching her son, happiness plastering a smile on his face. "Who's that with Dr. Hartman?"

"Noah Maxwell. He owns the Pizzeria chain. In fact, I wanted to talk to you about applying for a job. Would you be interested in working at one of his restaurants? I could talk to him for you if you are." Jacob had been right—again. She needed to see if Lisa wanted a job at the Pizzeria before approaching Noah.

"At the halfway house they were going to help me look for something. 'Bout the only experience I have is at a food joint. One of the things I learnt at the rehab center was to ask for help when I need it. Thanks."

"Then I'll talk to Noah."

Andy ran up to his mom. "Dr. Jacob said I could go on a bike ride with them on Saturday because my cast is coming off tomorrow." After his announcement, he twirled around and raced back to the group.

Lisa followed her son, plowing into the middle of the children all getting on their bikes.

"Do you want to start your lesson now?" Hannah asked Nancy, who kept her gaze glued to the ground.

She shook her head. "I don't wanna go on a ride. Can I stay here?"

"Why, honey?" Hannah lifted the child's chin.

Tears pooled in Nancy's eyes, and several coursed down her cheeks. "I just don't. I heard Mommy say bikes are dangerous." The little girl pulled away and stepped back toward the porch. She plopped down on the top stair, sucking her thumb and hugging her blanket.

"Nancy doesn't want to ride?" Jacob stood right behind her.

"No. She thinks they're dangerous." Hannah kept her voice low so no one else heard.

"Having seen my share of bike accidents, I can't totally disagree, but we've also gotten helmets for them."

"I'll see if someone can watch her while we go with the other children. I don't want to force Nancy. Hopefully she'll see the others enjoying it and want to learn to ride."

Dressed in black slacks and a gray pullover sweater, Noah approached. "I think our gift is a big hit."

"Did you have any doubt?" Hannah scanned the smiling kids and wanted to bottle this moment.

"No. But what are we going to do for Christmas? It will be hard to top this."

"You don't have—"

"This is the best way I can spend my money," Noah interrupted Hannah. "These kids' lives have been hard. Giving them some joy is priceless."

She realized Noah had as big a heart as Jacob. Too bad, according to Laura, he didn't want to settle down and have his own family. "I do have a favor to ask."

"If it's to go on the bike ride, I draw the line there."

"No. I'd like you to interview Andy's mother for a job at your restaurant. She needs a job and the only experience she's had is as a waitress."

When she started to say more, Noah held up his hand. "Done. I'll talk to her."

Hannah was at a loss for words. Realizing Jacob's misgivings about Andy's mom wanting to change, she'd practiced her speech to convince Noah to give Lisa a chance.

"I'll give her a ride into town and talk to her tonight. Where's she staying?"

"She's staying at a halfway shelter two blocks from your first restaurant."

"Fine. I know where that is." There must have been something in her expression because he added, "I know she just completed a drug-rehab program. I'm aware of what goes on at the refuge even though I don't get to spend as much time out here as Jacob."

"Thanks. I appreciate you giving her a chance." When Noah joined a couple of the boys by his truck, she said to Jacob, "It's a shame he isn't interested in having a family. Like you, he's good with the kids."

"You think I'm good with them?" A gleam glinted in his gaze.

"We might not always see eye to eye on certain issues, but I can't ignore the fact you have a way with the children. Are you interested in having a family?" The second she asked the question she wanted to retreat. Why in the world had she asked him *that?* As if she might be interested in him and the answer.

"Yes. Paul was a great example of what a father can be."

"Then why don't you have one?" The urge to slap her hand over her mouth swamped her. She was digging a deep hole with her inquisitiveness.

He threw back his head and laughed. "I wish it were that simple. It takes two."

Heat flooded her cheeks. She started to mention he was thirty-five, but this time she managed to keep quiet. "Oh, look at Gabe ride."

On Saturday Hannah came to a stop near the small lake and hopped off her bicycle. Susie pulled up next to her while Jacob flanked her on the other side. "This is beautiful. We'll have to come back in the spring when the trees are flowering. I see quite a few redbuds."

"That's our state tree." Susie put her kickstand down. "We've been studying Oklahoma history in school."

"I can see why it is. They're everywhere."

"Can we walk along the shore? We won't go too far."

"Make sure no one goes too close to the water." Hannah took a swig from her water bottle.

"She told me Thanksgiving that she wanted to be a doctor like me." After removing his ball cap, Jacob wiped his hand across his forehead. "I'd forgotten how much work bicycling is, especially that last hill."

"I thought you went bike riding all the time."

"When I was a child, I used to. I…" A frown carved deep lines into his brow.

"What?"

"My grandma gave me a bike one Christmas. I loved that bike. I would go all over the place. If I was quick enough, it became my way of escaping my mother when she went into a rage."

"What happened to it?"

"During one of my mother's rages, she ran over it with her car. I tried to fix it, but the frame was bent too much for me to do anything. I cried when the garbage man took it away." His gaze zeroed in on her. "That was the only time I cried. Not crying used to make my mom madder. She used to shout I didn't have a heart."

Her stomach knotted as she listened to him talk about his mother so dispassionately as though she were a stranger. But she'd gotten to know him well enough to hear the underlying pain that his words didn't reflect. "My mom and I had moved to a new town and I was desperate to impress the neighborhood kids." Hannah sipped some more cool water. "I performed a few tricks with my bike. They were properly awed until the last one. I fell and broke my wrist. I never got back on it after that. I stopped riding for years until college when I took it up for exercise."

"How did we get on a subject like this?"

"I don't know," she said with a shaky laugh.

"I know how." He shifted toward her. "I find it easy

to talk to you. I don't tell others about my childhood. I prefer leaving that in my past."

His words made her feel special. Surprisingly she found it easy to talk to him, too. Less than two months ago she'd thought of him as her enemy. Now she considered him a friend—a very good friend.

He inched closer, taking her hands in his. "I haven't had much time in my life for dating. I made a promise years ago to become a doctor and that's where all my energy has gone."

Children's laughter drifted to her, reminding her they weren't alone. She peered at the group near the lake. Terry was showing Gabe how to skip rocks. Susie was scolding the two youngest boys to stay away from the water.

When she looked back at Jacob, the intensity in his gaze stole her breath. He bent toward her. Her heart fluttered in anticipation. He released her hands and cupped her face. He lowered his head until their mouths were inches apart. The scent of peppermint spiced the air.

Softly he brushed his lips across hers. "I think we should go out on an official date."

"You do?" she squeaked out, her pulse racing through her body.

"Don't you think we've skirted around this long enough?"

"What's this?"

His mouth grazed hers again. "This attraction between us."

She wanted his kiss. His eyes enticed her to forget who he was, to forget the past and grab hold of the future.

A drumroll blared. Hannah gasped and shot back.

Jacob's eyes widened. He stared at her pocket as another drumroll sounded, loud and demanding.

She dug into her jeans. "That's my cell."

"A drumroll? What kind of ring is that?"

She pulled the phone out. "One I know is mine." She flipped it open. "Hannah here."

"I'm so sorry to bother you."

The alarm in Meg's voice alerted Hannah something was wrong.

"Nancy's missing. I've looked everywhere and I can't find her."

Chapter Nine

Heart pounding, Hannah raced up the steps and into the cottage with Jacob and the children not far behind her. Meg stood in the living room with Peter, Laura, Roman and a police officer. The older woman reeled around when Hannah came in. The anxious look on Meg's face tightened a band about Hannah's chest. She gulped in deep breaths, but she couldn't seem to fill her lungs. Bending over, hands on knees, she inhaled over and over. She'd never ridden so fast before.

Meg touched Hannah's shoulder. "She's been gone for at least an hour. We've looked all over the farm, especially the barn."

"You didn't find her in the pen with the puppies? She's taken a liking to one of them."

Peter moved forward. "No, but now that I think about it, I didn't see all the puppies. At the time I thought one was behind its mama in the back."

"Is anything missing from her room?" Jacob strode in with the children.

Meg shook her head. "I don't think so, but I'm not

that familiar with what she has." She snapped her fingers. "Except I know her blanket is gone. She had it with her while she was watching TV in here."

"I'll check her room. I know what she has." Hannah headed down the hallway, her hands shaking so badly she had to clasp them together.

She opened every drawer and the closet, then inspected under the bed and in Nancy's little toy chest. She finished her survey when Jacob appeared in the doorway.

"Anything?"

"Her doll she'd brought with her when she came to the cottage. I don't think she's been kidnapped. I think she's run away."

"Why? Where would she go?"

Her heartbeat pulsated against her eardrums. The constriction about her chest squeezed even tighter. "I don't know and tonight they are predicting it will drop below freezing with rain or snow."

"Let's hope they're wrong."

"Or we find her before then." Hannah welcomed Jacob's calming presence. She saw apprehension in his expression, but above everything his strength prevailed. He was a man used to emergencies and knew how to handle them.

Back in the living room the police officer tucked his notepad into his front pocket then peered at Hannah. "Anything else missing?"

"Her doll."

"I'll call this in and get things moving. Where's your phone?"

Meg pointed toward the kitchen. "I'll show you."

"We need to search the farm again." Jacob placed

his arm about Hannah's shoulder. "Anywhere she really liked?"

"The barn."

"Well, let's start there and fan out."

"How about us?" Susie came forward with the other children, unusually quiet, standing behind her.

"We'll get Cathy and Roman to organize the children and search both cottages, the unfinished one and the surrounding area. Susie, you can help Cathy with the kids in our house." Seeing terror on a couple of their faces, Hannah added, "Nancy will be found. She'll be all right."

"Let's go next door where Cathy and the others are waiting." Roman led the way with the children following.

"I'll have Alexa and Sean meet us at the barn. They can help us search that area." Laura left with Peter.

Hannah started forward. Jacob's hand on her shoulder stopped her. She glanced back at him, such kindness in his eyes that tears welled up in hers. He drew her to him.

"We will find her and she will be all right."

His whispered words, raw with suppressed emotions, fueled her tears. Forcing them down, she backed away from the comfort of his arms. "I don't have time to cry. We only have a few hours before it gets dark."

Two hours later Hannah paused near the creek that ran through the farm. Thankfully it wasn't deep, the bottom easily seen. She peered at Jacob downstream from her. Fifteen minutes ago he found Nancy's doll by a bush where it appeared the little girl had sat. With that they were now concentrating on this area. Nancy had to be near. Nightfall would be in another hour.

"Nancy," Hannah shouted for the hundredth time, her voice raw. She heard the child's name from the others intermittently.

Hannah forged forward into the thicker underbrush, so glad it was too cold for snakes. But there were other animals that could do harm to a small child. Thinking about that possibility, she again yelled the girl's name and heard the frantic ring in her voice.

Only silence greeted her.

Her shoulders sagged as the minutes ticked away. She pushed farther into the wooded area, sending up another prayer for Nancy's safe return.

In the distance she saw a glimpse of pink. Hannah squinted and picked up her pace, although it was slower than usual because of the dense foliage.

"Nancy."

A sound caused her to stop and listen.

The breeze whistled through the forest. Disappointment cloaked her. *Just the wind.*

She continued toward the pink. The little girl's blanket was that color. "Nancy."

Another noise froze Hannah.

A whimper?

"Nancy, honey, where are you?"

Hannah kept moving forward, straining to hear anything unusual, trying to be as quiet as she could so she could listen.

"Hannah," a faint voice, full of tears, floated to her. From the direction of the pink.

"I'm coming."

Hannah tore through the brush, bare limbs clawing her. A branch scratched across her cheek. She fumbled for her cell in her pocket to alert the others she'd found Nancy. She hoped.

"Nancy, say something."

"I'm hurt."

The nearer she got to the pink the stronger the voice. She reached the blanket, but Nancy was nowhere to be seen.

"Honey, where are you? I don't see you."

"I'm down here."

Hannah stepped to the side several yards from the discarded blanket and looked down an incline. At the bottom lay Nancy with the puppy cuddled next to her, a ball of white fur.

"I see you. I'll be right there." Hannah flipped open her phone and punched in Jacob's number.

After giving him directions to where she thought she was, she started down the hill, half sliding as it got steeper toward the bottom. With a tearstained face, Nancy struggled to sit up and watched Hannah's descent. Abby began to yelp and prance around in circles.

When she reached the child, Nancy threw herself into Hannah's arms, sobbing. "You're okay now, honey."

She stroked the child's back, whispering she was safe over and over until Nancy finally calmed down and leaned back.

"Abby ran away from me. I went after her and fell down here. My ankle hurts bad." Tears shone in the child's eyes. "I tried to climb up the hill. I couldn't."

Hannah heard her name being called. "Jacob, we're down here. Nancy's hurt."

"I'm coming. I see her blanket."

The most wonderful thing Hannah saw was Jacob's face peering over the top of the steep incline. "She fell. I think she did something to her ankle."

Jacob descended as gracefully as she did, speed more important than caution. "I called the others. They're coming." He knelt next to them, his gaze tracking down the child's length. "Which ankle hurts?"

Nancy pointed to her left one.

Jacob tenderly took her leg into his hands and probed the area. "I don't think it's broken. Probably a sprain. We'll have to get an X-ray to be sure."

"I don't want a shot. I don't want a shot!" Nancy's voice rose to a hysterical level.

Hannah hugged her to her chest. "Honey, don't worry about that. You need to calm down so we can get you back to the cottage."

Nancy straightened, wiping her eyes. "Where's Abby?" She scanned the surrounding terrain. "She's gone again!"

Jacob reached behind him and picked up the puppy. "She's right here, investigating a twig."

"Oh, good." Nancy sank against Hannah, grasping her as if she were a lifeline.

Hannah's gaze coupled with Jacob's. Everything would be fine now. He would take care of Nancy.

And he could take care of you.

The thought astonished Hannah. She looked away. Her feelings for Jacob were more than friendship.

"You aren't mad at me?" Nancy snuggled under her covers with her doll tucked next to her.

Hannah smoothed the girl's bangs to the side. "No.

I think you realize how dangerous it can be to wander off by yourself, especially when no one knows where you are."

"I thought I could take Abby for a walk. I thought if you saw how good I can take care of her, you'd let me keep her."

"That's a decision we'll all make at the family meeting tomorrow night. There's a cat Susie would like, and Gabe wants one of Abby's brothers."

"That's great! Abby won't be alone. She'll have playmates."

"No, it isn't great. We can't have a house full of children *and* pets."

"Why not?"

"Well…" Hannah couldn't come up with a reason Nancy would understand. The little girl wouldn't accept the answer that a lot of animals running around wouldn't work. All of a sudden Hannah wasn't looking forward to the family meeting tomorrow night.

"How's your ankle?"

Nancy plucked at her coverlet. "It still hurts a little."

Hannah leaned down and kissed the child's forehead. "Thankfully it wasn't broken. You should be better in a week or so."

"Yeah, Dr. Jacob told me that. I like him."

So do I. "Good night." Hannah rose, tucked Nancy's roommate in, then quietly made her way to the door.

In the hallway she heard Jacob talking to Andy and Gabe. Earlier he'd rounded up the boys and got them ready for bed while she had taken care of the girls. As though they were a team—a family.

Hannah crossed the large living room to the picture

window and stared at the darkness beyond. In the distance she saw the lights of Peter and Laura's house. Life was back to normal.

Who was she kidding?

There was nothing normal about her life at the moment. She'd discovered today she was falling in love with an enemy of her family—the man who was responsible for her brother's death.

Among all the feelings tumbling around in her mind, guilt dominated. What would her mother say if she ever found out? Mom hadn't mentioned Jacob Hartman in years, but Hannah could just imagine what her reaction would be.

Hannah shivered as if the cold weather that had swooped down on Cimarron City in the past few hours had oozed into the cottage, into her bones.

This was one problem she'd never thought she would have. How could they overcome the history between them. They both deserved a family—but together?

A sound of footsteps behind her warned her she wasn't alone. In the pane she glimpsed Jacob approaching. She tensed. Then she caught sight of his smile and melted, all stress flowing from her.

He grasped her upper arms and pulled her back against him. "For the time being all's quiet on the home front."

The use of the word *home* in connection with Jacob sent a yearning through her she hadn't thought possible where he was concerned. He had so much to offer a woman.

But how could she be that woman?

His breath washed over her as he nibbled on the skin

right below her ear, undermining all the defenses she was desperately trying to erect against him.

"After the day we had with Nancy's disappearance and our vigorous bike ride, I should be exhausted. But I'm not. I'm wide-awake."

How could this man affect her with that husky appeal in his voice? When had her feelings for him changed? The moment she had forgiven him? Or before?

He rubbed his hands up and down her arms. "Cold?"

The humor in his question told her he knew exactly the effect he was having on her every sense. Goose bumps zipped through her, and if he hadn't been holding her up, she would have collapsed against him. "It's dropped at least twenty degrees in the last hour."

"Outside. Not in here."

He swept her around so she faced him, only inches from her. "I don't think it's going to snow."

Why was he talking about the weather when his mouth was a whisper away from hers? She balled her hands to keep from dragging his lips to hers. "If it does, it won't stick. The ground's too warm." And now she was discussing weather!

"Yes, too warm," he murmured right before settling his lips on hers.

As her arms wound about him, he pressed her close. She soared above the storm, high in the sky. Nothing was important but this man in her embrace.

When he finally drew back slightly, their ragged breaths tangled, the scent of peppermint teasing her. She would never look at a piece of that candy and not remember his kiss.

"I'd better go. It's been a long day, and I have to be

at church early tomorrow." His fingers delved into her curls, his gaze penetrating into hers.

"Yes, I'm helping out in the nursery tomorrow, so I need to get everyone moving earlier than usual."

"You want me to come to the family meeting in the evening?"

She nodded, aware of his hands still framing her face as though leaving his imprint on her. "I'm new at the family-meeting stuff so I may need your help to get it right."

"Say that again." His mouth quirked into a lopsided grin.

She playfully punched his arm. "You heard me."

"Yes, but I like hearing you say you might need my help to get it right. I may never hear that again from your lips." The second he said the word *lips* his gaze zeroed in on hers.

She tingled as though his mouth still covered hers. When he lifted his regard to her eyes, a softness entered his that nearly undid her. In that moment she felt so feminine and cherished.

Pulling completely away, Jacob swallowed hard. "Seriously I'll help you anytime you need it. Just ask."

"I know." Bereft without him near, she meant every word. He was a good, kind man who had made a mistake when he was young. She realized that she could forget the past now in addition to forgiving him. Peace blanketed her in an indescribable feeling, underscoring the rightness of what she was doing.

He backed farther away. "I can find my own way out. See you tomorrow."

She watched him stride out of the room. Turning

back to the window, she glimpsed him descend the porch steps and make his way to his car.

Tomorrow she needed to go to her brother's grave and put an end to any lingering guilt. And tonight she needed to call her mother and tell her about Jacob Hartman's involvement in the refuge. She wanted to move on with her life.

Hannah made her way to her room and sat on her bed, reaching for the phone on the table nearby. Her hand quivered as she lifted the receiver and punched in her mother's number. She hadn't really talked to her in over a month. On Thanksgiving, her mother had been working and hadn't stayed on the phone for more than a minute.

"Mom, how's everything going?" Hannah asked when her mother picked up.

"Busy. Busy. You know how this time of year people seem to get sicker. My floor at the hospital has been packed this past week."

"I'm sorry to hear that." Her palms sweaty, Hannah shifted the receiver to the other ear. She didn't know how to tell her mother about Jacob. This was really something she needed to do in person. She thought about ending the conversation quickly and waiting until she could see her.

"It's late, honey. Is something wrong?"

Yes, I'm falling in love with a man you hate. "Since I didn't get to talk to you for long on Thanksgiving, I thought I would check in and see how things were going."

"Hannah, what are you not telling me? Something's wrong. I hear it in your voice."

Chewing on her lip, Hannah wiped one of her palms on her slacks. "Are you coming to see me at Christmas?"

There was a long pause, then her mother answered, "I don't know. It will depend on when I have to work. Why?"

"Because I want to see you." *Because I'm stalling.* She rubbed the other hand down her thigh. "Jacob Hartman is a doctor who lives in Cimarron City." Before she lost her nerve, she rushed on, "He's the doctor for the refuge, so I've seen him quite a bit."

"Jacob Hartman, the boy who killed Kevin?"

"Yes, Mom. I—"

"I can't believe it. I—" Her mother's voice roughened. "I—I…"

The line went dead. Hannah stared at the receiver for a few seconds, then called her mother back. She let it ring fifteen times before she finally hung up. She hadn't handled it well. She should have waited until she'd seen her mother. This news was the kind that should be given to someone face-to-face, the news that she was falling in love with the enemy.

After quizzing the groundskeeper about who was putting flowers at her brother's grave, Hannah hiked across the cemetery, enjoying the cold, crisp day. Several inches of snow had fallen overnight, but the place looked tranquil, as though the world was at peace. The quiet soothed her, especially after the night spent tossing and turning, going over and over in her head the abrupt conversation she'd had with her mother.

Near her brother's grave site, she saw a car—Jacob's new one. Since the groundskeeper had told her Dr. Hartman came once a week to change the flowers, she wasn't really surprised to see him. She stopped by a large oak and waited for him to leave.

She didn't want him to see her. The night before she had come to a decision. She needed to tell Jacob who she was, but she wanted to pick the right moment. This wasn't it. She hadn't prepared what to say to him. And because it was so important she had to consider carefully how she told him she was Kevin's younger sister, especially after messing up the phone conversation with her mother the night before.

After removing the old flowers, Jacob filled the vase with the new ones, paused for a moment, his head bowed, then pivoted away and sloshed to his car.

She waited until it had disappeared from view before she trudged to her brother's tombstone. The bright red roses, stark against the white blanket of snow, were silk. She stooped to finger the petals.

"Kevin, where do I begin?" She fortified herself with a deep gulp of the chilly air. "For so many years I was mad at Jacob Hartman for taking you away from us. I believed he had gone on with his life as though nothing had happened, living happily and unaffected by the wreck. Now I don't think that."

She reached out and traced her brother's name, chiseled in the cold marble. The dates carved into the stone were a permanent reminder of his death at a young age. She rose.

"The groundskeeper said he comes every week. That isn't the action of a man who has moved on. Occasionally I've caught a vulnerability in him that has stunned me. He's good at hiding it, but it's there. Is it a coincidence he became a doctor? Was it because he wanted to or because that had been your dream?"

Her throat closed around her last word. The cold burrowed into her. She hugged her coat to her. "I think the Lord brought me back to Cimarron City to help Jacob. It was time to let go of my anger and forgive Jacob. I have. For the longest time I'd forgotten what kind of person you were. You would have wanted me to forgive him long ago. Better late than never." She smiled. "You know how stubborn I can be."

Hannah touched the tombstone again, comforted by her visits to Kevin's grave. Was Jacob? She hoped so because after twenty-one years she finally felt she had said her goodbyes to her brother and he didn't blame her for telling on him that last day. Kevin had never held a grudge; she had forgotten that. "I love you. I love him. I will find a way to help him heal, and I will make Mom understand. I know that's what you would want me to do."

"I like your new old car," Hannah said as she took a bite of her pepperoni pizza early Wednesday afternoon. "How come you didn't get a brand-new one? I thought you would after that piece of jun—"

"Hold it right there," Jacob interrupted her. "You're speaking about a vehicle that served me well for years."

"And years."

His chuckles vied with the lunch crowd noise in the restaurant. "Okay. I get the point. It was an old rattletrap."

"There. That wasn't too hard to admit, was it?"

He snagged her look. "Yes. I thought I was being frugal."

"Is that why you didn't buy a new one?"

"It's hard to break a habit. I've been so used to saving to pay off my loans that I just automatically do it."

"You've got to enjoy some of the fruits of your hard work. Have a little fun."

"Are you telling me I don't know how to have fun?"

"Well, no, not exactly, but what do you do for fun?"

"Bicycling?"

"That's recent."

"Let me see." He peered up at the ceiling and tapped his finger against his chin.

"Just as I suspected. You work too much and play too little."

A twinkle glinted in his dark eyes. "And what do you suggest I do about that?"

"Why, of course, play more. I think you should join us in decorating the cottage for Christmas."

"Sounds like work to me." Jacob finished the last slice of pizza.

"Decorating is fun."

"You're a woman."

"I'm glad you noticed," Hannah said with a laugh.

"It's in your genes."

"The kids wanted me to ask you."

"Oh, in that case, I'll be there. What time?"

"Hold it right there. I think I'm offended. You wouldn't come when I asked, but I say something about the children and you're wanting to know what time to be there." She exaggerated a pout.

"I was going to come. I was just playing with you. Didn't you tell me I needed to play more?"

The mischief in his gaze riveted her. "I do believe you might be easy to train—I mean, teach."

His laughter filled the space between them, linking them in a shared moment. All of a sudden the noise, the crowd faded from her awareness as she stared at Jacob, relaxed, almost carefree.

"Hannah, Dr. Hartman, it's good to see you two."

Reluctantly, Hannah looked away from Jacob. "It's nice seeing you, Lisa. How's the job?" Lisa had been the reason she had insisted on coming to the Pizzeria to eat before they went to see Nancy's mother.

"It's only my third day, but I like it. I saw ya from the back and wanted to say hi."

Jacob wiped his mouth with the paper napkin. "Noah told me he hired you to fill in where needed."

"Yeah, I'm learnin' all the jobs." She squared her shoulders, standing a little taller. "There's quite a few I hafta learn, but I can do it."

"Great! I was just asking Jacob to come out on Saturday afternoon to help decorate the cottage for Christmas. If you aren't working, I'd love for you to join us, too."

"I hafta be here at five that evening."

"I can bring you back into town in time for your shift." Jacob picked up the check. "And I'll give you a ride to the farm. I can pick you up at one on Saturday."

"I'll be ready." Lisa glanced back at the counter. "I'd better get back to work."

"I know how you feel about Lisa being in Andy's

life. That was so sweet of you," Hannah said around the lump in her throat.

"Believe it or not, I would love for this to work out for Lisa and Andy."

"But you still don't think it will?"

"I just don't see it through rose-colored glasses."

"And I do?"

He looked her directly in the eye. "Yes, and I'm afraid you'll be hurt when it doesn't work out."

Hannah rose. "I'm not wrong about Lisa. Did you see her at church on Sunday?"

"She was like a deer caught in headlights."

"I realize it was all new to her. But God has His ways." She could still remember when she'd pledged her heart to the Lord. The transformation, a work in progress, was life altering.

Jacob removed his wallet and laid some money on the table. "Only time will tell." At the door he held it open for her. "C'mon, let's get this over with."

"I know Nancy's mother is a long shot, but I've got to try."

"Are you going to do this with every situation?"

She slid into the passenger seat in his car. "I will examine and evaluate every one to see if there's a way."

He gave her a skeptical look as he started the engine. "I hope you don't end up with your heart broken."

She was beginning to realize he was the only one who could do that. "Don't worry about me."

"But I do."

"That's sweet, but I'm tough."

"Yeah, right. You're like Nancy. You wear your heart on your sleeve."

She shifted, sitting up straight. "There's nothing wrong with that."

"As long as things work out."

"Like at the family meeting Sunday night?"

"Exactly." Jacob turned onto the highway that led to Deerfield. "You're blessed with the fact the kids in the cottage care about each other."

Hannah remembered the happiness on Nancy's face when the children voted for Abby to be their pet. "Like a family."

"Not any family I've been in."

The vulnerability, always below the surface, trickled into his words and pricked her heart.

Chapter Ten

Jacob pulled onto the dirt road. "I don't like the looks of this."

Hannah scanned the yard of the address she had for Nancy's mother. Trash littered the porch and literally poured out of a refrigerator without its door. Two old cars in various stages of rusting decomposition flanked the detached garage. The structure leaned to the side, threatening to crash down on the vehicle minus its engine.

"I'm glad you came with me." Hannah pushed her purse under the seat.

"Are you sure you want to do this? We can always leave." Jacob parked in front but left the engine running.

She studied the dirty windows facing them and thought she saw someone looking out. The curtain fell back in place. "No, we came this far. I need to finish this."

"No, you don't."

"Haven't you noticed how reserved and hesitant Nancy is when Andy's mother is visiting? When I try to talk to her, she won't say anything. She sucks her thumb and holds her blanket."

"As much as you'd love to fix every relationship between the children at the refuge and their parents, you won't be able to. Not every mother has maternal instincts."

"Like yours?"

"Exactly." A nerve ticked in his jaw. "I'm glad no one tried."

"You need to forgive your mother," she said, knowing firsthand how important it was to do that if you wanted to move on.

His hard gaze drilled into her, his hands gripping the steering wheel so tight his knuckles were white. "Why would I want to do that?"

"Because she's still affecting your life and will until you let go of the anger."

"I don't think I can. The things she did…"

"The Lord said in Matthew, 'For if ye forgive men their trespasses, your heavenly Father will also forgive you.'"

"I can't. I…" His voice came to a shaky halt. He drew in a breath and stared at the small house. "Someone's opening the door. Let's get this over with."

The finality in his tone ended the conversation. Hannah climbed from the car at the same time Jacob did, his expression totally void of any emotion. But waves of underlying tension came off him as he approached the house.

A woman in her midtwenties, dressed in torn, ragged jeans and a sweatshirt pushed the screen open and stepped out onto the porch. "We don't want any. Git off my land."

A medium-sized man with a beard appeared in the entrance. Hannah's gaze fixed upon the shotgun cradled in his arms, then bounced to his face, set in a scowl that chilled her.

"Ya heard her. Git. Now." The man gestured with a nod toward the road behind Jacob and Hannah.

Jacob edged to her side and grasped her hand. "Let's do as they say."

Hannah started to move back toward the passenger door when she remembered finding Nancy crying last weekend for her mama. The sight had wrenched her heart. She halted. "Are you Abby Simons?"

The woman stiffened, still between them and the man behind her. "Who's askin'?"

A stench—a myriad of odors she couldn't even begin to identify—accosted Hannah's nostrils. "I'm Hannah Smith. I run the place that Nancy is at."

"So? What's she gone and done wrong now?" Abby planted one hand on her hip, her eyes pinpoints.

"Nothing. She's a delight to have at the house."

Abby snorted. "That's your opinion. I have nothin' to say to ya." She turned to go back inside.

"You don't want to see her?" Her stomach roiled. Hannah resisted the urge to cover her mouth and nose to block the smells coming from the house and the couple.

A curse exploded from the woman's lips. "I say good riddance. All she did was whine." She shoved past the man with the weapon.

He glared at Jacob and Hannah. "What's keepin' ya?" He adjusted the gun in the crook of his arms.

Jacob squeezed her hand and tugged her back. "We're going." He jerked open the passenger door and gently pushed Hannah into the car, then rounded the back and climbed in behind the wheel, his gaze never leaving the man holding the weapon.

Fifteen seconds later dust billowed behind his car as he raced toward the highway. He threw her a look of relief. "We could have been killed. I think they're running a meth lab."

"You do?"

"You didn't smell it?"

"I don't know how one smells."

"When we get back to Stone's Refuge, I'm calling the sheriff, although I doubt there will be any evidence left when he arrives." Jacob pressed his foot on the accelerator.

Hannah waited for him to tell her he had told her so, but he didn't. Quiet reigned as the landscape flew past them.

She'd gone into social work to help others. But perhaps Jacob was right. She was too naive. She had a lot to learn. Even if Nancy was never adopted, she was better off where she was than with her mother.

"I was wrong," Hannah finally murmured in the silence.

"About Nancy, yes. The verdict on Andy's situation is still out."

"You think there's a chance it will work?" At the moment she needed validation she wasn't totally off-the-wall about trying to reunite children with their parents, if possible.

He slanted a quick look toward her, warmth in his

eyes. "His mother completed her drug-rehab program. That's a start. As well as getting a job. She's living at the halfway house for the time being, and they're wonderful support for people who are trying to get back on their feet." His gaze found hers again. "Yes, I think there's a chance."

His words made her beam from ear to ear. She felt as though she were shining like a thousand-watt bulb.

"Time will tell and don't be surprised if Lisa backslides. I remember when I quit smoking. I must have tried four or five times before I finally managed to."

"You smoked?"

"Yeah. I started when I was thirteen. I finally stopped when I was eighteen. But it was one of the hardest things I ever did. And staying off drugs will be the hardest thing Lisa does."

"Did you have help?"

He nodded. "Alice and Paul Henderson."

"I'll be there for Lisa."

"*We'll* be there for her."

Like a team. More and more she felt they were.

"I'm glad Peter suggested we cut down one of the pines on his property to use as a tree this year. Until he married Laura, I didn't do much at Christmas other than participate in some of the church functions." Jacob led one of the horses across the snow-covered meadow.

"So you don't mind doing this?" Carrying the ax, Hannah checked around her to make sure the children were keeping up with them.

"Mind? No. It's a good reason to leave work a little early this afternoon."

"This from a man who works all the time!"

"It was a little slow with the snow last night and this morning. Not too many people wanted to get out unless it was an emergency. I noticed the snow fort and snow figures out in front of the cottages. You all were busy today."

She laughed. "We had to do something with the kids home from school. I had a hard time keeping them away from the unfinished house."

"I imagine the kids are intrigued with it."

"You can say that again. I'm glad you don't mind driving in this weather. I haven't had much practice in snow."

At the edge of a grove of pines Jacob stopped and surveyed the prospective Christmas trees. "Okay, guys, which one do you want me to cut down?"

Every child with Jacob and Hannah pointed at a different one. Nancy selected a pine that was at least fifteen feet tall.

Hannah set her hands on the little girl's shoulders. "I like your vision, but that one won't fit into the living room." Then to the whole group she added, "We need a tree that is about six or seven feet tall."

"How about this?" Susie pointed to one near her.

"No, this is better." Andy went to stand by a pine off to the side.

While Terry started toward another, Hannah quickly said, "Hold it. Let's take a vote on these three. They're the only ones the right size." She waved her hand toward Susie's and two others.

Andy spun toward his. "What's wrong with mine?"

"It needs to grow a few more years." Jacob took the ax from Hannah and gave her the reins of the horse.

"Who wants Susie's?" Hannah called out, the wind beginning to pick up.

All the children raised their hands with Andy reluctantly the last one.

"Well, let's get the show on the road." Jacob approached the chosen one and began to chop it down.

The sound of the ax striking the wood echoed through the grove. The smell of snow hung in the air as clouds rolled in.

Terry bent down and scooped up a handful of the white stuff and packed it into a ball, then lobbed it toward Susie. That was the beginning of a small war held at the edge of the grove.

Hannah scurried toward Jacob to avoid being hit. "Do you want a break?"

He glanced up at the sky. "Nope. Not much time. I think it'll start snowing again soon. When that happens, I'd rather be back at the cottage sipping hot chocolate in front of the fireplace."

"We don't have one."

He paused and stared at her with a look that went straight to her heart. "Then we'll just have to use our imaginations. You do have hot chocolate?"

"Of course, with eight children in the house that's a necessity."

"We have marshmallows, too." Nancy came up to stand next to Hannah while Jacob went back to work on the seven-foot tree.

"Mmm. I love marshmallows. I guess I'd better hurry if I want a cup."

A snowball whizzed by Hannah's head. She pivoted in the direction it came. Suddenly she noticed the quiet and the reason for it. All the children were lined up a few feet from her with ammunition in their hands.

"Duck," Hannah shouted, and pulled Nancy with her behind a tree.

Jacob, in midswing, couldn't react fast enough. A barrage of snowballs pelted him from all angles. When he turned toward the crowd of kids, he was covered in white from head to toe. He shook off some of the powder, gave the ax to Hannah, then patiently walked a couple of feet toward the children with a huge grin on his face. The kids stood like frozen statues, not sure what to do.

Suddenly Jacob swooped down, made a ball and threw it before the first child could run. Another snowball ensued then several more after it. Kids scattered in all directions. Jacob shot to his feet and raced after the nearest boy, tackling Terry. As they playfully rolled on the ground, several boys joined them and it became a free-for-all.

Hannah, with Nancy beside her, watched by their chosen tree. The sound of laughter resonated through the meadow with the girls cheering on the boys in their endeavor to overpower Jacob. Although outnumbered, the good doctor was having the time of his life if the expression of joy on his face was any clue. She knew he wanted a family. He should be a father.

And you want a family. You want to be a mother. What are you doing about that?

When a snowflake fell, followed by several more, Hannah peered up at the sky. Another hit her cheek and instantly melted. She put two fingers into her mouth and let out a loud, shrill whistle that immediately called a halt to the melee on the ground.

"In case you don't know, it's snowing again. We need to cut down our tree and get back to the cottage. Playtime is over, boys."

Amidst a few grumbles Jacob pushed to his feet, drenched from his tumble in the snow. He shoved his wet hair out of his eyes and strode to the ax Hannah held out for him.

In five minutes he yelled, "Timber," and the tree toppled to the ground. "I always wanted to do that."

Having tied the horse's reins to one of the branches of a nearby pine, Hannah moved toward it, calling to the children. "Help Dr. Jacob with our Christmas tree."

After quickly securing the pine with some rope, Jacob guided the horse toward the cottage with their tree gliding over the snow behind the animal. Snow came down faster as they reached the porch.

"I'll take the horse back to the barn," Terry said when Jacob untied the pine.

"Come right back. It'll be getting dark soon." Hannah helped Jacob drag the tree up the steps and placed it to the side of the front door. "Who's up for hot chocolate?"

Hands flew into the air.

"While I'm fixing it, change out of those wet clothes then come into the kitchen." Hannah opened the door and went into the house.

Footsteps pounded down the hallway toward the various bedrooms.

"That'll give us a few minutes of quiet." Hannah's

gaze moved down Jacob's length. "I wish I had something for you to change into. Your jeans are soaking wet."

He started to remove his coat, but stopped. "I've got some sweats in my trunk. Can I use your bedroom to change in?"

Her step faltered. "Sure," she answered, trying not to imagine him in her room.

As he jogged to his car, she waved her hand in front of her face and thought about turning down the heater. Memories of his kiss swamped her. She wanted him to kiss her again. Oh, my. She was in deep.

As she prepared the hot chocolate and a plate of cookies under the disapproving eye of Meg, the children flooded the kitchen. They snatched a mug and one cookie then fled the room, nearly knocking Jacob down in their haste.

"Whoa. What was that?" He entered as the last boy zipped past him.

"Those cookies are gonna spoil their dinner," Meg grumbled while she stirred a large pot on the stove.

"Mmm. Is that your stew?" Jacob took the last mug sitting on the counter.

Still frowning, Meg nodded.

"Then you don't have a worry. The kids love it. There won't be a drop left at the end of the meal, especially if a wonderful cook invites a certain doctor to dinner." Jacob winked at Hannah right before he took a sip of his drink.

"Not my call." The beginnings of a grin tempered Meg's unyielding expression as she swung her gaze from Jacob to Hannah.

He turned a pleading look on Hannah. "I worked up quite an appetite chopping down *your* tree."

She took a cookie off the plate. "Here. This ought to tide you over until you can eat."

His fingers grazed hers as he grasped the treat. "The important question is where will I be eating dinner?"

"Meg, we might as well make a permanent place for Jacob at our table as often as he's been here for dinner." The image of him at one end of the table and her at the other darted through her mind. Like a family—with eight children! She should be fleeing from the kitchen as quickly as the kids did moments before. What was she doing thinking of them as a family?

"I heartily agree. Meg's cooking is much better than mine."

Meg barked a laugh. "You're cooking is nonexistent."

"Not from lack of trying."

Meg swept around with one hand on her waist and a wooden spoon in the other. "When? You work way too hard. I'm glad to see you spending more time with the children."

"I think that's our cue to leave the chef alone to create her masterpiece." Jacob grabbed the last cookie, held the door for Hannah and accompanied her from the room with Meg muttering something about him eating everything on his plate or else.

"She's a treasure. You'd better not run her off," Hannah said in mock sternness.

"I want to know what 'or else' means." He headed toward the sound of children talking in the living room.

"You're a brave soul if you dare to leave anything uneaten."

Jacob blocked her path into the room. "I enjoyed this afternoon. Thank you for inviting me. Other than the birth of Christ, the holidays have never held much appeal to me."

"I have to admit Christmas has never been my favorite time of year." After Kevin died during December, she and her mother hadn't done much in the way of enjoying themselves during the holidays. In fact, they had ignored it until they had become Christians.

"Shh. Don't let the kids hear you say that."

"That's why we'll be going all-out this Christmas here at the house and at church."

"I'd love to help you with your activities." His gaze captured hers.

Her pulse rate spiked. "I'm glad you volunteered. Next weekend we're going to the nursing home to perform the Nativity scene. Roman can't come because of a prior commitment, but we're taking some of the animals to make the play more authentic and I could use an extra pair of hands beside Peter."

"How many animals?"

"Two lambs for the shepherds. A couple of dogs. Maybe a rabbit or two."

"I don't remember there being any dogs or rabbits in the manger."

"We thought we would dress up two of the big dogs as though they're donkeys."

Jacob tossed back his head and laughed. "I'm sure they'll love that. This production could be priceless."

"Hey, just for that, you can help with the rehearsals, too. Every night after dinner this week. We aren't nearly ready."

He wiped tears from the corner of his eyes. "Definitely priceless."

"Be careful. That box has all the ornaments in it." Hannah hurried over to help Susie carry the oversized one to the living room where Jacob and Terry were setting up the Christmas tree in its stand on Saturday afternoon.

The scent of popcorn wafted through the large cottage. Meg came out of the kitchen with two big bowls of the snack. She placed both of them on the game table. "One is for stringing. The other for eating."

A couple of the kids dived into the one for consumption, in their haste causing some of the popped kernels to fall onto the floor. Abby pounced on it.

Hannah scooped the puppy up and gave her to Nancy. "There's enough for everyone." Hannah moved the one for stringing over to the coffee table where some of the younger children sat. "Nancy, you might put Abby in the utility room until we're done."

Meg settled on the couch behind the kids working with the popcorn to assist them while Hannah opened the box with strands of twinkling white lights.

She pulled the tangled mess out and held it up, "What happened here?"

"Peter. Last year he took them down and made a mess out of them." Meg gave Nancy who had returned without Abby a needle with a long string attached.

"Remind me not to accept his help this year with taking down the tree." Hannah sat cross-legged on the floor and searched for one end of the strand. "How many are here?"

"Four." Meg scooted over for Nancy to sit next to her while she worked on the popcorn garland.

"Maybe I should just go to town and buy new ones." Jacob squatted next to her.

"No. No, I'll figure this out. No sense in wasting money."

Fifteen minutes later Hannah finally untangled one strand completely and was on her way to freeing another.

Jacob bent down and whispered in her ear, "Ready to call uncle."

"No way. Here's one. By the time you've got it up, I should have the second string ready."

The doubtful look Jacob sent her as he rose fueled Hannah's determination, but the puppy's yelps from the utility room rubbed her nerves raw, pulling her full attention away from her task. "Nancy, please check on Abby."

Hannah had almost finished with the second strand when Abby came barreling into the room and raced toward her. The white puppy leaped into her lap, licking her face, her body wiggling so much it threw Hannah off balance.

"Nancy!" Hannah fell back with Abby on her chest now, one hand caught in the snarl of lights.

The little girl charged into the room. "Sorry. She got away from me." She pulled the puppy off Hannah.

Jacob offered her his hand, a gleam glittering in his eyes. When she clasped it, he tugged her up. "Okay?"

"Sure. Abby just gets a little enthusiastic. Laura's

teenage son is going to help us with her." Hannah glanced down at the lights and groaned. The second string was twisted in with the other two.

"Uncle?"

She picked up the snarl. "Uncle."

"Let me see what I can do before ya head into town." Lisa sat next to Hannah. "I'm good at stuff like this."

Ten minutes later the lights were ready to go. Hannah purposely ignored the merriment dancing in Jacob's eyes. She corralled the remaining children who weren't working on the popcorn garlands.

"Let's get the ornaments out, so when the lights are up, we'll be ready to put them on the tree."

Three kids fought to open the box. With two fingers in her mouth, Hannah whistled, startling them. They shot up with arms straight at their sides.

She waved her hand. "Shoo. I'll unpack them and give them to y'all. Lisa, want to help me?"

Andy's mother nodded.

"There. We're done with our part." Jacob stood back from the pine and gave Terry a signal to plug the lights in.

Nancy leaped to her feet, clapping her hands. "It's beautiful."

"Yes, it is. Just wait until the ornaments are on it. It'll be even better." Hannah peered toward Jacob who plopped into the lounge chair nearby. "And don't think your job is done. Look at this huge box of decorations."

Jacob shoved himself up. "Kids, remind me to find out what my duties are before volunteering next time."

A couple of the children giggled, setting the mood for the next two hours while everyone worked, first decorating the tree, then the rest of the house. Andy rode with Jacob to take Lisa to work. When they returned, Jacob brought large pizzas for dinner.

By the time the cottage quieted with the kids tucked into bed, exhaustion clung to Hannah, her muscles protesting her every move. "Getting ready for Christmas is tiring work." She collapsed on the couch in the living room.

"I know you may be shocked, but I have to agree with you." Jacob gestured around him at the myriad of decorations in every conceivable place. "Where did all this come from?"

"From what Laura told me, most of it was donated."

He picked up a two-foot-high flamingo with a Santa hat on its head and a wreath around its neck. "What's a flamingo have to do with Christmas?"

She shrugged. "Beats me, but it's kinda cute. Nancy sure liked it."

"She liked everything. We couldn't put it out fast enough for her."

"She's never had Christmas before. She told me her mother didn't believe in the Lord."

"Now, why doesn't that surprise me." Jacob eased down next to Hannah on the couch, grimacing as he leaned back. "After yesterday and today, I think I'll rest tomorrow."

"I think Terry said something about needing your help to build the manger Sunday afternoon."

Jacob's forehead furrowed. "And when were you going to tell me that?"

"Tomorrow when you came to help with the rehearsal."

His mouth twisted into a grim line that his sparkling eyes negated. He tried glaring at Hannah, but laughter welled up in him. He lay his head on the back cushion. "I haven't enjoyed myself like that in…" He slanted his gaze toward her. "Actually today has been great. Thank you again for including me."

The wistfulness in his voice produced an ache in her throat. "It was fun."

"It's what I think of a family doing during the holidays. The only time I had anything similar was when I lived with Paul and Alice. For three years I was part of something good." A faraway look appeared in his eyes as he averted his head and stared up at the ceiling.

Hannah dug her fingernails into her palms to keep from smoothing the lines from his forehead. She felt as though he had journeyed back in time to a past that held bad memories.

"That first Christmas with the Hendersons I was determined to stay in my room and have nothing to do with any celebration."

"Why?"

"Because in December the year before, I had killed a friend."

Chapter Eleven

Hearing Jacob say he'd killed her brother out loud tore open the healing wound. A band about Hannah's chest squeezed tight, whooshing the air from her lungs. Her mind raced back twenty-one years to the day she'd been told Kevin died in a car wreck. She heard her mother's screams then her cries all over again.

"I've shocked you, Hannah. I'm sorry. I shouldn't have said anything but…" He looked away, his jaw locked in a hard line.

His apology pulled her back to the present. She managed to shut down all memories and focus on Jacob next to her on the couch. "But what?" There was no force behind the words, and for a few seconds she wondered if he even was aware she had spoken.

When his gaze swept back to hers, the anguish in his was palpable, as if it were a physical thing she could touch. "Over the past month we've been getting closer. We've spent a lot of time together." His eyelids slid halfway closed, shielding some of his turmoil from her.

"I'm not sure where this... relationship is going, but I felt you needed to know."

"What happened?" She knew one side of the story, if she could even call it that. She needed to hear his side.

"It happened twenty-one years ago, but I'll never forget that day. Ever." He reestablished eye contact with her, a bleakness in his expression now. "Kevin borrowed his parents' car one night, and we went riding. We were bored, and he wanted to practice driving. Because we were fourteen, we drove in the country so no one would catch us. After he drove for a while, he let me get behind the wheel and try my hand. Everything was going along fine until..." Jacob pressed his lips together and closed his eyes.

"Until?" Hannah covered his hand with hers, his cold fingers mirroring hers.

Sucking in a deep breath, he looked directly at her and said, "Until I lost control of the car when it hit a patch of black ice. My friend didn't put on his seat belt when we changed places, and he was thrown from the car."

Her own pain jammed her throat like a fist. It was an effort even to swallow. "What happened to you?" She'd known little about what injuries he had sustained in the wreck.

"I had a concussion, some cuts and bruises, but otherwise I was okay—physically. But after that night, nothing was the same for me. At the time I didn't believe in the Lord and had nowhere to turn." Leaning forward, he propped his elbows on his knees and buried his face in his palms.

Her heartbeat roared in her ears. She reached out to

lay a quivering hand on his hunched back, stopped midway there and withdrew it. Words evaded her because she was trying to imagine dealing with something like that alone, without the Lord. He'd only been fourteen. A maelstrom of emotions must have overwhelmed him.

"How long before you went to the Hendersons to live?"

He scrubbed his hands down his face. "Too long. A year."

All the agony of that year was wrapped up in his reply. This time she touched him.

"I still have nightmares about the accident."

Her heart plummeted. All these years she had thought she and her family had been the only ones who had suffered. She'd been wrong—very wrong. "It was an *accident,* Jacob."

"Do you know one of the reasons I wanted to be a doctor? Kevin did. That's all he'd talked about."

Beneath her palm she felt him quake.

"I became a doctor. I tried to make up for my mistake, but there's always a part of me that remembers I took a life." Another tremor passed through his body. "I'll never forget Kevin's mother at the hospital. If I could have traded places with him, I would have."

Tell him who you are, Hannah thought. *No! I can't add to his pain. Not now.*

"I'm so sorry, Jacob. So sorry."

He shoved to his feet. "I'm not the one to feel sorry for. I survived."

His rising tone didn't match the despair on his face. "Yes, you survived. I thank God that at least one of you did. Your death would have deprived these children of a wonderful, caring doctor."

"You don't understand." Jacob flexed his hands at his sides. "These past few weeks with you I've been truly happy for the first time in my life. I don't deserve to be."

She rose. "Why not? How will you living a miserable life change the outcome of the wreck?"

He started to say something but snapped his mouth closed and stared off into space.

"Why are you telling me this now?"

"I thought we could date, get to know each other better, but I don't think we should now."

"Because you are happy with me?"

"Yes! These past two days getting the cottage ready for the holidays has shown me what Christmas can be like, what it would be like to have a family."

"How long do you have to suffer before it's enough?"

He plowed his hand through his hair, the tic in his jaw twitching.

"When will it be enough?"

"I don't know," Jacob shouted, then spun around on his heel and stalked to the front door. She sank down on the couch, her whole body shaking with the storm of emotions that had swept through the room. She couldn't forget that Jacob had opened his heart to her. She had to do the same. She would pray for guidance and tell him tomorrow after church.

Hannah stood at the window, watching Jacob help Terry, Gabe and Andy build a manger for the play. The sound of laughter and hammering pounded at her resolve to find some time to be alone with Jacob and tell him who she was. He'd avoided her after church, and by the time she'd gathered all the children together, he was gone. Even when he'd come an hour ago, he'd spent little time with her, as if he'd regretted sharing something so personal with her the night before.

He lived in a self-made prison, and she was determined to free him. This was why the Lord had brought her to Cimarron City, to Stone's Refuge—to heal Jacob, a good man who had made a mistake when he was a teen.

His eyes crinkling in laughter, Jacob tousled Andy's hair. The boy giggled then launched himself at Jacob, throwing his arms around his middle. The scene brought tears to Hannah. The only time today she'd seen him relax and let down his guard was with the children.

Hannah pivoted away from the window and froze when she saw Nancy in the middle of the room, watching her with her thumb in her mouth and her doll cradled against her chest. Hannah quickly swiped away her tears. "Hi, Nancy. Have you got your costume finished for the play?"

The little girl shook her head, plucking her thumb from her mouth. "Susie said she heard you talking to Meg about visiting my mother. Susie thinks you want to get me together with her like you did Andy and his mother." Terror inched into the child's expression. "Is Mommy coming to get me?"

"No, honey."

Nancy heaved a sigh. "Good. She isn't nice like ya and Andy's mother." The little girl held up her doll. "Can we use Annie for baby Jesus?"

"Yes," Hannah murmured, relieved to see the child's terror gone from her eyes.

The child beamed. "I told Annie she could be. No one will know she's a girl."

"We'll wrap Annie in swaddling and all that will show is her face. She'll fit perfectly in the manger." Hannah gestured toward the boys in the court finishing up with the cradle.

"I'm gonna try Annie in it." Nancy raced toward the sliding-glass door that led outside.

"Hannah!"

Out of the corner of her eye she noticed Nancy carefully lay her doll into the manger. At the sound of her name being shouted again, she turned from the window as Susie came into the living room.

"I can't get this to work." The girl dropped her arms and the white sheet slid off one shoulder. "Can you help me with my costume?"

"Sure. This won't be hard to fix." Whereas she wasn't sure about her relationship with Jacob.

"Jacob, you aren't going to stay for dinner?" Hannah moved out onto the porch that evening and closed the front door behind her so the children couldn't listen.

He stopped on the top step and faced her. "It's been a long day. I have a busy week ahead of me."

He'd made sure they hadn't had a minute alone to talk. She wasn't going to let him flee, not after working up her courage to tell him everything so there were no secrets between them. "I need to talk to you."

He stiffened. "Can we another time?"

"No."

He glanced around him as though searching for a way to escape. When he directed his gaze back to her, resignation registered on his face but he remained silent.

She pointed toward the porch swing. "Let's sit down."

He strode to it and settled at one end. Hannah sank down next to him. He tensed.

"This is about what I told you last night."

The monotone inflection of his voice chilled her. She hugged her arms to her and shored up her determination. "Yes."

She tried to remember what she had planned to say, but suddenly there was nothing in her mind except a panicky feeling she was wrong, that she should remain quiet. That she would only add to his pain.

"I understand if you don't want to see me."

"Is that why you told me?" She twisted toward him so she could look into his eyes. With night quickly approaching it was becoming harder to read his expression.

"I—I'm not sure what you mean."

"It's simple. Did you tell me about your past to drive me away?"

"You have a right to know."

"Why?" A long moment of silence eroded her resolve.

She started to say he didn't have to answer her when he said, "Because I'm falling in love with you and…"

His declaration sent her heartbeat galloping. "And?"

"Isn't that enough?" He bolted to his feet and took a step forward.

She grabbed his hand and held him still. "Don't leave after telling me that."

He whirled around, shaking loose her hold. "Don't you see, Hannah? I carry a lot of baggage. That's why I don't think it's a good idea for us to become involved."

She tried to look into his eyes, but the shadows shaded them. "We all do. Please sit."

"I can't ask someone to share that."

"Why not? It's in the past. Over twenty years ago."

"I've tried to forget. I can't. I'll never be able to."

"Forget or forgive?" She stood, cutting the space between them.

"Both! My carelessness led to another's death. That may be easy for someone else to dismiss, but not me."

She desperately wanted to take him into her arms and hold him until she could erase all memories of that night twenty-one years ago—from both their memories. But the tension flowing off him was as effective as a high, foot-thick wall—insurmountable and impregnable.

"Earlier you said you're falling in love with me. That's how I feel about you."

"How—"

She placed her fingers over his mouth to still his words. "No, let me finish."

The tension continued to vibrate between them, but he nodded.

She lowered her hand and took hold of his. There was no easy way to say this to him. "I need to tell you who I am. Before I married, my maiden name was Collins. I was Kevin's little sister."

Several heartbeats hammered against her chest before Jacob reacted to her news. He yanked his hand from hers and scrambled back, shaking his head. "You can't be."

"I am. I was eight when Kevin died in the car wreck. My parents split not long after the accident and Mom and I moved away. Actually we spent many years running away."

"What kind of game are you playing?"

"I'm not playing a game."

"I killed your brother! Why are you even talking to me?"

The fierce sound of the whispered words blasted her as if he had shouted them. "I'm not going to kid you. For many years I blamed you for taking my big brother away from me. I hated you."

His harsh laugh echoed through the quiet. "And now you don't hate me." Disbelief resonated through his voice.

"No, I don't. I didn't lie when I told you I was falling in love with you."

"Please don't. I don't want to be responsible for you betraying your family on top of everything else."

"I'm not betraying them."

"I'll never be able to forget your mother yelling at me that I had destroyed her life. I dream about that."

"This isn't about my mother. This is about you and me."

"There is no you and me. I…" He took another step back until he bumped into the railing post.

She quickly covered the short distance, planting herself so he couldn't easily leave. "If that's how you feel, so be it. But I wanted you to realize how I feel."

"I know. Now I need to go." He started to push past her.

She moved into his path. "No, you don't know it all. And the least you can do for me is to listen until I'm through."

He inhaled a deep breath.

She felt the glare of his eyes boring into her although darkness now cloaked the porch totally. "When I came back to Cimarron City, I discovered you were still living here and a doctor. At first I didn't realize you were the pediatrician for Stone's Refuge, but when I discovered that, I considered leaving. I didn't see how I could work with the man who killed my brother."

"It does seem unbelievable." Sarcasm inched into his voice as he tried to distance himself as much as she allowed.

"Have you forgotten what Christ has taught us? To forgive those who trespass against us?"

"Yeah, but—"

"But, nothing." She gripped his arms. "I have forgiven you for what happened to Kevin. It was an *accident*."

His muscles beneath her palms bunched.

"You're a good man who deserves to really live his life. You've paid dearly over the years for the wreck. Don't you think it's time you stop beating yourself up over it?"

"Because you say so?"

She thrust her face close to his. "Yes!"

For a long moment tension continued to pour off him, then as if he had shut down his emotions, he closed himself off. "Is that all?"

All! She nodded, her heart climbing up into her throat.

"May I leave now?"

"Yes." She backed away from him.

It didn't matter to him that she had forgiven him. He couldn't forgive himself.

The sound of his footfalls crossing the porch bombarded her. This was the end.

She couldn't let him walk away without trying one more time to make him understand. "Jacob."

He kept walking toward his vehicle.

"Jacob, stop!"

He halted, his hand about to open the car door. The stiff barrier of his stance proclaimed it was useless for her to say anything. He wouldn't really hear.

She had to try anyway.

Hannah hurried toward him, praying he didn't change his mind and leave. She positioned herself next to him, hoping he would look at her.

He stared over the roof of the car into the distance. The lamplight that illuminated the sidewalk to the house cast a golden glow over them. She could make out the firm set to his jaw and the hard line of his mouth slashing downward.

"When I realized I'd finally forgiven you for what had happened to Kevin, I was free for the first time in twenty-one years. That's what forgiveness can do for you. Let it go."

He cocked his head to the side. "And just when did you decide to forgive me?"

"It wasn't a sudden revelation. But I knew when you took care of me and the children during the strep outbreak."

"And all the time before that?"

"I was fighting my growing feelings for you."

"And you lost."

"I don't look at it as losing. I want to see where our relationship can lead."

"Nowhere, Hannah. Nowhere. So why waste our time?" He wrenched open the door and climbed inside his car.

A few seconds later the engine roared to life, and Jacob sped away. As the taillights disappeared from view, she vowed she wouldn't give up on him.

Hannah leaned against the wall in the back of the rec room at the nursing home as the children began their play about the birth of Jesus. She scanned the crowd one more time, hoping she had overlooked Jacob, but he was nowhere in the audience. Her gaze fell upon Lisa in the front row with Cathy and she was glad that at least Andy had his mother at the play. But no Jacob, although he had promised the kids he would be at their production, via a phone call to Terry. Jacob hadn't been at the house in a week. He was avoiding her. She didn't need it written in the sky to know what Jacob was doing. She'd even thought briefly—very briefly—that maybe one of the children would get sick and she would have to take them to see Dr. Jacob.

Not having dated much, she wasn't sure what to do now. She missed him terribly. She hadn't realized how much until day three and she had reached for the phone at least ten times to call him. She hadn't, but the desire to had been so strong she had shaken with it.

Laura slid into place next to her and whispered, "He'll be here. He doesn't break a promise to the kids."

"There's always a first time." Hannah checked her

watch for the hundredth time. "He has one minute before Susie and Terry appear as Mary and Joseph."

No sooner had she said Joseph than Jacob slipped into the room and eased into a chair in the back row at the other end of the room from where she was. Hannah straightened, folding her arms across her body.

Laura turned her head slightly toward her and cupped her hand over her mouth. "I told you he would be here."

"Shh. The play is about to start. I don't want to miss a word of it."

"Who are you kidding? You've heard the lines until I'm sure you can recite every one of them."

Hannah really tried to follow the children as they reenacted the story of the birth of Christ, but she continually found herself drawn back to Jacob, his strong profile a lure she couldn't resist. She came out of her trance when one of the lambs escaped and charged down the aisle toward the door by Jacob, baaing the whole way. The play stopped, and everyone twisted around in his seat to follow the animal's flight. Dressed in a gray suit, Jacob sprang to his feet and blocked its path to freedom, tackling it to the floor, its loud bleating echoing through the room.

"Got her." Jacob struggled to stand with the squirming animal fighting the cage of his arms.

As though the first lamb had signaled a mass bolt for all the animals, the other one broke free, probably because the young boy holding him had let go. Then the two dogs, portraying donkeys, up until this point perfectly content to sit by their handlers, chased after the second sheep. Kids scattered in pursuit of their fleeing pets.

Shocked at how quickly everything had fallen apart, Hannah watched the pandemonium unfold, rooted to her spot in the back along the wall. Then out of the corner of her eye, she saw a dog dart past her. She dived toward the mixed breed and captured it. Thankfully the mutt was more cooperative than Jacob's lamb. Taking the large dog by his collar, she led it back to the front where Peter was trying to bring some kind of order to the chaos.

Sprinkles of laughter erupted from the audience until all the elders joined in. One woman with fuzzy gray hair in the front row laughed so hard tears were running down her rouged cheeks, streaking her makeup.

"I think the show is over," Hannah said, clipping a leash on the dog she had.

"At least they were near the end." Jacob put his lamb down but held the rope tightly. "I'm not tackling this one again."

Hannah gave Jacob the leash then held up her hands to try and quiet the audience while Peter, Laura and Meg gathered the rest of the animals and the kids. Several times she attempted to say, "If everyone will quiet down," but that was as far as she got because no one was listening.

"Remember laughter is the best medicine." Jacob struggled to keep the lamb next to him.

Five minutes later only after Hannah whistled, the last strains of laughter died but whispering among the residents and children began to build. She quickly said, "There are refreshments in the lobby. The children made them."

The word *refreshments* sparked the interest of several elders in the front, and they started moving toward the exit.

Slowly the rec room emptied with Laura and Meg taking the children who were serving the food.

Peter took one of the lambs and headed for the door. "I'll be back for the others."

That left Hannah and Jacob trying not to look at each other. Unsuccessful, she finally stepped into his line of vision. "We should talk."

He swung his gaze to her. "I'm not ready. I don't know if I'll ever be ready now that I know who you are."

"You make it sound like I've changed somehow. That I'm a different person. I'm still Hannah Smith. That's my legal name now. Not Hannah Collins."

"And every time I look at you I see Kevin. I should have seen the resemblance. You have the same hair and eyes."

"Like millions of others."

He started to say something when Peter reentered the room. "I can help you with your animals." Jacob lifted the lamb into his arms, then tugging on the dog leash, walked toward his friend.

"Me, too." Hannah led her mutt along behind Jacob.

"I'll get the props," Peter called out.

Hannah barely heard the man, she was so intent on catching up with Jacob. She reached him in the parking lot at Peter's truck. He hoisted the lamb into its crate, then the dog. After taking care of the animals, Jacob stepped around Hannah and started to make his way back inside. She stopped him with a hand on his arm.

"Jacob—"

"Why did you tell me you were Kevin's sister?" His question cut her off.

And knocked the breath from her. The streetlight accentuated the harsh planes of his face, but distress rang in his voice. "Because I didn't want any secrets between us. You had shared yours. I had to."

"I feel like I'm reliving that night all over again."

She squeezed his arm as though to impart her support. "I didn't tell you to put you through that."

"What did you think I was going to do?"

"I don't know. But it was the right thing to do."

"For you."

She peered toward the building and saw Peter emerge. Through the floor-to-ceiling windows Hannah glimpsed the children playing host to the residents, serving them the refreshments and talking with them.

"The kids missed you this week. They've gotten used to you coming to see them a lot. Please don't stay away because of me."

Jacob shifted away from her. "I've been especially busy. It's flu season."

"They wanted me to ask you to Sunday dinner tomorrow."

Jacob closed his eyes for a few seconds. "I can't." He strode away, not toward the nursing home but toward his car.

Her legs weak, Hannah leaned back against Peter's truck as the man came up with a box full of props.

"What's wrong with Jacob?" Peter slid the items into the bed of his pickup.

"I think I've ruined everything."

Chapter Twelve

"**D**r. Jacob, you came!" Andy launched himself at Jacob and hugged him. "We've missed you."

"Where's Hannah? How's she feeling?" Jacob walked into the cottage, the scent of a roast spicing the air. His stomach rumbled its hunger.

"She's in her office," Susie said, looking too cheerful for someone who was concerned about Hannah's health.

"Office?" The way the twelve-year-old had described it on the phone to him half an hour ago, Hannah was dragging herself around the house, refusing to go to a doctor but desperately needing to see one. Reluctantly, he had agreed to come see what he could do.

Susie shrugged. "You know Hannah. She doesn't stop working for anything."

Knowing the way, Jacob headed back to Hannah's office. Before rapping on the door, he peered back at the end of the hallway and met several pairs of eyes watching him. The kids ducked back around the corner.

He knocked and waited for Hannah to invite him in. When half a minute passed and there wasn't a reply, he tapped his knuckles against the wood harder. Concerned, he decided to give her a couple more seconds before he went in without an invitation.

"Come in," a sleepy voice murmured from inside the room.

He inched the door open and peeped around it to find Hannah with her legs propped up in the lounger and only one dim lamp to illuminate the office. She blinked several times, as though disorientated, and straightened the chair to its upright position.

"Jacob, why are you here?" Drowsiness coated each word.

He slipped inside, aware of the children's whispering voices down the hall.

"Susie called and told me you weren't feeling well and wouldn't go see a doctor. She sounded very concerned, so I reassured her you would be all right. She wouldn't believe me until I agreed to come check you out." He crossed the room, pulling behind him a lattice-back chair to sit in. "What's wrong?"

She scrunched up her forehead, then rubbed her fingers across it. "Just a headache. Nothing serious and Susie knew that. I took some pills and came in here to close my eyes until they started working. I must have fallen asleep."

"Then you're okay? No fatal disease?"

She chuckled. "Not that I know of."

"I think Susie should take up acting lessons. She had me convinced you were at death's door."

"I appreciate the concern, but I'm fine. Well, except the headache isn't totally gone. Nothing I can't handle, though." She sent him a smile that went straight to his heart and pierced through the armor he had around it.

"Then if you're all right, I'll be heading home." He started to stand.

"What time is it?"

Weary from many sleepless nights and long days at work, he sank back down and looked at his watch. "Six."

"Stay for dinner. I think what's really behind this little incident is that the kids miss you and want to see you more." Her gaze bored into him. "And so do I."

"To tell you the truth I've missed…coming here." He'd missed seeing the children but most of all Hannah. Yet how could he be with her, knowing who she really was? This woman had haunted his dreams lately. It was hard to look at her and not remember Kevin.

"I'm not going away. You need to learn to deal with my presence. Don't let the children suffer because of the past. When I first came to Stone's Refuge, I had to do the same thing. And I did."

He released a slow breath. "You play hardball."

She scooted to the edge of the lounger. "On occasion. When it's important."

"And this is important?"

"Yes."

He agreed—not just because of the children but because of the woman whose smile played havoc with his heart. Although there was no way he could now see a future with Hannah, maybe he could find a compromise and be her friend, especially if there were always kids around them.

He rose at the same time she did and nearly collided

with her. Backing away quickly, he offered her a grin, hoping he appeared nonchalant when he didn't feel in the least that way. "Then I'll stay for dinner."

"No doubt Andy will want you to read him a bedtime story. He has a lot to tell you about him and his mother. She comes out here when she's not working and helps around the cottage."

"Noah's told me she's doing a good job at the restaurant."

"She's hoping to move out of the halfway house soon."

"What's the next step for her and Andy?" Jacob strode to the door but didn't open it yet.

"Once Lisa gets her own place, Andy will stay with her overnight, and we'll see how that goes."

"I hope for his sake that you're right about Lisa, but be careful. It doesn't take much for a drug addict to backslide." He hurriedly pushed away the memories of his own mother's downward spiral. Hopefully Lisa and his mother were different.

"Mom, let me help you with your bags." Masking her surprise behind a smile, Hannah opened the front door wider and scooped up one of the pieces of luggage. "Why didn't you tell me you were coming?" *Why didn't you return my calls?* was the question she really wanted to ask but not in the foyer where someone could overhear their conversation.

"I wasn't sure until a few days ago, and then I just decided to surprise you."

"How long are you staying?"

Karen Collins chuckled. "You know me. I never

travel lightly. The weather in Oklahoma can be so unpredictable. It could snow one day and be warm and sunny the next." Her mother came into the cottage. "Hon, once when I lived here I can remember the weather dropping forty degrees in half a day. So where do I stay?"

"In my bedroom. I'll show you, then I'll introduce you to the kids. They're in the kitchen helping Meg with the Christmas cookies for the birthday party for Jesus tonight at the church."

"All eight of them?"

"Yes, it's a big kitchen." Hannah walked down the hall to her bedroom door and pushed it open to allow her mother to go inside first.

"And this is a nice-sized room, too."

"My bathroom is through there." Hannah pointed toward the entrance on the other side of the large bed. "I also have an office off the kitchen."

"And you like living here with eight children?"

"I love it." For the first time in years Hannah felt as if she had put down roots. To her the cottage was her home.

Her mother lifted her bag onto the king-size bed and opened it. "Where do I put my things?" When Hannah glanced from one piece of luggage to the other, Karen hurriedly added, "I'll only unpack part of my clothes."

"Well, in that case I have enough space in my closet, and I can clear out a drawer for you in the dresser."

"I know how much you've wanted kids in your life. Any prospects of a husband?" Hannah's mom hung up a dress and started back toward the bed.

As though they hadn't talked about Jacob at all, her

mother as usual was avoiding the real issue and probably why she was here in the first place. "Yes, there is a man I'm interested in." Dread encased Hannah in a cold sweat.

Karen peered up at her as she shook out a shirt. "You are? That's wonderful. Who?"

The air in Hannah's lungs seemed to evaporate with that last question. She'd tried to tell her mother over the phone, but her mom had ignored all of her follow-up calls after the disastrous conversation. "Jacob Hartman."

Karen dropped the shirt. "I thought he was just the doctor here. Nothing more."

"Mom, I know this is a shock, but you wouldn't talk to me." Hannah rushed forward and drew her mother to the sitting area across the room. "Please don't say anything until you hear me out."

Karen pressed her lips together, surprise still registering on her face.

"I didn't realize Jacob was involved with Stone's Refuge until after I accepted the job here. I couldn't walk away. This is the perfect job for me." Hannah's heartbeat pounded like a kettledrum in a solemn procession. "Jacob is wonderful with the children. He's kind, caring and is trying desperately to make up for what happened all those years ago."

"You've forgiven him for what he did to your brother?"

The drumming beat of Hannah's heart increased. "It's the Christian thing to do, Mom. I know how you feel, but please give him a chance."

Karen shook her head slowly. "I don't know if I can.

I never imagined you were dating the man." Again she shook her head. "Working with him is one thing, but getting involved romantically…"

"Get to know him like I did, and you'll see what a good man he is."

"Until you called a few weeks ago, I hadn't thought about him in a long time. He consumed so much of my life for years that once I gave myself to Christ I just pushed memories of him away. I know how the Lord feels about forgiveness, but…" Tears shone in her mother's eyes. "It's so hard. Kevin is dead because of him."

"It was an accident, Mom."

"But he walked away from the wreck with few injuries."

"He may not have been injured much physically, but he was emotionally. His scars run deep."

"Will he be here tonight?"

"Yes."

"When is he coming?"

With a glance at her watch, Hannah rose. "He should be here within the hour. He promised the kids he would bring pizza tonight when he goes to pick up Andy's mother at the restaurant. She's going with us to church later."

"Is that the woman you've been helping?"

"Yes. I need to get back to the kitchen to help with the cookies." Hannah put her hand on the door. "Are you coming?"

Her mother pushed to her feet. "I'm really tired, honey. I'm going to rest for a while. You go on without me and don't worry about me."

Out in the corridor Hannah stared at the closed

bedroom door, her stomach in snarls. She was all her
mother had in the way of family, and she was afraid
her mom wouldn't come out whenever Jacob was at
the cottage.

*Lord, please help Mom forgive Jacob as You helped
me. I love both of them.*

Hannah opened the back door to admit Jacob, who
brought their dinner. "The kids were wondering where
you were."

"Just the kids?" He waded his way through the mob
of children, all wanting one of the pizza boxes.

"Me, too. I'm starved." She took several containers
from him and began opening them. "Everyone, act civil.
There's plenty to go around."

Jacob stepped away as soon as he lifted the lids and
brushed some snowflakes from his coat and hair. "What
have you all been doing? They've worked up quite an
appetite."

"Is it snowing bad?" Hannah glanced at the window,
but the curtains were drawn.

"No, not too much." Jacob removed his overcoat and
slung it over the back of a chair.

While all the children were filling their plates with
pizza, Andy stood off to the side, his gaze glued to the
back door. "Where's Mom?"

Jacob looked around. "She isn't here?"

"No." Alarm pricked Hannah. "She was supposed
to ride out here with you."

"The guy behind the counter said she left earlier.
I thought she hitched a ride here with someone else."

Jacob headed for the wall phone and punched in some numbers.

Concern creased Andy's forehead. "Where is she?"

"She's probably running late. Go on and get something to eat before there's nothing left." Hannah hoped she concealed her rising fear that all wasn't right with Lisa. She didn't want Andy to worry needlessly.

Coming up next to Jacob, she heard him say, "Give us a call if she arrives there."

When he hung up, she motioned with a nod for them to go into the hallway where Andy wouldn't overhear what they said. "Did you call the halfway house?"

"Yes, and they haven't seen her since she left for work this morning."

"What should we do?"

"Nothing."

"Nothing? We need to do something."

Jacob frowned. "What do you suggest?"

"I don't know. Go look for her."

"Where?"

Hannah shrugged, helplessness seizing her.

Andy poked his head around the kitchen door. "Something's wrong with Mom, isn't it?"

Hannah knelt in front of the boy and clasped his arms. "We don't know, hon."

Tears crowded his eyes. "Please find her."

Hannah glanced over her shoulder at Jacob, who nodded once. "Do you know anywhere she liked to go? A favorite place?"

Sniffling, Andy studied the floor by his feet. Finally he shook his head. "When she was gone, I never knew where she went."

Hannah rose. "I think Jacob and I have time to go to the halfway house and check with them before we go to church."

Andy's eyes brightened. "Maybe she went back to the old neighborhood."

"We'll go there, too." Jacob came forward. "Now, will you do me a favor, Andy?"

"Yes."

"Go eat some dinner and make sure everyone is ready to go to church on time."

"Sure." Andy straightened his slumped shoulders.

After the boy disappeared into the kitchen, Hannah asked, "Do you think she went back to her boyfriend?"

"Possibly. We've got a couple of hours to find her. Let's go."

"Will you tell Meg where we're going and if we aren't back in time to get Peter and Laura to take the children to church? I'll need to get my purse. Meet you back here in a few minutes."

Without waiting for an answer, Hannah hurried toward her bedroom. This wasn't the time for her mother to come out in case she had changed her mind. She needed to tell Jacob about her mom's surprise visit. In the quiet of his car would be the best place.

In her bedroom, she put a blanket over her mother who slept on top of her coverlet, then grabbed her purse and quickly left. Two minutes later she sat next to Jacob as he pulled away from the cottage.

"Everything okay in the kitchen?" Hannah fidgeted with the leather handle of her purse.

"Yeah. There's not much pizza left. I should have

bought another one. You won't have anything to eat when we get back."

She pressed her hand over her constricted stomach. "I couldn't eat even if pizza was my favorite food."

"It isn't?" Mock outrage sounded in his voice. "Don't tell Noah."

"It'll be our secret." She paused. "Speaking of secrets. Well, this isn't exactly a secret. More of a surprise."

He slid a look toward her as he turned onto the highway. "What?"

"My mother came to visit this afternoon for a few days. She wanted to spend Christmas with me, and her employer gave her the time off at the last minute."

His harsh intake of air was followed by silence.

"This is just like Mom. When the mood strikes, she gets up and goes somewhere. She doesn't like staying still for long in any one place. There were many times while I was growing up that I left my things in boxes rather than unpack. It was easier that way." She heard her nervous chattering and wished she could see Jacob's face but the dark hid it.

"Does she know about me being involved in Stone's Refuge?"

"Yes."

"Before or after she came."

"Before."

"I'm sure that made her day. Why is she really here?"

"That's a good question. One I don't have an answer to."

Silence ate into her composure. She rubbed her thumb into her palm and tried to think of a way to make everything all right. *Lord, what do I do? How do I fix this?*

"Hannah, I'm sorry you had to tell your mother. I imagine that wasn't a nice reunion for you two."

"I told my mother that I had forgiven you for what happened with Kevin, that I cared about you." *That I want to be more than friends with you,* she wanted to add but realized at the moment Jacob wouldn't want to hear that.

His derisive laugh taunted her words. "She was thrilled, no doubt."

"I love my mother, but we don't always see eye to eye on things. This will just be another item added to the bottom of a long list."

"Don't you mean, added to the top?"

Before she could answer him, her cell phone blared with a drumroll. She fumbled for it in her purse and flipped it open. "Hello."

"Hannah?" A voice, barely audible, came through.

"Yes, who is this?"

"I'm in trouble."

Hannah sat up straight. "Lisa, where are you?"

"I'm near my old apartment. He's so angry."

"Who?"

"My ex-boyfriend," Lisa said in a raspy whisper.

"Jacob and I are on our way. We'll be—" The connection went dead.

Hannah snapped her cell closed. "Please hurry. Lisa's near her boyfriend's apartment. Something's wrong. She sounds…" She searched for a word to describe what she heard in the woman's voice beside fear.

"High?"

"Likely."

Jacob pressed down on the accelerator. He remembered the times he found his mother stoned. The memories, one after another, left him chilled in the car's heated air. That last night before the state took him away from her, the paramedics had said she'd been a few minutes away from death. If he hadn't come home... He shuddered and increased his speed even more.

Chapter Thirteen

"Oh, great! It's snowing even harder now. Normally I love to see it on Christmas Eve. Not this year." Hannah gripped the door handle, prepared to jump from the car the second Jacob parked.

"Why did she go with her ex?"

"Some women have a hard time breaking ties with men who've been in their life, even ones who have abused them."

Jacob took a corner too fast, and the car fishtailed on a slick area. The color leached from his face as he struggled to control his vehicle.

She gasped. For a few seconds her brother's wreck flittered across Hannah's mind as a telephone pole loomed ahead.

Steering into the skid, he slowed his speed. Finally he managed to right the car, missing the curb and pole by a couple of feet. "Sorry," he bit out between clenched teeth, his white-knuckle grasp on the wheel tightening.

"It's okay. We need to get to Lisa before her boyfriend finds her."

"It's not okay!" Although the words came out in a harsh whisper, the power behind them hung in the air, reinforcing the barrier that he had erected between them. "I could have…"

His unfinished sentence lingered. She touched his arm.

He swallowed hard. "I know better. I couldn't live with myself if I caused something to happen to you, too." He retreated into stony silence as he negotiated the city streets.

"I forgave you, Jacob. There were no strings attached to that forgiveness."

"How could you?"

She felt as though she was fighting for the most important thing in her life. "Because I love you. Love yourself."

He shook off her arm, his jaw set in a grim line. His scowl told of the war of emotions raging inside him. She wanted so much to comfort him but knew he would reject it—reject her. All she could do now was pray and turn it over to the Lord.

When the apartment building came into view, Hannah bent forward, scouring the area around it for any sign of Lisa. Jacob brought the car to a stop in front. Hannah leaped from the vehicle and raced toward the entrance.

Jacob halted her progress. "What do you think you're doing?" His hand immediately fell away as if touching her was distasteful.

Snowflakes caught on her eyelashes. She blinked and looked up into his fierce expression. "Going inside to see if Lisa is with him."

"Let's check outside first. That's where she was when she called."

"Okay, I'll look down this side. You go over there." She waved toward the area across the street.

"No, we go together in case the boyfriend is looking for her, too."

"But it will go faster if—"

"I don't want you meeting up with him alone." His determination, a tangible force, brooked no argument.

"Fine. Then let's get moving. We're wasting time." Frustrated, worried, she stalked down the street.

Passing an alley, Hannah walked down its length, inspecting every place someone could hide. Nothing. Back out on the sidewalk, she continued, stopping at the quick market on the corner, the only place open on Christmas Eve.

"Let's check inside. Maybe she's hiding in here since it's cold and snowing," she said as she entered the store.

While she went up and down the aisles, Jacob questioned the clerk at the counter. When she finished her search, she came back to his side.

"If she comes back in, tell her Jacob and Hannah are looking for her and to wait here." Jacob took her elbow and led the way to the door. "She was here about fifteen minutes ago, using the phone in the back. When a man came in that fits the description of her boyfriend, she must have fled. The clerk didn't see her leave, but he thinks she went out the back way."

"Then he may not have found her."

"The clerk told the man she was on the phone in the back."

"No! How could he?"

"He was scared. He knows who Carl is and doesn't want to have any trouble with him."

"Did he call the police?"

"No."

Lord, please put Your protective shield around Lisa.

"We've got to find her first." Hannah rounded the corner of the store, making her way to the back where Lisa would have come out.

Footsteps in the continually falling snow led away from the door, heading toward an alley nearby. Another set had joined the first.

"She's running." Jacob pointed at the long stride between each print.

"He isn't, as if he's stalking her and knows he'll catch her."

"With this snow, it'll be hard for her to hide from him."

"But we can track her, too." Hannah hurried her pace.

The darkness of the alley obscured part of the footprints, but the occasional light from a window showed them the way—as well as Carl. At one place Lisa must have tried to go into a building, but the door was locked.

Jacob slowed, putting his arm out to halt Hannah. "Call 9-1-1."

She squinted into the dimness and glimpsed what he'd seen. A still body curled into a ball in the snow, a fine layer of the white stuff covering the person. She dug into her pocket and pulled out her cell, making the call while Jacob stooped and brushed the snow off the body, revealing Lisa.

After talking to the 9-1-1 operator, Hannah knelt next to Jacob. "Is she alive?"

"Yes." Removing a penlight from his pocket, he began to check out Lisa's injuries. "She's got a lump on the back of her head."

A snow-covered pipe lay a few feet away, a stream of light from the building illuminating it.

A moan escaped Lisa's lips. "No, don't." She raised her arm as though she were fending off a blow. Her eyes bolted open. She saw Jacob, and her arm fell to the pavement. "I'm sorry. I'm sorry." Tears streamed down her cheeks and blended with the melted snow on her face.

Hannah leaned close. "Lisa, I'm going to wait for the police and ambulance at the end of the alley. You're going to be all right. Jacob will take care of you."

Jacob paced the waiting room, wearing a path in front of Hannah's chair. "We should have heard something by now."

"Carl beat her up pretty badly. Thankfully Lisa was conscious enough to tell us what drug she took before she passed out again."

Jacob paused before her. "Let's hope the police have brought him in by now."

"One less drug dealer on the streets."

"But for how long?"

"Do you think Lisa will testify against him?"

"No." He pivoted and started pacing again. "She's afraid of him and rightly so."

"We've got to be there for her. Maybe then she will."

"Maybe." But skepticism drenched his voice.

An emergency-room doctor appeared in the doorway. "Jacob, I heard you found the woman. Does she have any kin?"

"A son staying at Stone's Refuge. Otherwise, I don't think so. How is she?"

"A concussion, two cracked ribs and some cuts and bruises. I think the man had a ring on that left his mark as he was pounding on her."

Chilled, Hannah stood and clasped her arms, running her hands up and down to warm herself. "May we see her now?"

"They're taking her upstairs to a room. Give them fifteen minutes to get her settled in, then you can see her. I want to keep her overnight for observation. If she does okay, she can go home tomorrow."

After the doctor left, Hannah sighed. "We need to get Andy. I promised him we would."

Jacob glanced at his watch. "He should be at the church with the others right now. I'll go pick him up and bring him back to see his mother while you go talk to her."

"She'll want to see you and thank you, Jacob."

"I don't know if that would be a good idea."

"Because she had a relapse?"

"Some things never change."

"Lisa is human. She made a mistake. We all do. God forgives us, thankfully, so the least we can do is try to do the same."

His gaze sliced through Hannah. "I'll be back later with Andy." Jacob strode from the waiting room before he said something he would regret. He'd heard the censure in her voice. But Hannah hadn't lived with a drug addict. He had. His mother had ruined her life and had been well on the way to doing the same with his.

No, you did a good job of that yourself that night you killed Kevin. What she started, you finished.

His guilt that was always there swelled to the fore-ground, threatening to swamp him. Up until the appear-ance of Hannah in his life he'd managed to cope with what he had done. Now he didn't know if he could con-tinue to work with the children at Stone's Refuge and see her. He'd thought he could, but he wanted more. He wanted a wife and a family—with Hannah. But how could they ever be really happy with what happened always hanging between them? How could she have really forgiven him?

Jacob found a parking space in the nearly full lot at the church and walked toward the entrance. The snow had stopped and a white blanket muffled the sounds, making it serenely quiet. Christmas music wafted from the sanctuary, reminding him how special this time of year was. He entered the place of worship and stood in the back, searching for the large group from the refuge. He caught Peter's gaze, and his friend leaned around Laura to let Meg know Jacob was there.

Andy exited the pew and started for him. Following close behind the boy was a woman whose image was burned into his memory. For a few seconds the remem-brance whisked him back to the hospital corridor where Hannah's mother had accused him of ruining her life, that he might as well have killed her, too. Emotions so strong he staggered back a couple of steps inundated him as his gaze locked with Kevin's mother's.

Around him the congregation sang "O Holy Night"

while Jacob desperately tried to compose himself enough to deal with her and Andy. He knew one thing as the distance disappeared between—that he didn't want the parishioners to witness the scene. Fumbling for the handle, he wrenched open the door to the sanctuary and escaped out into the empty lobby.

Why now, Lord?

No answer came as Andy and Karen Collins halted in front of him. His attention remained glued to the older woman, who was slightly heavier and with strands of gray hair, but otherwise the same as twenty-one years before.

"Dr. Jacob, is my mother all right? Did you find her?"

Andy's voice drew his gaze to the boy standing half a foot away, his head upturned, his eyes large with fear and worry in their depths.

Jacob forced a smile of reassurance. "She's going to be fine."

"Where is she?"

"At the hospital."

Panic widened the boy's eyes even more. "She's hurt!"

"Hannah is there with her. I've come to take you to see her." Jacob settled his hands on the boy's shoulders, compelling the child's full attention. "She has a lump on her head and some cuts and bruises, but she'll mend just fine. She's going to need you to be strong. Can you do that for her?"

Andy drew himself up tall. "Yes."

"Where's your coat?"

The boy pointed toward the hallway that led to the classrooms. "Back there."

"Go get it, then we'll leave."

The second the child disappeared down the corridor Jacob's gaze fastened on Kevin's mother. So many things he wanted to say swirled in his mind, but none formed a coherent sentence.

"Hannah said you were wonderful with the children. She's right."

Her words, spoken with no anger, confounded Jacob. He stared at her, speechless.

"When Hannah first told me today you two were more than associates, that you were…friends, I didn't know what to say to her. After she left to go with you, I had a long talk with God. I wanted to tell you that I've forgiven you for what happened, too. As my daughter pointed out to me, it was an accident that ended tragically for my son. What I said to you in the hospital that day was grief talking, but it took me years to realize that. It took finding the Lord and my daughter's example to see what I needed to do. I'm sorry for what I said."

Jacob heard her, but the words wouldn't register. "How can you say that?"

She smiled. "Stop blaming yourself for something that was out of your control."

Out of the corner of his eye, Jacob glimpsed Andy coming back. He rushed to the boy and clasped his hand. "We need to get to the hospital," was all he could think to say.

A few minutes later he headed his car away from the church, still grappling with what Hannah's mother had said.

"You aren't kidding me, are you? Mom is okay?"

"I promise. I'd never kid you about something like

that. She's staying overnight at the hospital and hopefully will go home tomorrow."

"I won't get to see her on Christmas?"

"I'll make sure you do. I'll pick her up and bring her to the cottage to spend some time with you if the doctor says it's okay."

Andy heaved a long sigh. "Good. I don't want her being alone on Christmas. She needs me."

Shouldn't it be the other way around? "You aren't mad at her for all that's happened?" The question slipped out before Jacob could snatch it back.

"No."

"Why not?"

"I love her."

Is love the key? If you love someone enough, you forgive them?

God loved us so much that he gave His only son for our salvation. Hannah had said Christ has taught us to forgive, that she had learned from the Master Himself.

Could he? Can the Lord forgive him for taking another's life? Could he forgive himself for surviving the car wreck? Could he forgive his mother for his childhood?

If he wanted any kind of life, he needed to figure that out.

"Where's Dr. Jacob?" Hannah asked as Andy came into the hospital room.

"He needed to go see someone. He told me Peter will come and take us home." The boy walked to his mother's bed and took her hand.

Lisa's eyes fluttered open. "Andy," she said groggily.

"How are you?" The child's voice thickened with tears.

"Hey, baby. Don't cry. I'm gonna be fine thanks to Hannah and Jacob." She closed her eyes for a few seconds. "I love ya."

Andy lay his head near his mother's. "I love ya, Mom. Dr. Jacob said ya could come to the cottage tomorrow if the doctor says so."

"That's…great. I can't…" Sleep stole Lisa's next words.

"Let's go home and let your mother rest. You'll see her tomorrow morning. We'll come up here early."

"Are ya sure?"

"Yep. It won't really be Christmas without your mother there." Hannah draped her arm over Andy's shoulder and led the way into the hallway.

At the elevator the doors swished opened, and Peter stepped off.

"We were coming downstairs to wait for you." Hannah let the elevator close behind her employer. "Church is over already?"

"No, but I thought I would come right away. It's been a long day for you all."

"Yes, and it's not over yet." She needed to find Jacob.

"My car is in the front parking lot." Peter punched the down button.

"Peter, can you do me a favor?" Hannah got on the elevator when it arrived.

"Sure."

"I need to pay a visit to someone. Can you drop me off then take Andy to the cottage?"

"Yes."

Andy glanced back at Hannah. "Hey, are ya gonna visit the same person as Dr. Jacob?"

"I might be," she said while Peter shot her a speculative look.

In Peter's car Hannah started to tell him to take her to Jacob's apartment. Then suddenly she realized that wasn't where he had gone. She knew where he was and told Peter.

At the cemetery Hannah saw Jacob's car parked close to where her brother was buried. "Right here. I'll have Jacob bring me home."

Peter looked out the windshield. Although nighttime, the snow brightened the surrounding area. "Are you sure about this?"

"I'm very sure." Hannah glanced in the backseat at Andy, who had fallen asleep. "I need to make Jacob understand what it means to really forgive someone."

"Forgive?"

"I'll explain later." Hannah slid out of the car, and without peering back, walked toward the man she loved.

The next few minutes would determine the rest of her life. She firmed her resolve when Jacob lifted his head and glanced toward her. His eyes widened.

"How did you know I would be here?"

"You come every Sunday afternoon and put flowers on my brother's grave. I've known for some time."

"But this isn't Sunday afternoon."

"True. But I figured you might be here. I had Peter drop me off, so I'll need a ride home. Will you give me one?"

Nonplussed, he blinked. "Sure," he said slowly, raking his hand through his hair.

A snowflake fell, then another one.

"This is the season for hope, for new beginnings. When I came to Cimarron City, I never thought I would come face-to-face with my past, but I did. The Lord gave me a chance to right a wrong by coming here. It's not right for you to stop living because of what happened. Kevin would be the first person to tell you that. I lo—"

Jacob pressed his index finger against her lips to hush her words. "I need to say something first, Hannah. Then you can. Please?"

She nodded.

The snow increased, causing Hannah to step nearer his body's warmth. He encircled her in a loose embrace, tilting her chin up so she looked into his eyes.

"Over the years this has become the place that I come to think, to work through my problems. I feel as if I've continued my friendship with Kevin. That was important for me to believe. It kept the pain to a dull ache. Then you came into my life and made me really feel for the first time since the accident. I wanted it all—a wife, children, my life back. I just didn't know how to go about getting it."

Hope flared in her. "And you do now?"

"You were right. I have to start by forgiving myself and asking the Lord for forgiveness. That's what I've been doing."

"It's not just yourself you need to forgive but your mother, too. What happened to you as a child has ruled your life too long. Don't let it govern your future, too."

One corner of his mouth lifted. "I'm working on that. Being around Lisa has helped me see another side to the situation. An addiction isn't easy to break. People with them need support and help, not condemnation."

She snuggled against him, seeking his warmth and nearness. "Realistic support and help. You have to know when to cut your losses, like with Nancy's mother."

"I want to be there for Lisa and Andy. I want it to work for them."

"Then we will be."

He tightened his arms about her. "I like how you use the word *we*. Hannah Collins Smith, I love you and I want to see where this relationship can go."

She chuckled. "Personally I'm hoping it leads to a house full of children, adopted and our own."

He bent his head toward hers. "I love your way of thinking."

Softly his lips grazed across hers, then took possession in a kiss that sealed an unspoken promise to love each other through the best and worst of times.

Epilogue

"This is my bedroom?" Nancy asked, standing in the doorway of a room with white furniture, a pink canopy on the bed and pink lacy curtains. "All by myself?"

Hannah entered and turned to face the seven-year-old. "Yep. Every square inch of it. What do you think?"

The little girl clapped her hands and twirled around. "I love it! I've never had my own room."

Hannah's gaze found her husband's, and a smile spread through her as she basked in the warmth of Jacob's regard. "We have a lot of bedrooms to fill."

Jacob placed his hand over Hannah's rounded stomach. "I don't think we've done too bad in a year's time. Two children and one on the way."

"Just think what we can do with a little more time," Hannah said with a laugh, thoughts of their wedding exactly a year ago producing a contentment in her that she had never thought possible until Jacob.

Terry skidded to a halt outside the bedroom and poked his head in. "Welcome to the family, Nancy."

The little girl beamed from ear to ear. "Thanks."

"Have you checked out the backyard?"

Nancy shook her head.

"C'mon. I'll show you the doghouse Jacob and I built for Abby."

As their new daughter raced after Terry, Jacob pulled Hannah back against him and ringed his arms about her. "We need to start working on the adoption papers for Gabe."

"And Susie."

His breath fanned her neck as he nibbled on her ear. "And then another of our own."

"We're gonna run out of bedrooms at this rate real quickly."

"Then we'll add on. We have the room, thanks to Peter."

Hannah swept around to face him. "Living in our own home on the ranch is the best of both worlds. I'm near my job as manager of the refuge and we have plenty of room for our children."

"Not to mention the pets they will have."

"Peter probably will never have to go out looking for homes for his animals."

"Especially with Terry as our son. With the addition of Abby we now have a cat, rabbit and two dogs."

"Just so long as we never have a snake as a pet. I draw the line at that."

"Sure, Mrs. Hartman," he murmured right before planting a kiss on her mouth. "Of course, you're going to have to tell Gabe he can't bring his garter snake with him when he comes to live with us."

She pulled back. "When did he get one?"

"He found it yesterday when Andy was visiting the refuge."

"Which reminds me, I'd better get downstairs and start lunch. Lisa and Andy should be here soon for Nancy's party. She's coming early to help me set up."

He draped his arm around her shoulder and started for the hallway. "You still don't trust me in the kitchen?"

"No, but I trust you with my heart."

* * * * *

Dear Reader,

Heart of the Family delves into a subject that is dear to my heart—our children. They are the future, and we must protect them and care for them. As a teacher, I have seen what happens when this doesn't occur. In this book, I present two situations that often happen with a child in foster care. Some go back to their family and some don't. Some get adopted and some don't. Good foster parents are important to the foster-care system in this country. My thanks go out to all of them. This book is for you.

I love hearing from readers. You can contact me at P.O. Box 2074, Tulsa, OK 74101, or visit my website, at www.margaretdaley.com, where you can sign up for my quarterly newsletter.

Best wishes,

Margaret Daley

Questions for Discussion

1. Hannah often talked to the Lord as though He were right there with her, a friend to listen to her troubles. How do you talk to the Lord? How do you pray?

2. Both Hannah and Jacob believe in Jesus, but throughout the book they must depend on their faith to make difficult decisions. How do you depend on your faith?

3. What is your favorite scene in the book? Why?

4. Jacob is tortured by something he did in his past. He can't get beyond it and forgive himself. Has anything like that happened to you or a loved one? How did you deal with it? Did you turn to the Lord?

5. Forgiveness is the cornerstone of this story. In certain situations, forgiving can be one of the hardest things you will ever do. Have you recently had to forgive someone who really hurt you? Have you ever held on to your anger and hurt because of something that was done to you? Did you pray for guidance and help? How did it make you feel when you let go of the anger and hurt?

6. Some of the children have lived rough lives in this story. How would you explain to a child that bad things happen to good people?

7. Being addicted to something can ruin a person's life because it takes over. Lisa has a hard time giving up her addiction. She realizes she can't do it alone. Have you ever dealt with an addiction or with someone who has one? What helped you to cope with it?

8. Who is your favorite character? Why?

9. What do you think is the heart of a family? Why?

10. Hannah feels the Lord has led her back to Cimarron City to help Jacob. Have you ever felt His hand in something you felt compelled to do? Have you ever felt the Lord pushed you to do something you didn't want to do? If so, how did you handle it when you were confronted with that difficult situation?

*Army Captain Jake Tanner is struggling
to find holiday cheer after he returns home
from overseas.
It'll take a beautiful widow, an adorable kid,
and a sweet four legged companion
to show Jake the true meaning of Christmas.
Read on for a preview of
HER HOLIDAY HERO by Margaret Daley,
from Love Inspired in December 2013.*

Chapter One

Jake Tanner had pulled out the desk chair in his home office and started to sit when the front doorbell chimed in the blissful quiet. He would never take silence for granted again. A long breath swooshed from his lungs as he straightened and gripped his cane, then limped toward the foyer. Through the long, narrow window with beveled glass, he could make out his neighbor standing on the porch.

Marcella Kime found a reason to see him at least a couple of times a week. He'd become her mission since he'd returned home to Cimarron City from serving in the military overseas. A few days earlier she'd jokingly told him she missed her grandson, and he would do just fine taking his place. He still wasn't sure what to make of that statement. He had returned to Cimarron City, a town he'd lived in for a while and visited often to see his grandma. Dealing with family, especially his father, the general, had been too much for him three months ago when he'd been released from the military hospital.

He swung the door open to reveal Marcella, probably no more than five feet tall, if that, with her hands full. "Good morning." She smiled as she juggled a large box and a plate of pastries. He reached for the parcel.

"The Fed Ex guy left this late yesterday afternoon. I meant to bring it over sooner, but then I had to go to church to help with the pancake supper. You're always home so I was surprised he couldn't deliver the package."

"Went to the VA hospital in Oklahoma City."

"Oh, good. You went out." She presented the plate of goodies. "I baked extra ones this morning because I know how much you enjoy my cinnamon rolls. I'm going to put those pounds you lost back on in no time. I imagine all those K rations aren't too tasty."

"I haven't had MREs—meals ready to eat—in six months, and no, they aren't tasty. In the hospital I was fed regular meals." But he hadn't wanted to eat much. He was working out again and building up his muscles at least.

"Oh, my. *K rations* certainly dates me. That's what they were called when my older brother was in the army."

His seventy-five-year-old neighbor with stark white hair never was at a loss for words. After she left, his head would throb from all the words tumbling around inside. He wanted to tell her again that she didn't need to worry about him, that in time his full appetite would return, but she continued before he could open his mouth.

"I'd come in, but I have to leave. Saturday is my day to get my hair washed and fixed. It needs it. Can't miss that." She thrust the plate toward him. "I'll come back later and get my dish."

After placing the parcel on the table nearby, he took the cinnamon rolls from his neighbor, their scent teasing that less than robust appetite. "Thanks, Miss Kime."

"Tsk. Tsk. Didn't I tell you to call me Marcella, young man? Your grandma and me were good friends. I miss her."

"So do I, Miss—I mean, Marcella."

When she had traversed the four steps to his sidewalk, Jake closed his front door, shutting out the world. With a sigh, he scanned his living room, the familiar surroundings where he controlled his environment, knew what to expect. Even Marcella's visits weren't surprises anymore.

Jake balanced the plate on the box, carried it into his office and set it on the desk to open later. It was from his father and his new wife—a care package as they'd promised in their last call. Finally, they weren't trying to talk him into coming to live with them in Florida anymore. He needed his space, and he certainly didn't want to be reminded daily that he'd let down the general—he wouldn't follow in his father's footsteps. He needed a sense of what this house had given when he was growing up—peace.

He snatched a cinnamon roll as he sat in front of his laptop, his coffee cup already on his right on a coaster. While he woke up his computer, he bit into the roll and closed his eyes, savoring the delectable pastry. Marcella sure could bake. Before getting started in his course work for his Ph.D. in psychology, he clicked on his email, expecting one from his doctor at the VA about some test results.

Only one email that wasn't junk popped up. He recognized the name, a message from the wife of a soldier who had served under him in Afghanistan. His heartbeat picked up speed. He should open it, but after an email a couple of weeks prior where he discovered one of his men had died from his injuries in an ambush, he didn't know if he could.

His chest constricted. But the woman's name taunted him. With a fortifying breath, he clicked on the message. As their commanding officer, it was his duty to know what happened to his men, even if he couldn't do anything about it.

His comrade was going in for another operation to repair the damage from a bomb explosion. Her words whisked Jake back to that day six months ago that had changed his life. The sound of the blast rocked his mind as though he were in the middle of the melee all over again.

Sweat beaded on his forehead and rolled down his face. His hands shook as he closed the laptop, hoping that would stop the flood of memories. He never wanted to remember that day. Ever. The walls of his home office began to close in on him, mocking what peace he felt in his familiar surroundings. He surged to his feet and hobbled around the room, dragging in breaths that didn't satisfy his need for oxygen.

I'm in Cimarron City. In my house. Safe.

In the midst of the terror that day in the mountain village, he'd grasped on to the Lord and held tight as He guided him through the rubble and smoke to save whomever he could. But where was God now when he needed Him? He felt abandoned, left to piece his life together. Alone.

He paced the room, glancing back at the computer a couple of times until he forced himself to look away. Lightheaded, he stopped at the window, leaning on his cane, and focused on his front lawn. Reconnoitering the area. Old habits didn't die easily.

He started to turn away when something out of the corner of his eye caught his attention. He swung back and homed in on a group of kids across the street—two boys beating up a smaller child.

Anger clenched his gut. He balled his hands as another kid jumped in on the lopsided fight. That clinched it for Jake. He couldn't stand by and watch a child being hurt. Adrenaline began pumping through him as though he were going into battle, pushing his earlier panic into the background. He rushed toward the front door. But out on his porch, anxiety slammed into his chest, rooting him to the spot.

Jake's gaze latched on to the three boys against the one, taking turns punching the child. All his thoughts centered on the defenseless kid, trying to protect himself. Heart pounding, Jake took one step, then another. His whole body felt primed to fight as it had when as a soldier he vied with the other part of him—sweat coating his skin, hands trembling, gut churning.

No choice.

Furiously he increased his pace until he half ran and half limped toward the group, pain zipping up his injured leg. The boys were too intent on their prey to notice him. When he came to a halt, dropping his cane, he jerked first one then another off the child on the ground. He tried holding on to the one he pegged as the leader while reaching for the third kid, but the boy yanked free and raced deeper into the park with the second one hurrying after him.

"What's your name?" Pain radiating up his bad leg, Jake blocked it as much as he could from his mind and clasped the arm of the last child, smaller than the other two who'd fled and more the size of the boy on the ground.

The assailant glared at him, his mouth pinched in a hard line.

The downed kid still lay huddled in a tight ball. As much as Jake wanted to interrogate the bully he held, he needed to see to the hurt child. He memorized the features of the third attacker then released him. As expected, the third attacker fled in the same direction as his cohorts.

That was okay. Jake could identify him. He wouldn't get off scot-free.

Adrenaline still surging, Jake knelt by the boy. That sent another sharp streak of pain up his thigh. But over the months he'd learned that if he concentrated hard enough, he could ignore the aches his injury still caused. "You're safe now. Can I help you? Where do you hurt?"

For a long moment the child didn't say anything. Didn't move.

Concern flooded Jake. He settled his hand on the boy's shoulder. "Where do you live? Can you make it home?" Should he call 911? Had the bullies done worse damage than he realized?

Slowly, the child uncurled his body. He winced as he turned and looked up. Jake took in the cut lip and cheek, blood oozing from the wounds, the eye that would blacken by tomorrow, the torn shirt.

"Let me help you home."

Wariness entered the kid's blue eyes. "I'm fine." He swiped his dirty sleeve across his mouth, smearing the blood.

"Who were those guys?"

The child clamped his lips together, cringing, but keeping his mouth closed.

"The least I can do is make sure you get home without those kids bothering you again."

The boy's eyes widened.

"Okay?"

The child nodded once then tried to stand. Halfway up, his legs gave out, and he sank to the ground.

Jake moved closer. "Let me help." He steadied himself with his cane.

When the boy stood with Jake's assistance, he wobbled but remained on his feet.

"I've been in a few fights. I know you have to get your bearings before doing too much."

The child tilted his head back and looked up at Jake, pain reflected in his eyes. "Did ya win?"

"Sometimes. Can you walk home? If you don't think you can, I'll call your parents." He dug into his pocket and pulled out his cell phone.

"No, I can walk." The child glanced over his shoulder. "Do you think they'll come back?"

"Not if they know what's good for them. I won't let them hurt you again."

"I wish that was true," the boy, probably no more

than ten, mumbled, his head dropping. His body language shouted defeat.

"It's getting worse," Jake heard the kid mumble to himself. That again aroused the protective instinct in him.

"C'mon. Show me where you live. Is it far?" He looked back to check for the trio who had jumped the child. A male jogger and a couple, hands clasped, were the only people he saw in the park. "I'm Jake. What's your name?" With his injured leg throbbing, he used his cane to support more of his weight than usual.

"Josh." The boy dragged his feet as they turned the corner onto Sooner Road.

"Why were those kids bothering you?" The question came out before Jake could censor himself. He didn't want to get involved. Yet, the second he took the first step toward the fight, he had become involved, knowing firsthand what the boy was going through.

Josh mumbled something again, but Jake could hear only the words, "like to fight."

"Have those guys bullied you before?"

The boy's pace slowed until he came to a stop in front of a one-story, redbrick house with a long porch across the front. "Yeah. The big one has since he moved here," he said, his head still hanging.

"Do your parents know?" Jake studied the top of the child's head, some blood clotted in the brown hair. The urge to check the wound inundated him. He started to bring his hand up.

Josh jerked his chin up, anger carved into his features while his eyes glistened. "I don't have a dad. I don't want my mom knowing. You can't tell her." He took a step back. His hands fisted at his sides as if he were ready to defend that statement.

"I won't."

The taut set of the child's shoulders relaxed some, his fingers flexed.

"But *you* will."

"No, I won't. I can take care of this myself. Mom will just get all upset and worried."

"She'll know something is wrong with one look at you." Jake gestured toward the house with a neatly trimmed yard, mums in full bloom in the flower bed and an inviting porch with white wicker furniture, perfect for enjoying a fall evening. Idyllic, as if part of the world wasn't falling apart with people battling each other. "Is this where you live?"

Josh stuck his lower lip out and crossed his arms, wearing a defiant expression.

Instantly, Jake flashed back to an incident with a captive prisoner who gave him that same look. His heartbeat raced. His breathing became shallow. His world shrank to that small hut in the mountains as he faced an enemy who had been responsible for killing civilians and soldiers the day before. He felt the shaking start in his hands. Jake fought to shut down the helplessness before it took over.

"Josh, what's going on?" A female voice penetrated the haze of memories.

Jake blinked and looked toward the porch. A tall woman, a few inches shy of six feet, with long blond hair pulled back in a ponytail that swished, marched down the steps toward them, distress stamped on her features.

"What happened to you?" Stooping in front of the boy, the lady grasped Josh's arms. When he didn't say anything, she peered up at Jake. "What happened?"

"Is Josh your son?"

"Yes." The anxiety in her blue eyes, the same crystalline color as the boy's, pleaded for him to answer the question.

Jake shifted. He'd done what he said he would do. He'd delivered the child safely home. It was time to leave Josh and his mother to hash out what had occurred in the park. He backed away, his grip on the cane like a clamp. He spied the imploring look in Josh's eyes. "Your son needs to tell you," he said.

She turned back to the boy. "You're bleeding, your eye is red and your clothes are a mess. Did you get in a fight?"

The boy nodded.

"Why? That's not you, Josh."

The kid yanked away from his mom and yelled, "Yeah! That's the problem!" He stormed toward the house.

Jake took another step back.

She whirled toward him, her face full of a mother's wrath. "What's going on?"

"He was in a fight."

"I got that much from him."

"I broke it up and walked him home." Jake could barely manage his own life. He didn't want to get in the middle of someone else's, but the appeal in Josh's mother's eyes demanded he say something. "Three boys were beating up Josh."

"Why?"

"That you have to ask him. I came in after it started, and he wasn't forthcoming about what was going on."

"But something is. I get the feeling this wasn't the first time."

"A good assumption."

"I'm Emma Langford." She paused, waiting for him to supply his name.

He clamped his teeth down hard for a few seconds before he muttered, "Jake Tanner. I live around the corner, across from the park." Why did he add the last? Because there was something in her expression that softened the armor around his heart.

The woman glanced up and down the street, kneading her fingertips into her temple. "I don't know what to do. It sounds like they ganged up on Josh. Have you seen them around?"

"No, but I know what they look like, especially one of them close to Josh's size. The other two were bigger than him. Maybe older." He could understand a mother's concern and the need to defend her child. He'd often felt the same way about the men under his command.

"So my child is being bullied." Weariness dripped from each word.

Jake moved closer, an urge to comfort assailing him. Taking him by surprise. For months he'd been trying to shut off his emotions. Hopelessness and fear were what had him in his current condition: unable to function the way he had before his last tour of duty.

"He never said a word to me, but I should have known," she said in a thick voice. "No wonder he's been so angry and withdrawn these past few months."

"That would be a good reason. Chances are he doesn't know how to handle it, either."

"Do you think they live in the neighborhood?" She panned the houses around her as if she could spot where the bullies lived.

"Maybe. They were in the park when the fight occurred."

"I need to find out who's bullying my son and put a stop to it."

"How?" Jake could remember being bullied in school when he was in the sixth grade.

"I don't know. Confront them. Have a conversation with their parents."

"Often that makes the situation worse. It did for me when I was a child." The reply came out before he could stop the words.

"But maybe it would put a stop to it. Make a difference for my son." Her forehead creased, she glanced back at the house. "I want to thank you for what you did for Josh. Would you like some tea or lemonade?"

He hesitated. He needed to say no, but he couldn't, not after glimpsing the lost look in the lady's eyes.

"Please. I make freshly squeezed lemonade." She started toward her house. "We can enjoy it outside on the porch."

Part of him wanted to follow her, to help her—the old Jake—but that guy was gone, left in the mountains where some of his men had died.

She slowed and glanced back, anxiety shadowing her eyes. "I'm at a loss about what to do. Tell me what happened to you when you were bullied. That is, if you don't mind. It may help me figure out what to do about Josh."

It was just her porch. He wouldn't be confined. He could escape easily.

He took a step toward her, then another, but with each pace closer to the house, his legs became heavier. By the time he mounted the stairs, he could barely lift them. He paused several feet from the front door and glanced at the white wicker furniture, a swing hanging from the ceiling at the far end. Thoughts of his mother's parents' farmhouse where he'd spent time every summer came to mind. For a moment peace descended. He tried to hold on to that feeling, but it evaporated in seconds at the sound of an engine revving and then a car speeding down the street.

The sudden loudness of the noise made him start to duck behind a wicker chair a couple of feet away. He stopped himself, but not before anger and frustration swamped him. His heartbeat revved like the vehicle, and the shakes accosted him. He clasped his hands on the knob of his cane and pressed it down into the wooden slat of the porch.

What was he thinking? He should never have accepted her invitation.

"I'm sorry. I can't. I have stuff to do at home." He pivoted so fast he nearly lost his balance and had to bring his cane down quickly to prevent it.

"Thank you for your help today with my son," Emma quickly got out.

Sweat popped out on his forehead and ran down his face, into his eyes. He concentrated on the stinging sensation to take his mind off everything rushing toward him. As fast as his injured leg would let him, he hurried toward his house and the familiar surroundings where he knew what to expect. The trembling in his hands had spread throughout his body by the time he arrived in his yard.

Once inside his home, he fell back against the door and closed his eyes, trying to slow his stampeding heartbeat. His chest rose and fell rapidly as he gulped air. He slid down the length of the door and sat on the tiled foyer floor, blocking the deep ache that emanated from his recent injury.

Rage at himself, at his situation swamped him, and he slammed his fist into his palm. Pain shot up his arm. He didn't care. It wasn't anything compared to how he hated what was happening to him.

What are You doing, God? I want a normal life. Not be a slave to these panic attacks. Why aren't You answering my prayers?

Chapter Two

From the front porch, Emma watched Jake Tanner limp down the sidewalk toward the corner at Park Avenue. Mr. Tanner had saved her son from getting hurt worse than he already was. Had the situation with Josh brought back bad memories of the man's childhood? Was that why he'd left so quickly? Why there was a poignant look in his dark brown eyes? She guessed she shouldn't have asked him about what happened to him when he was bullied. That couldn't be easy for anyone to remember.

Mr. Tanner rounded the corner and disappeared from her view. From what she'd seen of the man, it certainly appeared he could take care of himself, even with his injured leg. She was five feet ten inches, and he had to be a good half a foot taller. He might be limping but clearly that didn't stop him from doing some kind of physical exercise. Dressed in tight jeans and a black T-shirt, he looked well built with a hard, muscular body—a little leaner than he was probably accustomed to.

"Jake Tanner" rolled off her tongue as if she'd said it before. Why did it sound familiar to her? Where had she heard his name? Had she run into him somewhere in town? She wasn't from Cimarron City but had lived here for years. But then he would be a hard man to forget with his striking good looks.

Had he hurt himself recently? Was the injury to his left leg permanent? Questions began to flood her mind until she shook her head.

No. He made it clear he'd helped Josh, but that was all. Besides, she had her hands full with a child who was angry all the time. And there were her two jobs—one as a veterinary assistant at Harris Animal Hospital and the other as a trainer for service dogs with the Caring Canines Foundation with Abbey Winters, her best friend. Abbey had founded the organization that placed service and therapy dogs with people who needed them. Emma didn't want any more complications in her life, and she certainly wasn't interested in dating, even though it had been three years since her husband died, leaving her widowed at twenty-nine with a son.

Who is my top priority—Josh.

Emma threw one last glance at the corner of Sooner and Park, then headed inside and toward Josh's bedroom. They needed to have a conversation about what had happened today whether her son wanted to talk or not. Her child would not be used as a punching bag. The very thought tightened her chest and made breathing difficult.

She halted outside his closed door, drew air into her lungs until her nerves settled and then knocked. She half expected Josh to ignore her, but thirty seconds later, he swung open the door. A scowl puckered his face, and he clenched his jaw so tightly, a muscle in his cheek twitched, underscoring his anger. He left her standing in the entrance, trudged to his bed and flung himself on his back onto his navy blue coverlet.

"I'm not telling you who those guys are."

"Why not?" She moved into his room and sat at the end of the bed, facing him.

"You'll say something to them or their parents."

"Are you being bothered at school? Is that why you haven't wanted to go these past six weeks since school started?"

He clamped his lips together until his mouth was a thin, tight line.

"I'm going to talk to your teacher whether you say anything or not. I can't sit by and let someone, or in this case, several boys bully you."

"Don't, Mom. I'll take care of this. It's *my* problem."

The sheen in Josh's eyes, the plea in his voice tore at her composure. She wanted to pull him into her arms and never let go—to keep him safe with her. *Sam, I need you. This is what a dad handles with a son. What do I do?*

She'd never felt so alone as at this moment, staring at Josh fighting the tears welling in his eyes. "I know Mrs. Alexander would want to know. Every child should be safe at school. This is not negotiable. I can't force you to tell me, but I need to know who is doing this to you."

"I'm not a snitch. That's what they'll call me. I'll never live it down."

"So what's your plan? Let them keep beating you up? What if Mr. Tanner hadn't seen them and stopped them? What do you think would have happened?"

Josh shrugged, turned away from her and lay on his bed.

Emma remembered Jake Tanner's words about how talking with the bullies' parents sometimes only made the situation worse. Then what should she do? What could Josh do? "At least make sure you have friends around you. Don't go anywhere alone. It's obvious now you can't go to Craig's house through the park. I'll have to drive you to and from your friends' houses. I'll pick you up from school and take you in the morning. I'll talk to Dr. Harris and figure out a way to do that with my work schedule. If I can't, I'll see if Abbey will. She takes Madi to and from school." As she listed what she would do, she realized all those precautions weren't really a solution.

Then in the meantime, she'd talk to the school about the bullying. She had to do something to end this. The thought of her son hurting, physically and emotionally, stiffened her resolve to help him somehow whether he liked it or not. She hated that bullies were almost holding her son hostage.

"Don't say anything to Mrs. Alexander, Mom."

Emma rose and hovered over Josh. "I have to. It's my job as your parent. I can't ignore what happened."

He glared at her. "I hate you. You're going to make my life miserable."

The words hurt, but she understood where they came from—fear and anger at his situation. She knew those feelings well, having experienced them after Sam passed away. "I love you, Josh, and your life right now with these bullies isn't what you want or deserve."

Her son buried his head under his pillow.

"I need to check your cuts and clean them."

"Go away."

"I'm not leaving. You aren't alone."

He tossed the pillow toward the end of the bed. "I wish Mr. Tanner hadn't interfered. Then you wouldn't be making such a big deal out of this."

"Thankfully he did, and believe me, I would have made a big deal out of it when I saw you in this condition whether he'd stepped in or not. I'll be right back with the first-aid kit."

Josh grumbled something she couldn't hear.

As she gathered up what she needed, a picture of Jake Tanner flashed into her mind. Short, dark hair— military style like her brother's... Emma snapped her fingers. That was it. Ben had mentioned a Jake Tanner on several occasions because he was the army captain Ben had served under in his Special Forces Unit. Could this be the same man?

After she patched up an uncooperative Josh, she left him in his bedroom to pout. When she really thought about Josh's angry behavior and keeping to himself, she realized it had begun during the summer. She'd hoped his mood would improve when school started and he saw his friends more. But it hadn't. She'd tried talking to him. He'd been closemouthed and dismissive of her concerns. Why hadn't she seen it earlier?

She made her way to the kitchen to start lunch but first decided to call her brother. She knew it would nag her not to know whether the Jake Tanner she'd met was Ben's company's commanding officer. She remembered

Ben's commenting they both had lived in Oklahoma so it was possible.

She called his cell phone number. "Hi, bro. Do you have a moment to appease my curiosity?" Emma leaned against the kitchen counter, staring out the window over the sink at the leaves beginning to change colors.

"For you, always. What's going on?"

"Josh was in the park and some boys jumped him and beat him up. Apparently, this wasn't the first time they'd approached him."

"How's Josh?"

"Some cuts and bruises but I think his self-confidence is more damaged than anything."

"I wish I didn't live so far away. I could help him. With my new job I'm working weekends, so that doesn't leave a lot of time to even drive to Cimarron City when Josh isn't in school."

She didn't want Ben to feel this was his problem. He lived in Tulsa and was just getting his life back. "I'm going to talk to the school on Monday about it. But that's not what I wanted to speak with you about. A man named Jake Tanner broke up the fight and brought Josh home. He lives across the street from where it happened on Park Avenue. Could he be your captain? You said something about his living around here once. Am I crazy to even think it could be the same guy?" And why in the world did it make a difference, except that it would bug her until she found out?

"So that's where he is. Some of my buddies from the old company who made it back were wondering where he went when he was let out of the army hospital a few months ago. He has an email address but hasn't said where he is when he's corresponded with any of the guys. I've been worried. I should have thought about Cimarron City. He lived there for a while when his father was stationed at the army base nearby. And he used to visit his grandmother there in the summer. I think his grandmother died last year, but I thought since his father is stationed in Florida, that might be where he went."

"What happened to him?"

"I was stateside when my old company was ambushed and about a quarter of the men were killed, many others injured. Captain Tanner was one of them. A bullet in his left leg. Tore it up. I hear he almost lost it."

She recalled how emotionally messed up Ben had been last year when he was first released from the military hospital and honorably discharged from the army. He didn't have a job then—couldn't hold one down— and lived with their parents in Tulsa.

"How did he seem to you?"

"He couldn't get away fast enough. I invited him to share a drink for rescuing Josh, and he backed away as if I was contagious."

"What did you say to him?" Half amusement, half concern came over the line from her brother.

"Nothing. He wasn't mad at me. He was—" she searched her mind for a word to describe the earlier encounter "—vulnerable. Something was wrong. Maybe his leg was hurting or something like that. I did see his hands shaking. He tried to hide it, and he was breathing hard, sweating. That didn't start really until he'd been talking to me for a while. Do you think it could be…" She wasn't a doctor and had no business diagnosing a person.

"Post traumatic stress disorder?"

Ben had recovered from his physical injuries within months of returning stateside, but what had lingered and brought her brother to his knees was PTSD. Last year she'd trained her first service dog to help her brother deal with the effects of the disorder. "How's Butch doing?"

"He's great. You don't know how much he changed my life for the better."

Yes, she did. She saw her brother go from almost retreating totally from life to now holding down a job and functioning normally. He still lived with their parents, but she'd heard from her mom he was looking for his own apartment. "Are you having any problems?"

"Yes, occasionally, but Butch is right there for me. I can't thank you enough for him. Do you think you could pay Captain Tanner a visit? See how he is? I know what happened to him was bad, and as tough as he was, I wouldn't be surprised if he's dealing with PTSD. It can take out the strongest people."

Like Ben. He'd been a sergeant with an Army Special Forces Unit with lethal skills she couldn't even imagine. Yet none of that mattered in the end.

"Please, sis. I owe Captain Tanner my life. He pulled me out of the firefight that took me down. If he hadn't, I would have died."

"What if it isn't your Captain Tanner?"

"Was the person six and a half feet, dark brown hair, built like a tank, solid, with dark eyes—almost black?"

"That's him." She thought of the man she'd met today and realized she owed him, too. Not only for Ben but Josh. "I'll go see him. What do you want me to do?"

As her brother told her, she visualized Jake Tanner. The glimpse of anguish she'd seen in those dark eyes haunted her. He'd been quick to disguise it until the end when he started backing away from her. That black gaze pierced straight through her heart, and she doubted he even realized what he'd telegraphed to her—he was a man in pain.

The following Tuesday, Emma brought a terrier on a leash into the back room of the Harris Animal Hospital where she worked for Dr. Harris, the father of her best friend, Abbey Winters. "I think this gal will be great to train as a service dog. She's smart and eager."

"Even tempered?" Abbey, her partner in the Caring Canines Foundation, asked as she looked at the medium-size dog with fur that was various shades of brown.

"Surprisingly calm. That combined with this breed's determination and devotion can make a good service dog."

"I'll take her out to Caring Canines since you're working with the German shepherd at your house." The kennel and training facilities of the organization were housed at Winter Haven Ranch where Abbey lived with her husband, Dominic.

"Shep will make a good service dog, too. I've even

got a possible owner for him. You know I've been doing the same training with Shep as I did with Butch."

"How is your brother?"

"Doing so much better. I talked to Ben twice this past weekend."

Abbey's eyebrows lifted. "That's unusual. Doesn't your brother hate talking on the phone?"

"Yeah, he prefers video chatting where he can see a person's face, and the second time that's what we did. I got to see Butch. Ben looks better each time I see him. Butch has been good for my brother, and if what Ben thinks is true, Shep will be good for Captain Tanner."

"Another soldier? Is it a physical injury? PTSD?"

"Both. When those kids I told you about yesterday jumped Josh, Captain Tanner was the man who rescued him. After he left my house Saturday, I couldn't shake the feeling I'd heard that name somewhere. I finally remembered Ben served under a Captain Jake Tanner."

"So you called your brother to find out. I know how you are when you get something in your head. You don't give up until you find out the truth."

Emma laughed. "You've nailed me. I called him to see. Ben did some checking around after we talked on Saturday and found out that Captain Tanner has basically withdrawn into his house. Ben has a few connections, and one thought the captain was suffering from PTSD, although he doesn't seem to be participating in any therapy groups through the VA."

"How does Captain Tanner feel about having a service dog?"

"I don't know. I only talked to him that one time. I

plan on taking him some brownies as a thank-you for helping Josh. Shep will go with me. I'll introduce him to the idea of a service dog slowly."

She wasn't sure if Jake Tanner would even open the door. She'd use the excuse she needed more information about the three boys who attacked Josh. Not only did she want to help the captain if he was suffering from PTSD, but she did need descriptions of the boys to give her an idea who could be bullying Josh. His teacher had requested any information to help her with the situation at school.

"Shep could help him, but he needs counseling, too. Maybe he's getting private therapy."

"Possibly, but Ben doesn't think so from what he's hearing from his army buddies in the area. Do you have room in your PTSD group?" Though Emma's best friend ran the Caring Canines Foundation, she still conducted a few counseling groups.

"If he'll come, I'll make room. The members are there to support each other, and talking about it has helped them. But there aren't any soldiers in the group."

"Maybe you should start one for people who have been bullied." Josh was dealing with some of the same symptoms as someone with PTSD—anger, anxiety and depression.

"If I only had more time in the day. Even quitting work at the hospital hasn't changed much because I'm training more dogs now. There is such a demand for them. So you didn't get any answers about who's bullying Josh from your meeting with Mrs. Alexander yesterday?"

"She hasn't seen anything, and since I didn't know the bullies' names and couldn't describe them, there wasn't much she could do but keep an eye out for any trouble. Most of the boys in his class are bigger than Josh, so the bullies could be in Mrs. Alexander's room. Or from the other fifth-grade classes."

"They could even be sixth-graders. It was a good idea to get him off the bus. It's hard for the driver to keep an eye on the road and what students are doing at the same time." Abbey leaned down and stroked the terrier. "Did Dad give his okay on this dog?"

Emma nodded. "Your father checked her over and she's medically sound. It's Madi's turn to name the dog. Let me know what she chooses." Madi was Abbey's ten-year-old sister-in-law whom she and Dominic were raising.

"Madi takes her job as name giver very seriously. She'll stew on it for days," Abbey said with a chuckle.

"Not too long. I want to start right away and a name helps. Now that I'm winding down with Shep, I have a slot open." Since she still worked full-time at the animal hospital, she could train only one dog at a time.

Abbey took the leash from Emma. "Good. Before long we're going to need another trainer, or you're going to have to quit your job here."

"Your father might have something to say about that. I'm going to look at training more than one dog. Hopefully that will help."

"I know, but the requests for free service dogs have increased over the past few months, especially now that veterans have heard about our foundation and the

VA has stopped paying for service dogs. Many of the veterans can't afford an animal from the agencies that charge for them."

"How are the donations coming?" Emma leaned against the exam table, the terrier rubbing against her leg.

"They're increasing. My husband is very good at helping to raise money for Caring Canines. Dominic can attest to the good a dog can bring to a person after how Madi responded to Cottonball following her surgery to help her walk again."

Emma smiled. "And now Madi is running everywhere. You wouldn't know she had been in a plane crash twenty months ago."

"She's telling me she wants to learn to train dogs. I'm having her shadow me."

"A trainer in the making. There was a time I thought Josh would want to train dogs, but lately nothing interests him."

A frown slashed across Abbey's face. "Because he's too busy dodging the bullies after him."

"I know God wants me to forgive the boys, but I'm not sure I can. Josh has already had to deal with losing his dad. They were very close."

"Madi needed a woman's influence, and I suspect Josh could benefit from a male being in his life."

"He has Ben when he comes to visit."

"You don't want to get married again?" Abbey started for the reception area of the animal hospital, leading the terrier on a leash.

Emma followed her down the hallway. "I know you

found love with Dominic, but Sam gave me everything I needed. I've had my time." Abbey had loved her husband so much that when he'd died, it had left a big hole in her heart she didn't think any man could fill.

"That's wonderful, but he's been gone for three years. I realized when I met and fell in love with Dominic that we could have second chances, and they can work out beautifully."

"Says a lady madly in love with her husband. When am I going to fit a man into my life with work, training dogs and raising Josh?"

"When your heart is ready," Abbey said. They stood at the entrance into the reception area where a client waited with her cat. Abbey winked at Emma and started toward the main door. "See you later at the ranch."

"I'll be there today, but tomorrow I'm going to be busy baking brownies and scouting out the situation with Captain Tanner. At the very least, my brother wants a report he's okay. And if Captain Tanner needs Shep, I'll do my best to persuade him of the benefits of a service dog."

At the door Abbey turned back and answered, "He may need more than Shep. Animal companionship is great but so is human companionship." She gave a saucy grin then left.

Emma faced the receptionist and lady in the waiting room. "Ignore what that woman said. She doesn't know what she's talking about." Emma turned and headed for exam room one to prepare it for the next client. The sound of chuckles followed her down the hallway, and heat reddened her cheeks.

* * *

On Wednesday, Jake's hand shook as he reread the letter from the army. He was being awarded the Distinguished Service Medal for his heroic actions in the mountains in Afghanistan.

Why? I'm no hero. Not everyone came home. Those left behind are the true heroes.

Guilt mingled with despair as he fought to keep the memories locked away. The bombs exploding. The peppering of gunfire. The screams and cries. The stench of death and gunpowder.

The letter slipped from his hand and floated to the floor. He couldn't protect all his men. He'd tried. But he'd lost too many. Friends. Battle buddies.

He hung his head and his gaze latched on to the letter. Squeezing his eyes shut, he still heard in his mind the words General Hatchback would say when he gave him the medal during the Veterans Day Ceremony—six weeks away. And no doubt, his father would be there.

No, he wouldn't go. He didn't deserve it. He'd done his duty. He didn't want a medal for that. He just wanted to be left alone.

The doorbell chimed, startling him. He jerked his head up and looked toward the foyer. He went to the window and saw the delivery guy from the grocery store. Using his cane, he covered the distance to the door at a quick pace and let the young man in.

"Hi, Mr. Tanner. I'll put these on the counter in your kitchen."

While Morgan took the sacks into that room, Jake retrieved his wallet from his bedroom and pulled out some money for a tip then met the guy in the foyer. "Thanks. See you a week from tomorrow."

"I'm off next Thursday. A big game at school. Got to support our Trojans."

"When will you be working next week?" Jake handed him the tip.

"Friday afternoon and evening." Morgan stuffed the money into his pocket.

"Then I'll call my order in for that day."

"You don't have to. Steve delivers when I don't."

Jake put his hand on the knob. "That's okay. Friday is fine. I'll have enough to tide me over until then." He was used to Morgan. The young man did a good job, even putting his meat and milk into the refrigerator for him. He didn't want a stranger here. Jake swung the front door open for Morgan to leave.

"Sure, if that's what you want." The teen left.

When Jake moved to close the door behind Morgan, he caught sight of Emma and a black and brown German shepherd coming up the sidewalk. He couldn't very well act as if he wasn't home, and there was no way he would hurt her by ignoring the bell since she'd seen him. But company was not what he wanted to deal with at the moment.

Then his gaze caught the smile that encompassed her face, dimpling her cheeks and adding sparkle to her sky-blue eyes as though a light shone through them. He couldn't tell her to go home. He'd see her for a few minutes then plead work, which was true. He had a paper due for his doctorate program.

"Hi. How are you doing today?" Emma stopped in

front of him, presenting him with a plate covered with aluminum foil. "I brought a thank-you gift. Brownies— the thick, chewy kind. I hope you like chocolate."

"Love it. How did you know?"

"Most people do, so I thought it was a safe dessert to make for you. I love to bake and this is one of my specialties."

"Thanks. You and my neighbor ought to get together. Marcella is always baking," he said, with the corners of his mouth twitching into a grin, her own smile affecting him.

"And bringing you some of it?"

"Yes." He stared into her cheerful expression and wanted to shout there was nothing to be upbeat about, but something nipped his negative thoughts—at least temporarily. Her bright gaze captured him and held him in its grasp.

Since Saturday, he'd been plagued with memories of their meeting that day. He'd even considered going to her house and seeing how Josh was. He only got a couple of feet from his porch before he turned around. They were strangers, and she didn't need to be saddled with a man—even as a friend—who was crippled physically and emotionally.

Jake stepped away from the entrance. "Come in. I have to put away the rest of my groceries." For a few seconds, panic unfolded deep inside him. He was out of practice carrying on a normal conversation with a civilian after so many years in war-conflicted areas. Sucking in a deep breath, he shoved the anxiety down.

As she passed him, a whiff of her flowery scent

wafted to him—lavender. His mother used to wear it. For a few seconds he was thrust into the past. He remembered coming into the kitchen when his mom took a pan of brownies out of the oven. The aromas of chocolate and lavender competed for dominance in his thoughts, and a sense of comfort engulfed him.

Emma turned toward him with that smile still gracing her full mouth. It drew him toward her, stirring other feelings in him. He'd had so little joy in his life lately. That had to be the reason he responded to a simple grin.

"It's this way." He limped ahead of her through the dining room and into the kitchen.

"I like this." Emma put the plate on the center island counter. "It's cozy and warm. Do you cook?"

"No, unless you call *cooking* opening a can and heating up whatever is in it. My meals aren't elaborate. A lot of frozen dinners." Jake's gaze landed on the German shepherd. *Beautiful dog to go with a beautiful woman, but why did she bring the animal with her?* Had his strange behavior the other day scared her somehow? When a panic attack took hold of him, it was hard for him to do much about it, which only made the situation worse.

"That's a shame. You need to come to my house one evening. I love to cook when I have the time."

"What keeps you so busy you can't cook very often?" Jake asked, resolved to stay away from any topic about him as he began emptying the sacks on the countertop. Focus on her. A much safer subject to discuss.

"Training dogs, working a full-time job at the animal hospital and trying to raise a child who's giving me fits."

"Things aren't any better?"

"No. The Cold War has been declared at my house. He didn't appreciate my talking to his teacher."

Jake whistled. "Yep, that will do it."

"Are you taking his side? Are you saying I shouldn't have talked with his teacher about his being bullied?"

Jake threw up his hands, palms outward. "Hold it right there. I am not taking anyone's side. That's between you and your son."

"I could use your help with this situation."

He scanned the room, looking for a way out of the kitchen and this conversation. He didn't want to be in the middle between a mother and son. "I don't know the boys who ganged up on Josh."

"But you saw them. Can you describe the culprits? Even one of them?"

"Maybe the smallest kid. Brown hair, brown eyes."

"Good. Do you have a piece of paper and a pencil?"

"Yes, but…" Staring at the determination in Emma's expression, he realized the quickest way to get rid of her was to give her what she wanted—at least the little he knew. He crossed to the desk under the wall phone and withdrew the items requested.

Emma took them. "I love to draw. If you tell me what he looks like, I'll try to sketch a portrait of him. Brown hair and eyes as well as a small frame fit a lot of kids in Cimarron City. So let's start with what shape his face is—oval, oblong, heart shaped? Is his jaw square, pointy, round?"

Staring at the dog sitting near the back door, Jake rubbed his day-old beard stubble. He'd forgotten to shave this morning. He was doing that more lately. When he glanced down at his attire, he winced at the shabby T-shirt and jeans with several holes in them. If someone who didn't know him walked in right now, that person would think Jake was close to living on the street. Suddenly he saw himself through Emma's eyes. And he didn't like the picture.

The military had taught him always to be prepared and to keep himself presentable. Lately he'd forgotten his training. The least he could do was change clothing. He wouldn't shave because her visit was impromptu, and he didn't want to give her the wrong impression— that he cared. He knew better than to care, not with the upheaval in his life.

"Your visit has taken me by surprise. I'll be back in a minute." He gestured to the kitchen. "Make yourself at home. I have a large, fenced backyard if you want to put your pet outside. A big dog like that probably requires a lot of exercise." He wanted to add: *I won't hurt you. I'm only hurting myself.*

"That's great."

As she walked to the back door, Jake slipped out of the kitchen and hurried to his bedroom. He felt encouraged she wasn't afraid of him since she was putting her German shepherd outside. Somehow he would beat what he was going through…but he didn't think he could by the time of the medal ceremony on Veterans Day.

After rummaging in his closet for something nicer to wear, he began to change. He caught sight of himself in the full-length mirror on the back of the door and froze. He didn't know the man staring back at him in the reflection. He sank onto his bed and plowed his fingers through his unruly hair.

I just want some hope, Lord.

Four sweet, heartfelt stories from fan-favorite
Love Inspired® Books authors!

**TIDINGS OF JOY and
HEART OF THE FAMILY**
by Margaret Daley

**LASSO HER HEART and
MISTLETOE REUNION**
by Anna Schmidt

Get two inspirational Christmas romances
for the price of one!

Available in December 2013 wherever books are sold.

www.Harlequin.com

LIC1213R

REQUEST YOUR FREE BOOKS!

2 FREE INSPIRATIONAL NOVELS
PLUS 2
FREE
MYSTERY GIFTS

Love Inspired

LI13R

SPECIAL EXCERPT FROM

Love Inspired

*Bygones's intrepid reporter is on the trail of the town's
mysterious benefactor. Will she succeed in her mission?
Read on for a preview of COZY CHRISTMAS
by Valerie Hansen, the conclusion to*

THE HEART OF MAIN STREET *series.*

Whitney Leigh rolled her eyes. "Romance! It's getting to
be an epidemic."

Because she was alone in the car she didn't try to temper
her frustration. Fortunately, this time, the editor of the
Bygones Gazette had assigned her to write a new series
about the Save Our Streets project's six-month anniversary.
If he had asked her for one more fluff piece on recent
engagements, she would have screamed.

Parking in front of the Cozy Cup Café, she shivered and
slid out.

As a lifelong citizen of Bygones she was supposed to
have been perfect for the job of ferreting out the hidden
facts concerning the town's windfall. Too bad she had failed.
Instead of an exposé, she'd ended up filling her column
with news of people's love lives. But she was not going to
quit investigating. No, sir. Not until she'd uncovered the
real facts. Especially the name of their secret benefactor.

She stepped inside the Cozy Cup.

"What can I do for you?" Josh Smith asked.

Whitney was tempted to launch right into her real reason
for being there. Instead, she merely said, "Fix me something
warm?"

"Like what?"

"Surprise me."

She settled herself at one of the tables. There was something unique about this place. And, truth to tell, the same went for the other new businesses on Main. Each one had filled a need and become an integral part of Bygones in a mere five or six months.

Josh Smith was a prime example. He was what she considered young, yet he had quickly won over the older generations as well as the younger ones.

He stepped out from behind the counter with a steaming cup in one hand and a taller, whipped-cream-topped tumbler in the other.

"Your choice," he said pleasantly, placing both drinks on the table and joining her as if he already knew this was not a social call.

"I see you're not too busy this afternoon. Do you have time to talk?"

"I always have time for my favorite reporter," he said.

"How many reporters do you know?"

"Hmm, let's see." A widening grin made his eyes sparkle. "One."

Will Whitney get her story and find love in the process?
Pick up COZY CHRISTMAS to find out.

Available December 2013 wherever
Love Inspired® Books are sold.

A troubled past has hardened millionaire
Tomas Delacorte, but when he hires the bubbly
Callie Moreau as his landscaper, she'll show him a
world full of light and love.

Bayou Sweetheart

by

Lenora Worth

*is available January 2014
wherever Love Inspired books are sold.*

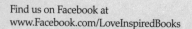